The
SAINT LAURENT
MUSE

Also by C. W. Gortner

The American Adventuress

Marlene

Mademoiselle Chanel

The
SAINT LAURENT MUSE

A Novel

C. W. GORTNER

WILLIAM MORROW
An Imprint of HarperCollinsPublishers

THE SAINT LAURENT MUSE. Copyright © 2025 by CW Gortner. All rights reserved. Printed in the United States of America. No part of this book may be used or reproduced in any manner whatsoever without written permission except in the case of brief quotations embodied in critical articles and reviews. For information, address HarperCollins Publishers, 195 Broadway, New York, NY 10007.

HarperCollins books may be purchased for educational, business, or sales promotional use. For information, please email the Special Markets Department at SPsales@harpercollins.com.

FIRST EDITION

Interior text design by Diahann Sturge-Campbell
Fashion illustration © YuliaBu/Stock.Adobe.com

Library of Congress Cataloging-in-Publication Data

Names: Gortner, C. W., author.
Title: The Saint Laurent muse : a novel / C.W. Gortner.
Description: First edition. | New York, NY: William Morrow Paperbacks, 2025.
Identifiers: LCCN 2024008280 | ISBN 9780063319837 (trade paperback) | ISBN 9780063319844 (e-book)
Subjects: LCSH: La Falaise, Loulou de—Fiction. | Fashion designers—Fiction. | Fashion—Fiction. | LCGFT: Biographical fiction. | Novels.
Classification: LCC PS3607.O78 S25 2025 | DDC 813/.6—dc23/eng/20240226
LC record available at https://lccn.loc.gov/2024008280

ISBN 978-0-06-331983-7

25 26 27 28 29 LBC 5 4 3 2 1

For Erik,
then, now, and always

The
SAINT LAURENT
MUSE

Prologue

When your mother baptizes you in a perfume named Shocking, you can expect to live an exceptional life.

Have you seen the container? The glass torso of a woman, the scent inside like liquid rose, under the gauzy exterior engraving of an Amazonian breastplate. Inappropriate for a teenage girl, let alone a baby, though I didn't realize it until later—and it wouldn't have mattered anyway.

My mother had worked for the perfume's extravagant creator, Elsa Schiaparelli, whom Coco Chanel so despised that she once set fire to Elsa's dress at a party. Born Maxime Birley, my mother was an Irish aristocrat. Her father, Sir Oswald Birley, painted royal portraits, and her mother, Lady Rhoda Birley, fed bouillabaisse to her rosebushes and rode the fox hunt in a sari. My mother never believed in their way of life. To her, lineage was no excuse for settling for whatever the world happened to fling at you.

And she didn't settle. Her extramarital affairs so enraged my father, Count Alain Le Bailly de La Falaise, who could trace his ancestry back to the seventeenth century, that he sued her for divorce after only four years of marriage. It was 1950, so the French courts ruled in his favor, declaring her an unfit mother, and assigned us to Papa's custody. I was three years old. My brother, Alexis, was two.

It was only much later in life that I understood how deeply her desertion had affected me. Even so, I never resented her for it, though people often thought I should. She was the first person who taught me to be unexpected and create my own existence, though it would take many years for me to nurture that seed of wisdom from her chaos. I was expected to be so many things, you see, except for who I became.

Now I can honestly say I have lived an exceptional life. A very unexpected one.

I witnessed a time that will never come again. An age of incandescent innovation and daring—not for nothing was Shocking my baptismal fount. An era of stunning acclaim and seismic rivalry, of white-powdered nights refracting on cube-mirrored walls and operatic mayhem under throbbing strobe lights. Of girls in swathed turbans and enamel bracelets stalking palatial catwalks, and fawning celebrities desperate to partake in our decadence. Of dagger-angled boutiques crowned by the initials of a prince whose reign was so supreme it made him a legend, and of secrets that tore us apart.

I lived in the time of Yves Saint Laurent.

They called me his muse.

PART I

THE SCANDAL COLLECTION

1970–1973

I do not want to find myself in the past.
—Yves Saint Laurent

1

Mama was mixing cocktails for us in her Riverside apartment when she made the statement that changed my life: "You're wasting your time here. There is no fashion in America."

I was rolling a joint on her coffee table. "Not even Halston?"

"I suppose he might prove an exception, though it's still not couture." She rattled the martini shaker to punctate her statement, her auburn hair coiffured and her still-lithe figure in an A-line minidress I'd bought for her in London. "Diana says he has enough financing now, so maybe you could work for him."

Diana was Vreeland, editor in chief of *Vogue*, with her finger on every fashion pulse.

I lit up the joint. "He has plenty of staff already."

"I see. You'd rather hang out at Warhol's Factory, doing nothing."

"You go there more than me," I said with a laugh. "You love how the drag queens coo over you for cooking shepherd's pie and giving them makeup tips."

"Someone has to feed them and teach them not to use so much mascara." Pouring out the martinis, she brought a glass to me. I coughed on my toke on the joint. "Besides, Andy is the one chasing after me," she said archly, sitting opposite me. "He wants me to be in one of his silly movies, like a groupie or whatever it is he calls them."

"He calls them 'superstars.' Berry's been taking wonderful photographs of them."

She made a disdainful moue. "While her sister, Marisa, is

becoming a successful model. She and Berry are Schiaparelli's granddaughters. I don't see why Berry is wasting her time at the Factory, either."

"Because Andy's launching a magazine, and Berry wants to photograph for it. He just designed the cover with the Fondas for *Time*. Even your husband thinks Andy's paintings should be exhibited at the Met."

"Those baffling soup cans." She sighed. "My John can be very persistent when it comes to his wayward waifs. The Met is appalled by the suggestion, of course—some nonsense about crass commercialism—but perhaps I should do it. What do you think? Should I make a movie with Andy and shock the museum board? Heaven knows they need something to rattle them off their lofty perches."

Reclining against the sofa, I savored my buzz. As often happened, the conversation had veered from my aimlessness to her need to shock. Until she said, "We can't rely on our youth forever. Eventually we all need an anchor. I married the Met."

"And I married Desmond FitzGerald, Knight of Glin," I reminded her.

"Well." She sniffed. "You were nineteen at the time and said yes to the first man who proposed. An Irish baron with an estate—what did you expect? I did warn you, he's what we call an 'aristocrat,' with all the baggage that entails."

Of course, she had never warned me. She'd treated my marriage as a lark, to which she'd arrived late and overdressed. But then, it was typical of her to reinvent the past, so I merely said, "Well, I didn't expect busloads of tourists every weekend to tour the grounds and hear him lecture on the estate."

"Nor, I imagine," she added dryly, "did you expect to oversee a perfect table setting for twenty of his ilk, with a butler hovering at your shoulder."

"Did *you* know what to expect when you married Papa?" The words popped out before I could stop them. In the subsequent silence, the click of her cigarette lighter sounded too loud in my ears. I'd trespassed over an invisible demarcation between us: my past mistake was fair game, not hers.

"It was a different time," she said at length, drawing on her cigarette. "Are you blaming me for your very brief marriage?"

"Of course not." I resisted rolling my eyes. "I was the one who said yes to him. Then I went mad with boredom. I just think you would have divorced him, too."

She fingered her wedding band. "I did. I divorced your father. Be glad you didn't have children. According to the French courts at the time, I wasn't only leaving a husband; I was deserting my children. They declared me 'une mère indigne.'"

An unfit mother. Her rare admission took me aback. "We never blamed you, Mama. Alexis and I know how unhappy you were."

"Desperately so. It must be our family curse. We have orphaned childhoods and miserable first marriages." With her cigarette poised in one hand, she sipped her drink with the other. "And then we must go off and earn a living."

Many things could be said about my mother, but not that she wallowed in self-pity or regret. She'd never outright acknowledged that upon her absconding, my brother, Alexis, and I had been dispatched to foster families by our father, who had no interest in raising two young children. What followed were boarding schools in England, with holidays split between him in France and our maternal grandparents in Sussex, as Mama was always off on some adventure.

When I married Desmond FitzGerald, Twenty-Ninth Knight of Glin—properly handsome and titled, ten years my senior— Mama unearthed an antique piece of familial lace for me to don like a wimple on my wedding day, an uncanny prediction of how the marriage would go. Perhaps she'd considered it as her warning that I was shackling myself to a cloistered existence, where spontaneity was eschewed, and sex as prescheduled and unimaginative as the table setting for twenty.

Nevertheless, she celebrated the occasion by showing up at the reception with her hair bobbed in the new Vidal Sassoon style, wearing a silver-sequined flapper dress and chandelier earrings, one of which she lost as she cavorted on the dance floor. My husband's best man, John McKendry, a photography curator at the Met, flung himself into the chaos to search for her bauble. I could still remember her laughter when he breathlessly found it and returned it to her.

"It's a fake, darling," she'd said with a coy gaze at him, like a scandalous debutante, though she was forty-five at the time, and he eleven years younger, and so thin he disappeared when he turned sideways. "You needn't have gone to the trouble."

Watching them as they'd danced together, Mama unleashing her full arsenal of charm, my brother had hissed in my ear, "She just found her ticket to America."

He was right. Maxime wed John within the year, moving with him to New York. It was how Mama survived. She charged ahead and never looked back.

She now said, "Life will have its revenge in the end. We must find something we love to do, more than anything else. I found it in Paris. Don't you remember when I'd bring you to see the collections? You were always mesmerized by the clothes. You're half French, after all."

I didn't remember. My lone memory of her during my boarding school years was when she'd materialized for a meet-the-parents afternoon, wearing a little veiled hat and a body-hugging white jersey dress designed by Schiaparelli, printed with surrealist eye motifs by Dalí. She incited consternation in the school's headmistress, who believed cardigans and discreet pearls ought to be a uniform. Mama attended the tea in the hall, flirting with one of the students' fathers and provoking sidelong glances from his wife and the other parents. Then she insisted on viewing my cramped bed in the dormitory, sniffing, "Where on earth is the closet space?" before she sallied away again to Paris.

It was a few months before my sixteenth birthday. Less than a year later, I was expelled for insubordination and sent to live with my grandparents, where my grandmother, in her gardening hat, informed me very precisely, "You must find yourself a husband by the age of twenty. I'll not have you become a burden under my roof."

Shuddering at the memory, I said, "I don't know anyone in Paris."

"You have that French boyfriend designer. What's his name again?"

"Fernando Sánchez. He's Belgian, and he designs furs for Revillon Frères. He's not my boyfriend."

"He still lives in Paris, doesn't he? Surely he must know plenty of people." She rose to add more martini to her glass. "It's not as if there's anything keeping you here."

"Are you trying to get rid of me?" Again, the question escaped me before I realized what I was about to say. "I thought you liked having me in New York."

"Naturally I like having you here." She shrugged. "But really, darling, you have such style. You inherited it from me. Style is the fearlessness to do as we please. Only the French know how to appreciate it."

"I always thought French fashion was stuffy. We never covered it at *Queen*," I said, citing the London fashion magazine I'd also briefly worked for.

She regarded me in amusement. "Chanel. Dior. Balenciaga.

My own ex-employer and sacred monster, Schiaparelli: they became legends because they established themselves in Paris. If you're serious about a career in fashion, Paris is the place."

Quite to my surprise, I thought she might have a point, though I rarely agreed with her. Her unexpected, voluble concern for my future might be unnerving, but I had followed in her footsteps in more than a disastrous first marriage. I'd also adopted her habit of dabbling in fashion, where aristocratic lineage had cachet. Not that my lineage meant anything to me. I'd seen its underbelly: my father's manor roof caving in from perennial disrepair; my grandparents' isolating snobbery. But it meant something in fashion, because the fantasy of it sold clothes. Indeed, no sooner had I left my husband in a polite divorce and moved to London than *Queen* offered me a position.

The new editor in chief of the modest society publication was targeting winsome girls with long hair who dropped out of school and slept with musicians. I suggested pooling resources to promote emerging British designers, such as Ossie Clark, who co-owned the popular boutique Quorum. I spent my spare time there, assisting in the raucous in-store fashion shows, doing window displays in a miniskirt with black garters and stockings. When passersby stopped to stare, I flashed them.

The war in Vietnam was televised nightly. Young people were marching in the streets demanding an end to the war, chanting for civil rights and equality. None of us wanted matching appliances or our parents' repression. We pursued love and freedom, a life without rules, and didn't plot our futures in advance. London was our playground.

During a trip to New York to visit Mama, she'd introduced me to Vreeland, who was so enthused by my medieval flounced shirt and scarlet breeches, which I'd acquired at a theater costume auction, she had me pose for *Vogue* in lamé and a monkey-fur bolero designed by Fernando. He styled the shoot. I liked his glossy black curls, gaunt cheekbones, and nimble fingers. He spoke French, Spanish, and English. He told me I was a natural in front of the camera. I found his attention flattering, even if I had no ambition to be a model.

Nevertheless, I decided to stay in New York to see how things went.

At a Factory party, I met Berry, whose grandmother had employed my mother. She was looking for a roommate for her walk-up on Second Avenue and Fifty-Eighth, where we shared a pull-out bed and shrouded our lopsided lamps in tea-dipped scarves. Berry was exploring her passion for photography. I continued to take whatever odd fashion jobs came my way. We partied at the Factory, among Andy Warhol's corn-fed boys in tank tops and gold briefs, and long-legged girls chasing fame and millionaires.

Halston had opened his namesake Madison Avenue boutique; during a cocktail reception there, he admired my shawl, which I'd silk-screened while high on acid at the Factory. I offered to tie-dye samples for him in his bathtub, staining his imported Carrera tiles. He used the fabrics in a collection.

Fernando came often to New York to peddle his portfolio; we went dancing, got high, and slept together. I didn't think anything of it. I'd just turned twenty-three and had already been married and divorced. I wasn't looking for permanency.

"He did say I could visit him whenever I like," I thought aloud, warming to the idea.

"Then do it." Mama downed her martini. "If I were your age, I certainly would."

2

Is that what you're wearing?" Betty's drawl preceded her elongated form in the full-length mirror propped against the bedroom wall. Fernando's sketches were taped around it like confetti. I'd been posing for him, a live model to draw inspiration from.

"The airline lost my other suitcase," I said. "This is all I have."

Tightening the fringed belt about my short-panted waist, I watched her stalk toward me, her slashed cheekbones framed by her straight white-gold mane, her endless legs encased in trousers, a starched, collarless white shirt unbuttoned to her navel.

"It's . . . how would you say it? Groovy?" A smile curved her light pink lips as she rolled out the compliment. We'd met at Chez Régine, a nightclub on Montparnasse, on the very day of my arrival. I'd been jet-lagged and determined to enjoy myself, when she and her suave husband, François, cut a swath through the crowd, all of whom seemed to either know or want to know them. Fernando did know them—rather well, as it turned out. Having rarely tested my fluency in French—I'd learned it in childhood, but my mother and I spoke in English, and I hadn't lived in France for sixteen years—Betty declared my accent appalling, as if I'd just moved to Paris from some dreadful province. It made me laugh.

She liked that. "An English girl with a sense of humor. How rare."

"Anglo-Irish on my mother's side," I corrected. "French on my father's."

"Only the French part matters in Paris," she replied, and we'd proceeded to dance together until dawn. As we said goodbye on the street, shoes twined in our hands, she invited me to a Saint Laurent couture fashion show as casually as if it were brunch.

Now she lit a cigarette and blew out smoke. "Did I tell you I once modeled for Chanel? A hideous woman. She likes her models like her suits: cut to the bone."

I upended my lone suitcase on the futon, searching among the upheaval of clothing I'd thrown into it without forethought. "Will she be there today?"

"Never. In her mind, there are no other designers, though her time is over and she knows it. If you wish to impress *Yves*," she added, as I scavenged for my suede boots, "he prefers women who wear his clothes."

Locating the boots, I held them up, noticing they were stained from tromping about New York in the winter slush. "I have these."

"Ah, Rive Gauche. His prêt-à-porter. The affordable line. 'A boutique for every woman. No one-of-a-kind dresses for rich ladies.' Or so he tells the snobs who criticize him for selling to the masses."

"Is couture really so different?" I pulled the boots over my white knee-high stockings and looped a scarf about my head, tucking in my short hair, still growing out from a botched bleach job when all of us at the Factory decided to mimic Andy's penchant for wigs and greeted him like an assembly of replica dolls.

Surveying my maroon velvet vest and the costume shirt with its tarnished ruffles, I squeezed a bangle over my wrist and roped fake jewel pendant necklaces across my shallow cleavage.

"You'll see soon enough." Betty tapped ash into the ashtray at the bedside. "You don't know anything about couture, do you?"

"Not really." I laughed. "I never paid attention to it."

"That would explain why you dress like a rebellious schoolgirl in castaways."

"Well, I did get kicked out of boarding school. Twice."

"How could you not? Your mother is Maxime de la Falaise." Betty watched me sweep everything back into the suitcase. "How is she, by the way?" She spoke as if they personally knew each other.

"Still married. Or she was the last time I saw her."

"Yves has a fatal weakness for aristocrats who survive a revolution."

I stuffed my cigarettes into my pocket. "That sounds like her. And my childhood."

"He'll admire you for surviving it, too. Not to mention throwing over the titled husband with a castle to be a hippie in London." Betty tossed her shoulder-length hair over her shoulders. "Would you consider working for him?"

My careless smile belied the sudden leap in my pulse. "Is he hiring?"

"He might hire you," she replied.

"Betty, stop it," called out Fernando from the living room, where he was turning over the sofa cushions in search of his car keys. "Loulou isn't here for a job."

She flipped her hand at me. "Do you have one already?"

"No," I said. "Should I?"

"I don't. But at least you're available, if Yves asks."

"Won't Pierre Cardin have something to say about it?"

"*Cardin?*" She snorted. "You must tell Yves that. In front of Pierre."

I paused in confusion. "I thought Pierre was his boyfriend and business partner."

"A Pierre is. Pierre *Bergé.*" She linked her arm in mine.

"A schoolgirl in castaways who doesn't care about couture. Yves will adore you."

FERNANDO NAVIGATED THE soot-stained city in his VW Bug, the traffic choking to a halt on rue Spontini in the sixteenth arrondissement, the Eiffel Tower a spindle in the distance. Betty sat crammed beside me on the back seat, her legs folded up to her chin.

"Never any parking." He turned into a labyrinth of side streets, fenced by elegant Haussmann town houses. "A mob scene. I never understood why they chose this place."

"Because Yves loved the hôtel—and what Yves wants, Pierre gets for him," said Betty. They glanced at each other in the rearview mirror, a frisson between them.

Bergé, I remembered. Not Cardin.

"Just drop us off here." Tugging at the door handle, she forced Fernando to slam on the brakes as she catapulted onto the sidewalk. "Come with me, Loulou."

I met Fernando's hooded dark eyes. "Go," he said. "Yves and I went to school together. He doesn't care if I'm late. He cares if Betty is. Do you have anything on you?"

Fishing a joint from my packet of Gauloises, I handed it to him, then hastened after Betty as she strode toward the hôtel.

"He's gay," she remarked.

"Who?"

"The bedroom-eyed Spaniard you're sleeping with."

"Then it's a good thing I'm not planning to marry him."

She chuckled. "They're so irresistible. They want us body and soul, but only if we're what they wish to see. We must be their mirrors."

I discerned a barbed undertone to her voice. "All of them?"

"All those who design clothes for us." She guided me into back corridors circling the salon, where I discerned a crowd. "His couture is by invitation only. Pierre charges three thousand francs for the privilege and assigns seating in advance. Any journalist who criticized a past collection is excluded. They fight over the front row like animals." Rounding a corner, she pointed to a doorway. "You can watch it from there. It's a great spot to see the show and avoid the backstabbing. I'll come get you afterward."

Stepping to the doorway, I gazed upon an immaculate, white-painted salon, surprisingly small, with an open walkway on the carpeted floor leading from a curtained archway hemmed on both sides by rows of little gilded chairs.

All I knew about couture was that it was handmade, impossibly expensive, and accessible only to the wealthy, who made semiannual pilgrimages to the Parisian couturiers. As I took in the women in hats and white gloves, as if they were attending a garden soiree, I envisioned a collection of elaborate ball gowns, stiff as palace curtains and ballooned with petticoats—the sort of thing a princess would wear coming down a marble staircase.

At some unheard cue, the audience took to the gilded chairs, those in the front row with flutes of complimentary champagne. I spotted Vreeland's distinctive raptor profile among them and thought of approaching her, but held myself back. She'd be surprised to see me here, lurking in the back, without an assigned seat.

When the models began to walk out from under the curtained archway, silence thickened the pall of cigarette smoke congesting the air.

My breath hitched.

The palette was black, navy, beige, and gray, featuring scholastic blouses tucked into pleated trousers and slope-shouldered peacoats that reminded me of my boarding school uniforms.

Knit zigzag-patterned pullovers over wide skirts had a subdued, café society air, while the belted gabardine jackets evoked exotic getaways. Wispy trench coats paired with black cotton jumpsuits might have been worn by any of the leggy girls vying to catch Warhol's eye at the Factory, though the models in the show were expressionless, each pivot and pause precise as clockwork before they rotated and disappeared behind the curtain.

There was no music. No sound.

If this was couture, it didn't look sacred or inaccessible to me. I found it boring, to be honest. Yet something must have been off, for a woman in pearls sitting near me in the back row hissed to her equally demure companion, "What is he showing us this season? Clothes for *boys*?"

I'd failed to recognize it, but as soon as she spoke, I realized the ensembles were indeed staples in a male wardrobe, interpreted for a stylized female form. The subtle twist struck me with its covert rebelliousness, an undernote of defiant intrigue stamped on every piece, like Betty.

His controversial le Smoking suit preceded monochromatic eveningwear: flared tuxedo pants under a satin-lapeled jacket unbuttoned over a translucent organza shirt, enhancing the sheen of skin. Sequined jumpsuits, girdled by sashes of pink taffeta, followed, and tapered halter-style dresses slit to the thigh, with medallion-studded chain belts.

When the finale bride appeared in a sheath of see-through cigaline, it roused a collective gasp. Black marabou feathers sprouted from the flame-haired model's hips; a serpentine silver belt clasped about her impossibly slim waist. Her naked torso showed under the fabric in a marbleized silhouette—a symbol of female empowerment, for women who reveled in independence and saw themselves as equals, with every right to wear, or not wear, whatever they liked.

Women like me, if I could afford it. I suddenly wondered how it would feel to wear something exclusively tailored to my body, fitted on me by the designer himself.

Vreeland came to her feet in fervent applause, along with John Fairchild of *Women's Wear Daily*, whose opinion, I'd learned in New York, dictated seasonal orders for American department stores.

Then Yves Saint Laurent emerged to take his bow.

He was tall and slender as a shadow. His black velvet jacket and paisley shirt were pasted to his long form, a gauzy scarf knotted about his throat, and low-slung pants with a wide, metallic notched belt hugged his narrow hips. With his wispy beard and shoulder-length tawny hair framing his etched features, he could have been Betty's twin. As he nudged the oversized tortoise-shell glasses on his prominent nose, he put his other hand at his heart in humble appreciation, a smile playing at the corners of his wide mouth. Swerving about, he vanished, leaving a breathless hush in his wake.

The fashion editors converged in eager debate. The woman in the pearls and hat, along with her friend, shoved past me with a snarl: "Is this what we've come to? Pornography in Yves Saint Laurent's salon?"

I had to stanch my laughter.

"Loulou." Betty's voice jolted me around; she beckoned from the corridor.

He stood behind the archway, surrounded by naked models divesting themselves of the garments for white-smocked assistants to return to the racks. One hand was cocked high at his waist and his head was lowered, staring at the floor as though nothing could breach his placid stance. It made me wonder if he understood the furor he'd stirred.

Then I recalled his sly half smile as he took his bow.

A short, stocky man in a blue suit, his receding salt-and-pepper hair bristling like a badger's fur, barked instructions at the assistants. He murmured to Yves, who gave a weary nod; then the man marched into the salon, bellowing greetings at the editors. He apparently knew all of them by their first names.

Yves exchanged a glance with Betty. She rolled her eyes. "Impossible," she said. "Let him play the bull and round them up. They obviously loved the collection."

"Did you?" He turned to me, his voice barely a whisper.

"Very much. It was . . ." I searched for the right word. "Unexpected."

He gave a brief nod. "That's how it should be." A moment of quiet stretched between us that should have been awkward, between strangers, yet felt almost tender. "Betty tells me you design for Halston." His limpid blue eyes met mine. "Are you wearing something of his?"

"I don't design for him. Everything I'm wearing is secondhand. Except the boots."

He blinked. "Even the bracelet?"

His observation caught me by surprise. "A napkin ring. I filched it from le Petit Saint Benoît. I can be an incorrigible thief."

"Did you steal the boots as well?" His mouth quirked as if he fought back a smile.

"I bought them in New York. On sale."

His entire person thawed. "How long are you in Paris?"

"I don't know. I never plan too far ahead."

He considered me. "I'd invite you to join us for dinner, but Pierre has booked our entire evening with the editors. So tedious."

"Another time, perhaps." I kept my tone light, because he sounded as if I might think him rude for not including a stranger in his evening plans.

"You can see each other on Sunday." Betty squeezed his arm.

"Loulou's staying with Fernando. He'll be hosting his afternoon tea. You promised to come this time. You've finished the collection and deserve to have some fun."

"If I don't go, when will I see you again?" He let out a fraught sigh, his gaze still fixed on me. "I designed this collection for Betty."

"Yes," I said softly. "I thought it looked like her."

He went quiet for another moment before he inclined his head. "It was lovely to meet you, Loulou. I wish we could talk longer. Please, excuse me."

As he went into the salon to another round of applause, I realized we hadn't been introduced, yet he knew my name.

"What did you tell him about me?" I asked Betty, curious.

She gave me a shrug. "Nothing. There's not much to tell, according to you."

I had to smile. "Not even that only my French half matters?"

"He likes that you're half English." She tossed her mane. "Forget New York. You excite him. You must stay here with us."

IN BED THAT night with Fernando, I asked, "Is he always so polite?"

Fernando chuckled. "At Dior, they called him 'le petit prince.'"

"Betty says I excite him, whatever that means. She wants me to stay."

"She would know. They're like brother and sister. But she doesn't take any of it seriously. She started modeling for money, then she met François and married him. Fashion is dress-up to her." He paused. "Do you want to stay? I don't mind."

I didn't answer, my hand on his hair-matted chest. I thought I should probably bring up what Betty had told me. It hadn't upset me—most men I'd met in fashion swung both ways—but if he preferred men, we should be open about it.

"Was that his lover Pierre, in the blue suit?"

"That was him. Formidable as Napoleon."

"How long have they been together?"

"Almost thirteen years. Pierre is forty, six years older than Yves. They had a fling the year Dior died, but Pierre was living with the painter Buffet. He went to Yves's first show and started chasing him. They didn't get together until things soured at Dior."

"What happened at Dior?"

"Yves's collections became too daring." Fernando sighed. "It was a bad time for him. He wanted to make the house more current, and Dior executives rescinded his exception from the draft during the Algerian War, to avoid officially firing him. He was called to military service and had a nervous breakdown."

I recalled Yves's shy air. "How awful for him."

"The military locked him up for a month in a mental ward. Pierre fought every day for his release." Fernando reached to the side table for a cigarette. "Yves never talks about it, but he was devastated. He didn't want to design couture anymore. Pierre went on the attack, selling everything he owned to hire a lawyer and sue Dior on Yves's behalf. They used the money they won to start their own house. Without Pierre, Yves would never have done it. He'd have gone into theater design instead."

"It's like a fairy tale: the knight in armor, rescuing his captive prince."

Fernando said wryly, "I've heard Pierre called worse."

"And they don't hide it. It's unusual, isn't it?"

A shutter seemed to roll down behind his eyes. "It shouldn't be."

I decided to let it go. "Do you really host tea parties for them? It sounds very posh. I don't have a thing to wear."

He chuckled. "*My* parties aren't posh. You can wear anything."

3

For the rest of the week, while Fernando sketched in the flat, I ran errands, buying baguettes, wine, and cold cuts for us. Wandering his neighborhood on Place Furstenberg, I had coffee at Café le Flore, where artists and fashion aspirants nursed attitudes at the tables. In a corkscrew alleyway not far from the café, I stumbled upon a secondhand clothing shop, to my delight.

With my suitcase lost forever, I needed new clothes, but I didn't have much money to spare. Resisting a gendarme-style cape I fell in love with, I opted for a less expensive pair of wrap-around blue silk pajama pants and a pleated gray skirt. Then I strolled for hours on the boulevard, enjoying the sooty gleam of Paris in the late June heat.

On Sunday, I helped Fernando pull back the beige sofa to make extra room, setting out the tray of cakes he'd sent me to purchase from a local patisserie, along with a teapot—English style, with loose tea and silver strainer—but accompanied by painted-glass thimble cups, "Like Arabs," he said with a wink. As he removed his recent sketches of lingerie-style dresses from his corner desk, I rolled joints on a silver tray.

"Why don't you leave your drawings out?" I asked, licking the joints' seams.

"Yves might be coming today." Fastening his portfolio, he tucked it into a drawer. "Loulou, you saw his collection. Everyone's raving about it."

"I saw some of the ladies walk out, like he'd showed center-folds from *Penthouse*."

"The last of the couture dragons. No one cares what they think." He lit a joint and drew in deep, as if he required fortification. "We worshipped Balenciaga when we were at school, but he closed his atelier last year because he said he had 'no one left to dress.' Chanel survives on her name alone; once she dies, it's the end for couture. Yves knew it would happen. He uses his couture to test ideas and reinterprets them in an entirely new way for Rive Gauche, so high fashion can be worn by women on the street. It outrages the Chambre Syndicale de la Haute Couture."

"The what?" It sounded like a nefarious James Bond villain.

"Tyrants who impose regulations on who's allowed to make couture, and defend it at all costs. They're terrified ready-to-wear will destroy them."

"And Yves isn't?"

"Rive Gauche is making millions. He can barely keep up with the demand."

"You never wanted to work with him? You're his friend, and very talented."

"I designed some lingerie for him when they were starting out, but they had no money. I took the offer from Revillon. When I first met Yves at our Syndicale design courses, he'd just arrived from Oran. He was already exceptional. His sketches anticipated Dior's spring collection before anyone had seen it; Dior hired him because of it. He has a sixth sense for fashion." Fernando handed me the joint, regarding himself in the mirror over his mantel. "There's no room for another designer at his house. A kingdom can only have one prince."

I went quiet, thinking I didn't belong here. To me, fashion

was madcap adventure, wearing whatever caught my fancy, not a rigid arena, under siege with rules.

"Besides," he went on, "I'm preparing my own ready-to-wear line."

I sat back on my heels. "The new sketches."

"Having you here inspired me. And I know someone who can help. You'll meet her today. Paloma Picasso."

"Like the painter?"

"Her father is the painter. She designs costume jewelry. Marvelous shapes and colors; she takes apart vintage pieces to make new ones. Yves put art on the runway with his Mondrian dress. I'll put art on the runway with her jewelry on my clothes. Paloma wants to collaborate with me."

"How wonderful!" I clapped my hands. "Can I help?"

"You can. I need all the help I can get. As soon as Revillon pays me for the season, I'll have samples made and start hunting for investors." He put a finger to his lips. "Don't say a word to them."

"I promise. My lips are sealed."

We busied ourselves straightening throw pillows and odds and ends, lighting incense and scented candles. When his flat bell rang, he threw the door open with an expansive smile to welcome Betty and her husband. With them was a fascinating young woman.

She wore a turban and a square-shouldered flowery dress, accessorized with a colored rhinestone necklace and square-heeled, lace-up shoes. Her large black eyes under plucked brows dominated her arresting face, her lips painted garnet red—not beautiful but utterly unconventional, exuding old-fashioned glamour, just as Betty in her wide-bottomed denim and hip belt over a black tunic personified the relaxed style of today.

Fernando said, "Paloma, this is Loulou de la Falaise. Loulou, Paloma Picasso."

"Very nice to meet you." I was awed by her, though surnames usually didn't impress me. But she wasn't an inherited title. She was the daughter of one of the world's most celebrated artists.

"And you." A warm smile widened her lips. "What a charming outfit. You must like to rummage in your mother's attic. Like me."

I was barefoot, in my wraparound silk pajama pants and the same ruffled shirt I'd worn to the show, bracelets heaped to my elbows. I heard myself chime as I kissed her cheeks and inhaled a sultry scent. "You smell wonderful."

"It's Y." She extended her wrist to me. "Yves's perfume."

Betty sprawled on the sofa with François. "Speaking of Yves, isn't he here yet?"

"No," said Fernando. "He hasn't called, either."

"But we're hours late." She lit a cigarette in exasperation. "Pierre probably told him he can't come. He doesn't want Yves doing anything with us. He's always—"

"*Quiet*," hissed Fernando. "They're coming up the stairs."

The short man I'd seen at the show, Yves's lover, entered with a resolute air. Behind him, shoulders sloped in a belted khaki jacket and matching tight pants, was Yves.

"We couldn't find parking," he murmured.

The atmosphere in the room expanded at his arrival, like an exhale of pent-up breath. He kissed Paloma; greeted Betty, François, and Fernando; and gave me a downcast look as Fernando said, "Now you know how it feels when we try to get to your shows on time."

"Come sit by me." Betty slid against her husband, patting her vacated spot for Yves. She immediately began to whisper in his ear, making him snigger. Paloma perched on the sofa arm, while Fernando hunkered at the table, plying them with tea and joints. Betty's husband smiled in placid contentment; François never seemed to say much.

Pierre seemed oddly out of place in his starched dress shirt and pleated trousers, like a chaperon on a school outing, his charge on the sofa giggling and getting high.

Then he thrust out his hand. "Pierre Bergé. You must be Loulou de la Falaise."

His grip was firm, his close-set dark eyes bright and intense. He had creases about his stubble-framed mouth, a premature frown line scored between his eyebrows, and he made no effort to disguise his appraisal of me, as if he were tallying my net worth.

Or lack thereof.

"Your mother, the Comtesse de la Falaise, is well-known in Paris," he said.

"She'd be delighted to hear it. She loves it when people talk about her."

"It's not gossip. She worked for Schiaparelli." He spoke concisely, reciting inarguable fact. "After the war, our economy was in ruins; couture was something we could export. Modeuses like your mother became essential for attracting international clientele. They were hired to wear the clothes in public." He gave me a curious look. "The comtesse was so successful at it that when Schiaparelli shut her atelier, Collard hired your mother. She designed separates before Givenchy, though he claims she stole his idea."

He spoke in such a staccato burst it took a moment for me to digest it. Once I did, I couldn't curb my incredulity, thinking it must be one of her many exaggerations, seeded like pollen in her wake.

"My mother designed a *collection*?"

"Just one that I'm aware of." He removed a yellowed newspaper clipping from his pocket, unfolding it. "It was shown in 1955. She had the samples made in London because it was cheaper at the time. It's also against couture regulations, so French customs seized her samples. In less than two weeks, she had the collection remade here and modeled the clothes herself at the Plaza Athénée. It was very well received."

I stared in amazement at a winsome illustration of a silhouette in a crisp raised-collar blouse and wasp-waisted satin skirt, with an accompanying photo of Mama, a pencil in hand, seated at a desk in a studiously artful pose.

"As I understand it," he went on, "she had offers to invest in her own house."

Lifting my eyes to him, I recalled her words: *We must find something we love to do . . . I found it in Paris.*

He smiled. "You must keep that, as a souvenir."

"Thank you." I refolded the article and pocketed it, resisting the urge to ask him why he'd gone to the trouble of excavating it from some dusty fashion archive. Obviously Betty had also told him about me, or, specifically, about my mother. And while the revelation that Mama had done more than run around in daring dresses caught me aback, the purpose for delivering an old newspaper clipping about her work eluded me.

Betty was passing a joint to Yves, who melted into the sofa with boneless ease, his blue eyes behind his glasses glazing over. Paloma pulled off her turban to show it to him. He explored it as if it were flesh, his fingers interpreting the subtle folds and seams.

"If we wanted to hire you," said Pierre, startling me, "what would you like to do? Yves designs our lines. We're expanding the house and he could use the help."

I must have looked dumbfounded. No one had ever asked me what I wanted to do in fashion. I'd never asked myself. I did whatever came naturally to me. A fleeting impression of enameled stones twined in metal flittered across my mind; I saw myself at a desk, like Mama in the photograph. The rest was blurry, unformed.

"I don't know," I said. "I've never worked in couture."

"You know how to dress," he replied, like it was another in-arguable fact. He glanced at Yves. An invisible wire seemed to thrum between them. Close to thirteen years together, Fernando had said. I couldn't imagine a relationship lasting that long.

Smoke drifted through Yves's hair as he smoked, and Paloma pirouetted for him, swirling out her dress. He appeared en-grossed in her, blind and deaf to anything else, until he said, without looking at me, "Loulou, how would you wear this?"

Paloma turned to me with implicit challenge. On the sofa, Betty snorted. "She can wear it however she likes. Isn't that the point? What she doesn't know, she'll learn."

Were they *testing* me?

I feigned indifference as I studied the dress. It was second-hand; I'd shopped in enough flea markets and thrift stores to recognize the dated, overpadded shoulders and nipped waist. Hints of leaves nested in the flowery pattern, like bits of clover. I envisioned a movie star of the era in it.

"With a green feather boa," I said. "Like Dietrich."

Sudden silence fell, as if I'd pronounced the unthinkable.

Paloma exclaimed, "Marvelous!" She wagged a finger at me. "You *do* like rummaging in the attic. I found this dress in my mother's closet; it's from the forties. I made the rhinestone neck-lace for it. Yves likes it so much he's asked me to design jewelry for his boutique. A green boa would be sublime. *Why* didn't I think of it—"

She suddenly stopped herself, realizing what she'd admitted aloud. Fernando's attentive smile didn't waver. Betty shrugged as if it were inevitable.

I sensed the wire vibrate again between Pierre and Yves.

"Well?" asked Pierre, of no one in particular.

Yves raised his face to me. His slow smile brimmed with intimacy, as though he and I were accomplices in a newfound secret.

"I think," he said, "you should come see me at my studio in Hôtel Forain."

HOURS LATER, THEY left in a cloud of intoxicated laughter. Fernando declined their invitation to dinner, claiming he was tired. I saw Paloma approach him, a brief, apologetic exchange, but otherwise, he behaved as if nothing were amiss, even after the door shut behind them.

"That was unexpected," he finally said. He was also unsettlingly sober despite the afternoon of indulgence, piling dirty cups in the sink and emptying ashtrays.

"I'm not doing it," I said.

"What? Of course you are."

"No. I don't like what they did." My voice faltered. "He stole Paloma from you."

"He didn't steal her." Fernando rinsed the teapot. "She explained it to me. They ran into each other at a Rothschild dinner party, where he admired her jewelry. Paloma asked him what he thought she should charge for it. He offered to test pricing for her at the boutique. She'd be crazy not to take him up on it. So would you."

"Fernando, it's not fair—"

He turned from the sink to stalk into the living room, where the pungent smell of cigarette and marijuana lingered. Suddenly, he went still, as though he couldn't bear to see their hollowed indents on the sofa. "You can stay here as long as you like. Go see him. It's why you came to Paris."

Behind me, water dripped into the sink. "I came to see you—"

"Loulou." The look he shot over his shoulder cut off my protest. "You want this. I saw it when we went to his show. I saw it again today. He must want it, too."

"I barely know him. I don't know what he wants." Or, I thought, what I did.

"You do. You're not like Betty."

"What does that mean?" I heard the icy shake of my mother's martini.

Style is the fearlessness to do as we please.

"She doesn't take it seriously," he said. "Plus, she's pregnant."

I stared at him. "She is?"

"That's what she told Yves. She doesn't want to model anymore. Though"—he gave a curt laugh—"I can't imagine her raising a baby or turning down free clothes."

"And they think I can *replace* her?"

"She's never worked for them. Yves dresses her to attend his boutique openings and pose for pictures. His ideal woman. That's all she does—and all she wants to do. Betty isn't interested in going to work every day."

"What do they want from me?" I hated that I'd failed to grasp the undercurrent of intrigue, even as it swirled around me. "Because of this?" I pulled the folded clipping from my pocket. "Because my mother sold clothes for Schiaparelli and designed one collection? I might not be Betty, but I'm also nothing like my mother."

"You're not. You're different. Yves sees it. His sixth sense." Fernando removed his coat from the peg by the door. "I see it, too."

I started to move toward him. He held up his hand. "I'm going out to clear my head. After that, I'll renew my contract with Revillon and book a flight to New York. Back to my fur coats and illustrations for *Vogue*. I'll be fine."

"Then I'll go with you. We can have your samples made there, do your show at the Factory. Andy loves to host fashion events."

He shook his head. "Loulou, you're not thinking clearly. The chance to work for Yves is a once-in-a-lifetime opportunity."

"It wasn't for you. You asked me first."

"I don't have a job to offer. I don't have a house. I'm nothing, compared with him."

My throat tightened. "You're someone to me."

Fernando went silent for a painful moment before he said quietly, "You're not going to tell me you're in love with me?"

"No." I tried, and failed, to muster a smile. "I'm not. I know it's—"

"Impossible." He let out a sigh. "Whatever this is between us . . . it can't last."

"I understand." I spoke softly, because I did understand. I'd known it all along, deep down inside, before Betty even mentioned it. "You prefer men."

Though I hoped saying it aloud would ease the burden of the weighted air between us, he seemed to flinch. "Then let's not make this more complicated than it is. We can still be friends. Good friends. I don't want to lose that."

"I'll always be your friend. I didn't mean for any of this to happen."

"No one ever does. Don't wait up." With a nod, he left.

I washed the dishes, tidied the living room, and paced the flat, toking on a joint with the windows open, the laughter of passersby and honking cars filling the night.

My head reeled, the euphoria of the day crushed by my disappointment for him. That we'd just ended our romantic association, if it could be deemed that, hurt me far less than the nagging thought that I'd unwittingly betrayed him. He'd been so welcoming, entrusting me with his hopes for his new line.

I'd wanted to realize those dreams with him, though I had known we wouldn't last other than as friends, only for it to be pulverized in his very apartment, by people whom he also called friends.

Eventually I peeled off my clothes and tumbled into bed, brooding.

As I drifted to sleep, I saw Yves's secretive smile.

You should come see me at my studio.

Fernando didn't return that night.

4

Fernando departed for New York that week. He'd appeared at the flat two days after the party, disheveled and bruise-eyed, but no worse for the apparent wear. I had the impression he'd been with a man, a rough, salty aroma about him. I didn't ask. He showered and took a nap, then packed his bags. We had dinner at a local bistro, talking about nothing in particular, evading any raw edges, until he said, "I'll be away for a while. The rent is covered this month. It's not much, so just tell me when you can afford it."

Then he was gone.

I was alone in Paris. In his flat; he'd left me a set of keys. I had enough money to buy food, if I was frugal, but paying rent right now was out of the question. I regretted splurging at the second-hand store. I couldn't eat my new pleated skirt or pajama pants.

Coming to Paris seemed like a mistake. I felt lost, as I had as a child at boarding school, in dire need of escape. Snooping around in the bathroom cabinet, I located a stash of Mandrax and popped two, then impulsively phoned my mother, reverse-charging the call. It rang and rang until she picked up, somewhat breathlessly.

"Darling," she said, after she accepted the charge. "How are you?"

"I don't know." I lit a cigarette, starting to feel the Mandrax's hypnotic effect. I loved it for going out dancing, the energy it induced. But if I combined it with alcohol or took too many at once, I passed out and didn't remember afterward what I'd done.

"How so?" Ice clinked as she fixed herself a drink. "You'll have to make it fast. An overseas call is outrageously expensive, and John and I are due at the Factory. Andy has a new protégée he wants us to meet. Another of his waif photographers, God help us. The slinky, dangerous kind, who apparently likes to photograph large penises. You know Andy. He likes his penises like his gossip: the bigger, the better."

"I think Yves Saint Laurent wants to hire me," I blurted out.

"Oh my, that didn't take long. Right to the top." She paused. "You *think* he wants to hire you?"

"I'm not sure. We met at his couture show and spoke for a minute. Then he came to a party here and invited me to his studio."

"Well." She took a moment. "Did you go?"

"Not yet." I really wanted another Mandrax.

"Why not?" At my silence, she made a semi-commiserative sound that made me realize how upended I must be, to have phoned her for maternal comfort. "The not-your-boyfriend designer. He's jealous."

"He broke up with me. Or we broke up. Something like that."

"Something like that happens at your age. Quite often, as I seem to recall."

I smiled weakly. "Mama, Fernando asked me to help him with a line he's designing, but then this thing with Yves happened. He thinks I'd be crazy not to do it."

"He's right. You won't get a better offer." She covered the receiver, hissing at her husband, "Just a minute, darling. It's Loulou from Paris, in a bit of a froth."

"Why didn't you tell me?" I glanced at the folded clipping I'd put on the bedside table. "About your collection in 1955. Pierre, Yves's lover, gave me an article."

"Did he? I'm flattered anyone remembers. But I designed it for Collard. Surely I must have said something about it at some point."

"He also said you had offers to finance your own house."

She laughed. "One offer. From an admirer who wanted me to be his mistress on the side. I said no. I love the work, not the responsibility. I saw what happened to Schiap. All the acclaim and hard work, and then it was over. Fashion changes. We can't all endure like Chanel. It's a brutal business, especially at that time. Especially for women."

I let the reality of her words sink in. "He didn't say what they want me to do, but how can I possibly contribute? He's already famous." As soon as I admitted it, I wished I'd taken the extra pill and passed out.

"He makes clothes, darling. You know how—"

"How to dress. Yes, Pierre told me that, too. It's not a credential."

"In fashion, it's the only credential. You're selling yourself short, as usual. I'm sorry the boyfriend/not-boyfriend didn't work out, but—"

"Fernando is gay."

"Of course he is. The ones who break our hearts always are. Look, I must run. The car is here, and John is fit to burst." I started to hang up when she said, "Chin up. You're perfectly capable of whatever it is. I'm rather envious, to be honest."

She hung up without saying goodbye, which was also typical of her. Putting the receiver on the cradle, I stared at the walls. All of Fernando's sketches were gone. The bedside clock ticked toward two p.m. The entire city felt empty to me, like a desert.

Pulling out my address book, I dialed Betty's number.

"Oui?" She came on the line as she did in person, languid and slightly irritated.

"Can you talk?"

She yawned. "Barely. I was asleep. We had a late night. A new club opened on rue Sainte-Anne. Fabulous. We phoned you to join us, but no one answered."

"We?"

"François and I. Yves, Pierre, and Paloma. They kept asking me about you."

My stomach lurched. "I must have been at dinner with Fernando."

"Everything well?"

"Not really. He went back to New York."

"Oof." A pause. "Was it dramatic?"

I swallowed, stubbing out my cigarette. "I feel bad for him."

"Don't. He understands how these things go."

I imagined one of her shrugs. "Did you know?"

"About Paloma selling her jewelry at the boutique? We all did. Fernando must have known it, too. Or maybe he didn't want to know." Betty stifled another yawn. "He has his job with Revillon. It pays the bills, but he wants his initials on a logo, his headline in *Vogue*. He might get it. You belong somewhere else."

"With Yves?"

"We think so."

The room tilted about me. "I don't understand."

"There's nothing mysterious about it. He's always on some impossible deadline. Two couture collections a year, plus the prêt-à-porter. They have twenty-two boutiques worldwide and are about to launch a menswear line, plus God knows what else. Pierre wants to conquer the world. Yves wants to hide in Marrakesh. Whenever we lure him out, he goes wild, like a child in a candy store. You're not what he's used to. You didn't treat him as if he were so terribly important. You didn't try to impress him."

"Betty, we only just met."

"That's all it takes with him. A spark. Infatuation. Did you get his gift?"

"Gift?"

"He sent you a gift."

I tossed my gaze at the flat doorway. "The concierge delivered a box today. I thought it was for Fernando. There's no label on it."

"It's for you. Open it."

I went to retrieve it, feeling how light it was. Setting it on the futon, I tore open the sealed flaps, the scented tissue inside—the same perfume I'd smelled on Paloma—crinkling as I tugged out a folded garment.

"Oh." I had the phone tucked between my shoulder and ear, the garment dangling in my hand. It wasn't monochrome, not a design from his show. It was almost weightless, made of iridescent ocher-and-russet cotton with pale saffron swirls, with a high, ruffled neckline.

"He made it for you," Betty said into my stunned silence. "The day after the party. He said you made him think of a gypsy in a peasant dress."

I felt close to tears.

"He sees us, Loulou. Inside and out. It's glorious. And a little terrifying."

"All right." I curbed the tremor in my voice, which I wasn't sure was the drug taking too much effect or my surge of insecurity. "I'll go see him."

"He won't stab you with his scissors. He's a perfect gentleman. I used to visit him at the studio all the time, but I'm too lazy now. Spoiled. I have my husband, my life. Pierre thinks I'm a bad influence on Yves. I don't like to fight. I love them both."

"I'll go tomorrow," I said, more firmly.

"If you don't want to work for him, just tell him no."

She hung up. I contemplated the dress. A dress. He'd made me a dress.

As I pulled it over my head, a card tucked in its folds floated to my feet: a hand-painted snake motif, coiled around the word "LOVE," and his signature.

When I turned to the mirror I saw how he'd captured my essence, without having measured an inch of my body. Light from the window penetrated the fabric to ghost my silhouette, my small breasts and jutting hip bones, my skinny, coltish legs.

I saw another woman in my reflection, in a dress I'd never have chosen for myself. As if a stranger hid inside me, surfacing under my skin.

And I felt it. The power of his seduction.

You want this.

I WAITED IN the salon. Without the anticipation of a show, the milling crowd and conversation, it resembled any empty drawing room, like the one in my ex-husband's castle or my maternal grandparents' Sussex estate. All that was missing were the excess chintz and clutter of historic paintings.

Wondering if I could smoke, though everyone had been smoking the day of the show, I was fishing in my pocket for my cigarettes when the crisp clack of heels on the creaking floor turned me around.

A short, plump woman came toward me. Her fine tweed skirt and jacket matched her flame-tinted hair, styled in beauty parlor affectation, a black band holding back her bangs from her close-set green-brown eyes, full cheeks, and stubby nose. She had the pretty banality of a secretary, but the authority in her approach made me straighten my spine.

She reminded me of a headmistress at one of my boarding schools.

"I'm Clara Saint." Her greeting was cool, her English slightly accented. "I manage the press office for Rive Gauche. Monsieur Saint Laurent has been expecting you."

She hadn't asked for my name, and I hadn't called in advance. Maybe Betty had alerted them to my arrival. As I plucked at my gray pleated skirt, which I'd paired with a cardigan and ropes of fake pearls, along with my battered suede boots, the slight arch of her brow made me think she'd anticipated someone altogether different.

I was glad to see it. After trying on various outfits at the flat, including the dress he'd sent, I recalled what Betty had said, about not trying to impress. I'd opted for demure, which now seemed like an act of rebellion.

"If you'll follow me." She led me past the salon and up a wrought-iron-railed staircase to the second floor, where I glimpsed a room through an ajar door with a block-color modern painting on the wall and a stolid desk.

"Monsieur Bergé is out at the moment," she said, sharp-eyed at my curiosity. "My office is next to his; we work together. The workroom and monsieur's studio are down the hall. The ateliers are located on the third floor, and the cabine is off the salon."

"Cabine?"

"For our house mannequins. They present our most recent collection for our clients, and monsieur fits his designs on them for each new collection."

"You keep models here all the time?" I imagined a group of plasticized women languishing in a shrouded room, painting their eyes and lips, waiting to be summoned.

"It's required for couture."

As she steered me past an open room where women in white

smocks toiled over wide tables, corkboards on the wall pinned with drawings and rows of shelves crammed with fabrics, with additional bolts stacked in every corner, I barely heard a sound. A hermetic hush cocooned the place, like in a church or laboratory.

At a black-painted door bearing his name on a plaque, she paused. "I'll let monsieur know you're here." She knocked to announce herself, then slipped inside, closing the door behind her.

The sudden urge to break a rule, as I'd so often done at school, propelled me into the space where the women were working.

They had their heads bent over their tasks, dressmaker dummies at their sides pinned with colorless cotton calico. I paced to one of the dummies, trailing my fingers over the visible seams of a safari-style jacket, intrigued by how they conceived these initial spectral incarnations of his designs.

A voice rapped, "Please don't touch it." A short, dark-eyed woman in a beige blouson smock that demarcated her from the others, her severe chignon mirroring her stern expression, trudged out from behind a table. "You'll ruin it."

"Just by touching it?" Her vehemence took me aback.

"Even the cleanest hands carry impurities. Oils on our skin. Monsieur Saint Laurent's modèles are made to his exact specifications. Each one takes us hours to complete." She marched to me, armed with a pincushion.

I had the feeling she was perfectly capable of stabbing me with her scissors and retreated as she rounded the dummy, making a minute adjustment.

She released a sigh. "Who are you? The studio is off-limits to sales personnel."

"Anne-Marie, she isn't personnel." Yves spoke from the doorway. A cigarette smoldered between his fingers; he wore a kneelength white smock like his assistants. "I invited Loulou to visit us. She is my guest."

"A guest who spoiled your specific modèle." I couldn't stanch my mortified laugh.

"Anne-Marie is the director of my studio. She's very particular about our modèles." As he stepped to us, I noticed every woman in the room stopped whatever she was doing to give him her full attention. "You haven't spoiled anything. It's a sample."

"That was perfected for hours. I'm sorry," I said to Anne-Marie. "I didn't know."

"Evidently," she replied, but her manner softened. "This is the wild girl you told us about? She doesn't look wild to me. She looks as if she's about to apply at the lycée in her mother's pearls."

Yves's throaty laugh extinguished the tension. Laughter exploded around me, the women giggling in unison as I felt my cheeks flush.

"It's true, yes?" said Yves. "You're a new student here."

I joined in the mirth to conceal my embarrassment, giving Anne-Marie a contrite shrug. "Not a very good one, it seems."

She clucked her tongue. "As you say, you didn't know." Her voice turned brisk. "We can review the modèle whenever you're ready, monsieur."

"Later." With a flick of his fingers, he made another adjustment to the sample that was imperceptible to me. "I'm taking my new friend out to lunch first."

My new friend . . .

I regretted my recklessness as I followed him into his studio, dominated by a white desk heaped with books, papers, and pencils. Shelves of art volumes encompassed the wall behind it. Floor-to-ceiling mirrors occupied the opposite wall. By the entry to the workroom, the back of the door was festooned with fabric and thread swatches. It had the feeling of a sanctuary, like the workroom, but also creative dishevelment, a place where magic was brewed.

"My little kingdom," he said. "I'm glad you decided to come."

"Anne-Marie probably isn't," I remarked, perusing various objects on his bookshelves: little statues, a misshapen lump of rock, a framed playing card (the ten of clubs).

"The rock is from my villa in Marrakesh," he said, as I turned it over in my hands. "I found the card here, in the cellar, when Pierre and I were looking for a house. We had limited funds, and hôtel particuliers like this aren't easy to find. Pierre thought it was too far away from the other fashion houses. No one had ever opened one in this district. As soon as I saw that card, I knew this was the one."

"Because the card would bring you luck?"

"It did. It still does." He smiled when I bumped against his desk and a burst of furious yapping erupted from underneath it. A Chihuahua was ensconced in a cushioned basket. Beside it on a pillow was a stout black-and-white bulldog, growling at me.

"My petite Hazel," he said. "And my Moujik. Careful, they might bite."

"Not me." I kneeled to proffer the back of my hand. Hazel sniffed me warily. After a moment, she licked my fingers.

"She must like you." He didn't sound surprised.

I caressed the little dog's ears and cooed at the bulldog. He growled again, not baring his teeth but unwilling to submit to my touch.

"Moujik needs to know you better," he said. "Like Anne-Marie."

"I've always gotten along with dogs." I stood. "I rescued a Saint Bernard puppy once when I was at school. The poor thing was lost and hungry. I fed him scraps and hid him in the school garden shed until they discovered him."

"What happened?"

I shrugged. "They took him away. I hope he had a good life. I never saw him again. They kicked me out of the school four months later." Pausing at his desk, I retrieved a sketch from among the pile without thinking. "This is pretty."

He stepped to my side, lighting another cigarette. He offered me the pack—Lucky Strikes, an American brand—and I shook my head, sifting through his sketches, drawing out another. "I like this, too."

Lifting his chin to exhale smoke over our heads, he regarded the sketch in my hand before returning his gaze to me. Behind his glasses, his blue eyes were unblinking, taking in my entire person without leaving my face.

"Why?"

"It's different. The shoulder . . . you made it sharper." At his quick intake of breath, I said, "It reminds me of Paloma's dress. Is this what you're designing next?"

"I'm thinking of it. Anne-Marie tells me it'll be too much of a scandal."

I thought of his braless models in see-through shirts, of the last of the couture dragons denigrating his line as pornography. Compared with that, I didn't see anything remotely offensive in these sketches.

"Why would it be a scandal?"

"The war. The occupation. It wasn't a romantic time."

"So, they won't appreciate you rummaging in their attic," I said.

He smiled. "Which of the others do you like?"

I paged through the sketches. Some were sedate, as if he were tiptoeing around his impulses, but the majority captivated me with their depiction of old-style glamour. When I chose the ones that I liked best, he asked, "Do you think it would be a scandal?"

"I don't see why. They're beautiful. Only . . ." I paused. Was he really asking for my opinion, or was he indulging me after I'd taken it upon myself to remark on his work?

"What?" He cocked his head. "You can be honest with me."

"There's no color. It's all black and white."

"I haven't decided on colors yet," he said, a bit defensively to my ears. "Once I finish my drawings, Anne-Marie and I choose which designs to make, then select the fabrics."

"You never use color when you draw a collection?"

"I do. Just not this time."

"Maybe because it's safer to dress them in mourning?"

"Mourning?" His eyes widened a fraction. "I'm thirty-four. I didn't live through the war. I was a child when it ended, living in Oran with my parents."

"I didn't live through it, either. None of the young women who wear your clothes did. To us, it's history." As a frown fretted his forehead, my intimation taking seed, I added quickly, "I'm just saying, if you dress the past in mourning, how can it be a scandal?"

He went still, giving me the disquieting sensation that I'd gone too far. "A funeral. My respectful homage to the dead."

My mouth parched as he riffled through the stack of sketches I'd chosen, crunching pages in his fist. A few drawings eluded his grip to drift to the floor, and I hastily retrieved them, fearing he'd trample over them.

"I *won't* be a prisoner." He spoke with vehemence. "I'm tired of living by their rules. Pierre did all of this for me, to give me a house, a name. He found our American investor. I owe him everything." He turned his eyes on me. "Him—and no one else. The world thinks they *know* me. They don't. I'm not such a good boy."

I didn't know how to respond.

"Did you like the dress I sent?" he asked abruptly.

"Very much," I replied.

"But not enough to wear it. Was it too predictable, like this collection?"

The moment went taut between us. I thought of lying to him, then thought better of it. "You don't know me well enough to dress me."

His jaw clenched. Swerving about, he strode into the workroom. As I went after him, clutching the sketches, Moujik bounded from under the desk. Yves came to a halt before the shelving stuffed with bolts of fabrics: hundreds of variations in silk and velvet and cotton, linen and wool. A surfeit of luxury that he seemed to dismiss in resentment when he said, "*Show* me."

The women sat frozen at the tables. When Anne-Marie hastened toward us, hearing the clamp in his tone, Moujik barked. She stopped.

Yves snapped his fingers. Moujik dropped at once onto his haunches.

Setting the sketches I'd rescued onto a worktable, I focused on the first one: a padded-shouldered coatdress with buttons halfway down the front. Taking a breath to ease the tightness in my chest, I let my eyes rove over the shelves.

"This." I pulled out a rich velvet, spilling it like ink onto the table.

"It's black." Dry rebuke blistered his tone. "Mourning."

"Yes, but you drew these lips on it." I pointed at the surrealistic detail on his sketch, extracted a bloodred bolt of silk from another shelf. "If you do them in this color, appliquéd in glitter or sequins, it's her lipstick: the undercover spy, stealing secrets."

Anne-Marie was staring at me as if I'd lost my mind. Or she feared Yves had lost his, her mouth ajar as he directed his gaze to the fabric, the sketch juxtaposed against it.

Clarity surfaced in his eyes. "What else?"

"For the double-breasted pantsuit, a charcoal-gray wool with pinstripes, like—"

"A gangster." He put a hand to his chest. "Yes, I see it. I *see* her."

Moujik whined, pawing at Yves's legs. I looked past the dog to the bolts propped in a corner, wrapped in cellophane. As I started to them, Anne-Marie said, "We've scheduled those fabrics for return. None of them fit our needs—"

I tore off the plastic on one, toppling the others, unspooling gold-and-black pleated silk, silk-screened with mosaic images of Grecian athletes. I indicated the sketch of a peplum dress with a deep V-shaped décolletage. "The Hollywood starlet."

Yves lit a cigarette, pacing around the table. "We need more. The contrabandist. The chanteuse. The femme fatale. All of them."

"Polka dots for the femme fatale." Hauling a nearby stool, I perched on it to extract a white-polka-dotted red fabric bolt from an upper shelf, unraveling it to the floor as I recalled the other sketches on his desk, seeing Paloma twirling her dress in Fernando's flat. "For the turban and blouse. A green feather boa for the chanteuse—"

He laughed. "Or my le Smoking, with very short pants." Beckoning Anne-Marie, he said, "Look at it now. Is it a scandal? Or a challenge to free women from the past?"

Anne-Marie allowed herself a tentative step forward, as if it were against her better judgment. She took in the collage of colors, ripped from her tidy shelves.

Moujik took advantage of the moment to roll about on the silk I'd spilled onto the floor, shedding fur and splaying his paws in the air.

Yves giggled. "If Moujik approves, it's a sign that fabric is meant to be used."

Anne-Marie lifted narrowed eyes to me. "Where did you learn to do this?"

"I didn't do it," I said. "The designs are his."

"And you've never seen them before today?" Suspicion notched her voice.

"No," cut in Yves, before I could answer. "I only showed them to you."

He handed me his half-finished cigarette as I stepped off the stool. The nicotine jolted my veins. My mouth scorched on the filter, tasting burning tobacco and him.

"Then she has a gift for it." I couldn't tell if Anne-Marie spoke in admiration or intimidation. "An instinct for color." Another pause ensued. "It's still a risk, monsieur. We've never shown a collection like this. What would you like to do?"

He said briskly, "Order in lunch from the bistro. I must start over. The silhouettes need refinement. I also need all our fabric books, any new swatches we have in stock. What I don't find, we can request from our vendors. Everything must look authentic."

Anne-Marie nodded. "At once. Sylvie, please see to lunch." A blond woman at one of the worktables jumped up to scurry to a telephone. "You'll let us know, monsieur, when you finalize the silhouettes? If we wish to present this collection for spring, we haven't much time."

I detected an undertone to her inquiry, an uncertainty that she still exerted control over the process they'd established in the studio.

He blinked. "Of course. I can't do any of this without you." He cast another look at the table. "We'll work together, as always."

Taking me by my arm, he guided me back to his studio, the

women watching us. As he closed the door, I heard whispering break out among them.

"Will you stay?" he said. "Work on it with me?"

I couldn't believe he'd still want me to, after I'd challenged his vision and raided his workroom like a pirate, to Anne-Marie's obvious disconcertion.

You're perfectly capable of whatever it is.

"We can try." Inexplicably, even as I realized how much I did want to collaborate with him, I restrained my eagerness, as if I had to be certain I could walk away.

"Then just between us." He smiled. "Nothing official until you decide."

I met his eyes. "Anne-Marie still thinks it's a risk."

"I need to take risks." He held my gaze. "Do the unexpected." His fingers coiled about my arm. "Let's do it together, Loulou. Let's cause a scandal."

5

"oulou! What is taking you so long? They're waiting for us." Betty shoved open the bedroom door and laughed. "Did you lose another suitcase?"

I stood in my black panties before the mirror, the carnage of my closet strewn about me. "I can't decide what to wear. None of it feels right."

"Andy's been here over a month." She eyed me. "You already met him in New York." Her hand swept out, encompassing the mess. "You're obviously taking advantage of the clothing allowance. You must have the entire Rive Gauche boutique in here."

"It's a night out with Andy and Yves." I bent down to pick up a khaki skirt, holding it uncertainly against my hips. "There'll be photographers. Reporters."

"And? They'll mob us at the entrance, as usual, and then they're banned. You know Fabrice's rule: Only he says who gets into the club, and he never allows the press. The queens. The basement. The glory hole in the bathroom. It's our place, not theirs."

"Right." I let out a nervous laugh. "I'm overthinking it."

"Just wear something you can dance in. Not *that*. François has been circling the block for half an hour. And Yves must be there by now, wondering where we are."

Discarding the khaki skirt, I rummaged in my overstuffed closet. When my hand fell upon the dress in the far back, I pulled it out.

She chuckled. "*Now* you're going to wear it?"

"No." I returned it to the rack, selecting a scarlet Rive Gauche blouse instead, paired with le Smoking trousers and red pumps. Ruffling my hair, I affixed a fringed sash about my waist, tying it off at a rakish angle, and ladled on as many bracelets as I could. I turned to her. "Voilà."

"Perfect." She smiled. "Yves loves to see us in his pants."

As we turned off the lights and I locked the front door, she said, with that prescient sense she could display, despite her apparent indifference to everything, "It's not about being seen in public with Andy and Yves. It's because no one besides us really knows if you're working at the house. Does Fernando even know?"

I swallowed, turning to the stairs. "He must. But he might not be there tonight."

"Or he might." She followed me down, her vinyl thigh-high boots rustling on her bare legs. "He came from New York with them, and he's staying with a friend while Andy shoots his movie in Lagerfeld's apartment. Or Andy's boyfriend shoots it for him, so Andy can go shopping with Pierre for overpriced antiques."

"While I live in his flat. I'm covering the rent now, but it's still his place."

"Talk to Yves about getting your own place. He must be paying you enough to afford one. And don't tell me you're still feeling sorry for poor Fernando."

I lit a cigarette at the curb, the Parisian autumn night chilling my skin. "I should have brought a jacket."

"We'll be in the car. And inside the club. Loulou, look at me." As I did, Betty's eyes narrowed. "You have to stop feeling guilty for doing what was right for you."

I drew in the nicotine. I'd taken a few pills as I'd scavenged for something to wear, but I still felt too sober. "I don't know why I do."

"Neither do I. Maybe you need to get laid." Her frank declaration made me cough. "Well?" she said. "How long has it been?"

"Not that long," I admitted. "Just no one I liked enough to see again."

"You go out all the time. There must be a man, or a woman, in Paris you like enough to see again. And no, the gay men you sleep with don't count."

"Betty, I don't have the time. I'm at the studio every day from nine in the morning to sometimes late at night. The knitwear girl quit after a horrid row with Anne-Marie."

She rolled her eyes. "Who hasn't had a row with Anne-Marie?"

"I haven't. She's the studio director. The girl up and left us in the lurch, so I volunteered to take over. Then Yves kept asking for my opinion—this scarf or those shoes—until before I knew it, he put me in charge of accessories for the show."

"Now you know why I wear the clothes and don't set foot near the hôtel until the day of the show." She searched the street for François. "You end up without a life."

"I love it," I said. "Especially after everyone leaves, and it's just me and Yves. He forgets to eat, so I fetch us food from the bistro. We talk for hours while he draws."

"He's always like that. He craves the company, but he's in another world. All he thinks about are his dresses."

"How can he think about anything else? He's responsible for every creative decision. Pierre won't interfere, if he can avoid it. He's in charge of the business side and has made it very clear to me he doesn't want to be involved in atelier drama."

"What about Clara? She's capable." Betty laughed. "She helped Nureyev defect from the Kirov, after all. He's living and dancing in Paris because of her."

"Yes, she told me. She has so much to do already: dealing with Pierre, organizing coverage for the boutiques, fielding requests for shoots and interviews. She works more than anyone gives her credit for. I've seen her in her office after midnight."

"She still has a lover. If she can manage it, so can you."

"We're almost done with the collection; the final fittings are next week. Except yesterday, Yves decided we need new models for the show. Different faces. I have a slew of headshots to review with him tomorrow."

"Ooh-la-la." She whistled through her teeth. "You thought you might not want a job and now you have ten. He probably isn't paying you enough."

"It's enough. I've no reason to feel bad. My mother saw Fernando at the Factory; he seemed fine. He was with Halston, who said he's dying to meet Yves."

"I'm sure Halston is. He might be taking America by storm with his Ultrasuede nonsense, but he's not selling any of it here." She put her hand on her belly. She was showing now, a knot under her black smock belted below her waist, not that it was going to stop her. "Anyway, I was right. Working with Yves is where you belong."

As François pulled up in the car, she hissed, "You still need to get a lover."

We drove to rue Sainte-Anne, near the Palais Garnier and Bourse de Paris, where the gay nightclub scene thrived. When Betty passed me a vial, I dug in with the little spoon and inhaled the white powder. It stung my nostrils and fired my nerves.

She pouted when I handed it back to her. "I can't do a fucking thing because of the baby. As soon as I give birth, I'm getting stoned for a year."

Her husband patted her leg, swerving us into the back area to avoid the swarm of photographers at the club entrance.

Le Sept's exclusive policy of invitation only—a canny ploy by its proprietor, a former hairdresser named Fabrice—had exploded its popularity, with queues of hopefuls lining the street. He stood by the nondescript black-painted door in a tailored suit and his coif of bleached-blond hair like a genial dictator, pointing at those he approved, who shrieked in elation, and annihilating those who failed to make his cut. In his club, celebrity was unimportant and sexual preference superfluous. Beauty and style were all that mattered to dance the night away with all the beautiful, stylish people around you.

"Loulou!" Fabrice kissed my cheeks as a surge of people pressed in around us. "And Betty. Where have you been, ma belle Viking? It's been too long."

Betty jutted her belly. "Where does it look like I've been?"

He guffawed, stepping aside to let us pass, the burly doorman blocking the crowd as Fabrice chided, "Get back, bitches! Or none of you gets inside tonight."

The exterior facade was deceiving. Beyond the nondescript door lay an intimate restaurant with upholstered banquettes and original nineteenth-century gas fixtures, wired for electricity, bathing patrons in a lustrous glow. It was always crowded, the carpeting beneath my feet throbbing with the heartbeat of the dance floor in the basement.

I spotted Andy at once at a reserved table, shrouded by the scrim of smoke that turned his silver wig metallic. His posture was almost inanimate, like a porcelain doll, while the others around him gesticulated and drank from bottles of champagne in ice buckets, laughing and leaning into each other, packed tight as sardines on the banquettes.

Yves saw us coming toward them and waved, shelved between Pierre at his left, talking to Andy—besides me, only Pierre spoke enough English to carry on a conversation—and Paloma at his right in black satin, a jeweled ornament on her turban. By her side sat Clara Saint in her uniform tweed, though she rarely joined us at le Sept, preferring opening galas at the opera or evenings at the ballet when Nureyev danced, followed by civilized dinner parties in her well-appointed apartment on rue Jacob, in Saint-Germain, not too far from Fernando's. Seated by Clara, a cigarette poised between strong fingers, dressed in a linen suit the color of fresh-churned milk, was one of the most handsome men I'd ever seen.

"Thadée Klossowski de Rola," Betty whispered to me. "Clara's lover. His father is Balthus, the painter. He wants to be a writer. Isn't he divine?"

He was. He turned to us as we squeezed in, saying hello to everyone, Betty declaring she was *starving*. His eyes shone lucent gray blue under thick, naturally arched brows, his nose broad like a boxer's and his jawline defined, enhanced by chiseled cheekbones. As he ran a hand through his unruly mop of auburn hair, I wondered if it felt like a horse's mane, a rough grain to its heft.

Clara said, "Loulou, you've not met my Thadée."

My smile felt too wide on my lips. "We haven't. Lovely to meet you."

"And you. Clara says you've brought a dose of excitement to the house." His wide-lipped mouth quirked as he caught me staring, and I laughed, glancing away only to be trapped by Yves's knowing regard. He gave me a complicit raise of his eyebrow.

"I'm enjoying it," I said. "Clara's been helping me learn the ropes."

"Until you can sail your own ship," replied Thadée, reaching over to pour me a glass of champagne. Thinking everyone must have noticed my attraction to him, I gulped at my glass and babbled to Andy: "How's the movie going?"

"Okay, I think." He tugged at his lower lip, shifting his basilisk stare to me. "Karl's apartment is perfect. Very 2001: A Space Odyssey.

Jed is around here somewhere, probably downstairs dancing. He's been managing the shoot for me."

Betty nudged me under the table.

I remembered Jed from the Factory. He and his twin brother, Jay, were all-American beefcake. Jed had snagged Andy's attention while sweeping the floors, working as a janitor. By now, everyone suspected they must be lovers, ever since Andy was shot in '69 and Jed moved into his apartment to help him recuperate, never leaving his side. But for all his stated disregard for conformity, Andy refused to admit he was gay.

"Is Karl here?" piped Betty, ever ready to poke the hive.

"Yes," said Andy. "Over there, with Corey and Donna. Corey's doing makeup for the movie, and Donna's playing a gold digger. Antonio Lopez, in the red vest, is their friend, a fashion illustrator. The other one is Karl's new protégé, Jacques something or other. He claims to be an aristocrat. I'd like to photograph his crotch."

I turned to the other table. The brash trio flung charged glances in our direction.

Corey was doe-eyed, lithe as a ballet dancer, with the blond ringlets of a Botticelli cherub, and in a white T-shirt molded to his torso. The striking olive-skinned Antonio was pencil-stroke thin, conveying the carnality of a connoisseur. Between them writhed Donna, her bleached brows and curls offset by a bright blue satin minidress. Corey had his hand in her lap, and she pursed her gap-toothed mouth in a staged orgasmic O.

Presiding over the antics was a square-jawed character out of a penny dreadful. Jet-black widow-peaked hair swept back from his mien to his starched collar; a cravat swaddled his thick throat, studded with a cameo; and stony dark eyes that didn't deign to acknowledge us.

At his side sat a striking young man with cut-glass features.

He had arresting, narrow hazel-gold eyes and copper-brown hair slicked to his skull; his wispy mustache was waxed to fin de siècle tips. He was dressed with matinee-idol drama, in an oversized black bow tie and wing-tipped collar under a wide-lapeled white smoking suit stamped in a swirling pattern of pink-and-green nightingales, like chinoiserie, and was smoking a cigarette in a long white filter. When he saw me staring, he whispered in the other man's ear.

Yves said dryly, "The one dressed like Dracula is Karl."

Karl Lagerfeld had been friends with Yves, a fellow classmate; I knew because Clara had mentioned it to me. Or rather, she'd warned me that we didn't mix with Karl's clique. Betty later explained why: Yves and Karl had entered a fashion competition when they were students, and Yves won first prize, incensing Karl. Their friendship cooled after Dior hired Yves. Once Yves established his own house, it simmered into a détente—all of it, Betty assured me, entirely on Karl's part. He worked for Chloé, a ready-to-wear luxury label, as a styliste—the catch-all term for freelance designers hired to design prêt-à-porter. He didn't make couture, so Clara deemed him beneath our standards.

"Don't pay attention to them," snarled Pierre, jolting me back around. "It's what they want. They've been acting like idiots all night."

Yves shrugged. "They're American. I think it's cute. We should hire the girl to model."

I made a mental note of it, refraining from indulging my curiosity. As Donna let out an exaggerated moan that sent Corey into hysterics, Yves smiled.

When the waiter arrived with Betty's plate—I was too jittery to eat—I remembered no one had mentioned Fernando. His name stuck in my throat while I lit a cigarette, drank too much champagne, and did whatever I could to avoid Thadée's regard.

Clara fidgeted with her napkin, glaring under her lashes at the other table, where Donna was calling out for "a cigarette for moi, pleeze!" in a mocking French accent.

Pierre monopolized Andy about an upcoming auction—he was an avid collector—while François engaged Paloma and Betty devoured her roast chicken.

At length, I had to say, "Is Fernando here?"

Yves tapped ash onto his plate, glancing at the trio as Karl paid the bill and they went, tumbling and giggling, downstairs.

"Fernando might show up later." Thadée's voice wrenched my attention to him. "He said he had some sketches to finish. He's staying with us; we're just a few blocks away from his place."

Just a few blocks away, from an apartment that was his, yet he hadn't come to see me. Was he avoiding me? A stab of remorse propelled me out of my chair. "Excuse me, please."

I could feel Thadée's gaze following me as I weaved into the crowd, the restaurant booked solid with fashion people and their entourages, along with a few famous actors. Finding a long line at the ladies' restroom, the women eager to touch up their makeup before hitting the dance floor, I started toward the back stairs leading to the basement, where the music—Diana Ross, "Ain't No Mountain High Enough"—thundered.

There was a tiny restroom in the basement, off the dance floor, that I'd used before in a pinch. Tripping down the narrow stairs in my red heels, I removed them and went barefoot, turning into the darkened corridor, the walls painted pitch black.

The basement wasn't large; by now, the dance floor was filled to over capacity. A top-heavy bar jutted from a corner, and the floor-to-ceiling mirrored walls refracted the neon lights strung above them and the dancing bodies. Men together, women together, or with each other, flinging sweat-sopped hair, lubricated in the metallic aroma of amyl nitrite to heighten the rush. Past the dance floor was a small, enclosed courtyard where they could indulge release. Police raids were never a concern at le Sept. Fabrice made sure of it.

The bathroom reeked of urine. I discerned moaning in the lone stall. Not wishing to intrude, I retreated into the corridor, wedging my feet back into my pumps when a hand touched my shoulder.

"You shouldn't be here alone."

Thadée.

"I've been here before." His touch seared me as he withdrew his hand. "Men always have sex in the stall. It's better than hiding in a back alley or under the bushes in a park. I like it. I like that they can be so free. They've earned it."

His chuckle was low in his chest. "Then it's true, what they say."

"What do they say?" I sounded too flippant. He was too close. We could barely stand side by side in the corridor, which was as thin as a snake.

"That you're fearless. Clara told me you waltzed into Yves's studio and showed him what to do with his collection, in front of the gorgon, Anne-Marie Muñoz."

"I didn't show him what to do. I just—"

"Gave him a push. He gets stuck in his ways. You pushed him."

I smiled, moving past him, my legs brushing against his. "No one pushes Yves."

He said, "Dance with me."

I paused. "Now?"

"Why not?"

"Because they're still upstairs—"

"Talking. About art and fashion. About the sexy boys and girl with Karl, though it infuriates Pierre. Ordering more champagne. Clara is tired. She doesn't enjoy places like this. She's going home. She has to get up early for work."

The dismissive way he said it made me think it was commonplace with them. I didn't know his exact age, but he must be close to mine. I'd discovered at the house that Clara was thirty-two, so probably not much older than him. She might behave as if she were middle-aged, but she wasn't.

"So do I. She and I work together, in case you've forgotten."

"I haven't. She won't mind if I stay a while longer." He didn't reach for my hand, but I felt his fingers anyway, twining in mine. "Come dance with me, Loulou."

I drifted with him onto the floor, into the oily mass, Corey from Karl's clique gyrating with Donna and Antonio; Karl and Jacques nowhere to be seen. Corey made way for us, throwing brazen kisses in our direction. Donna whirled her legs and arms like a cyclone. Yves was right. She was stunning. We should hire her.

Thadée moved as if he swam underwater, the neon limning him in iridescence, his hips swerving into mine.

Suddenly, the music, the cocaine and pills, the champagne— they all hit me like a tidal wave. It pulled me under. I peeled open my blouse to my waist, watching his eyes turn heavy-lidded, sweat lathering his shirt, so I could see a dusting of dark chest hair under the drenched cloth and the sculpture of his body, like Yves's models on the runway.

The crowd was chanting the lyrics, leaping up and wailing. Colliding and breaking apart. Lost in our haven for the beautiful.

Corey thrust his pelvis into Donna as she bent before him, waggling her buttocks, exposing a red thong under her skirt. Their abandon made me forget myself, submerged in the joy of dancing with a beautiful man who was showing me his desire, as they were showing theirs, buoyed on the desires of everyone around us.

Nothing to hide or be ashamed of. We could be and do whatever we wanted.

And as I parted my mouth to kiss him, Thadée shook his head and pulled back.

I froze. They were here, joining in: Betty and François, Yves, and Paloma, laughing and drunk, Yves shedding his reticence to mouth the song in pantomime to Betty as she gyrated in her thigh-high boots. Andy staked a spot by a wall with Pierre, who stood with his arms crossed at his chest. He often left us to dance, wandering into the courtyard to find his own entertainment. Tonight, he stayed put, like a sentinel.

A few steps away, splashed in neon flickers against the black wall, stood Karl, motionless and alone. He wore oversized sunglasses to shield his eyes.

His friend Jacques materialized beside Yves without his shirt, his bow tie unraveled about his olive-skinned throat. Suckling a finger, he trailed it across Yves's shoulder. He was shorter, around my height: a wisp of skin and enticement.

They stared at each other before Yves lifted his hand to trace Jacques's taut stomach to the waistband, inches above his prominent bulge. A charge sparked between them as Jacques, slit-eyed, mouthed something inaudible and slipped away to Corey, Donna, and Antonio, who were grinding into one another.

The crowd roared and opened space for them. Reveling in the voyeuristic display, Corey tore off his T-shirt to reveal taut musculature. Donna dropped her minidress to her ankles and kicked it aside, prancing naked but for her red thong and high heels.

Thadée vanished. Reeling about to crane on tiptoes, I searched above the bobbing seam and caught sight of him moving up the basement stairs in his now semitranslucent damp clothes. His abrupt departure tore at me like a talon.

Yves hooked an arm about my waist to pull me close. Doling out powder from a vial on the crook of his hand, he held it to my nose. As I inhaled, he murmured, "You'll see him again. I can invite him to Marrakesh."

I wanted to see him again. I was young and high on Paris.

I thought every night would be like this.

6

I'd just arrived at the hôtel with a considerable hangover, hastily dosed with a couple of aspirin, a coffee, and a gobbled croissant, when Clara called me into her office.

As I stepped inside, she checked her wristwatch over her perennial stack of papers. "Never a minute late, though I hear the fun went late last night."

"It did. You should have stayed. Anyway, I can't be late today." I forced out a smile, my temples throbbing from rushing up the stairs. "Yves and I are looking at headshots."

"Yes. I heard he wants new faces for the presentation." She extracted a note from her purse by her chair. "I believe he may be interested in this."

The note was handwritten: an address on boulevard Saint-Germain. Seeing my puzzled expression, she said, "Thadée mentioned how taken Yves was with the Americans. I took the liberty of inquiring. Karl rents that apartment for them."

"Oh. Thank Thadée for me." Pocketing the note, surprised and touched that he'd undertaken the effort, I began to turn away.

"You can always thank him yourself," she said, halting me. "Though at the risk of sounding presumptuous, I suggest you don't take his charms too seriously."

I didn't discern hostility in her voice, yet it felt as if she'd flung ice water on me.

"He can be so terribly romantic." She affected a sigh. "A titled mother and a famous painter for a father—it's irresistible. But as you surely know, titled mothers and painter fathers have no money, and for someone without it, he's extraordinarily idle. Not," she went on, inflectionless as if she were discussing a passing acquaintance, "that I mind what he does with his time, providing he doesn't waste mine."

Looking over my shoulder, I saw her mouth part into something that might have been a smile.

"We're not exclusive anymore."

I struggled for the appropriate response. "He—he was just nice to me."

"One thing he's never lacked is manners. I'm giving you friendly advice, woman to woman. His little—how shall I say it? His little *interests* never last very long." Her phone rang, and she picked up the receiver, adding as she did, "Remember what I told you about Karl and his clique."

I tasted bile as I went into the studio. None of it had seemed friendly to me. I had no idea what type of arrangement she and Thadée had, but evidently his flirtation with me had riled her, perhaps because things had gone stale between them. Whatever the reason, I thought it petulant of her. I wasn't about to get into a tussle over her lover, no matter how attractive or romantic he might be.

Yves was seated at his desk, looking over the headshots. He glanced up with a frown at me. "Loulou, I don't like any of these models. They all look the same—"

I tossed the note onto the desk.

"What's this?" He blinked through his glasses. He was also nursing a hangover.

"The Americans," I said through my teeth.

WE STOLE DOWN the hôtel's back stairs like errant children, getting into his black MG sports car and putting on sunglasses to block the sunlight as he drove us to Saint-Germain.

By the time we arrived at the building, I was starting to reconsider. Perhaps Clara's advice was only that, particularly her reminder about Karl's clique.

"We've a lot of work to do," I said. "Maybe we should wait and see—"

He bounded from the car to the building entry, punching the apartment number on the call panel. "If you're worried about running into Karl, he doesn't live here."

"I'm not worried about Karl. It's just that . . . they're his friends, not ours."

He rang the door buzzer again. "What of it? Karl and I aren't the enemies everyone makes us out to be." He leaned toward me, lowering his voice as if he might be overheard. "He's always idolized me. He wanted me to notice his friends."

I heard Thadée in my mind.

Talking. About art and fashion. About the sexy boys and girl with Karl, though it infuriates Pierre.

Clara's unsettling smile also returned to me. We were going behind Pierre's back. Had she given me the address on purpose to undermine me? Things had always been perfectly cordial between us—until today. Even if Thadée had gone to the trouble of locating the Americans, I shouldn't have been so quick to tell Yves.

"We've other models we can choose. We shouldn't—"

The buzzer rang, opening the entry door. "We're dropping in for a visit," he said. "It's not like we're doing anything bad."

"Who the fuck is it?" grumbled a hoarse voice from a floor above us. Yves pushed me ahead, attempting in vain to muffle his laughter.

Corey was peering into the stairwell, his ringlets askew, wearing nothing but leopard-spotted briefs and the bewilderment of someone who'd been out all night and wasn't fully awake.

At the sight of us, his eyes snapped wide. He rushed into the apartment, leaving the door open, so that once we reached the landing, we could see the chaos within.

A tangle of limbs sprawled on a mattress on the floor. Clothing was strewn everywhere, the tables littered with makeup, ashtrays, and pill bottles.

"Donna!" Corey was shaking the girl on the bed. "*Wake up!*"

She groaned, shoving her head under a pillow—"Eat me, Corey. I'm wrecked"—but when Yves purred from the threshold, "Too wrecked for me?" she bolted into an upright position, stark naked, her face creased and her bleary eyes smudged with mascara.

To my surprise, she snatched at the sheet to cover herself—a modesty I wouldn't have thought she had in her, considering her unabashed display at le Sept.

"You're—" Her voice caught. "This can't be happening."

Yves sketched a bow. "With my assistant Loulou de la Falaise."

"Oh my god." Corey gaped at us. "Antonio will *die* when we tell him." His astonishment was genuine and, without his insolence of last night, undeniably sincere. They couldn't be much older than me, only in their early twenties, and obviously starstruck. Yves might complain about his celebrity, dodging paparazzi who chased him around at night, but right now, he was reveling in the fluster.

Corey said, "Antonio's gone to fetch our friend Pat at the airport. She's fabulous. She models in New York, but she's getting a lot of rejections because she's black."

"Oh?" said Yves, his interest piqued.

Scrabbling to search the mayhem on the floor, Corey extracted a rumpled color headshot of an oval-faced girl with skin like raw honey and arresting, heavy-lidded eyes.

Yves took one glance at it. "Bring her, too. Be at my studio at, say, around two this afternoon? We can see about fitting her and Donna for my show, if that's okay?"

"*Okay?*" squealed Donna. "*Oui!*" She let the sheet drop in her enthusiasm. She didn't bother to retrieve it, stumbling from the bed to bark at Corey, "Make them some coffee or . . ." Her demand faltered. Every inch of counterspace was heaped with belongings; judging by the upheaval, they had nothing available to offer.

"We have weed. Some leftover blow," said Corey hopefully.

Yves glanced at me. "Maybe later." He roamed his gaze over Corey, pausing on the low-slung leopard-print briefs. Corey squirmed when Yves drawled, "I'd like to put you in my menswear. Come with them. The men's line debuts next season, and we can always use extra help at a show. Andy mentioned you do makeup."

"I do," exclaimed Corey. "I taught Donna and Pat everything."

Again, I had to stifle my laughter at his excitement, my apprehension vanquished as we turned to leave. Yves tripped down the stairs, while Corey came out after us to whisper, "Is he serious? He really wants *us* to come to his studio and be in his show?"

I met his eyes. "He does. Don't be late. And wear some clothes."

He blushed to his roots.

In the car, Yves chuckled, switching on the ignition. "See? That wasn't so bad."

EVERY SEAT IN the salon was filled; invitations fanned before expectant faces in the indoor heat, while outside the hôtel, January sank its teeth into the Seine.

Ten days ago, Chanel had passed away in her suite at the Ritz. Weeks before her death, she gave an interview in which she

denigrated the past decade—"Flower power? *What* is that?"—
and anointed Yves as her successor, saying only he had the talent
to carry on her legacy. It was an imperious designation from
a woman whose fame had superseded her designs. When the
news came that she was gone, Yves wept—he'd admired her
all his life—even as Pierre sniped, "She was a relic, her house
a museum. We put women without bras on the runway. She
believed a woman should never be seen in public without a hat
and stockings."

Behind the salon curtain, I attended to last-minute panic,
after I'd arranged all the accessories in order of appearance. The
models were unclear as to how Yves wanted their makeup; Corey
hovered nearby, armed with eyeliners and brushes. With an impatience that betrayed his escalating anxiety, Yves said, "Will
someone please *show* them again?" and together with Corey,
we instructed the models on the plum-red lips and smoky eyes
devised for the show. In couture, maquillage was supposed to
be minimal to exalt the clothes, but Yves wanted everything to
match his vision.

As the models finished applying their makeup and began to
dress, I peeped out to catch sight of Paloma in the front row, in a
crimson turban, a black boxy dress, and a fur stole, designed by
Yves for her to demonstrate how the collection ought to be worn.
She was with the cover model Marisa Berenson and Betty, the
chair between them reserved for me.

"Go sit with them," said Yves. "It's time for the disaster to
start."

Inexorably, as the show loomed closer, he'd been overtaken by a
foreboding that he combatted with compulsive attention to detail,
so that we'd barely slept in the last two weeks as we finished the
clothes.

"It won't be a disaster. You're just nervous because it's different."

"*Too* different. You should say you had nothing to do with it." He lit a cigarette, staking out the journalists in the front row. "How could *Vogue* fire Vreeland? She's irreplaceable. And that new editor, I don't recall her name—I hear she worships Halston and wants to modernize the magazine to bring in more advertisers. Diana understood me."

"She's Grace Mirabella," I reminded him, having assisted in overseeing the invitations. "She was Vreeland's associate editor for years. She understands you." I kissed his cheek. "You'll see."

Taking the long way around, I entered the salon through the door where Betty had first left me to see his show, though by now I was no longer an unknown.

Rumors had spread of my presence at the house, with speculation running amok. Photographers who sold candid pictures to fashion magazines and tabloids had started besieging me when I went out. I didn't know how they managed it, given my erratic itinerary, never the same club on any given night, yet somehow, they found me, flashing cameras in my face, barraging me with questions about Yves. My answer was always the same: I was Yves's friend, nothing more.

I belied my declaration now, sporting a cropped pink satin jacket he'd designed for me, paired with purple satin shorts over black tights, my hair curled into ringlets to match the collection's theme.

Taking my seat, I saw by the probing glance that Grace Mirabella directed at me that she'd already deduced why I was here.

Marisa had come at my request through Berry, who was dating a movie star in Los Angeles. One of the most highly paid print models, discovered by Vreeland herself, Marisa's glamorous presence asserted that our spring Libération collection was not to be missed, diluting a bit of the sting of Vreeland's absence, if not Yves's apprehension.

The lights lowered to highlight the path from the curtain—a new theatrical lighting device Yves had incorporated. He'd wanted to use songs from the era, too, but musical accompaniment was unheard of for couture, and Anne-Marie had expressed such voluble alarm that he let himself be dissuaded.

The models began to appear.

I'd thought we had no reason for concern. We'd even burst into laughter during the fittings, Yves crying out, "No, no! It's too grotesque, like Carmen Miranda exploded all over her," while I reassured the model in the offending outfit and conferred with him as to how we might adjust it. I hadn't stopped to dwell on the collection's overall impact, which to me had an insouciance that hardly deserved condemnation.

Yet as the six models entered the salon and rounded it before returning behind the curtain to quickly change into their next outfit, the impact was visceral—an unmistakable shattering of high-society refinement. With our plunging necklines in clinging chiffon; cropped fox-fur jackets, dyed electric blue or green; the coatdress spattered in lipstick kisses; and day dresses with lace-corset insets, along with the sharp-angled shoulders of the suits, the turbans and cloche hats, we'd depicted a gallery of seductive wartime glamour for women who took the Pill and burned their bras.

The salon went quiet as a tomb.

Then the Americans came out.

In barely-there culottes and a puff-shouldered le Smoking jacket, Pat strode arm in arm with Donna. Pat's bare chest was crisscrossed by diamanté-studded straps, the scarf I'd knotted at her throat a corsage of bloodied petals. Donna's eyebrows and her lips had been painted chalk white by Corey. Pat had astounded us with her limber beauty and her inability to stay still. She didn't pose; she whirled, and her raw exuberance captivated Yves.

During the run-through, once he'd ensured she and Donna could take off their jackets without turning the sleeves inside out, he encouraged them to play to the audience.

They were doing just that.

Pat arched her spine, curling her red-nailed fingers into mock claws, a sleek chanteuse on the prowl. Donna sashayed her hips in her polka-dotted blouse, matching turban, and sleek cream trousers, the spotlight revealing she wasn't wearing any underwear. Yves had shown nudity before in his collections, but she wasn't an idealized silhouette veiled in gossamer. She moved with animalistic ease, her lips parted by her gap-toothed O, delighting in the palpable dismay she generated.

The silence weighed on my nape. The journalists sitting around me seemed paralyzed in dread that the girls would leap into their laps and start unzipping flies.

Then a male reporter hissed, "Clothes to be worn on the bidet. *Shame!*"

Lunging to his feet, he charged from the salon. Within seconds, others stampeded behind him, the entire front and second rows emptying of occupants, save for Paloma, Marisa, Betty, and me. And Grace Mirabella, who maintained an unreadable expression.

I kept my chin up for the finale bride in her floaty white hat and pantsuit, after which Yves would take his bow. But as the lights flickered to full brightness in the now near-deserted salon, he didn't step out from backstage. Having heard the hostility, he was underscoring it by his disdain.

Betty looked at me and shrugged.

Paloma sighed. "It was glorious. I'd wear all of it."

I won't be a prisoner.

By emptying the attic of its secrets, Yves had proclaimed not only his battle cry for women to free themselves of the past, but his own emancipation from it.

He wasn't such a good boy anymore.

"UNANIMOUS." PIERRE DUMPED the newspapers on the glass table of their spacious living room in their art deco duplex on rue de Babylone, which they'd spent the past three years renovating and had recently moved into. "They hate it."

Hunched in his bathrobe, smoking cigarettes, Yves brooded at the double doors to the terrace, a rarity in Paris for his beloved Moujik and Hazel to enjoy.

The dogs slumbered by the sofa. Yves didn't glance at the papers. He'd barely spoken a word since I'd arrived, summoned by Pierre from the hôtel, where I'd seen the empty salon first-hand, devoid of clients scheduled for fittings—for the first time in the house's history, Anne-Marie informed me. The workroom was equally awash in silence; and as I'd left with my heart in my throat, Clara remarked from her press office that I should inform Pierre that one publication thus far had requested a photo shoot.

"Every single editor," Pierre went on. "'Saint Laurent Receives Boos for New Collection.' 'Yves Goes Bitchy.' 'Saint Laurent: Truly Hideous.'" He glared at us. "The orders as of this morning are no better. As in, we have none."

"Clara told me . . ." I summoned a frail smile. "*Vogue* wants to feature the collection in a spread, with actress Anjelica Huston."

"*Vogue Italia.* We need American and British coverage—the ones who count—and the editors refuse to take my calls. They must think we're crazy."

"I'm not crazy." Yves turned to us, his eyes sunk in shadow. He hadn't slept well. He'd anticipated controversy, but its manifestation had proved as unnerving to him as it was to me. "I didn't design the collection for them. I designed it for women like Lou-lou, who don't care about the past. Couture has become nothing but nostalgia and regret. An old woman locked in her bastion. A relic, like you called Chanel. I'm done with it."

"*Done* with it?" exclaimed Pierre. "We *built* our house on couture."

"Today's woman wants what's affordable and modern, some-thing to wear with ease, not whatever couture dictates. I'll adapt the collection for the boutique." Yves flicked ash outside and moved from the terrace doors, his white robe crumpled about his spare frame. "They can cling to their outdated taboos while the world changes around them, but I—" His voice snagged. "I must change with it. My work is meaningless if it doesn't speak to today."

"You can't change everything overnight," snarled Pierre. "That's what you tried to do at Dior. Look at what happened."

"What happened," said Yves frostily, "is we started our own house. I thought this was reason why: to do as we like."

He proceeded toward his bedroom downstairs, the dogs leap-ing up to follow him past the golden Buddha and white book-shelves, the porcelain vases of immaculate lilies and newly acquired Matisse.

"You and *she*"—Pierre scowled at me—"went out of your way to provoke. We can't do as we like, with American investors to satisfy. What am I supposed to tell them?"

Yves paused. "Tell them it was my decision. All Loulou did was help me see how blind I've been." His voice was dead quiet. "If you must blame someone, blame me."

Pierre's hands bunched at his sides. "It still won't explain what we plan to *do* about it. The collection cost us a lot of money. Without orders, it's a loss."

"I don't care. I'm going to Dar el-Hanch. All this outrage in Paris stifles me."

Pierre swerved to me as soon as Yves disappeared. I'd seen his temper flare in the hôtel, bellowing over a mishap and threatening business associates on the phone. He expressed fury as easily as he breathed, and I braced myself for its explosion.

Instead, he gave an arid chuckle. "The worst reviews of his career, and he's finally learned to give a speech. Even if he expects me, as usual, to balance the accounts."

I swallowed. "He put his heart and soul into the collection."

His stare bore into me. "Did you think I doubted it? I was there when he first put women in trousers, despite the law in France prohibiting it. That law still stands. To this day, a woman wearing pants can be arrested."

Slumping onto the sofa, he raked a hand through his hair. "I was also there when we started the house, and he could barely utter three words to the press; he let me do all the talking, until everyone thought I must be a tyrant. I've protected him all these years by letting them continue to think it. He just threw himself into the fire all by himself."

"We—we never imagined the reaction would be like this," I said nervously.

"*You* might not have. Yves knew exactly what he was doing."

Feeling as if the entire world had turned upside down, I lowered myself onto the edge of the sofa. "Can we sell it in the boutique?" I was grasping at any thread of hope.

Pierre heaved out a sigh. "More money to simplify the line and see it into mass production. Months of effort down the drain in the meantime, while he ignores the outrage."

I couldn't have felt any worse. "Is there anything I can do?"

Pierre snorted. "You've done enough."

Let's do it together, Loulou. Let's cause a scandal.

"Are you . . . firing me?"

In the subsequent hush, my chest tightened. What had started out as a daunting proposition had transformed into an identity, shaped for me with the same precision as Yves cut his fabrics. I couldn't envision life without him, not working at his side every day.

Then Pierre chuckled again. "You just heard him. He won't let you take any blame. And despite the fiasco, he's right. Women of today don't care about couture. To stay relevant, we must adapt."

I sagged in relief.

"But if you stay," he went on, "you work for us. For *our* house. Your position will be made official. We pay you a salary. No more indecision. If you don't like it, you can leave. Today."

"I want to stay," I said.

"Then pack your bags. I need you to make sure he doesn't lie around the villa smoking kif. He has work to do. The menswear. Our new cologne. We can't let one badly received collection be our last. We need to prove we're still the best."

As I moved to the apartment door, his next words brought me to a halt. "Was it your idea to hire the Americans?"

"No. Yves—he wanted to hire them. He likes their energy."

"They certainly have enough of it." Pierre paused. "I assume you also didn't know that Lagerfeld had already hired them for his new line at Chloé?"

Clara's warning flashed across my mind; I bit down on the urge to throw the blame on her. But she'd merely passed along an address, knowing Yves had expressed interest. If she hadn't, someone else would have. Moreover, she was Pierre's right hand, his most trusted employee. She'd advised me against it, albeit obliquely, and I'd ignored her out of anger over her catty remarks about Thadée. A rift with her, especially now, was the last thing I needed.

"They didn't mention it," I said.

"Why would they? Karl hasn't shown his line yet. They're not under exclusive contract. But Yves must have known it. He deliberately hired them to put them in our salon first." Pierre's voice took on a razored edge. "Lagerfeld has always lived in our shadow. He won't forgive or forget this."

I RETURNED TO the flat in a daze, fumbling to fit my key into the lock. The door swung open on its own. Someone was in the bedroom, pulling open drawers.

As I stepped backward to the staircase, Fernando emerged, carrying a suitcase. He went still as a shaky exhale escaped me. "I didn't expect you."

He set the suitcase down. "Loulou, it can't be as terrible as all that."

Stumbling across the threshold, I fell into his arms. "It's worse," I heard myself choke out. "I failed. It was a catastrophe."

He drew me to the sofa. "You didn't fail." Lighting a cigarette from a pack in his pocket, he handed it to me. "The collection is divine."

"That's not what anyone's saying. I think Pierre wanted to fire me."

"Bah. He's like Napoleon. He blusters to instill fear. Listen to me." His voice turned somber. "I was there. In the back row, late as usual because of the parking. I met up with Betty afterward. We both agreed it was unlike anything Yves has shown before. You did the impossible: you inspired him to break his couture mold."

"He says he's done with it."

Fernando smiled. "He always says that. 'Mon Dieu, it's killing me. How I *bleed* for my dresses.' Then he goes right back for more."

I didn't want to laugh, but his imitation was so uncanny, I couldn't help it, the unexpected mirth thawing some of my bitter disappointment.

"He had to knock himself off his own pedestal," Fernando said. "Give them a shock. It wasn't only the clothes; it was the attitude. The makeup. Everything about it screamed flesh and blood, not decorous lady. He threw the editors' prejudices in their faces. They're enraged because he refuses to be another Chanel, reinterpreting the classics until he drops dead of boredom. And he'll do it again, if I know Yves."

"You really think . . . ?"

"Why would he stop now? He's grabbed every fashion headline. The publicity alone is priceless—and of everyone in this business, Pierre knows how to use it."

"I was just with him and Yves. Pierre didn't sound enthusiastic."

"I'm sure he isn't right now. He cultivated the editors to rule in the house's favor, and they turned against him. He'll find a way to strike back. He couldn't have been oblivious to what Yves was doing. He sees every collection before it's presented."

"He attended the run-through. He didn't say anything about it."

"Because he knew it would be a scandal, and Yves wouldn't back down. This revolt against couture has been coming for a long time. Pierre must play the scolding father to remind Yves what's at stake, but he also called me and Betty to rally around Yves in Marrakesh. Betty says she's too nauseous to go, and you've never been. Pierre will take Yves to the villa to see him settled, then return to Paris to deal with the problem. We'll take their jet on our own." He nudged me. "They only travel by private plane. It's very luxurious. Free booze on board."

"I've missed you," I said. "I thought you hated me for choosing him."

"Right now, I do." He gave me his impish smile. "I'd kill to have a scandal. I can't get anyone to look at my sketches, much less a headline that says 'Sanchez Goes Bitchy.' Now, pull yourself together. We're going out dancing at the seediest dive on rue Sainte-Anne we can find."

"*Not* le Sept." I shuddered. "I can't bear it tonight."

"Oh, no. We're in no mood to be seen by the beautiful. What if they boo us off the dance floor?" At my unwitting laughter, he said gently, "He'll survive this. So will you."

"We thought it was perfect. We worked so hard on it."

"The world wasn't ready for it. There'll be other triumphs. Other failures." He patted my hand. "Fashion is a bitch. But where would we be without it? Don't give up."

I nodded. "Okay."

"I'm sorry for keeping my distance. I had to . . . well, get over my injured pride. But I saw your influence in every one of those slutty outfits. In every accessory. There's Loulou, I told myself. She wears it as she pleases and doesn't give a damn."

"Maybe I should," I said dryly. "Pierre is making my position official."

He met my eyes. "Yves hired you because you don't."

7

Talitha floated naked on a raft in the mosaic-inlaid pool, her hair spread in a wet aureole around her. Palm trees rustled in the dehydrated afternoon breeze, carrying a hint of dusty lemon over the villa's yellow-washed plaster walls.

An ululation of prayer drifted from the medina. We reclined on upholstered cushions in the garden of Dar el-Hanch, Yves and Pierre's House of the Serpent in Marrakesh, enclosed by the splendor of the villa they'd acquired and restored, which reflected the desertic childhood colors of Yves's birthplace of Oran.

Like Yves, I'd fallen under Marrakesh's spell, its red jagged mountains and crooked byways, the taste of dates and olives ripened by the North African sun. We'd spent hours wandering in the bazaar, where he relished his anonymity and browsed for rustic fabrics, leaving me to peck among treasure troves on threadbare rugs, seeking odd stones and ornaments that I later threaded into fanciful necklaces and bracelets for us to wear while dancing barefoot under the star-spattered night.

"Is she okay?" I said to Fernando, keeping an eye on Talitha, while he sketched me in my black kaftan and a cascade of amber beads.

"As much as can be expected. She's clean, and she asked Paul for a divorce. They have a little boy. Paul won't stop using. It scares her."

I hadn't known about Talitha's struggle with heroin until she arrived unexpectedly from London, bathed in the aura of everything money could buy. Estranged from her husband, John Paul Getty Jr., she'd left her son with friends in Rome to visit Yves. They'd met when he and Pierre first bought the villa. The Gettys had spearheaded a wealthy expatriate exodus to Marrakesh, a place where anything went, and I'd seen at once the potent effect she had on Yves, with her boundless wealth and casual hippie chic that suited her small-boned frame.

Nevertheless, she'd abstained from our nightly revels, floating aimlessly to the music Fernando played for us on the record player, a new album by an androgenous British singer named Bowie. She waved aside the copious joints and alcohol we consumed. When I taught Yves how to eat hashish instead of smoking it, he gobbled so much in one sitting that he vomited. After tempering his excess, now he became giddy, performing impromptu floor shows on the table, hiking his kaftan to his thighs, and singing throaty chansons made famous by his longtime friend Zizi Jeanmaire, the ballet dancer and singer, whose stage costumes he designed. He made Talitha burst into gales of laughter at his antics. Her bond with him was like mine, an innate recognition of a kindred spirit.

"I should check on her," I said. "She must be getting sunburned." Rising to cross the heat-seared patio, I passed Yves in a white kaftan under a parasol on a chaise longue, papers and pencils strewn about him, oblivious as ever in the throes of his work.

Her somnolent brown eyes fluttered open at my approach. Her body was tanned to dark copper. "Would you be a sweetheart, Loulou, and fetch me a cigarette? I'm turning into a crisp." Rolling off the raft, she slipped into the pool.

I took a cigarette from Yves; he smiled when Talitha called out, "You should come swimming with me. You have such a beautiful body, and you never show it off."

"In a bit," he said absently, returning to his drawing.

As I brought the cigarette to her, the phone rang inside the villa. I saw her pause with a shudder. She'd confided in me about Paul's increasing desperation, beseeching her to halt the divorce proceedings and reconcile with him.

"It's probably Pierre," I reassured her. "This is the time when he always calls."

She reached for a towel. "Yes, of course." Rubbing herself dry, she took up her discarded kaftan from a stool. "You've been so kind to me. And you're so good for Yves. He's so at ease with you. Are you in love with him?"

I laughed in surprise. "Not like that."

"Then you have more willpower than me. I fell madly in love with him when we first met." Her eyes gleamed. "I tried to seduce him. I thought it very unfair that he only likes men. If he can dress us so exquisitely, imagine what his hands could do to us in bed."

"He's never slept with a woman?" I lowered my voice.

"Not that I know of." She glanced mischievously at him. "But he's always so secretive. I always thought he might have had a fling with Betty."

"Betty? No. They're too much like twins."

"Exactly. Who hasn't fantasized about going to bed with their twin?"

We both started giggling. She was so easy to talk to, like a sister I'd never had, and we were whispering in conjecture over Yves's predilections when the butler came out to announce, "Mademoiselle, Monsieur Bergé is on the phone. He says it's urgent."

Yves grumbled, "Urgent, again? I don't understand *why* he keeps calling. It's not as if Anne-Marie can't manage without me. Tell him I'm taking a nap. Or we're all taking a nap together," indicating, despite his apparent obliviousness, that he'd over-heard Talitha and me.

Fernando wagged a finger. "Don't you dare tell Pierre that. He'll be here first thing tomorrow to take a nap with us. We're being chaste as nuns, and Yves is chained to his desk, finishing the menswear."

"Maybe he misses you." Talitha went to sit cross-legged beside Yves.

"I doubt it. He was furious he had to stay in Paris to clean up my mess, as he called it. He wants to make sure I'm fully informed of how terribly difficult I've made everything." He handed her the drawing. "What do you think, Tally?"

"Oh, yes," she murmured, bending over the sketch pad.

I followed the butler into the house. I'd been fending off Pierre daily, assuring him that we weren't lying around doing nothing. After our late dinners, Yves would sometimes shut himself in his study to return the barrage of calls, but he didn't like to be bothered until he'd had the day to himself, as though he needed to forget about the house and all the obligations hinging on his return.

"Loulou?" Pierre barked at me over the line. "*Where* is he?"

"Outside by the pool. It was very hot today. It's just started to cool off."

"I need to speak to him. Now."

Even as I hesitated, a hand plucked the receiver from me. With a resigned sigh, Yves said, "What is it? Has the mob set fire to our hôtel?"

Talitha leaned against the fluted archway with a smile, the drawing in her hand.

I saw Yves's posture stiffen. "When?" he said, after what felt like an eternity. "No. It's too soon. I won't cut short my time here. Tell them to wait."

I heard Pierre start to shout.

Yves endured the tirade in silence. Then he said, "Then I suppose I can be back by the end of next week. No—" he interrupted firmly. "Not before then. Let Anne-Marie see to the measurements. She can schedule the fitting as well."

Hanging up the phone before Pierre could raise further protest, he turned to us. His expression was indecipherable.

"Well?" I blurted out. "What happened?"

He looked past me to Talitha. "Did you do this?"

"Guilty as charged." Her smile broadened. "I hated reading all those awful things they wrote about your collection in the papers. When he confided to me that he was going to propose to her, I told him only you could dress her."

"Who?" I darted my gaze between them.

"Mick Jagger," she said. "He's a friend of mine. He's getting married to his girlfriend, Bianca, a model from Nicaragua. They're planning an intimate ceremony in Saint-Tropez because she's already pregnant."

"Mick Jagger," I echoed, "of the *Rolling Stones*?"

Yves said, "Bianca wants to wear the bridal suit from our collection, but I need to change the pants into a skirt for her, in case she starts to show."

From behind us, Fernando clapped. "Bravo, Pierre. If publicity alone can't sell it, Bergé will find a way."

Yves murmured, "Look at my drawing, Loulou."

Talitha extended it to me. He'd sketched a nude man in bold black lines, seated on a cushion, with an oversized bottle jutting between his legs.

"My advertising campaign for the new cologne," he said. "Tally loves the idea. We'll have to find the perfect model. Someone to catch everyone's attention."

I raised my eyes to him. "You want to feature a naked man in an advertisement? Pierre will kill us."

"It's never been done before." Yves laughed. "Why not? It's a cologne for men. Don't worry about Pierre; I know how to handle him. He can beat me with his ruler and chase me around the apartment for being a very naughty boy." His laughter faded. "They accused me of being crazy. I'll show them just how crazy I am."

BIANCA WAS FERRIED incognito into the hôtel in the early evening, to dodge paparazzi who might be lurking outside, the press having caught wind of something illicit in the air after Jagger was spotted swaggering about the city with his entourage. For a man hoping to marry in secret, he didn't seem very interested in concealing it.

Yves and I waited in the studio, the window shades drawn, and only Anne-Marie from the staff to assist with the outfit, which Yves had based on our bride-gangster pantsuit and his le Smoking, tailored for her in crisp white satin.

As she removed her sunglasses and an enveloping headscarf, a mass of black hair tumbled about her face. Her eyes were dark liquid pools against her olive-tinted complexion, her enviable figure rounded but not showing overt sign of pregnancy. She appeared to be in awe of Yves as he kissed her cheeks, though she was about to marry one of the most famous rock stars in the world.

I set myself to putting her at ease, drawing her behind the screen we'd set up for her to undress. Once I helped her into the ensemble, I brought her before the mirrors, Anne-Marie fussing over the bias-cut skirt under the wide-lapeled satin jacket.

"Très belle," said Yves. "Bianca, what you think?"

She regarded her reflection with a model's practiced instinct, pivoting and plucking at the lace-edged chemise she'd kept on. She seemed unsure.

I said on impulse, "Let's try it without the blouse."

"You think?" Her expressive eyes widened.

I looked at Yves, who nodded. "Yes."

Without hesitation, Bianca removed the jacket and pulled off the chemise. I rebuttoned the jacket for her, so that beneath it her full breasts showed enough to tantalize without being exposed.

"Here." Taking a pin from Anne-Marie, Yves pinched excess fabric at the waist. "We'll add an extra stitch to keep the jacket in place when you sit down. The hat, Loulou."

Extracting the hat from its box, I tucked the trails of tulle about her throat.

"Exquisite." Yves sighed. "A modern bride, without fuss or frills."

Tears glistened in Bianca's eyes. "You must come to the wedding. We're sending out invitations a day in advance to avoid alerting the press. I want you there. Both of you," she said, smiling at me. "You've made me something so beautiful to wear."

"We simply couldn't," demurred Yves. "A designer should never upstage the bride."

After she departed in her limousine, Anne-Marie took the outfit into the workroom to add the extra stitch and finish the lining.

"She's gorgeous," I said. "The suit is perfect on her."

"She'll be a sensation. But they can't keep the wedding a secret. Look." He drew up the window shade. "There's at least one reporter on that corner. He's not even trying to hide. I can see him smoking from here."

Stepping beside him, I caught the glow of a cigarette, held by a shadowy figure.

"They're vultures," I said in revulsion.

"They are. They'll also find out about the wedding, and the

entire world will see Bianca in our suit. We can't be there in person, but"—he smiled at me—"we'll be there anyway. Every woman will want to follow her example."

"Talitha's gift," I said softly.

Our hands touched as the lights of Paris glimmered in the oncoming night.

DECLINING YVES'S OFFER to drive me home, as he was tired, I went out the back door to walk to the boulevard, avoiding crossing paths with the reporter.

My heels struck a dull percussion on the quiet street, steeped in unseasonable mist for late spring. With the memory of Marrakesh still warm in my veins, I shivered and pulled up the collar of my peacoat, pausing to light a cigarette at the corner.

When I heard the footsteps behind me, I said, "I'm not answering any questions—"

"I'm sorry. Did I scare you?"

It was Thadée, in an overcoat and a beret. The white scarf wrapped about his throat reminded me of the bridal tulle on Bianca.

"You snuck up on me. Again." I gave an uneasy laugh. "You're like a thief."

"I'm not brave enough to steal. All I do is covet." Seeing my pause at his odd turn of phrase, he added, "I was outside the hôtel and saw you leave."

He must have been the figure Yves had seen, mistaking him for a reporter.

"Clara left hours ago. We had a client who requested privacy."

"Mick's fiancée." He smiled at my startlement. "Don't worry. The secret is safe with me. Clara coordinated it when Jagger called; they've known each other for years. She must have forgotten to tell me she was leaving early."

Raising my cigarette to my lips, curious as to why he'd lingered on the corner after discovering Clara was elsewhere, I asked, "Shouldn't you be with her, then?"

His subsequent silence spurred heat in me that I hoped didn't show on my face.

"Perhaps," he finally said, "I prefer to be with you."

Though he didn't move any closer, I felt as if he were pressed against me, like the night we'd danced together. I could feel the fog-wet wool of his coat, the cool weft of his scarf; smell the tobacco on his person. I imagined breathing him into me, kindling flame.

"I don't sleep with married men."

He met my eyes. "I'm not married."

My throat clogged. I had to force my next words out. "You're still her lover."

"The lover part has been over a long time. Does it matter so much to you?"

Dropping my cigarette to grind it under my heel, I said, "It obviously matters to her. She went out of her way to tell me she knew about us dancing at le Sept."

He said quietly, "I don't ever lie to her."

"Yet here you are." I considered him. "It's too complicated."

His voice thickened. "It doesn't have to be."

Leaning toward him, I savored his disconcertion. "It is. You should go home."

He sighed and stepped back. "I can wait."

As he began to walk away, the mist crept in around me. "Wait for what?" I said, though I knew I shouldn't give him encouragement.

His reply floated back to me. "For you."

Left alone, I shivered again, only this time it wasn't from the cold.

Thadée might not be a thief, but he could still steal my heart—if I let him.

8

As Yves predicted, Bianca and Mick Jagger's wedding was swarmed by paparazzi, with every publication featuring pictures of Bianca in our white suit. She was, as he knew she would be, a sensation. Overnight, our collection, dubbed a "debacle," was in demand. Lauren Bacall placed a substantial order, as did Catherine Deneuve, whom Yves often dressed for her films.

Ordinary women flocked to the boutiques to buy whatever we had in stock, prompting us to increase the production of our prêt-à-porter. With Yves vindicated, Pierre issued the headline-inducing statement that the house wouldn't present a fall couture collection. Orders from private clients would be accepted, but going forward, Yves would focus his efforts on Rive Gauche.

With the press reeling from the announcement, Pierre confirmed my hiring and located a one-bedroom artist's loft for me on rue des Grands-Augustins, a scenic twenty-minute walk across the Quai d'Orsay to the hôtel. Fernando helped me move in with my mountainous boxes of clothes, and he gasped at my sunlit living room with its aerial view. "You're across the street from the studio where Thadée's father used to paint."

As soon as he said it, the bizarre, unintentional coincidence wasn't lost on me. I shrugged it aside. "Imagine that. I just wanted enough closet space."

Fernando cackled. "You got your wish. You can use the entire apartment as a closet."

Women's Wear Daily called me for an interview a few weeks later at my loft. I answered the questions over the phone, hopping around as I dressed. I was apparently careless, for no sooner was the interview published than Clara invited me to lunch. I couldn't think of a reason to turn her down; and over our meal at the bistro, she said with deceptive lightness, "You should direct press inquiries for the house through me."

I dug my fork into my quiche, my stomach souring. "Diana Vreeland introduced me to John Fairchild of *Women's Wear Daily* when I modeled in New York. They called me. I didn't think I needed to bother you with it."

"Diana Vreeland no longer works at *Vogue*. In the interview, you said you hate black and navy. You must have spoken in jest, since Yves favors those colors in his designs."

"They asked me what I prefer to wear, not what Yves favors."

"Loulou." The precise way she enunciated my name set my teeth on edge. "When you speak to the press you speak for all of us. Hiring you was an experiment that I think we can agree didn't start out well. We're fortunate Pierre salvaged the situation." She clipped her sentence as if to underscore that I'd been saved only by a celebrity wedding and Pierre's tenacity. "You're now on our staff. I'm the house press officer. I must ask that you consult me on future interview requests. We have our image to protect."

"Then I will." I refused to rise to her bait, though I longed to toss my glass of wine in her face, and tell her exactly what I thought of her dowdy image while I was at it.

"Thank you. I understand you're still unaware of how things are done." She gestured at the waiter for the bill, terminating the subject.

Once the bill came, I calculated my share and set the francs on the table.

"There's no need," she said. "It's a company lunch. I'll put it on our account."

"No." I stood, slinging my bag over my shoulder. "It wasn't a company lunch."

Her lips pursed. "I see."

"Do you?" My flat tone brought her face up from the receipt, her hair-sprayed red coif barely shifting on her tweed-clad shoulders. "I'm not a threat to you. Yves hired me to assist him in the studio. That's all I want to do."

"All of us are hired to assist him. Without him, there'd be no house, no work." She signed the receipt with a flourish of French-manicured fingers. "We're not so different."

"We aren't?" I said, not caring to hide my skepticism.

"Like you, I was born into a privileged family." Clara stood, straightening her peplum jacket over her A-line skirt. "Mine was in Argentina. My mother also left my father and moved to Paris. I was six years old. At twenty, my father died and left me his coffee company. I hadn't seen him since I was a child; I didn't want to run the company, so I sold it. I went through all the money, spending it on couture, boyfriends, and my love for the arts, particularly the ballet. It's how I met Pierre, who shares my passion for it. He introduced me to Yves and offered me a job."

"My family was never rich. I never had an inheritance or money to lose."

"Yes, but you and I both know what a family name is, and how little it can mean. We are women who must make our own way in life. It's never easy for us."

Besides our shared gender and need to work, which I appreciated, I thought we had nothing else in common. She was just seven years older than me, and acted like she was my mother, or how I imagined a mother might behave. Though at least she was being candid, and in some ways, she did remind me a bit of Maxime. She even had a younger man, though her age gap with Thadée wasn't as pronounced. But she was more sensible, not given to dresses with surrealist eyes, if still under no illusion that the world owed her anything.

"Then I trust working together won't be a problem," I replied.

Her laugh was sharp. "Certainly not. Whatever gave you that idea?"

WITHOUT A NEW couture line to present and the summer lull vacating Paris, Pierre decided to take Yves, Clara, and Thadée on holiday to Italy. They often traveled together and made plans to visit Talitha in Rome, inviting me to join them.

I declined. Clara and I saw each other daily at the hôtel; we were pleasant, but not friends. Much as I would have liked to see Talitha again, I couldn't imagine spending ten days on vacation with Clara and Thadée, overseen by Yves's knowing smile as Pierre marched us about to visit museums and browse antiques. Instead, I made the excuse that I could stay in the studio with Anne-Marie to ensure everything proceeded on schedule while they were away.

Yves pouted, but I suspected Clara was relieved.

The studio felt empty, with Yves gone. It was my first experience of that certain kind of desolation his absence conjured. The patchwork of swatches and threads slung on his door seemed drab; even the shelves of fabric blots seemed to wilt. The remaining staff like Anne-Marie, mostly older and not given to going away on holiday, turned shadowy, stilted, as if they required his physical presence to animate them. The missing cloud of his cigarette smoke and rodent-scratch of his pencils, his sudden laughter or coo of approval over the whisper of his hands draping cloth on a cabine mannequin—without him, the hôtel sank into the patient pining of a devoted lover, who must resign themselves to awaiting their beloved's return.

To stave off the gloom, I set myself to learning about how our prêt-à-porter was made, as it differed vastly from the highly specialized, regulated industry of petites mains, artisans employed for couture who inherited and passed on their skills in generational veneration. Anne-Marie explained that despite its immense profitability, the ready-to-wear process was commercial, and distressing for Yves. After selecting fabrics and sending off his designs, he had to wait for samples to return from the factory. With couture, he oversaw every step in-house, selecting every button and trimming, fitting his designs on the mannequins, and making changes to the last minute before the garment was presented. Ready-to-wear, once approved by him, was set in stone. Couture was a garden, with each hemline and seam seeded and nurtured by him.

"Prêt-à-porter is a business," she concluded. "Haute couture is art. He learned it under Monsieur Dior, who wanted him to carry on his legacy. Couture is in his blood."

I didn't argue the point, though I was fascinated by the distinction and her lesson. The more I knew, the more useful I could be.

The menswear line arrived ahead of schedule, so I called Corey to be fitted. He arrived in thigh-baring cutoff jeans and a white mesh tank top that revealed more of his physique than some of the older women in the studio were accustomed to seeing. He undressed to his tiny briefs without a hint of abashment, causing those same women to avert their eyes, and then donned the loose-sleeved cravat-styled shirt, wide-bottomed suede pants, and fringed western jacket Yves had designed for him, transforming from street urchin to urbane cowboy.

He brought Pat and Donna with him. Their manic laughter as they chased after a furiously barking Moujik, whom Yves had left behind in Anne-Marie's care, brought a welcome burst of irreverence. Anne-Marie rescued the indignant bulldog. The women from the workroom crowded into the salon to watch Corey practice his runway strut with Pat, while Donna lolled splay-legged on one of the gilded chairs and popped her chewing gum, flicking ash from her cigarette onto the carpet.

Anne-Marie sniffed. "They have no manners. I suppose none of us do at that age."

I had trouble envisioning her young. She seemed locked in ageless maturity, never a hair out of place; but her steadfast discipline and forbearance, as she chided Donna to close her legs and please use one of the ashtrays, spoke volumes about her character.

As they tumbled into the simmering tin of the late afternoon, Corey begged me to meet them at their apartment later; they were going dancing at le Sept. Seeing me hesitate, Anne-Marie said, "I'll lock up tonight. You're young, too. You should enjoy it."

I rushed home to change and phone Betty, who moaned she was still too fat to be seen in public, having recently delivered a baby daughter. "The child hates me. She refuses to breastfeed. I'm leaking milk like a cow."

Fernando, however, was eager. "A night out with the Americans. How naughty of you to play with the kittens while the big cats are away. I'll bring Paloma. She has a family friend here, some architect from Barcelona. We'll meet you there."

Recalling Clara's tidy smile as she put me in my place steeled my nerve. She might disapprove, but a night at le Sept with our models was hardly an act of treason. If Yves were here, he'd have willingly joined in the escapade.

The Americans' apartment in Saint-Germain looked as if a storm had swept through it, half-filled suitcases brimming with articles of clothing, makeup scattered everywhere among torn stockings, discarded briefs and panties, and mismatched pairs of shoes.

"We're off to Saint-Tropez next week," Corey trilled. "Karl went there ahead of us with Antonio, who's doing sketches for him. Oh, and Jacques. He'll be there. Ugh."

At the sting in his voice, I said, "Don't you like Jacques?"

"Not really," he said, as I perused sketches pinned to the walls with thumbtacks, recognizing Donna and Pat drawn to sleek, wind-blown life. I could see why Lagerfeld had hired Antonio to sketch for him. There was a vivid sensuality to the work, a marked absence of the rigor so often seen in French fashion illustration.

A moment of silence followed before Pat said, "But Karl sure likes him."

"Are they lovers?" I wasn't sure why I asked, other than curiosity. I remembered how Jacques had sidled up to Yves, like a serpent proffering the forbidden apple.

"Not according to Karl," said Corey. "Jacques is his 'protégé,' whatever that means. But they must be fucking. How else did Jacques weasel his way into our group? He showed up out of nowhere, just as we were getting along. He says he's from a rich old family, counts or dukes or something. Karl laps it up, but we"—he glanced at Pat and Donna—"we think it's bullshit."

I turned to the girls. Though I didn't know Karl, my initial impression of him wasn't of someone who was easily taken in. "You think Jacques is lying?"

"He's a hustler." Donna popped her gum. "We've seen the type. They're a dime a dozen in Times Square. But Karl pays for everything, including our rent, so . . ." She shrugged. "We have to put up with his 'protégé.'"

Corey came to me with a compact in hand, his deep-set eyes rimmed in liner, his curls gelled in a golden riot about his face. "Until Karl kicks us out."

"He wouldn't do that," I said at once.

"Sure he will. Jacques wants Karl all to himself. He'll find a way to kick us out. We'll be okay." Corey daubed glittery powder on my cheeks. "Antonio can take care of us. He's making money with his drawings, and Donna got hired by French *Vogue*. She and Pat are also modeling in Karl's ready-to-wear, and I'm in Yves's show. We came to Paris with nothing. Now we have something." He smiled. "You should wear more makeup, Loulou. You're so pretty."

His warmth touched me. In the smudged mirror, his touch of silver gleam highlighted my cheeks and brightened my eyes. As the girls crowded in around me, Donna coiling a gauzy scarf about my shoulders, it struck me that a year ago, I'd been like them, adrift without a destination. I might have never found one, had I not met Yves. Inflamed by their youth and someone else's largesse, they were fuel for fashion's voracity. They could be so quickly consumed.

"You must let me know if he kicks you out and you need help," I said.

"Oh, you've helped us so much already." Corey emptied a packet of cocaine onto his compact mirror, slicing up lines with a razor blade. "We wanted you to come out with us tonight to thank you."

We snorted the coke and squeezed into a taxi to the club. Within a half hour of our arrival, they were partially undressed and provoking lust on the dance floor, Donna squealing as Corey sprayed her with a bottle of champagne, and Pat flung off her top for the roaring crowd. I danced with them, until Fernando arrived with Paloma and her friend, a matador-handsome architect named Ricardo Bofill.

Fernando glowered as Ricardo eyed my sweaty dishevelment, my breasts showing under my wet shirt. With the coke and several whiskeys in my veins, I returned his stare. He wasn't the sort of man I found attractive—too self-confident—but his smoldering appreciation and lithe build were undeniable.

With the success of her jewelry in the boutique, Paloma had received an offer to design for the exclusive Greek jeweler Zolotas. As she gushed about the proposal, I squeezed Fernando's hand under the table. Now that I was employed by Yves and Paloma reaped recognition, he probably thought he'd be designing fur coats for Revillon for the rest of his life, the dream of launching his own line unattainable.

But the reason for his sour mood became evident when Ricardo remarked, "None of what you sell is necessary. It's needless luxury."

Fernando glared as I said, "You don't think fashion is necessary?"

Ricardo leaned back in his chair. "I design buildings for a living, where people work and live. Shelter and food are necessary. Not fashion."

"Should we run about naked?" I countered, widening his smile.

"I wouldn't mind if you did," he said.

Fernando growled, "Everyone needs clothes. Yves sells a lot of them."

"I'm aware." He eyed Fernando, indicating he wasn't averse to male appreciation, either. "In Spain, as you should know, we have a fascist dictatorship. The last thing most Spaniards can afford is designer dresses from Paris."

"I'm not Spanish," retorted Fernando. "I'm Belgian."

When Ricardo went with Paloma to dance, Fernando hissed to me, "He's been like that all night, talking down to us. A macho pig."

"Well, he's not wrong about everyone needing a roof over their head," I teased.

"He probably comes here to cruise men. I am half Spanish—not that I'd tell him—so I should know. Besides not being able to afford designer dresses from Paris, you can't be gay in fascist Spain. It's a crime. They imprison you."

"He's not gay," I said. "Look at him. He's ignoring Corey. Would you?"

Ricardo followed my gaze to where Ricardo was behaving as though he didn't notice Corey, already shirtless, casting lascivious glances at him.

"No," Fernando said grumpily. "That American boy is too beautiful to be ignored. So, maybe he's just a macho pig. A hetero one, which makes it worse. At least if he were in the closet, he'd have an excuse for being so insufferable."

I laughed and dragged him from his chair onto the dance floor, where his bad mood vanished as Corey flirted with him instead. Slipping between us with generous abandon, eager to please as a puppy, Corey put the smile back on Fernando's face.

Toward dawn we staggered out, leaving the Americans behind to wring out the last bit of the fun. At the curb, Ricardo murmured, "I'd like to see you again," and pressed his card into my hand before he got into a taxi with Paloma.

I smiled as they drove away, Paloma waving drunkenly at us. "Maybe he will."

Fernando made a gagging sound. "I can't believe you *like* him."

"He likes me. I thought you might be going home with Corey."

"So he can blab about me to Karl?" Fernando gave me a

haughty look. "I still have my dignity. My dick doesn't get hard as easily as yours."

Laughing, we said good night with the promise to get together again soon. By the time I reached my loft, the sun peeped over the city. I had an hour or so to shower and change, take an upper to keep from keeling over, and go to the hôtel.

I was rinsing the excess from my pores when I heard the phone ring. I ignored it, certain it was Fernando, checking to make sure I'd made it home and not run off with Ricardo, but once it started to ring again, I padded out to answer it.

Sobbing came over the line—a deluge of despair. My chest closed in. "Yves? Oh god. What is it? What's wrong?"

"She's gone." His voice was strangled. "Talitha . . ."

Pierre snapped in the background, "Let me talk to her," and he barked into the phone, "We're coming home tomorrow. Have the car pick us up at the airport."

"What—what happened?" I saw Talitha in the pool, her lazy smile.

You've been so kind to me. And you're so good for Yves . . .

He said grimly, "She was found dead in Rome, from what looks like an overdose. Paul called to tell us. Yves is hysterical. We're trying to calm him down."

I heard Yves weeping, Clara murmuring to him.

"I'll come there," I said. "Book the first flight I can."

"No. We need you at the studio. Loulou, don't talk to reporters if they call. It's already all over the news. She was Getty's wife, and the Italian authorities questioned Paul; they warned him not to leave the country, though he had nothing to do with it. We don't want the press mobbing us. Talitha was our friend."

"Yes. Call me at the hôtel with your itinerary. I'll send the car."

He hung up and I sank to the floor, tears flooding my eyes.

YVES SECLUDED HIMSELF in rue de Babylone, refusing to answer my calls. Pierre heaved a sigh and told me not to worry. Yves was grief-stricken, taking it to the extreme, but he knew we had the menswear show to prepare, as well as the launch of the cologne. He couldn't hide away forever like an inconsolable widow.

I worried anyway.

Then he showed up without warning on my doorstep, as I was about to depart for work. In a black turtleneck and jeans, he looked thinner, his hair longer and untidy, his face hollowed, with the shadow of loss in his eyes.

"I missed you," he said, as I embraced him.

"I'm here," I whispered. "I'm always here for you. I'm so sorry about Talitha."

He blinked back tears. "She was healthy when we saw her. I never thought . . ."

"Neither did Fernando. He told me she was clean, and scared of it."

"She went to see Paul to insist on the divorce." His voice hardened. "Pierre thinks Paul can't be held responsible, but he is. He had heroin in the apartment. He killed her."

"I'm sure he didn't mean to," I said softly. "Yves, she already had a problem with it."

He gave reluctant assent. "I should have brought her back to Paris. I kept telling her she could stay with us, but her son, the divorce . . . she said she had to finish with Paul."

"Don't blame yourself. It's horrible, but you couldn't have known."

After a moment, tears filling his eyes again, he said, "There's something I want to do for her. Will you come with me?"

I nodded. "Of course."

We drove to the studio of his friend, the photographer Jeanloup Sieff, who was making his name in fashion with his distinctive black-and-white portraiture. He had the studio readied with a neutral backdrop, in anticipation of our arrival.

While I sat on a stool, Sieff and Yves spoke out of earshot. I heard Sieff say, "Not the bottle. You alone. It will be such a powerful statement."

Yves began to shed his clothes.

My mouth went dry.

His long, lean limbs soaked in the light. Sieff arranged him naked on a stack of flat black leather cushions. The spotlight in the foreground haloed him in a messianic aura, his oversized glasses in stark contrast to the nubile pallor of his skin.

You have such a beautiful body, and you never show it off.

At thirty-five years old, he'd reached the cusp in a man's life when the last of boyhood has been shed. Yet Yves retained an elusive quality of it, a pentimento under the surface of his skin. He seemed to me like someone who could never age.

And he looked so vulnerable. So achingly beautiful. Like a living statue, bathed in the glow of his incandescence.

Sieff clicked the camera, roving about him to capture various angles.

It was done in less than an hour. Yves dressed and we said goodbye, driving together in his car to the hôtel. We didn't speak.

We both knew that the prince had just declared himself a rebel king.

9

The advertisement featuring Yves in the nude, accompanied by the beguiling tagline "For three years, this eau de toilette has been mine. Now it can be yours," roused another torrent of outrage. French publications refused to print it, citing schoolchildren might see it, never mind that they trafficked in skimpily clad female imagery all the time. Others described Yves as a "bespectacled Christ," with covert titillation.

Yves smiled. Another controversy was what he'd set out to make; only this time, Pierre was primed to capitalize on it, the furor over the ad doing more than the ad itself to alert the public to our new men's cologne. Seating at our menswear presentation became so avidly sought after that Clara had to rent a larger showroom on Place des Victoires. Pierre brutally excluded the most vocal critics of our maligned Libération couture, reducing them to abject apologies to appease him and gain entry.

Once again, I witnessed Pierre's indomitable resolve to keep the House of Saint Laurent center stage. When ready-to-wear designers complained that all the press focus on Yves was distracting from their upcoming lines, Pierre responded by forming a coalition to oversee a formalized annual prêt-à-porter presentation schedule. He earned himself a knuckle-rapping from the Chambre Syndicale de la Haute Couture, along with the accusation that he was setting a dangerous precedent that could undermine both the House of Saint Laurent and couture's future. By championing the legitimacy of ready-to-wear, he was placing it at the same level as couture—an unforgivable negation of the Syndicale's very purpose.

Which, of course, made Pierre harrumph. "Do they have an issue with making money? Or maybe they think we'll put Yves naked in the salon, too? They're the ones who are burying themselves in their archaic tradition."

He'd changed his tune, declaring to all and sundry that as the champion of innovation, Yves alone had foreseen that prêt-à-porter was the future.

By the day of the menswear show, the crowd had swollen to standing room only. Corey was so flustered at the sight that I had to slip him a downer to dampen his coke-induced anxiety. Yves fluffed his collar and murmured, "You are très chic," prompting Corey to stride onto the runway with his le Sept swagger, eliciting applause. He returned backstage with tears streaming down his face to whisper, "I can die happy now."

We followed the success of our menswear with our women's prêt-à-porter. Yves had retooled our designs, adding a hundred new pieces. He, Anne-Marie, and I spent day and night in the studio, pushing the manufacturer to its limits. To celebrate the line, Yves also designed a striking black-and-blue packaging for a brand-new perfume to sell in the boutique, called simply Rive Gauche.

With proverbial baton in hand, Pierre directed our queue of models into the salon, clad in our billowing palazzo pants, belted smocks, retro pantsuits, and satin tuxedos—all of which I'd accessorized with beaded accessories and hand-dyed scarves from Marrakesh. To avoid our past mistake, we chose only French mannequins, erasing the savage memory of the Americans, though Yves sighed and whispered to me, "We need more Pat and Donna, and less Mademoiselle Fifi."

Nevertheless, in a rush to ingratiate themselves with Pierre, every editor present hailed it as Yves Saint Laurent's most exciting collection in years.

We went out to celebrate at la Coupole. Over oysters and champagne, Pierre informed us that the department store orders for the men's cologne and the new perfume exceeded expectations. Production had been increased. The American investor, who'd taken a chance on Pierre and Yves after Yves's abrupt dismissal from Dior, had negotiated a deal with the parent holding company, Squibb, to safeguard the house upon the investor's imminent retirement.

"We will surrender our shares in the fragrances, but keep full right of approval over new scents, plus royalties on everything sold," Pierre explained. "In exchange for our shares, and a million-dollar loan at low interest to be repaid over fifteen years, Squibb will relinquish control of the house back to us."

Yves blinked and glanced at me, though I was in no position to offer an opinion.

Pierre guffawed. "Ten years in business, and you have no idea what I'm talking about."

"You know I detest talking about money," said Yves. "It's bourgeois."

"For someone who hates talking about it, you have no issues spending it." Pierre pierced us with his regard. "We'll have autonomy. No one to question our decisions."

"If that's the case," conceded Yves primly, "then you should accept the offer."

"There's another matter to discuss before we do." Pierre sat back to allow the waiter to clear our plates and serve the second course of veal. "Couture sales are declining everywhere; it's too expensive for overseas department stores to fly their buyers here twice a year to see the shows and license designs for reproduction. They're stocking ready-to-wear. It's more economical for women to buy off the rack. But they need other licensed products to complement the clothes: a perfect opportunity for us. We no longer need anyone's approval," he added again, as Yves lit a cigarette in bemusement. "Between our Rive Gauche and new licensing, we can expand our international reach, but only if we don't abandon couture."

At this, Yves stiffened. "Why?"

"Because we have our prestige to maintain. Prêt-à-porter is getting crowded, with new stylistes leaping on board like rats. We're unique in that we can do both. We will dominate the market on both ends."

A frown darkened Yves's face. "I thought we agreed couture isn't viable anymore. It's too costly to make and takes up too much time. Now you want me to keep designing it, as well as Rive Gauche, along with other licensed products? I'll perish."

"You haven't yet," retorted Pierre. "I ask you the same question that I asked the Syndicale: Do you have a problem with us making money? Because I don't."

"Always money with you." Yves's entire person tensed, like a wire about to snap. "Our fashion house isn't the corner charcuterie. I don't slap two pieces of fabric together and call it a dress, as you should know by now."

Before they erupted into an argument, I said quickly, "I can help you with it. We can do all of it together."

At my echoing of what he'd once said to persuade me to work with him, Yves murmured, "I can't fight both of you at the same time."

"Then don't." Pierre sliced into his veal. "You do it together. Let me see to the rest."

I WENT TO New York for Christmas, reuniting with my brother, Alexis, in Mama's apartment.

We hadn't seen each other in years, though we'd kept in touch through occasional phone calls. When I burst through the door, ladened with tinsel-wrapped boxes of sample clothing from the studio, I almost didn't recognize his willowy figure in blue jeans turning toward me.

In my mind, he was cemented as a frightened little boy with scraped knees, clinging to my hand after our mother's departure, both of us inconvenient strangers to our father, who sent us away. Now twenty-two, Alexis was building a career in furniture design. He had our mother's expressive eyes and wealth of dark hair, along with our father's innate reserve, submitting a bit stiffly to my embrace.

"You're so handsome." I drew back to admire him. "You could be a model."

"And you're so famous. Every other week there's something about you in the dailies: the hippie-aristo muse to Yves Saint Laurent."

"'Hippie-aristo muse'?" I laughed. "They'll print anything to sell a headline."

From the kitchen came a clash of pans and Mama's amused remark: "Tabloid coverage aren't headlines. In my day, we called it gossip—and there's nothing wrong with it. Now, we have company tonight, so whatever awful gossip you must say about me, do it before they get here."

"Let's grab a smoke." Alexis pulled up the living room window, crawling out with me onto the fire escape, the chill winter air dispelling the pungent smell of spices choking the apartment.

"What is she making?" I asked, lighting a joint for us.

"A feast of God-knows-what." He made a helpless gesture. "She's writing a food column for *Vogue* and wants to publish a book of old recipes, so she's trying them out on us. We never get anything normal with her, do we? It's Christmas, and we'll be dining on Tudor boar's head or something equally outrageous."

I paused, noting the tightness to his jawline. "Is she driving you crazy?"

"No more so than usual." He toked on the joint and coughed, indicating he wasn't used to smoking grass. "She insisted we spend the holidays together. I'm getting married next year."

"You are?" I stared at him. "Why didn't you tell me?"

"I'm telling you now. We haven't set the date yet. She has your same name: Louisa."

"What about Papa? Have you told him?"

Alexis eyed me. "When was the last time you spoke to him?" At my resultant silence, he said, "Well, it's the same for me. I phoned him months ago, after I proposed to Louisa. I left a message with his butler, I think. He never called back."

Our father was a lost cause—for both of us—refusing to answer our calls or patch up our broken relationship, so I said, "Mama must be overjoyed."

"She is. Louisa really wanted to meet her. You can imagine the scene when Mama stormed into London."

"Overbearing," I said, recalling my own wedding and laughing.

"To say the least. She dragged Louisa off on an insane bridal shopping spree and left me with the bills." His voice lowered as he inclined his head to me, as he'd done when we were children, always wary of proclaiming his discontent aloud. "I can't afford the things she bought for us. Who needs two monogrammed dinner services for fifteen people? As soon as she left, we returned everything. We want a simple wedding and a simple life."

"I'm so happy for you." I clasped his hand. "Really, I am."

His smile reached his eyes. "We survived her. Are you happy in Paris?"

"Yes." I finished the joint. "Very much. I love my work."

"Anyone special, besides Yves?"

For a moment, I saw Thadée, the white scarf coiled about his throat . . .

"Just my work. I've no time for anything else."

As I moved to crawl back into the flat, he said, "John is dying."

"What?"

"His liver is failing. Cirrhosis, I think."

I heard Mama chopping up something in the kitchen. "Did she tell you?"

"Not in so many words. But she mentioned tests, a week in the hospital. You can see it. His color is terrible. Not that it's stopping him from having an affair."

I was freezing from the wind, snowflakes spiraling around us, speckling Alexis's hair, though he didn't seem to feel it. "He has a lover?" I didn't know why I should be surprised. Mama had never been a proponent of marital fidelity.

"A photographer he met through Warhol. Apparently, he's besotted."

"The slinky, dangerous kind, who apparently likes to photograph large penises," I said, echoing Mama's words when I'd called her before I first went to see Yves.

"She doesn't care. Robert Mapplethorpe is very talented, according to her, and John needs the diversion. She's helping him to promote Mapplethorpe's work at an upcoming exhibition."

I met his eyes. "She's . . ."

"Overbearing and indefatigable." Alexis sighed, and we both inched back inside, closing the window. He brushed his sleeves to dispel the snow.

"Well?" Mama stood in the kitchen doorway, her hair in a clipped wave, an apron tied about the black couture dress I'd sent her from our collection, with a lime-green lace-corset inset. "Done with gossiping about me?"

I went to her; when I saw a flinch in her gaze, I hugged her. "Merry Christmas, Mama."

She laughed. "I have my children with me, all grown up and earning their own way. Who would have thought?"

"Not Papa," said Alexis with a droll smile. "Aristocrats aren't supposed to earn their own way. We're supposed to subsist off the peasants."

"Your father never had any peasants or money. He has a title. And we were never aristocrats," she said tartly. "We always preferred tinkers and gypsies." She pinched my cheek. "Don't we, my Loulou? You've both done me proud. An unfit mother, indeed."

Dinner was a bacchanalia of pies and stews we could barely identify yet proved surprisingly tasty. Sunken and fragile, John told us about his most recent exhibition at the Met, Robert Mapplethorpe smirking at his side. Mama treated the shaggy-haired, long-faced young man like an extended member of the family, and I admired his silver bracelets and tangle of pendants, which he claimed were his designs, worn by Joe D'Allesandro, a muscular actor who played male prostitutes in Andy's art house movies.

Alexis didn't say much. We opened the presents at midnight, Robert snapping pictures of us on his Polaroid as Mama exclaimed over the clothes I'd brought her from the studio and proceeded to model each ensemble before the Christmas tree, her head thrown back and her eyes slitted, in practiced repetition of her time as Schiaparelli's modeuse. She was drunk; it wasn't long before her hands were roving over Robert's thin body as he started to pose her, John watching them with an indulgent smile.

My brother paled. I'd booked a double-bed hotel room for my stay and offered him the spare. He hastily agreed, packing an overnight bag. Against our mother's feeble protests, we left her with John and Robert, saying we'd return the next day for lunch.

"She's not only promoting his work," I said, during the taxi ride to the hotel, doing my utmost to refrain from judgment, as it really wasn't my concern.

My brother let out a snort. "When does she ever do only what she says?"

ANDY INVITED US to his New Year's Eve party at the Factory. John wasn't feeling well, so Mama mandated that I attend the party in their stead, to not offend Andy by their absence. He was lending his cachet to Mapplethorpe's exhibition.

I wore cream wool trousers by Yves with a chain belt, a purple blouse; ladled myself in bijous; and obliged Alexis to go with me. He would rather have tread barefoot over hot coals, but in the patterned wide-collared silk shirt and suede bell-bottomed pants that Corey had modeled for our menswear, which I'd had adjusted to give Alexis for Christmas, my brother attracted more than his share of complimentary attention.

Muttering under his breath, "When in Rome," he downed a glass of champagne and let himself be fawned over, drawn into the raucous party, where everyone was high and sporting a camera.

Andy sat at a table with Mick and Bianca Jagger. She'd given birth to a daughter and was radiant; after she and I spoke at length, Andy drew me aside to say, "Halston will be here later. I'm sure he'll want to see you."

True to form, Halston didn't show up until well after midnight and the New Year countdown, sweeping into the party-wrecked warehouse in his signature black turtleneck and trousers, and a full-length white mink coat. A bevy of rowdy models accompanied him, wearing his backless or one-shouldered dresses in vibrant jewel tones like a flock of tropical birds.

Donna and Pat burst from the group to rush over to me. "You're here," Pat cried. "No one told us!"

"I didn't know you were in New York, either. Is Corey with you?" I noticed Halston glance at me in practiced disinterest, followed by his deliberate pivot to Andy.

"He's still in Paris." Donna pouted. "We miss him so much, but he wanted to stay a while longer and try his luck. Antonio came back with us. Things were getting too weird; he got into an argument with Karl, who, of course, kicked us out."

"Where's Corey staying? I can look him up when I return."

"He was renting a hotel room somewhere. He said he'd call us."

"I'll find out," I said. "Are you modeling for Halston now?"

"I am," said Pat. "Donna did her cover shoot in Paris, then we both did Karl's show. After Antonio fell out with Karl, we had no other bookings, so we decided to come home. Halston hired me. It's so exciting! I'm going to model in his show at Versailles."

"Versailles?" My bewilderment must have shown, as Donna yelled across the room at Halston. He looked around from his chat with Andy in feigned surprise, as if he hadn't seen me until that precise moment.

Of course, he expected me to go to him. At the table, I kissed his tanned cheek.

"Why, Loulou," he said, in his nasal-tinged voice, which he'd cultivated to erase any trace of his humble roots in Iowa. "You're looking so chic. Happy 1973."

"You, too." I saw by his polished demeanor that he must be reveling in his success, fueled by his company's recent acquisition by a conglomerate and his celebrity friendship with movie star Liza Minnelli. "Congratulations on everything. I saw Liza in her television special, wearing your clothes. She was spectacular."

"Liza always believed in me. As for the rest, all it took was style and elbow grease." He toyed with his cigarette. "Speaking of which, is Yves going to say yes?"

"Say yes to what?"

"Versailles, of course." His unblinking blue-gray eyes were intent on me. "Hasn't he mentioned it? My friend Eleanor Lambert, president of the Council of Fashion Designers of America, is hounding me. She's organizing the project through Yves's dear friend, the Baroness de Rothschild. Apparently, Marie Antoinette's palace is in shambles. Eleanor suggested a fashion charity fundraiser to restore it. I could invite Liza to perform, but unless Yves agrees, neither she nor I will have the time."

My smile didn't slip. Pat had mentioned the show, so he was either seriously considering it or already enlisted. Andy licked his lips at my hesitation, fully cognizant I'd been caught unawares, his favorite social sport.

"You'll have to ask Yves," I said at length. "He's also very busy."

"Well." Halston's smile revealed too-perfect, capped teeth. "I think you're in a better position to ask him. Tell him I'll consider it an honor if he invites me. The cause is, after all, worthy enough for both of us to find time in our very busy schedules."

"I will. It was lovely to see you."

As I started to turn away, he sniped, "You're making quite a name for yourself. A step up from bunking with Berry Berenson and tie-dyeing rags in my bathtub."

Andy giggled maliciously.

I glanced over my shoulder. "Is Ultrasuede hard to dye? I've never worn it."

Halston's perfect smile fractured. Andy cawed his laughter aloud.

Searching for Alexis among the crowd, I extricated him from a corner where he was fenced in by stoned girls and eager boys of Andy's clique. I hissed, "We're leaving."

I hailed a taxi to take him back to my mother's, then went directly to my hotel. It was too early in France to call; as I paced, checking the clock, I thought Yves and Pierre were probably not at home. They must have gone out to celebrate the new year.

Nevertheless, I dialed their number as soon as the hour was right. No one answered at rue de Babylone, so I called the hôtel. At no answer there, which I'd fully expected, as it was New Year's Day, I dug out my address book.

I had Clara's home number. Should I call and tell her? Gritting my teeth, I did, about to hang up after several rings before Thadée's tired voice came on the line.

"It's Loulou," I said. "Sorry. Did I wake you?"

He went silent for a moment before he replied, "We haven't gone to bed yet. Happy New Year. You sneaked up on me this time."

"I need to talk to Clara." I kept my tone polite.

"She's taking off her shoes. We were with Yves, Pierre, and Rudi, dancing at le Sept. You can imagine. Rudi had to seduce every man in the club."

Rudi was Nureyev, Clara's friend, whom she'd helped escape from the Kirov's clutches. I was about to tell Thadée to forget it, it wasn't important, when Clara said briskly, "Loulou, Bonne Année. Is anything the matter?"

I swallowed. Then I told her about Halston.

"A fashion event to restore Versailles?" She sounded as taken aback as I'd been. "As far as I know, no, it hasn't been mentioned. Unless Marie-Hélène spoke to Pierre and Yves about it in private. Perhaps she did, and nothing has been decided."

"Yes, I thought . . . it sounded like the proposal was serious."

"It may well be. I'll pass it on to Pierre. Thank you. I appreciate it." She clicked off, and I dropped the receiver onto the cradle as if it had scalded me.

I had five days left before I went back to Paris, and resolved to spend the rest of my time with my family, avoiding the Factory and everyone in fashion.

PART II

THE BATTLE OF VERSAILLES

1973

Beautiful things have to be maintained. Versailles must be heated. Beautiful things must go on.
—GÉRALD VAN DER KEMP

10

Yves was in the midst of finishing his new couture line when I arrived. Plunging into work, I didn't mention to him what I'd heard in New York; it was Clara's purview now, and when I asked her, she assured me Pierre had been informed. I mentioned Corey, too, relating he was in Paris, but I wasn't sure where. Had he called her with a forwarding address? She kept records of all our models.

She thumbed through her Rolodex. "I don't have a notation of any new address for him. Wouldn't he be at the same one?"

"No. Could you ask around? He must be working somewhere."

"I will make inquiries."

I intended to follow up with her, but then Yves became distracted, his temper too quick to flare over an ill-fitting fabric or inaccurately pressed sleeve, though such mishaps were common when putting together a collection.

A few days before the show, his favorite cabine model, Delphine, came in late for her fitting. Her outfit had vexed Yves no end; as soon as she arrived, flustered and apologetic, she froze before his icy stare.

"Your lipstick is garish," he said. "Your hair is a fright. If you can't show me respect by doing as I ask and be on time, don't bother coming in."

Flinging his tape measure aside and yanking off his white coat, he stalked from the studio. Delphine gave me a teary look.

Anne-Marie hastened to her, clucking, assisting her into the outfit, while I went downstairs in search of Yves.

He was sitting in the salon among the tidy rows of empty chairs, smoking and staring blankly at the wall. Taking a seat beside him, I said, "What's wrong?"

"Nothing." He averted his eyes.

"Yves." I put my hand on his. "You're upset about something."

"All this." His voice quavered. "For what? I don't live anymore. I live to work."

I took a moment to let him settle. "We can always reduce the number of pieces—"

"It's *not* that." He drew on his cigarette. "Whether we show twenty or a hundred pieces, it's never enough. Ever since we regained control of the house, Pierre is licensing deals for everything: Sunglasses. Ties. Pillows. Even cigarettes. YSL cigarettes. It's absurd." He turned to me. "He keeps saying he'll make us very rich. I just didn't know how much it would cost me. I'm his slave."

"Have you spoken to him about it?"

"What for? So he can yell that he's sacrificed his entire life for me, and if we want to stay on top, we must do whatever is necessary? We don't talk. We fight. It's utterly exhausting." ·

"Then let me talk to him." I nudged up his glasses, sifted a lock of hair from his forehead. "Maybe you can design one couture line next year instead of two. I know you didn't want to design it anymore, but Pierre is right. We must—"

He cut me off. "Maintain our prestige." Stubbing the cigarette in the standing ashtray by the chair, he went silent before he said, "He's looking for a new location, with more room. He thinks this hôtel is too far away, and too small for our needs."

I nodded. "I hate to say it, but we're tripping over fabric bolts upstairs."

"More room and a better location just mean more work." He came to his feet, paced a few steps from me. "He's building his empire on my back."

I stayed seated, marking the weary slope to his shoulders. "I can finish the fittings today. Why don't you go home early and rest?"

Without looking at me, he said, "I . . . I've met someone."

He spoke so softly, I almost thought I'd misunderstood. Then he moved back to me and sat, his long hands hanging between his knees. "I don't know what to do about it."

"'Met someone'?" I echoed tremulously. "When?"

He shook his head. "It hasn't been that long. He makes me feel so young and alive, so desired again. But I barely see him. Whenever we do, we must hide like criminals."

I remembered Talitha.

He's always so secretive . . .

"Why must you hide? You and Pierre have an agreement, don't you?"

"Supposedly. We were faithful at the start, but after all these years . . ." He exhaled a fraught breath. "We have rules. How far it can go. For how much time. Never anyone who'll threaten us as a couple. We've done it together sometimes. But he won't like it."

I struggled for my voice. "Why?"

"Because I don't want to share it with him."

"Does he know?"

"He hasn't said anything. But he was furious with me on New Year's Eve over nothing. He said I was drinking too much, when we all were. He made a scene at le Sept in front of everyone. Clara had to take him aside to calm him down. I left."

"Who is it?" I asked.

Yves lifted his gaze. A fist punched my heart when he said, "Jacques de Bascher."

My breath evaporated. I darted my eyes to the salon doorway, suddenly fearful that we'd be overheard, half expecting to see Pierre standing there, glaring at us.

"Jacques?" I whispered. "Karl's lover?"

"They're not lovers. Karl leased an apartment for him at 12 rue du Dragon, near Café de Flore. They don't live or sleep together."

"You can't believe that."

"I do." Yves held my gaze. "Karl has always been strange that way. When we first met and became friends, we went to bars together. He never had lovers. He showed no interest in sex. He likes to possess things, to show them off. That's what Jacques is to him: a possession to dress up and parade on his arm to make everyone envious. Karl always gets bored eventually."

Images of Jacques in his matinee-idol guise, whispering in Karl's ear, crashed against what Corey had told me of Karl's callousness and Jacques's outlandish lies.

And Pierre's snide chuckle.

Lagerfeld has always lived in our shadow. He won't forgive or forget this.

"You can't trust it," I said abruptly.

Yves recoiled. "Why would you say that?"

"You're overworked. Unhappy. You're not thinking clearly."

"You've only seen him one time. How do you know he can't be trusted?"

I drew in a ragged breath. "Donna and Pat. Corey. When you were in Italy, they told me Jacques wanted Karl all to himself. They think Jacques had them kicked out of the flat. Donna and Pat went back to New York because of it. Corey stayed behind." As I spoke, I thought of my promise to Pat and Donna. "I told them I'd check up on Corey, but I don't know where he is."

"Neither do I," said Yves. "You should ask Clara; she might know. But wherever Corey is, you can't blame Jacques for it. He wasn't paying their rent. Karl was, and he used them. He found them amusing until he got bored. He would have kicked them out eventually, no matter what. Karl always gets bored."

"Not with Jacques," I countered. "He's renting an apartment for him."

Yves hesitated. "For now. Until he finds someone new."

"What if he doesn't?"

He went quiet, knotting his hands. "He will," he said at length, but I discerned hesitation, a doubt he wouldn't admit.

"Yves." I steadied my voice. "You don't trust it, either."

He let out another sigh. "I haven't seen him enough to be sure. I think about him all the time. If he doesn't call me, I fall into despair. Haven't you ever wanted someone you're not supposed to have, and miss them day and night?"

"No," I said, too quickly.

"You're a terrible liar." He gave me a smile. "You do want someone you think you shouldn't. But you're brave enough to fight it." As I met his eyes, he said, "I'm not."

"You are. Promise me you'll not rush into anything. Enjoy the infatuation, but keep your head. You can always confide in me."

He kissed my cheek. "I do confide in you. And yes, I promise to be careful. I won't do anything catastrophic. How can I? I work too much."

I CARRIED HIS secret, keenly aware of when the phone rang on his desk at a certain time in the afternoon and he hurried to answer it, closing the door for privacy. If I happened to be with him, choosing fabrics or chattering as he sketched, I withdrew. The calls were never long. I imagined brief exchanges: a place to meet, a stolen hour or two.

I didn't say a word.

After our couture was presented, Yves designed an exuberant ready-to-wear line featuring culottes tucked in mid-calf boots, maxi skirts, and halter-necked pleated dresses, as if a floodgate of inspiration had opened in him. He didn't complain about the overwhelming workload or ceaseless demands on his time as Pierre approved a swift succession of licensing deals that put Yves's logo on an ever-expanding array of products.

To free up his schedule, Yves assigned me to oversee preproduction of Rive Gauche, the selection of models and accessories for our shows. I also started designing a few stand-alone pieces under his tutelage to fill gaps in the lines; he adjusted the silhouettes to blend with his, uniting us as one.

By then, I'd convinced myself he sought solace in a transient passion. He was given to volatility, as I'd experienced firsthand, and his creativity was flourishing, as though he needed to believe he could still fall in love to create. He didn't seem troubled anymore, apologizing to Delphine for his outburst and resuming his uproarious laughter at our inevitable blunders. He seemed to have taken my advice.

But the guilt gnawed at me, even as Pierre carried on in his bullish focus to exalt the house. As the head of the new prêt-à-porter coalition, he weathered clashes with the Syndicale over the standardized ready-to-wear presentation schedule for buyers and editors. His decision to present our collection last demonstrated that regardless of his public avowal of indiscriminate support for ready-to-wear, Yves's silhouettes—and his alone—must define the season.

As a result, sales for Rive Gauche soared, and the Syndicale raged at Pierre for putting his own interests in "confection" above those of haute couture. Battle lines were drawn, though by now, every remaining couture house had a prêt-à-porter label they had to promote to survive. No one could afford to ignore the sweeping changes shaking up the industry, no matter the history of the house or its vaunted exclusivity.

My unwavering loyalty to both Pierre and Yves warred with my knowledge that underneath our feet ran an unseen fault line, should Yves give in to his tempestuous nature. How many places could he hide with a lover before he was discovered? What if Karl tossed Jacques out on his ear and vengefully told Pierre? Though we didn't socialize with Karl, everyone in fashion knew one another. Everyone talked about one another. The merest whisper of treachery could explode into a full-blown scandal overnight.

I couldn't imagine it. To me, Yves and Pierre were inseparable, a "double-headed eagle," as they were dubbed in the house. No one, much less a young man with nothing to his name, could divide them, or pitch their life and empire into tumult.

By the time summer arrived with its sopping humidity, heralding our exodus to Marrakesh, nothing had changed. Our busy days in the studio were followed by wild nights. We went dining and dancing together at le Sept, as we always had. We partied till dawn and braved epic hangovers to do it all over again.

I decided there was no reason to foresee trouble ahead.

WE WERE STAYING at the villa.

Clara and Thadée had joined us, along with Fernando, Betty, and her husband, François. Pregnant for the second time, Betty reclined like an odalisque under a parasol, soaking up the sun and munching on dates while François rubbed tanning oil on her enlarged belly.

Clara stayed with Thadée at la Mamounia, a hotel in town a short taxi ride away. Yves expressed bewilderment; the villa had plenty of extra room. But Clara's stated reason that the hotel had air-conditioning was reasonable enough, and not having them under the same roof was better for me. The sight of Thadée's lean torso emerging from the villa's pool, glistening in his white swimsuit, had me smoking kif constantly, so that I dwelled in a stoned haze.

Then Paloma arrived with Ricardo, flush with success over her partnership with the Greek jeweler, her designs now worn by movie stars and royalty.

Our casual indolence adopted a more illicit flair.

As far as I could tell, Ricardo and Paloma were just friends. When Pierre bluntly asked, Ricardo replied that he visited from Barcelona on a regular basis because he had architectural projects in Paris. If I had any cause to doubt that they were only friends, Ricardo's overt stares at me across the low, brass-topped table where we sat on embroidered leather cushions purchased in the bazaar dispelled it. He made no attempt to disguise his interest, and again, I wasn't the only one to take notice.

Fernando was appalled. "He's flirting with you right under our noses."

"And? I'm single." We strolled in the luscious gardens of la Mamounia, where Clara had invited us to dinner. A palace gifted by some sultan to his son, it had been converted into a hotel in the '20s. Fifteen hectares of intricate Moroccan stonework and enameled tile, enclosed open-air patios, and sandalwood screens, with curved art deco additions. Very lavish and suitably expensive, the gardens offering a paradise of vegetation and cascading fountains.

Yves and the others were drinking and gossiping on the garden-side terrace when Fernando seized my arm and hauled me off for a scolding.

"You're not sleeping with him, are you?" he demanded, coming to a halt.

I eyed him. "Why would you care?"

"Because he's not—" Fernando's voice tightened. "Not right for you."

"I'm not looking for a boyfriend or another husband."

"He's a cheater. He probably collects women like trophies in every city he visits. Paloma told me he lives with an Italian actress in Barcelona. They have a child."

"Are they married?"

"No. He's still looking to cheat on her."

"That's between him and her. I don't need anyone to tell me what I should or shouldn't do."

"I'm just trying to warn you," he exclaimed. "He's a shark."

"I can swim. And I'm on the Pill."

"You are?"

"I don't recall you using contraception with me," I said. "I'm also not a virgin."

He glowered. "I don't know why I even bother. Just go ahead and do it. You always do." Swerving around before I could detain him, he stormed back to the terrace.

My sudden solitude among the jasmine-scented greenery, the clustered palm trees sketched in spiky ink against the crescent-mooned sky, struck me with its unfamiliarity. Surrounded every day by people in the studio, by Yves and his cares and the demands of our work, I rarely found time for myself.

I couldn't remember the last time I'd been alone.

Pausing by a fountain, I dipped my fingers to rinse the sweat off my nape. I longed to throw off my kaftan and plunge into the water to frolic like a Fellini movie siren.

Then I heard him behind me, the weighted pause.

Not Fernando.

"He's not wrong," said Thadée. "Ricardo Bofill doesn't deserve you."

I spun about. "Since you were obviously eavesdropping, you must have heard what I think about people telling me what to do."

"I'm not telling you what to do." He moved past me to sit at the fountain's edge, his light linen pants and billowy shirt evoking the milky suit he'd worn at le Sept. "But Fernando is still right. That Spaniard wants you as another notch on his belt."

"Perhaps I want him as a notch on mine. Would that surprise you?"

"Not really. Women can want just sex. You want more."

"You don't know me well enough to say what I want. As I said to Fernando, *why* would you care?"

"You know why." Scooping up a handful of water, he moistened his neck. Droplets slid into his shirt, darkening the cloth against his sun-bronzed skin.

I had to look away. "You shouldn't say that to me."

"And you don't need to be so headstrong and independent." His gentle rebuke lifted my gaze. "I care about you. We all do. Even Clara, though you think she doesn't."

His citing of her roused my anger. "I'm independent because I never had a family growing up, except my brother. He needed me to be headstrong for him."

"I'd be strong for you, if you'd let me." In the interplay between the hotel's distant lighting and the overhead moon, the trickling water in the fountain cast wavering reflections on his face, softening its angular planes.

"Don't." I took an unwitting step back. "Don't start this again. It's—"

"Too complicated." He rose to his sandaled feet; suddenly, I yearned to throw caution aside. He was right. I did want more, and not from Ricardo.

You do want someone you think you shouldn't. But you're brave enough to fight it.

I could see the trace of moisture on his throat, like a translucent scarf. As he stepped to me, I went still, incinerated by the incline of his head toward me, the searingly light brush of his lips on mine, rooting me to my spot.

He murmured, "I told you I would wait. I will. For however long it takes."

"We can't do this—" My whisper was smothered by his mouth, his body melding to mine. I couldn't pull away; I returned his kiss as if I were drowning, my arms winding about his neck, my feet arching on tiptoes to drink him in—

"*Loulou!*"

Yves's drunken shout, followed by a burst of laughter and the tromp of approaching feet. I leaped back from Thadée as Yves, Pierre, and Clara emerged from the darkness, their cheeks flushed and eyes bloodshot.

"There you are." Yves blinked, swaying. He was intoxicated. "We thought she'd wandered off and gotten lost like Persephone in the underworld."

Pierre barked his curt laugh, taking us in with disturbing lucidity. "It seems Thadée has rescued her, like Hermes."

Disgust washed over me. They'd almost caught us kissing, and I hated that I couldn't distinguish if I was more upset by their intrusion or my recklessness.

"I suppose everyone does care about me," I muttered, darting my gaze at Clara, suspecting she must have initiated the search to catch me in the act.

But she merely slurred, "Everyone is tired and wants to go to bed." She stumbled to Thadée to grasp his hand. "We've all had a little too much to drink, I'm afraid."

"Yes," said Thadée softly. "Loulou and I were talking."

I didn't think he sounded believable. Yves seized my hand as Thadée led us with Clara over the garden paths. Yves staggered. I had to tighten my hold on him to keep him upright.

On the terrace, François had his arm slung about somnolent

Betty. Fernando, Ricardo, and Paloma idled nearby. Requesting their car and a taxi at the front desk, Pierre glared at Yves, who burped, giggled, and released me.

The driver pulled up outside with the car, followed by the taxi.

Ricardo gave me a sharp-toothed smile. "Ride with us."

I nodded, turned to Thadée and Clara. "Good night."

"Bonsoir, Loulou." She smothered me in a sloppy hug, reeking of martinis and hashish, and then fell back against Thadée. I'd never seen her high, and found myself hoping that if she'd had any suspicion at finding me alone with him, she was too inebriated to remember it tomorrow.

Still, I couldn't meet his eyes as Thadée said, "Sleep well," and I got into the taxi with Ricardo and Paloma, while Betty, François, Yves, and Pierre piled into the car. Fernando made a point of squeezing in with them, straddling Yves's legs while Pierre scowled at the inconvenience.

During the brief ride to the villa, Paloma dozed off. Ricardo pressed his thigh against mine and said in my ear, "Tonight?"

"Yes," I hissed. "After everyone goes to bed."

I had to forget the kiss. I had to forget *him*.

RICARDO TOOK ME in my bedroom with a vigor that banged the painted headboard against the wall. I rolled over to mount him, hushing his groans.

"Quiet. We'll wake everyone up."

"They drank like Cossacks and smoked everything in sight," he panted, thrusting up into me. "An earthquake couldn't wake them."

Then he had me gasping and crying out, unable to contain my pleasure, no longer caring who, or what, we woke up.

THE NEXT MORNING, Yves huddled by the pool, wincing from his hangover behind his sunglasses. Betty and François ate breakfast, and Paloma sprawled in a bikini on the tiles. Fernando was sketching. He avoided eye contact with me.

Pierre was submerged in his morning paper, specially flown in daily from Paris.

"Good morning," Betty chirped. "We slept like rocks, in case you were wondering. We're meeting up with Clara and Thadée later to visit the bazaar."

Ricardo served himself a heaping plate of scrambled eggs and toast.

Yves grimaced. "How can anyone eat in the morning? I feel sick."

"Then stop drinking so much," snapped Pierre, without looking up.

I had to get away. They all knew what I'd done.

"We're going to visit the Zagora Desert," I announced, out of nowhere. It just popped from my mouth, the first place that came to mind.

Yves gaped at me. "In this infernal heat? The desert is six hours away by car."

"We'll rent one. Take plenty of water." I served myself a cup of strong black coffee and nibbled on a piece of toast, though my stomach was also in an uproar.

Ricardo said dryly, "I'll bring her back safely, in case you're afraid I'll abduct her," as though we'd discussed it before-hand. We hadn't. We'd barely talked at all, having sex until we were exhausted and then falling asleep on opposite sides of the bed. When I woke up, he was gone, taking a shower in his room.

"Fine," said Pierre. "Go to the desert. Have fun."

"No, it's *not* fine," cried Yves. "You can't just leave. We have work to do."

"We're supposed to be on vacation. You can survive a few days without her." Pierre finally lifted his eyes to me. "Don't listen to him. He's being dramatic, as usual."

I gave Yves an apologetic smile. He hastened after me to my bedroom.

"What is this?" he demanded. "Why are you leaving?"

"I've never been to a desert." I started tossing clothing into a bag.

"Where are you going to stay? There aren't any hotels near the desert. Loulou, this is crazy. You're running off with a man you barely know."

He'd nicked the wound where it stung. "I said we'd rent a car. We can sleep in the back. I'll bring a cooler. I'm not crossing the desert on a camel. I'm just going to see it."

"You're going to not see Thadée," he said.

I paused for a moment that went on too long, then resumed packing.

"You were with him in the hotel garden," Yves went on. "He went after you and Fernando. He didn't come back with Fernando because he stayed with you. Alone."

"Hermes to the rescue. Except I'm not Persephone."

He sat on my rumpled bed. "Is he the one you think you shouldn't want?"

My hands started to tremble as I shoved things I didn't see into the bag. "Don't be silly. I want to visit the desert and spend some time alone with Ricardo."

He reached out his hand to enclose my wrist. I froze.

"I know that's not true." He pulled me to him, sitting me beside him. "You must tell me what happened last night."

"You know what happened. Everyone does."

"Not with Ricardo." He paused. "I confided in you. Don't you trust me?"

"Of course I trust you. It's just—" My voice hitched. "Thadée kissed me."

"Ah." Yves stroked my hand. "Did you kiss him back?"

"I . . . I did. Then you, Pierre, and Clara showed up."

"I'm sorry. Everyone was drunk and tired. Pierre insisted we go find you."

I swallowed against the barb in my throat. "Clara might have seen us. They've been together for years. I shouldn't have done it."

"They share a history together. It's not passionate anymore." He cupped my chin, turning my face to his. "He likes you, too. Very much. I can tell."

"If you can tell, then so can she."

"I doubt it. When she called us this morning, she said nothing about it. Clara rarely drinks, and we overdid it last night."

It was what I'd hoped to hear; it didn't make me feel less guilty.

"And now you're going to the Zagora with Ricardo. That'll look worse, as if you're running away from something."

"I can't stay." Extricating my hand from his, I said, "Please. I can't."

He nodded. "You must be careful with him."

"Fernando already warned me last night. He thinks Ricardo is a shark. It's not anything serious. I'm not going to elope with him to Barcelona."

"I mean be careful with Thadée. He has a tender heart. If he took a risk by kissing you, then you must mean a lot to him. He's always been very discreet."

"I can't live on hope. It's not smart or safe."

As soon as I spoke the words, his face shadowed. "Then I must be a fool."

He left me with the unsettling sensation that I was setting something into motion that could spiral out of my control.

THE DESERT UNDULATED in an endless expanse, the waning sun bringing out a rich cumin yellow in the sand and vivid nectarine in the sloping shadows.

I envisioned a vast discarded dress, stained in desertic rust.

Ricardo and I had taken our time along the rutted roads in our rented station wagon, eating sandwiches from the cooler, resting on sleeping bags in the back, and rocking the car with our couplings. We saw a goat herder, swatting his belled animals with a switch as he trudged to a hamlet. When we came upon a young couple hitchhiking in cutoff jeans and with grungy backpacks, I demanded we pick them up. They had us drop them off at the nearest bus stop; they were famished, so we also shared our sandwiches with them as they related that they'd wandered from Marrakesh in search of adventure, and ran out of food and water.

They gave us hits of acid to thank us. Ricardo didn't take his. He kept watch over me as I twirled in the night with my arms flung into the air, weaving glimmering rainbows for hours until I eventually came down from the hallucinatory high.

Now the desert rippled before us like an immense flashback. I was tired, dirty, and hungry. And entranced. I'd never seen anything so beautiful and inhospitable.

"Well," he said. "They were right. It's infernal."

I hugged my knees as I sat to watch the sun descend. Subtle violet unfurled in its wake, pleating the sky, the stars pinpricking the twilight like beads.

"Will we see each other again after this?" he asked. "Or are we done?"

I turned to him. I found it so strange. I'd roved his body, taken him inside me, yet I could never see him again and not miss him.

He hadn't made me forget Thadée. The memory of the garden was lodged in me like a splinter.

"If you like," I said at length. "You know where to find me."

He grunted. "Chained to Yves's ankle. I should probably get you back before they send out a rescue helicopter. We said we'd be gone a few days."

"I'm perfectly capable of returning to Paris on my own."

"Why bother, when you can take their private jet? I'd also prefer not to have them accusing me of stealing you away and ruining their vacation, in a villa they own and can visit whenever they like."

I smiled. "You don't like them, do you?"

"I don't like their monstrous egos. Paloma keeps a sane head about it; she understands it's just clothes and jewelry. But the rest of them are self-indulgent, spoiled, and utterly oblivious to reality. I don't know how you put up with it."

Coming from anyone else, I'd have been swift to jump to our defense, but Ricardo's blunt candor washed over me. He wasn't a lover. He was a distraction, and we both knew it.

"I like them." I gave a decisive shrug. "Fine. Let's go back." I really didn't care what he felt. Truth was, I'd seen the desert, and had my fill of him.

He went ahead to the parked car. I took a lingering glance at the fiery sunset as it faded into night and memorized the colors, wishing I'd brought a camera with me.

I would have to tell Yves.

We could design such a gorgeous collection.

11

We'd just finished presenting our fall lines when Pierre informed us that Baron Guy de Rothschild and his wife, Marie-Hélène, had invited us to dinner at their Parisian residence of Hôtel Lambert.

"You'll have to dress up," Pierre told me. "The baroness is formal."

"Me?" I was taken aback.

"Marie-Hélène asked to meet you. She heard you're working for us." Pierre glanced at Yves. "See that she doesn't show up in those gypsy scarves and spangles."

"The Baroness de Rothschild wants to meet me?" I turned, incredulous, to Yves after Pierre left. "What for?"

"She must be curious. The collection. She sees a new influence," he said, smiling. "She's a very loyal client."

"Well, I don't have a thing to wear to meet a baroness that isn't 'gypsy spangles.'"

"We have an entire sample closet here." He stood, wagging a finger at me. "Don't you dare try to get out of it. If I must go, you're going, too."

He selected and adjusted a satin-lapeled couture le Smoking for me from our sample closet, with a bow-tied red silk blouse. I had no real jewelry, as I tended to lose valuable things, so I piled on my assortment of cheap bangles, earning myself a glare from Pierre and a giggle from Yves. They both wore formal tuxedos. Yves had pinned a white orchid to his lapel to lessen the severity.

I expected a regal gathering with members of high society and too many forks at the dinner table. When we arrived, however, it was only us, although the magnificent cream stone town house situated on the eastern tip of Île Saint-Louis—one of the few privately owned hôtel particuliers remaining in Paris—blazed with light. A footman escorted us through a central courtyard with lichen-spotted statuary to the upper floor, where the Rothschilds kept their city abode.

It was like entering a museum. I'd seen priceless antiques and paintings in Yves and Pierre's home on rue de Babylone, but the Rothschilds had accumulated centuries of wealth and status to bestow on their surroundings. The quantity of treasures adorning the gilded coffered-ceiling enfilade of rooms—the medieval tapestries and crystal chandeliers suspended on velvet-trussed cords, along with countless alabaster and marble statues, Sèvres vases, and Limoges-enameled fixtures—stupefied me.

It was the kind of display I'd seen only in Hollywood movies about royalty.

Marie-Hélène was the city's foremost social hostess, as close to royalty as France had these days, even though she'd been born in New York before she moved to Paris to wed Guy de Rothschild. She greeted us serenely, her honey-blond hair in a lacquered pompadour, wearing a cream silk couture jacket and skirt by Yves, and a dazzling suite of ruby earrings and bracelet.

She wasn't beautiful, I noticed as she kissed Yves's cheeks and her shorter, balding husband greeted Pierre. She was too tall and equine-faced, with wide-spaced brown-green eyes. But what she possessed transcended beauty, as I was about to find out.

Over an intimate dinner replete with the excess cutlery, she queried me politely but with an expert instinct for lineage. I was forthright, citing my father's titled yet penurious station, as well as my mother's aristocratic ancestry and rebellious spirit.

"To have worked with Schiaparelli." The baroness sighed. "What an unforgettable experience. I own couture pieces by her, given to me by my mother, who was a client."

"Your mother might have seen my mother posing in the lobster hat," I said, my fingers hovering until Yves nudged me toward the correct fork for the watercress salad with glazed walnuts, a palate cleanser before the main course. "My mother always claimed Elsa despised her for being too beautiful."

Marie-Hélène smiled. "Women of strong character rarely see eye to eye. But look at you, carrying on the family tradition with Yves."

"Loulou's a joy," Yves piped up. "She went to the desert and described the sunset to me. We designed Rive Gauche this year in those colors."

"Yes, I've seen how she inspires you." At some unseen gesture, the baroness alerted her staff to remove our salad plates, while at the other end of the table, Baron Guy and Pierre engaged in conversation. "Your collections are so youthful now."

"It's all because of Loulou." Yves pressed my hand.

"Then we must hear what she thinks of our Versailles proposal," said Marie-Hélène. "I understand she received advance word of it from Halston."

A sudden hush fell over the table. The staff served garnished lobster thermidor, and Pierre finally cracked both the silence and the shell on his plate with a gruff "Clara and I were under the impression everyone had decided against it."

"I decided otherwise." Her authoritative tone left Pierre slack-jawed; I'd never seen him as taken aback as he was in that moment. "The palace curator, Gérald van der Kemp, and his wife, Florence, are dear friends of ours, and they tell us funds are urgently required for the château's restoration. The roof is leaking. The Hall of Mirrors has termites. There's no modern heating. It is a matter of national pride; we cannot let Versailles fall to ruin because our government refuses to see to its maintenance."

"Pompidou has always been tightfisted," said Pierre. "So, we're obliged to do a charity event to pick up his slack."

"Oh, Pierre." She laughed. "I'll make sure it's a grand divertissement to be remembered, like my Proust Ball. A very exclusive one." She managed to make both the term "exclusive" and eating lobster exercises in opulent restraint. "Cardin, Givenchy, Emanuel Ungaro, and Marc Bohan of Dior have agreed to participate. Therefore, Yves must; he's our foremost couturier. Eleanor Lambert proposes five Americans from New York. They're acceptable enough, only . . ." She gave another sigh, this time with a hint of distaste. "Eleanor thinks it will look better in the press if we're seen to 'invite' them."

I recalled Halston's words to me.

Pierre asked, "Who are the American designers?"

"I'm not sure about one of them: Stephen Burrows. I've never heard of him. The others are Oscar de la Renta, Halston, Bill Blass, and Anne Klein. All established names in the United States and, as I said, acceptable enough."

Pierre frowned. "Klein isn't a designer. She mass-produces sportswear for women to wear at the office. Mix-and-match separates."

"Givenchy designs separates," Yves said. "So do we."

"Hers are priced for temporary receptionists," retorted Pierre.

"As I understand it," injected Marie-Hélène smoothly, "there's been opposition among the Americans over Anne Klein's inclusion. Eleanor insists her business is very profitable, more so than the others. That is how America defines quality: by money in the bank. We needn't be concerned. We have the crème de la crème of haute couture. If they choose to show sportswear at Versailles, so be it."

"When is it scheduled?" said Pierre, in clenched-jawed sub-mission. "We can't interrupt our season for a charity event."

"None of the designers want their season interrupted. We've decided to hold it at the end of November as a winter gala."

Yves gasped. "*November*? That's less than four months away. I can't possibly design anything new for it in so little time, with all my other obligations."

"There's no need to go out of your way, my dear." She dabbed her mouth with her monogrammed napkin, without smudging her neutral lipstick, which was applied to appear as if she wore none. "You and the others can present clothes from previous collections, unless you wish to design the costumes for your seg-ment. I encourage you to consider it, as you have such a deft hand for the theater. I'm overseeing the arrangements, including the guest list. All you need do is approve your decor and appear the day before in the Théâtre Gabriel at Versailles for dress rehearsal, on the twenty-seventh. The gala will take place the following eve-ning. I've approached Jean-Louis Barrault to direct and design the sets. He designed my Proust Ball, as you know, and he's eager to do us justice in Versailles. He's also hiring dancers and the orchestra."

"Barrault?" Pierre's lukewarm tone thawed. "I'm impressed."

Yves whispered to me, "A famous mime and director. He oversaw the Comédie-Française before the war, and starred in films."

"Oh," I said. He sounded a tad dated to me, an impression validated by Marie-Hélène's patriotic declaration: "Barrault is one of our finest. We cannot disappoint. This event demands the very best France has to offer."

Pierre nodded begrudging approval. I took a moment before I said, "When I saw Halston in New York, he mentioned he'd be honored if Yves invited him."

"Absolutely not." Though she issued her refusal with a gracious smile, it was emphatic. "Yves will invite Oscar de la Renta from the American contingent, as is appropriate. It's a public relations exercise to nurture a sense of mutual collaboration, and de la Renta studied under Balenciaga. Halston must content himself with an invitation from Cardin. He's not a couturier. Indeed, none of them are. De la Renta, however, has the training. He also dresses women of status, not actresses."

She sat back as the server removed her plate. She'd barely eaten, which was how she must maintain her svelte figure, making me feel like a hog for consuming everything on my plate. But then, I never fretted over my weight, with all my running around at work and dancing at night. If anything, I was too thin.

"We must humor them," she said. "But not to our detriment. Did Halston mention anything else we ought to consider?"

I thought of Pat's excitement. "He's hired a black model for the show; he'll probably bring others. He also said he could ask Liza Minnelli to perform."

"Mademoiselle Minnelli's performance is confirmed. She made a point of inserting a no-filming clause in her agreement, as if we'd ever allow cameras inside a royal theater. We reached out to Nureyev and Josephine Baker, both of whom will perform for us. I understand Ungaro is inviting Louis Jourdan and Jane Birkin to perform in his segment. Yves, feel free to invite someone of your choosing for yours."

She made another indiscernible motion for dessert and coffee to be served. "As for black mannequins, it's to be expected. The racial tension in America led to civil unrest and riots; they've much to atone for in their past. We keep different standards here."

I thought she was wrong, as "standards" were changing everywhere, and France had its own sordid history to atone for, but I refrained from saying it. Yves tensed at my side, as though he were thinking the same thing.

After repairing to their salon for after-dinner cognac and cigars—Yves and I smoked a joint, pretending we were sharing a cigarette—we said good night, Marie-Hélène kissing my cheeks. "Yves thinks the world of you. I can see why. Such inimitable style and heritage. I'm so pleased."

I murmured, "Thank you," thinking she'd stamped her approval on me as if I were a Thoroughbred with established pedigree. It reminded me of my mother mixing cocktails and declaiming America had no style, though I doubted the baroness had ever fixed her own cocktail or put on a dress by herself in her entire life.

During the chauffeured drive to drop me off at my flat, Yves said, "If they're bringing Minnelli, who just won an Oscar, to perform and American models like those we hired, it won't look good for us."

Pierre snorted. "We were crucified for hiring those models. Minnelli might have Hollywood cachet, but she's nowhere near the stature of Nureyev or Baker. Cardin has Birkin and Jourdan. We can invite Zizi Jeanmaire to perform in your segment and give Minnelli a run for her Oscar. Marie-Hélène demands excellence; it's a matter of national pride. They don't stand a chance against us."

"Isn't it supposed to be a mutual collaboration, not a competition?" I asked.

As usual, Pierre spoke with the aggression of someone gearing up for a fight: "When you put ten fashion designers on the same stage, it's always a competition."

WHILE AN UNSEASONABLE chill for early September stole over Paris, scattering the desiccated leaves from the chestnuts in the

Tuileries, Barrault sent over his set design for Yves's approval. Pierre brought it to us: a 1920s scene, with a cardboard cutout of a car from the era, and—

"Female impersonators?" Yves glanced at Pierre. "Men in drag at Versailles?"

Pierre snorted. "There were plenty of them during the Sun King's reign, mincing in heels and wigs up to the ceiling. We can count ourselves lucky. Givenchy has an enormous pumpkin to deal with."

Yves grimaced. "It's a farce. A preposterous folie."

"Marie-Hélène has charge over it. Who are we to argue? Design the costumes for the drag queens and Zizi Jeanmaire's number, then wash your hands of it. It's a society gala for one night. All anyone will care about is the guest list, not the clothes or the sets."

Having rendered his brusque verdict, Pierre turned to the studio door. Yves rolled his weary eyes at me before Pierre came to a halt.

"I almost forgot. Karl is having a birthday celebration next week. His fortieth. Or his thirty-fifth, if he's to be believed. He isn't. His boyfriend—or again, if he's to be believed, *not* his boyfriend—is organizing the party and called Clara to invite us."

Yves went still, the column of ash from his cigarette tumbling onto the sketch of the set on his desk. "What?" he said in disbelief.

"A party. For Karl." Pierre shot an exasperated look over his shoulder.

"And we—we're going?" quavered Yves.

"We need to keep up appearances. Nurture a sense of mutual collaboration," said Pierre, with a deliberate echo of the baroness, and pointedly stared at me, where I stood as if paralyzed by Yves. "Our long-suffering president of the Syndicale has announced her retirement; she's finally fed up with defending couture. I'm rallying votes to be elected to the position. Once I take over, the Syndicale will oversee both haute couture and prêt-à-porter under a single organization, which is how it should be. No more divisiveness. So, in answer to your question, yes. We're going to the party."

"Why? What does any of that have to do with Karl?"

"He's been made the lead styliste at Chloé. He also signed a lucrative deal to launch a Chloé perfume, which you would know if you read anything in the papers that isn't about you. They're sending him on an American tour to promote it. He's gained recognition. I won't have him connive behind my back when I'm running the Syndicale."

Yves managed to square his shoulders. "I won't go."

Pierre tugged at his jacket sleeve, checking his wristwatch. "You will. I'm late for a dinner. I already had Clara confirm our RSVP. She and Thadée will be going as well. You, too, Loulou. You can wear whatever you like this time, as long as it's ours."

He didn't wait for a response, stalking out.

Bracing his hands on the desk, Yves whispered, "Jacques will be there."

I jolted up to shut the studio door, though it was late and everyone except us had left for the night.

"Do you think Pierre knows?" It would be just like Pierre to round us up like gladiators to thrust us into the arena for combat with Karl.

"Never. He'd go berserk. He suspects I was seeing someone, but not anymore, and never Jacques. I've been very careful." Yves flinched as his cigarette burned to the filter and scorched his fingers. He stubbed it out and immediately lit another, pacing to the window. "So careful that I've only seen him once since we came back from Marrakesh. The day after, in fact. We met at his apartment." Though I could see him struggling to remain calm, a tremor clogged his voice. "He was angry with me because it had been so long. I tried to explain I'm busy with the collections, Pierre dragging me off to view new hôtel particuliers to move the house. He said he was busy, too, researching a château in the countryside for Karl to buy. A cousin of his was coming to stay with him. We argued for the first time."

I took a step toward him. "About what?"

"About us. Sneaking around, hiding. He says I'm ashamed of it. He's twenty-two, fifteen years younger than me. He's a different generation, and doesn't understand why we can't openly see each other if Pierre and I have an arrangement. He thinks maybe it's impossible, and we shouldn't do it anymore."

"What do you think?" I said quietly.

"I couldn't bear it, Loulou. I *can't* lose him." His voice fractured. "I'm in love with him."

The unseen fault line I'd thought to sidestep yawned beneath me. "In love . . . ?"

"I've never felt like this before. I want to be with him all the time. I need to stop hiding how I feel and be brave. It's what people in love must do to be together: they find a way. I promised him that I'll leave Pierre."

Panic gripped me. "You can't promise him that. Jacques is with Karl."

"Not in that way. They live apart. Karl makes no demands on him."

Urgency clamored in me. "Yves, he *is* with Karl, whether they live together or not. He takes Karl's money. He's planning a birthday party for him. If he's having doubts about you, then you can't give up your entire life for him. You have much more to lose."

His fingers traced the sketch, smudging the cigarette ash

into it. "That's what I keep telling myself. How much I'll risk. My reputation. The house. The clients. What will people say?" He gave a terse smile. "'Yves is crazy' is what they'll say. 'He's lost his mind.' I don't care. Don't I deserve to be happy?"

"Of course you do." The studio wavered around me, like a facade tumbling in a gale. "You deserve every happiness. But Pierre won't just let you go. You know he won't. It's been—"

"Fifteen years," he cut in. "Fifteen years, and we don't touch each other anymore. I can't remember the last time we did. I don't think he's any happier than me. He's just better at being unhappy. He buries his feelings in the business. Now he'll get himself elected as president of the Syndicale. More power and status. Pierre Bergé, the fashion conqueror. That's how he seeks his happiness. He's never needed what I do."

"Just wait a while longer." I brushed his hand with mine. "Yves, do it for yourself, if nothing else. You can't go back once you decide. You can't undo it."

He let out a little sigh. "I don't mean to burden you with all this."

"You're not burdening me. I just think you're overreacting because you quarreled with Jacques, and now the party, all of us in the same room. You don't have to decide anything yet. You had an argument. It happens. He'll understand if he cares about you."

His gaze shifted to the window, toward some distant place. "Yes," he said faintly, as if to persuade himself. "Maybe he will understand."

AS THE NIGHT of the party neared, I couldn't shake off a feeling of impending doom. Yves designed red velvet dresses with glittering headbands for the female impersonators in his segment. Zizi came to the studio in a pixie-cut black wig—an indication that she feared Minnelli might outshine her—and was fitted for her Marlene Dietrich–inspired tails-tuxedo ensemble. She chattered and flitted about, all the women in the studio in fawning awe over her. She and Yves went out to dinner, leaving me to see to the adjustments of her tuxedo with Anne-Marie.

I went home late to kick off my shoes and find my fridge empty, except for a carton of yogurt and a stale baguette. I hadn't shopped for food. Dumping the bread in the trash, I smoked a joint and tried to eat the yogurt, which had soured, then rounded my loft restlessly, thinking I should go out dancing, dispel my gloom at le Sept.

Ricardo was in Barcelona. Fernando had installed an answering machine, with a scratchy message that he was away in New York. Betty was too tired, so I resigned myself to a night of sleep, which I needed more, when the phone suddenly rang.

Clara said, "I'm sorry to bother you. It's about Corey."

"Did you find him? Is he okay?"

She went silent for a moment. "He's in some trouble. Can you come to our apartment? He's here with us. Thadée will come there for you."

I grabbed my boots, yanking the phone cord with me. "I'll be downstairs waiting."

Thadée appeared minutes later, hunched against the evening wind. "I have a car," he said, "but parking in this area is impossible. It's a ten-minute walk to the apartment."

"Tell me about Corey," I said, lighting a cigarette as we moved down rue des Grands-Augustins to the intersection with rue de Saint-André des Arts.

Thadée related harrowing details. "He's been living in a rundown hotel in the Marais. We left messages, but the concierge hadn't seen him in weeks." Thadée glanced at me. "He's twenty-four years old and in a foreign city. When he called us, he was desperate, thinking of killing himself."

I bit back a surge of tears, in the blast of wind at the intersection. "I should have made the effort to chase Corey down myself. If the messages at his hotel had been from me, he might have answered sooner."

"You can't blame yourself for it. He's alive, so we can still help him. He needs to go home, Loulou. If he stays, Paris will end up killing him. We'll pay for his airfare. He can stay with us until then. But you must convince him to go. He asked for you, said you were always kind to him and offered to help."

"I didn't help," I said, angry at myself. "I abandoned him, like everyone else."

He shook his head, his coat flapping about him. "You probably saved him. Clara only found him because you asked her. She called a fashion house where he'd been hired to do makeup for a show; they had his hotel address. If you hadn't asked, none of us would have thought twice about him. Another pretty thing who came and went, like so many others. They have no idea what this world of ours is like. How many wolves wait to devour them."

I didn't speak as we reached the white stone apartment building on rue Jacob. Their tidy apartment was on the top floor, decorated with curated objets d'art, including an exquisite small painting of ballerinas by Degas, and other paintings of half-naked pubescent girls lolling on beds or chairs, by Thadée's father. Clara was always spare in her dress and behavior, despite her binge in Marrakesh. It showed in her surroundings.

Framed photographs of her and Thadée with friends were displayed on a lacquered Venetian table in the entry. I avoided looking too closely at them as she brought me to a spare bedroom. The gaunt figure on the bed in an oversized robe, his tangled hair wet from a shower and hanging about his face, couldn't be Corey. He looked as if he'd aged years.

"Loulou." He tried to smile. "I really messed up."

I took him in my arms as he started to cry. Clara said, "We'll be in the living room. I left a mild sedative on the bedside table, so he can rest."

She closed the door. After he expended himself, I dried his tears with my scarf.

"My life is over," he said brokenly. "I'm not a model. I'm not an artist. I'm not anything. All I had was my looks, and now I'm washed up, old." His haunted eyes searched mine. "I'll never be anything. Anyone."

"Corey, you will. You have your whole life ahead of you. You're so young."

So very young, in ways I'd never been. Innocent in ways I'd not known, despite everything he'd been through. I'd been fighting all my life to fend off my uprooted childhood, the indifference of my parents. I learned early to rely only on myself for my sense of safety. No one was going to do it for me.

They have no idea what this world of ours is like. How many wolves wait to devour them.

As if a veil had been torn from my eyes, I saw how fashion ate its prey, digesting the flesh and discarding the bones. He'd come to Paris with dreams, and we'd shattered him. We allowed him a fleeting moment of glory, then turned our collective backs.

"You have to go back to New York." I enfolded his hand in mine. "We'll help you."

He sniffled. "I—I want to go back. Antonio's in New York. Whenever I called him, he begged me to come home. Donna and Pat did, too. I didn't listen."

"They miss you. I saw Donna and Pat last Christmas in New York. They all miss you so much. They're your family, Corey. You belong with them."

"I thought I belonged here." A raw sound that wasn't a laugh scraped his throat. "For a second, I did. On the runway for Yves."

"He wouldn't want to see you like this." Once more, I fought back overwhelming sorrow and guilt. "He thinks you're très chic. Remember?"

"Every day." His hollow smile surfaced. "I'll always remember it."

"Then remember me, too." I leaned to him, kissing his cheek, like a sister. Or a mother. "Remember, I'll never forget you. I'm so sorry for what we did to you."

"You didn't do anything. None of this is your fault."

"It is. We should have protected you." I stood, turned down the bedcovers, and handed him the pill. "Go to sleep. You can stay here as long as you want. When you're ready, we'll book a flight for you to go home."

He crept into the bed. With his damp curls on the pillow, he looked heartbreakingly angelic again, like when I first saw him at le Sept, laughing and playing with Donna, enticing us with his flirtatious impudence.

It seemed a lifetime ago.

I waited until I thought he was asleep. Tiptoeing to the door, I heard him say, "I saw Yves the other night. He was with Jacques."

My hand froze on the door latch, my lungs abruptly short of air. "Where?" I asked faintly.

"At a club for men. Les Bains. They didn't see me. I wanted to warn Yves."

I've only seen him once since we came back from Marrakesh. The day after, in fact.

"Jacques is dangerous. He likes pain and degradation." Corey's voice drifted as he succumbed to the sedative. "Protect Yves. Keep him away."

My blood turned to ice. In the hallway, I had to pause, take a calming breath, before I went into the living room. Thadée was smoking. Clara sipped a cognac. I should have felt awkward in their home. But the memory of the hotel garden also seemed like a lifetime ago. I could barely acknowledge my discomfort.

"Corey agrees to go back to New York," I said.

"Thank God." Clara set her glass aside. "It's terrible, what's happened to him."

Without warning, I swayed, lightheaded. The room overturned around me. Thadée leaped from the sofa to catch me. As he helped me to sit, Clara hastily poured another cognac from the corner bar tray and thrust the glass at me. "Drink."

I gulped it down. "I'm okay. I haven't eaten today. We had so much work at the studio."

"You can't work yourself into starvation." Taking the glass from me, she said to Thadée, "Bring some baguette and brie."

"No, please. Don't bother—" I started to say, but he bolted to the kitchen.

Clara regarded me. "It doesn't do us any good for you to kill yourself."

I forced myself not to look away. "Do you know Jacques de Bascher?"

She went still. Only for a moment. "Not well. I know he's Karl's friend. I've had no personal dealings with him."

I clamped down on my revulsion. "But he called you to invite us to Karl's party."

"Karl wasn't about to put himself in the position of inviting us himself. He had Jacques do it for him. I consulted Pierre before giving them an answer."

"Why wouldn't Karl want to invite us himself?"

"Oh, Loulou." She gave an impatient sigh. "Don't be naive. Yves went and hired those American girls from under Karl's nose. Pierre and Karl have never gotten along. Honestly, I'm surprised Karl made the effort, through his friend or otherwise."

She stepped back as Thadée returned with a tray and put it on the table, pushing aside a stack of art books. Slathering brie on a chunk of bread, he handed it to me. I needed the sustenance but didn't taste it. I might have been eating stale air.

Clara said, "Why are you asking me about Jacques de Bascher?"

"Corey said something to me." I plucked out my words like shards.

"Oh? I imagine whatever he said wasn't pleasant."

"Karl was paying for the apartment where Corey was staying with Donna and Pat. Jacques got them kicked out." It wasn't the entire truth, but it wasn't quite a lie, either. I wouldn't divulge the rest of it to her.

Thadée gave me a quick look as Clara retrieved her glass. "Then Corey must blame Jacques and Karl for his situation," she said. "It was awful of them to put that poor boy out in the streets, but it's their doing, not ours."

She might have been talking about a stray dog, found tied to a lamppost. I wrestled again to subdue my disgust. "So, we have to play nice with them."

Her smile was a sliver. "Surely we can manage it for one night."

"Fine," I muttered. What little hunger I had deserted me. "I should go home."

"I'll walk you back," said Thadée.

At the door, Clara kissed my cheeks and murmured, "We'll take care of Corey. No need to worry about him."

"I'll check up on him later," I replied firmly.

DURING THE SHORT walk back to my flat, the wind having abated, silence thickened like a pane of glass between us before Thadée said, "Whatever's going on, you can trust me."

When I lit a cigarette, the nicotine hit me with a nauseating jolt.

"It's not just Corey," he added, when I didn't answer. "You're worried about something else."

"I'm worried about pretending everything's fine," I said through my teeth.

"Isn't everything fine?" He slowed his pace as we turned onto my street, where the bistro was closing for the night. "Or did Corey say something else to you?"

I found myself not wanting to talk about it. "I can go alone from here. It's getting late—"

"No." He came to a halt on the sidewalk. "Tell me what Corey said to you."

Suddenly, I couldn't keep it to myself. It was consuming me inside. "Yves is having an affair with Jacques. Corey saw them together."

Thadée went still. "Where did he see them?"

I wished I'd kept my mouth shut. But it was in the open now, so I said warily, "At a club called les Bains. Promise me you won't tell anyone."

"Of course not. I would never do that to you or Yves. How long?"

I hesitated again.

"Loulou, I swear to you, I won't tell anyone. Yves is one of my best friends."

Huddling in a doorway, my cigarette tossing embers as the wind abruptly kicked up again, I said, "Yves confided in me about the affair earlier this year. He was unhappy with Pierre, all the licensing and extra work, the plan to move the house to a new location. It seemed like an infatuation to me. Nothing serious."

"His affairs are never serious. They also don't last months."

"He . . . he thinks he's in love," I said.

"What?" He stared at me.

"He's afraid Jacques is going to leave him."

Thadée frowned. "He's the one who always leaves. Isn't Jacques with Karl?"

"Karl supports Jacques, but Jacques told Yves it's not a physical relationship. Yves was very upset when Pierre told us we had to go to Karl's party. I thought Pierre had found out. Yves says he hasn't; he's been careful. He's only seen Jacques once since we returned from Marrakesh. They met at Jacques's apartment and had an argument."

"About?"

"Jacques was angry at Yves for not being open about them. Yves tried to explain why, but . . ." I swallowed, crushed my cigarette under my heel. "Jacques suggested they should stop seeing each other, so Yves promised to leave Pierre. He said to me, 'It's what people in love must do to be together.' They must 'be brave' and 'find a way.'"

"My god," said Thadée. "He's never spoken once of leaving Pierre in all the years I've known them. They have their ups and downs, like every couple; but a separation is unimaginable. Pierre runs the business. Yves can't possibly do it on his own. He has no head for it. He'd be lost without Pierre."

"There's more." I met his stunned eyes. "Corey says he saw them the other night at that club. It sounded more recent to me. He also said Jacques is dangerous. I think . . ." I had to clear my throat, if not my conscience, for betraying Yves's confidence.

"You think Yves lied about the last time they were together."

"Yes, but he has no reason to lie to me. I already knew."

"He does have a reason, if he's doing things that he doesn't want anyone to know about. He can be like a rebellious child that way." Thadée contemplated me. "It's not that he doesn't trust you. He lies whenever he's afraid someone will put a stop to what he wants to do."

"What else could he be doing, besides seeing Jacques?"

"Well, les Bains, for one. I don't have firsthand experience, but it's known as a gay bathhouse. Not a safe place for Yves."

I imagined a warren of dimly lit backrooms and saunas. "I don't understand."

"Yves isn't anonymous. All it takes is for one malicious person to recognize him, like Corey did. A reporter or photographer. Imagine the feeding frenzy in the press. It could cost Yves his reputation. Pierre would be enraged."

"Why?" I was genuinely confused. "They've never hidden that they're together. They have an arrangement. I assume Pierre also has affairs on the side."

"He has one-night stands. Pierre never lets anyone get in the way of what truly matters to him: Yves and the house. If the press finds out Yves is cheating on him, Pierre will be forced to explain it. They might not be hiding they're a couple, but doing so in private, among friends, is very different from being open about it to the entire world."

"I still don't understand. How is it any different? They're gay. So what?"

"Loulou, you really don't get it, do you?" At my emphatic shake of head, he explained, "Not everyone lives in London, New York, or Paris. The house has international clientele; foreign clients tolerate it, if it's not front-page news. Drugs. Bathhouses. Anonymous sex. Now do you understand?"

I did, but it didn't make me feel better. "That's ridiculous. It's none of their business."

"But it will affect Pierre and Yves's business, if it gets out."

Talking about illicit affairs roused the searing memory of my kiss with Thadée in Marrakesh. It crept underneath everything we said, like a secret we, too, were hiding, fearing its exposure to the world. We were standing alone on the street, a few passersby hurrying past. It would be so easy to take him in my arms and kiss him again. Lovers in Paris, kissing in doorways; it was seen every day in the city.

"Corey's also been going to that bathhouse and doing drugs," I said, skirting my thoughts and the underlying tension. "Maybe he's confused about what he saw."

"He modeled for Yves and detests Jacques. Do you think he's confused?"

Protect Yves. Keep him away.

"No," I admitted.

"Yves would be drawn to it." Now Thadée paused, as if he'd suddenly said too much.

"Drawn to it? The drugs and sex, or the risk of being outed by the press?"

He took a moment. "The thrill of the forbidden. Yves can be extreme."

"How so?" I shoved my hands into my pockets, my fingers numb from the chill in the air. "I know he can be temperamental in his work, but he's also very successful at it."

"That's part of the problem." Thadée fumbled in his coat for his cigarettes, lighting one and giving it to me, then lighting another for himself. "He found success very young at Dior. He's never known a normal existence. He acts out sometimes. On New Year's Eve, he drank so much that Pierre started yelling at him. Yves stormed out and disappeared until late the next day."

"He told me they had a fight over nothing."

"Well, he was gone for over ten hours. Pierre kept calling us. He was about to start contacting emergency rooms when Yves came home, high out of his mind. He wouldn't say where he'd been, but he must have been in a bad enough state for Pierre to threaten him with a sanatorium, like that mental ward at the Val-de-Grâce when he was drafted."

My anger flared. "That's a terrible thing to threaten him with. Everyone goes overboard. We were all doing it in Marrakesh.

It's not . . ." I faltered, seeing Corey in my mind, what it had done to him, the physical decline and despair.

"Unlike us, Yves doesn't know when to stop," said Thadée. "Pierre always does it for him. He yanks the reins. Yves can get out of hand very quickly, if he's running around in secret. You're right to be worried. I'm worried, too."

My heart began to pound. "We can't stop him. It's his body. His life."

He let the moment extend, then he said, "Let me get you home." As we hastened toward the square, he ventured at length, "We could find out more."

A metallic taste soured my mouth. "More?"

"About Jacques. He doesn't strike me as someone who's hiding. He craves attention, to be seen and admired. He invited us to the party, so he and Karl must want us there, which must also mean that Karl has no idea about the affair."

"What are you saying?"

"That everyone at the party will behave as if everything's fine. It may be a bit awkward, seeing as we made the rule of avoiding Lagerfeld and his clan, but Yves broke that rule when he hired the Americans. Pierre wants us to play nice, as you say. If we don't act suspicious and enjoy ourselves, we can invite Jacques out later, for drinks. Dinner. Go dancing with him at le Sept. Get to know him. He should find it irresistible. It's what people in love do, isn't it? They're always eager to impress their lover's friends."

"Pretend we want to be his *friend*?" I started to shake my head, appalled by the subterfuge. Then I paused. "Why are you doing this?"

His eyes lowered. "I haven't done anything particularly useful with my life. People assume I don't need to, because of my father. I've learned to go a long way on a smile. But I care about Yves. If Jacques is a danger to him, I won't stand by and let it happen."

"You didn't say as much in front of Clara."

"She can't hear it. None of them can. Everyone has their assigned role. Betty is there to amuse Yves and wear his clothes. Clara oversees press for Rive Gauche. You're Yves's assistant. Pierre has made it very clear that he has sole responsibility over Yves. But he doesn't know about Jacques. And we can't tell him."

I shuddered at the thought. "Yves would never forgive us."

"So, we get Jacques into our confidence. If he's harming Yves, we stop him. He depends on Karl for the roof over his head. The last thing Lagerfeld wants is for *his* private life to become a public scandal. The humiliation would be intolerable to him."

"And if we find out Jacques and Yves are truly in love?"

"Then we step aside and hope for the best," he said.

At the flat's front portal, I inserted the key, pulling the door open before I found a reason to regret this. "Only if no one else knows," I said, turning to him. "Not Betty. Not Pierre or Yves. Especially not Clara. No one else."

"Only us." He nodded as I moved into the foyer to climb the stairs, not looking back at him outside, though I knew he'd stay put until I was gone.

Once in the flat, I dumped my bag on the kitchen counter and sat on my bed in my coat.

What was I doing? Like Yves, I'd just made a pact with a man I shouldn't be involved with. Even as I told myself we were doing it for Yves, I knew that what was driving me to my own extreme might be more tangled than I cared to admit.

Thadée was also dangerous—to me. I'd just agreed to sneak around with him, to ensure Yves's safety, by befriending the man Yves was sleeping with.

It was another secret we could share. And secrets could be our undoing.

12

I chose an ensemble from our fall collection: a cream-colored mousseline blouse, gray cuffed trousers with a thin golden belt, and a scalloped gold tricot cardigan. To complete the look, I added fake pearl drop earrings.

Yves gave me a twitchy smile when he and Pierre picked me up in their new Rolls-Royce. Pierre wore a tobacco-colored velvet suit and paisley cravat, while Yves had opted for demure elegance, his thick hair shorn to his shoulders and his face clean-shaven, complementing his dark blue suit, a white gauze scarf about his throat.

Pierre grimaced as the driver pulled before the elegant white building on the northern corner of Place Saint-Sulpice, where taxis and limos dropped off guests. Clara and Thadée were waiting outside; she was in a Rive Gauche black silk dress and camel hair cape. He wore a light blue suit that brought out the nascent gray in his eyes.

"Ready for battle?" Thadée quipped at Pierre, who grunted. "Trust Karl to turn his birthday party into a night at the Palais Garnier."

The flat boasted an intact drawing room with high windows festooned in lace curtains to highlight the view of the famed eighteenth-century church in the square. I had expected mini-malist decor, the *Space Odyssey* pastiche Warhol had mentioned when he came to film his movie, but everything was staged for grandeur. Heavy gilt-framed paintings and seashell chairs upholstered in blue Chinese silk. Porcelain urns flanking rich lacquered tables; mahogany bookshelves crammed with leather-bound volumes. A damask-hung daybed sprawled incongruously in the salon, as though someone might suffer an attack of vapors and require respite. Cathedral-sized candles burned in sconces, shedding a melted, flattering glow.

Pierre's scowling appraisal indicated none of it was fake. "He's developed a taste for antiques, though as usual for him, it's in bad taste. Designing prêt-à-porter and furs must pay enough to feather the nest. But for all his lord-of-the-manor air, he won't see the Baroness de Rothschild or any of her circle here."

Seizing a glass of champagne from a circulating waiter, he bulldozed into the crowd, greeting those he knew, which seemed to be everyone, effusive as always in his bluster.

Yves lingered with Clara, who chatted to him as if indeed nothing were amiss.

"Betty's not coming," I told Thadée in a hushed voice, taking my own glass from the waiter. "She called at the last minute to say she wasn't feeling up to it. Fernando's still in New York, but I see Paloma over there with Karl."

"Then our trap is ready," he murmured. "Any sign of our new best friend?"

I scanned those around Karl. He stood by a marble mantel, his muscular arm straining the fit of his tight sleeve and propped on the veined stone. A high collar framed his square, black-bearded face. Ruffles cascaded over the double-breasted front of his long jacket. Along with his codpieced pants and thigh boots with silver-studded cuffs, he exuded the menacing glamour of a story-book pirate.

In a scarlet satin dress with puffed sleeves, Paloma conversed with him. The man at her side had his back to me, but even before he turned around, I knew it was Ricardo. His gaze lanced me, his sardonic smile curving his lips.

He must have found the ambience ludicrous.

"No," I said to Thadée. "I don't see him. Let's spread out and mingle."

Drifting into the milieu, I weaved my path toward Karl. Ricardo leaned in toward Paloma; her red-lipped mouth parted in genuine happiness to see me.

We kissed each other's cheeks. "How lovely you look," she enthused. "The new collection is so ideal for your figure. I saw the show. It was gorgeous."

After complimenting her dress and jewelry under Ricardo's mordant stare, I said to Karl, "Bon anniversaire. Thank you for inviting us."

His jet-black eyes were reflectionless. "Thank you for coming. Do you like my flat?"

"Yes." I fabricated a bright smile. "It's very beautiful. So . . ."

"Excessive, no?" Karl smiled. It didn't change his expression, as though his mouth were manipulated by invisible wires. "It's already starting to bore me. I'm considering an auction next year to rid myself of all of it."

"Oh." Seeing as these were the first words that we'd exchanged, I wasn't certain how to respond. "It must have taken a lot of time and effort to decorate."

"Out with the old, in with the new. I've no patience for nostalgia." He glanced at Thadée, nearing us in a circuitous pattern, on the heels of Pierre's trajectory. Pierre appeared intent on stopping to talk to everyone present, forestalling the inevitable greeting of Karl. "But there's a particular piece I'll always keep." Karl shifted his gaze back to me. "Would you like to see it?"

I nodded, drinking my champagne as he set his blunt, multi-ringed fingers on my arm and propelled me through various rooms into a formal dining area with a large, age-burnished painting dominating the far wall.

"*La salle ronde*," he said. "Do you know it?"

"No," I said. The painting depicted a gathering of wigged, frock-coated men inside a florid pillared rotunda, partaking of a meal, while liveried footmen stood watch. The men engaged in animated conversation, some inclined to others to share witticisms. A tiered crystal chandelier overhead refracted the aged yellow in the pigments, the deep crimson and gold-edged black of the men's apparel. A doorway slung in white drapery at the painting's edge lent the illusion of entry into a garden of delights.

"It's by Menzel." Karl's tone bordered on reverential. "Frederick the Great, receiving his friends at Sanssouci. At the age of seven, on Christmas Eve, I had a coup de foudre when I saw this reproduction in my hometown in Germany. I refused to leave until my parents persuaded the antique dealer to let them purchase it for me. It wasn't inexpensive, but I had to own it, to see it every day. I immediately decided it represents a life worth living, which I could strive to achieve."

It fit his surroundings and manner of dress: a choreographed refinement that contained, I thought, more frivolity than substance.

And then, as if on cue, a side door in the dining room wainscoting opened.

Jacques appeared.

He wore a high-collared shirt like Karl's, except instead of ruffles, he had on a silver-and-black-striped tie. A silver-threaded scarf draped across his shoulders, emphasizing his slim frame in a tailed ivory waistcoat, his narrow legs in high-waisted, pleated cream trousers with suspenders, the cuffs breaking perfectly upon patent-leather shoes.

I found myself riveted by the tiny satin ribbons on his shoes before his chuckle brought my face up to his: a sharp jaw and feline eyes, his hair lighter than I recalled, a tawny-brown wave tousled across his forehead. Without the matinee-idol artifice of le Sept, his long, sculpted nose and unwaxed mustache above his thin-lipped mouth gave him a fey quality—an elfin schoolboy in costume, waiting in the wings for the play to start.

"Jako," purred Karl. "There you are. Say hello to Loulou."

"Nice to meet you—" My voice cut short as Jacques took my extended hand and raised it to his lips. The gesture should have struck me as contrived, only he performed it with a spontaneity that caught me off guard. I discerned not pretense or ridicule in it, but rather oblique recognition of my importance to Yves.

"I'm so happy you could come." His voice was light, with a smoky undertone. "Having you and Monsieur Saint Laurent here tonight is our honor."

"Speaking of which," said Karl drolly, "I haven't spoken to Yves yet. I should return to our guests. Please excuse me."

Suddenly, I was alone with the quarry Thadée and I had come to hunt.

"What do you think?" Jacques gestured at the painting.

"Lovely, but not my era," I replied.

"No? Which era do you prefer?"

"This one," I said. "I'm a woman."

He laughed. "I prefer this one, too. Much more freedom. But Karl adores telling that story. The origin of his evolution. Was it Christmas Eve for you?" He glanced past us to the doorway as he lowered his voice. "Sometimes it's New Year's Day. Or a surprise birthday gift from his parents. The point is never how the revelation happened; it's what the revelation led to. The creation of his imagined self. I find it fascinating, the ways in which we first discover who we yearn to be, and how we live to fulfill it. Don't you?"

"I work in fashion." I spoke casually, though the sophistication of his insight was also unexpected. "That's what fashion is: we wear clothes to reflect who we want to be."

"Yes." He gazed fondly at the painting. "That's why I love fashion, too. We can be seen only as we wish to be seen. It's also why I never tire of Karl's bedtime story. He saw perfection in this painting, and he had to re-create it in the world for him to inhabit."

"Do you work with him?" I shouldn't be dawdling out of sight with him, but my curiosity had the better of me. I'd been braced for a repellent shadow with a chokehold on Yves. Instead, he reminded me somewhat of Corey, without the gleeful exuberance. He seemed both too young and too old at the same time.

"Sometimes." He tugged at his scarf. "I help him find rare books, pieces of art to inspire him. I dress up for him. He's quick to translate whatever he sees into a design."

"He doesn't design for men, does he?"

"I wear dresses for him." His smile was mischievous. "I can be Garbo or Valentino, depending on his mood. You must do the same for Yves. We are their muses. The raw clay they mold into their ideals."

"I've never thought of it like that," I said, once more surprised by his maturity. "What else do you do for Karl?"

"Whatever he asks." He met my eyes. "Did Yves send you to question me?"

The moment suspended, charged, between us.

"No," I said. "Is there anything for him to question?"

He sighed. "I want him to be happy. He's not. He's so much like Karl that way, even if they think they're nothing alike. Neither of them can abide reality. Karl fears everything mundane. Yves fears he's unloved."

"And you?" I asked. "What do you fear?"

"That I'll die before I can truly live. Does that seem very banal?"

"I think we all fear that," I replied, though I'd never heard anyone admit it. I had sudden empathy for him, caught up in the fantasies of others, as if he had none of his own. Had Karl or Yves ever thought to ask him what he dreamed or longed for?

It was on the tip of my tongue to delve further, especially about his relationship with Karl. I couldn't bring myself to do it. The smile on his face now was almost prescient in the knowledge that I was searching for reassurance on Yves's behalf.

Then he held out his arm with timeless gentility. "Shall we?"

Amused, I let him escort me into the party, where the champagne was overflowing, joints and mirrors now being shared. A classical symphony lilted in the background—Handel or Beethoven, to exalt the scene.

Jacques disengaged from me to welcome the guests. Karl had resumed his arch pose at the mantel, chatting with Yves and Pierre. He had a squat appearance beside Yves's willowy length, but as they started laughing together, Pierre grimaced, betraying he wasn't enjoying himself at all, biding his time before he could make a polite exit.

Then Jacques rang a utensil against a glass. The chime silenced the room.

He lifted the glass. "To my benefactor, Karl. Happy birthday. May you grow younger and more creative every day. And to our friends, for celebrating with us."

We lifted our glasses in unison, chanting "Bon anniversaire!" Karl acknowledged us with a nod. I watched Yves, his reaction to his secret lover's evident affection for Lagerfeld. Without warning, Yves embraced Karl, revealing a friendship begun when they were students, dreaming of their ideals. Karl visibly thawed, kissing Yves on his cheek.

Depositing his glass on the mantel, Pierre marched over to Clara.

I caught Thadée's questioning look from where he stood with Paloma and Ricardo. Ricardo gave me one of his fanged smiles to convey his opinion of the party.

"No more violins," cried Jacques. Pouncing at a cabinet stereo system, he hit a switch to flood the room with synthetic tribal drums and breathy crooning. Tossing away his scarf, he scanned the avid crowd to select a partner.

When he seized my hand and whirled me around, the guests applauded and cleared space, like the crowd at le Sept.

An enamel box manifested as if by magic from within his jacket, along with a tiny attached spoon. Scooping rosy powder from the box, he put the spoon to my nostril.

I inhaled. It was high-quality cocaine, a glorious rush thrumming into my veins. He did two quick snorts, and we began to dance, the music quickening me to euphoria. He moved like quicksilver, his eyes slitting in pleasure as he gave in to his abandon. Joyous and exuberant now, a beautiful young man without pretensions or cares.

Thadée joined us, languid in his movements. Clara hastened to bob beside him. Paloma danced with Ricardo; all at once, everyone in the room was dancing, the music like elastic bands snapping our waists, tossing our arms over our heads.

Yves had gone wide-eyed in surprise. I yanked him into our midst. He shed his reticence, kicking out his long legs and swiveling his hips, dispelling the threads of the atelier, his glasses slipping on his nose and a grin breaking across his face.

Only Karl remained apart, a trace of mirth in his stolid expression.

And Pierre, stoic against our joy, on the opposite side of the room.

I RETURNED HOME at dawn. The party had gone on all night, Jacques spurring us like an inexhaustible ringleader, spreading enthusiasm and cocaine in endless supply. He stripped off his shirt and shoes to dance barefoot in his waistcoat, his hair dripping and his slender limbs sheened in glossy perspiration. At one point, he danced with Yves and me; the attraction between them was hypnotic, though no one else seemed to notice it.

Pierre departed with Yves before I did. Clara left soon after. Thadée, Paloma, and Ricardo stayed until it was over, all of us kissing Karl and Jacques goodbye.

The pressure of Ricardo's thigh against my leg as we shared a taxi with Paloma indicated he'd like to finish the night in bed with me. I pretended not to notice, stumbling out of the taxi to watch the sunrise alone from my flat.

After I showered and dressed for work, I walked to the hôtel to sober up. Anne-Marie was already in the workroom, directing the atelier premieres on the pieces approved by Yves for Versailles. He hadn't decided on everything yet, and I consulted with her on narrowing down the ample choices from our collections to items that would complement the set's theme.

Yves arrived in the afternoon, bleary-eyed. Once he was in his studio, armed with his cigarettes, I brought him the list Anne-Marie and I had compiled.

"Yes, yes. It all seems perfect." He didn't glance at it. "You heard Pierre. No one cares about the clothes. Only the guest list."

As I retrieved the list, he said shyly, "Last night was fun. You liked Jacques? He obviously liked you."

"I did like him. He's . . ." I searched for the right adjective. "Enchanting."

He blinked against sudden tears. "Now you see why."

"You must give it time." I hugged him. "I think he cares for you."

Against my chest, he whispered, "Do you think he can love me?"

I drew back. "Only he can tell you that. For now, let's focus on Versailles. No one may care about the clothes"—I forced out a laugh—"but we have our prestige to maintain. Vive la France."

He nodded vaguely, his smile surfacing and fading.

That night, after we ensured the selections were accessorized and ready for a trial run on our house mannequins, the workroom phone rang. Anne-Marie handed it to me.

Thadée said, "I came to the corner kiosk to buy cigarettes and call you. Clara went to bed. Too much of everything last night. When do we start?"

"I'm not sure we should," I said.

He went silent for a moment. "Are you having second thoughts?"

I abruptly changed the subject. "How's Corey?"

Again, he hesitated before he said, "Corey went back to New York."

"What?" I stifled the rise in my voice, Anne-Marie only a few feet away.

"Clara took him to the airport early, while we were still at the party. She booked him a flight and gave him money."

Dark suspicion prickled in me. I glanced over my shoulder. Anne-Marie was gathering her coat and handbag; she nodded good night to me as she left.

"Just like that," I said, "without giving us the chance to say goodbye to him?"

"According to her, Corey insisted on leaving as soon as possible."

"Or maybe *she* wanted him gone."

"I thought we agreed it's for the best. He couldn't stay; he's in terrible shape."

I resisted the fury building in my voice. "He needed some time to recover. He also saw Yves and Jacques together. If he's no longer in Paris, he can't tell anyone."

Thadée drew in a troubled breath. "That never occurred to me. But if Clara does know or suspect something, she only did it to protect Yves."

"And we only have Corey's word that Yves needs protection. I spoke to Jacques at the party. You saw him. Does he seem like a threat to you?"

"No." He coughed. "He seems charming. I enjoyed his joie de vivre, so I understand why you'd be having doubts."

"But?"

"But people aren't always what we think they are, when we first meet them."

I had to concede the point. "True, but that doesn't mean they're dangerous, either."

"We should still be sure of it, shouldn't we? We have good reason."

Do you think he can love me?

I found myself conceding again, reluctantly. "After Versailles. We'll invite him out. One time. If there's nothing to be concerned about, we don't interfere."

"Of course. Good night, Loulou. Sleep well."

A sense of emptiness came over me. As I turned off the workroom lights, I kept telling myself he was right: we had a good reason, and it couldn't do any harm.

Even if I couldn't escape the thought that I might be enticing a danger with Thadée that we shouldn't pursue.

13

The Palace of Versailles had seen better days.

Against storm-clouded skies and the remnant of protected woodlands, the royal palace that had once been a potent bastion of the French monarchy brooded on the edges of the small city that had sprouted up to profit from the annual tourism. Its limestone facade was darkened by centuries of grime, less a majestic symbol of the past than a crumbling relic.

Today, there was plenty of activity in the central courtyard, the Cour Royale behind the gilded gates, where the monumental château splayed in diminished glory. Catering trucks unloaded supplies alongside vans with the dismantled stage sets. Workmen trudged in and out of the palace carrying boxes and backdrops, assistants directing new arrivals to designated areas.

After our van pulled into the Cour d'Honneur and reserved parking area, Anne-Marie, along with Sylvie and four other women from the atelier, oversaw the removal of our garment-bagged clothes on wheeled racks. I shouldered the bag of accessories.

A young woman with a clipboard hastened to me. Her name tag bore her name, Suzanne, and the Rothschild crest of a fist clutching five arrows—a livery badge.

"Loulou de la Falaise, for Yves Saint Laurent," I informed her, noting how weary she looked as she checked the documents on her board, as if she hadn't slept a full night in weeks. I could only imagine the demands Marie-Hélène de Rothschild had volleyed to those hired to ensure her winter divertissement went off without a hitch.

"Ah, yes." She mustered a wan smile. "We've set aside a room for you near the Théâtre Gabriel." Her gaze searched the women behind me with the racks. "And monsieur?"

"Messieurs Saint Laurent and Bergé will be here this afternoon for the dress rehearsal and preshow dinner. Our models should already have arrived."

"Let me see." She checked her board again. "Yes. Your mannequins are here, in the room. Bien sur, mademoiselle. Please follow me."

In the Cour Royale, troops of people came and went with a precision that impressed me—a striking contrast to the now-familiar chaos before a fashion show, and one boasting ten designers from two different countries no less.

Within the fabled Hall of Mirrors, wan sunlight struggled to pierce the filth-encrusted windows. Workers perched on ladders were submitting the hall to a thorough dusting and polish of the age-speckled mirrors. Filaments of cobweb dangled from the enormous chandeliers, and bits of peeled gilding floated like confetti in the air, drifting onto the marble and porphyry statuary. A harried man in oversized glasses was on his knees sketching on a swath of white paper unfurled like a banner over the inlaid wood floor running the length of the hall.

A familiar nasal-twanged voice exploded in rage: "Halston will *not* tolerate this humiliation a second longer! It's an outrage."

Stalking toward us with arms akimbo, his cigarette trailing smoke like a dragon, Halston paused to glare at the man hastily composing what appeared to be a minimalist rendition of the Eiffel Tower. A visible shudder went through him as an unmistakable petite woman with tousled, cropped black hair and magnetic, wide-spaced dark eyes came up behind him, placed a long-nailed hand on his arm.

"Darling, calm down. It's just a mix-up." Her giggle, girlish and impudent, reached me. "The French measure things in meters, not feet. Who knew?"

"They knew," he snarled. "It's their fucking country. They misled us on purpose. Halston won't stand for it."

"Honestly." Liza Minnelli rolled her expressive eyes, tugging at a red cashmere sweater slung about her shoulders. "Would you please stop referring to yourself in the third person? It's driving everyone crazy."

Halston's glare lifted and fell on me.

"Mon Dieu," muttered Suzanne under her breath. "Monsieur le monstrueux américain, who thinks he's the new Sun King."

"Loulou!" Halston's voice whiplashed through the hall as though he were indeed the reincarnation of Louis XIV, summoning a wayward courtier.

"Go on," I told Anne-Marie. "I'll be there in a minute."

Suzanne marched the women onward, bypassing the sketching man. The rolling racks squeaked loudly on the creaky floor. Halston went rigid at their passage, scouring the bags as if his glare could x-ray through them.

Liza cocked her head in exasperation when he swerved to me and spat, "Yves was supposed to invite me. I specifically asked *you* to tell him."

I thought it might not be the time to kiss his cheeks in the traditional French greeting. "Nice to see you, too," I said dryly instead. "Did you have a good flight?"

"I did not. And I'm not having a good time, either. So, quit the chitchat." Jet-lagged shadows bruised his eyes, his tall, lean figure in black a menacing tower. "Halston's had enough of the 'bonjour' bullshit."

"Though if Halston needs to take a shit," piped up Liza, moving to us with a supple dancer's poise, "he needs to use his own toilet paper. Thank God, I always bring extra rolls in my suitcase for foreign engagements, like Mama taught me. She always said you never know what you'll find behind the curtain."

At my startled look, she burst out laughing. In person, she was more gamine than her brazen screen persona. Other than her exaggerated trademark eyelashes, mascaraed to butterfly antennae, she wore no makeup, and flaunted no trace of her glamorous birthright as the daughter of the legendary Judy Garland.

Halston sneered, "I doubt Yves needs to carry extra toilet paper around with him. Unless Loulou has it stuffed in one of those oversized couture bags."

I returned Liza's amused regard.

"Don't bother answering him," she said. "He's been in an awful mood over—"

"The basement," he interrupted. "They put us in the fucking basement, like servants. All of us together, in leaky rooms that stink of mold. With one toilet that doesn't flush half the time, and no paper. Fuck them. How *dare* they?"

"The accommodations," Liza went on, overriding his tirade. "The set, which Joe has to improvise because the measurements should be in meters. The temperature—and I have to say, it's a refrigerator. Guess no one thought to bring in space heaters. The lousy toilet. What else?" She glanced at him with a wry intimacy I recognized, as I shared it with Yves. "Oh, yes. The invitation."

"You didn't tell Yves." Halston narrowed his eyes at me.

"I did," I replied. "I told him and the baroness. She made the decision."

"Then she can also go fuck herself." He dragged on his cigarette's monogrammed white filter, seeming about to flick the butt on the floor and crush its smoldering remains into the ancient wood before he thought better of it. "Had I known, I would never have agreed. My company just got bought by Norton fucking Simon Incorporated for sixteen million dollars. I don't need to waste my time salvaging this shipwreck. And you can tell the baroness that—from me. Tell her, Halston is *out*."

"Halston is not out." Liza's firm rebuttal brought him to a standstill. "We have thirty-six models here from New York depending on us. I badgered my stepmother into choreographing our segment, and her arthritis is killing her. She wrote the final song for us. So, Halston is *in*. We don't bail on our crew at the last minute."

He blinked at her, chastened.

"Darling." She softened her tone. "It's show business, not the end of the world. We've both survived worse gigs. Let's get back to work and show them what we're made of."

"Even though we have to share a toilet and provide our own paper," he groused. "What's next? Dinner in tin cans and shovels to dig up holes in the gardens?"

"Like I said, I brought extra rolls." She laughed again. "I also had the models raid their hotel bathrooms before we boarded the bus. You need to take a crap? We got you covered. Do us a favor in return and cover our asses onstage tomorrow night. Now, go apologize to Joe and help him with the backdrop. We've got one day to pull this shit show together."

With a rancorous nod, Halston retreated to the illustrator working on the sketch.

I met her eyes. "You know how to handle him."

"I adore him," she said with a shrug. "He's my dearest, closest friend. But he's also a man, and most men, in my experience, think fame and money are their ticket to respect. They have no idea of how much women put up with, every day of our lives, to get the job done, whether we have money and fame or not."

A chuckle escaped me. "Very true."

"I'm Liza, by the way." She thrust out her hand; her grip was warm and friendly.

"Loulou. I recognized you at once."

"Did you? Can't say anyone else has so far. But here I am, freezing my tush off to help a friend. The place is a dump, as Bette Davis would say, but the show must go on. I bet you know the drill." She winked. "Pity we're on opposing sides. It's going to be a battle."

OUR ROOM WAS spacious, but also palpably damp, and decorated in faded crimson-and-gold trompe l'oeil depictions of rubicund gods and goddesses in diaphanous fragments, lolling and eating grapes among clouds. Anne-Marie had arranged the racks in order of the models' scheduled appearance; the girls shivered in their underwear under their coats, while the women employed handheld steamers to smooth out wrinkles in the clothes before the fittings for dress rehearsal.

"How much time do we have?" I asked Anne-Marie, lighting a much-needed cigarette. I wouldn't have done so inside the palace, if I hadn't just seen Halston puffing like a train going off the rails in the Hall of Mirrors. While what we'd been allocated wasn't a leaky basement, it was hardly Coco Chanel's suite at the Ritz.

She indicated a clipboard on the collapsible table, evidently left for our edification by the overworked Suzanne. "Four hours," Anne-Marie intoned, as I flipped through the typed instructions. "Lunch, and then we're second to last in the lineup for rehearsal."

"We're on before Givenchy. Pierre will have something to say about it." Setting aside the clipboard, I started to unwrap the accessories in their labeled bundles to distribute on the garment racks, slinging them on the hangers of each ensemble.

"Monsieur Bergé approved the schedule weeks ago," said Anne-Marie, meticulously snipping errant threads from linings. "The final segments in the French presentation are Nureyev, the cabaret dancers, and Madame Baker. Then the Americans present theirs."

"Right." I curbed my grimace. In my rush to finish our outfit selections and house fittings the Russian danseur, cabaret girls, and Madame Baker had slipped my mind.

I found myself wondering what Liza would think of it. The stallion of ballet, Nureyev was still a powerful attraction, regaled for his beauty and leaping pas de deux charisma, but the popular Crazy Horse cabaret on avenue George V in Paris specialized in highbrow burlesque of feather boas and sequined thongs. As for Madame Baker, she was now in her late sixties, enshrined in France for her banana skirts and slinky nude catsuits, but no longer the scandalizing zeitgeist of her youth.

Pity we're on opposing sides. It's going to be a battle.

And then some.

If we had Nureyev's muscled thighs, burlesque, and Baker crooning "J'ai deux amours" to punctuate our couture presentations, the Americans had more to overcome than an unreliable toilet and moldering accommodations.

AFTER A CRISP, catered lunch of ham sandwiches and green salad delivered to our room, we proceeded to the Théâtre Gabriel for the dress rehearsal.

My breath vaporized into clouds as we entered. We'd requested a space heater in our rooms, which was promptly located for us, after the models started turning blue in the frigid late-November cold seeping through the palace. But the royal opera house was, as Liza had remarked, a refrigerator.

The massive proscenium stage was framed by towering Romanesque columns and swaths of gold-fringed velvet curtains, with a gold-soaked heraldic flourish of wind-blown angels cradling the crown over a fleur-de-lis-studded shield sprouting bladed sunrays. But the stage itself was nearly overwhelmed by the cavernous orchestra pit, the elaborate faux-marble walls featuring depictions of mythological frolic, and triple tiers of balcony seating. Seven crystalline chandeliers were suspended overhead, with a larger one over the king's loge, completing the overwrought excess.

The orchestra seats were taken over by the French designers and their staff. The Americans huddled in the back rows, whispering among themselves, as the French segment began. Or failed to begin, barked arguments soon erupting between the famed Comédie-Française director Barrault and the stage and lighting crews—who were, evidently, in no rush to hasten things along, their hours of work ordained under union contract.

Spotting Halston as he stalked out, stabbing a cigarette into his filter and lighting it as he went, I saw Pat waving at me from among the Americans, sidestepping through them to reach me.

She flung her arms about me, her kiss on my cheek icy.

"God," I said, "you're freezing."

Her whispery laugh was accompanied by a shudder, her tiny frame wrapped in a turban, an oversized neon-colored patchwork coat, and a muffling scarf.

"Hell has frozen over," she said. "Everyone's getting pitchforks and frostbite."

"They must have some kind of heating in here. Let me go ask—"

"Don't bother. We already did. Like, a hundred times. All this painted wood, they say it's a fire hazard. Union regulations. Until the night of the show, no heat. I should have brought my fur coat. Frostbite in here, and a yeast infection from the mold in the basement." She leaned to me. "If you ask me, I'm okay with burning it all down."

"That bad?" I met her amber-brown eyes, her eyelashes as artificial as Liza's.

"Honey, don't ask. Halston is livid. He wants to sue." I almost laughed, until she added, "The frogs are gonna destroy us. Got a cigarette? Or a joint? A pill or line? I'm dying here."

"All the above," I said, leading her outside, where the blast of cold had us hunkered by a wall, cupping our palms to light the joint.

Pat drew in a deep inhale. "Better. I need to be stoned out of my mind for this."

"Your coat . . ." I'd been admiring it. "It looks like macramé."

"Jersey wool. Stephen made it." She smiled at my bewildered expression. "Stephen Burrows. I'm walking the show for him. Well, I'm walking for all of them; we're not that many to go around, though Halston flew over an army. But Stephen's my brother."

"Your brother designs fashion?"

"Oh, no." She cackled again, toking on the joint and passing it to me. "Good stuff, Loulou. You always have excellent party favors. He's not my brother in the biblical sense. He's black, from New Jersey. I met him at the Factory. A friend of Halston's; they party together on Fire Island. He sells his clothes at O Boutique on Park Avenue South, close to Max's Kansas City. We took a shine to each other, so I started modeling for him at his studio. As his muse. You know, like you do for Yves."

"His work is very unique." I thought Yves would be enthralled by it, the clashing colors that should have been too garish, blended into a vivid mosaic.

"He's a free spirit. Stephen doesn't care about any of this shit. He came along for the ride, because, hell, why not? It's Versailles. Once in a lifetime. We all did. But Halston—*what* a diva. If it weren't for Liza calming him down every six seconds, he'd be back on a plane to New York, spitting nails and calling the big guns to sue everyone."

"I ran into him earlier." I coughed on my exhale. "He wasn't happy."

"Nope." She lowered her voice, though there was no one nearby to overhear us except stagehands taking a cigarette break. "He thinks Anne Klein is a hack and shouldn't be here. He puts up with Blass, because Bill dresses rich society ladies, but he's up in de la Renta's face every chance he gets. He's insecure and jealous."

"Because Yves invited de la Renta to the show, not him," I murmured.

"And he's an asshole." She underscored the words with a puff of smoke. "Stephen just keeps quiet and stays out of everyone's way. You wait. We'll be destroyed by the French, but Stephen— at least he'll wipe the stage with them."

Finishing the joint, I gave her an extra, plus a bunch of uppers from my pocket, then we went, teeth chattering, back into the theater.

"Donna sure dodged a bullet," she said, kissing my cheeks once more. "She got a shoot for *Harper's Bazaar*. She's going to laugh her bleached eyebrows off when I tell her."

"Corey," I said belatedly, halting her before she returned to the now-glowering Americans wreathed in ice-bound breath. "He went home."

"Poor baby. We were so worried about him. He got himself in some deep shit here. Gay Paree." She rolled her eyes. "Not so gay after all. Karl and Jacques did a number on him. Thanks for the high. Catch me later at the dinner party, okay? If they let us in. I'm stealing a mink coat—from the baroness, if I have to."

I watched her sidle into the seats and then hurried backstage, barely paying attention to the enormous cardboard pumpkin being lowered by wires onto the stage.

The frogs are gonna destroy us.

Not until I was accessorizing our models in the tumult behind the scenes did it occur to me that I hadn't seen or heard a word yet from Yves or Pierre.

THE PRESHOW DINNER was in the curator's palace apartments and specified black tie, so I wore the black velvet couture coat-dress spattered in lipstick kisses from our Libération collection, my eyebrows depilated to arches, my hair curled in loose ringlets, along with heavy eye shadow and Romani-inspired, beaded faux-silver earrings I'd put together out of leavings on a whim one day in the studio.

The rehearsal had turned interminable, frequently interrupted by Barrault, whose expertise in managing a nationally sponsored theater was put to the test by the oversized sets and cold-stiffened models. Once our segment went through his demanding paces, sans the female impersonators, I left early to return to my hotel room in the town, to luxuriate in a hot bath and get ready for the dinner.

As I was leaving, the clerk at the reception desk hailed me to say an envelope had been delivered for me. It was letter-sized, with the initial *J* handwritten on it in Yves's telltale calligraphy. On my way to the palace in a taxi, I probed it, detecting a folded paper and a smaller envelope inside it; my pinching of the smaller envelope indicated a stiff notecard, like those he made for people he loved, hand illustrated for birthdays and Christmas with his beloved Moroccan snakes coiled around hearts, one of which he'd sent to me with the dress to lure me to the studio. With the card, there was a metal object, shaped like a key.

I pocketed it, thinking Yves would explain it at the dinner.

The van der Kemp apartments were lavishly appointed, as befitted the couple who were propping up the palace's endangered foundations with their social cachet and fundraising prowess. The apartments also brimmed with the baroness's promised roster of elite jet-setters and aristocrats, as well as a bevy of well-heeled American socialites. Princess Grace of Monaco hadn't arrived, no doubt saving her regal entrance for the gala tomorrow night, but many others had, having indulged themselves for over a week in profligate anticipation, from the star-studded private party held by Norton Simon at Maxim's for Halston and Minnelli, to various other dinners hosted by everyone willing to foot the staggering bill.

Threading my way through the crowd to the buffet tables and pausing to greet acquaintances, I spied some of our couture clients: Lyn Revson, wife of the founder of the Revlon cosmetics empire, her hair sprayed into a towering coiffure. Dazzling diamonds sparkled at her wrists and throat as her gold-flecked tulle ball gown swept the oriental carpeted floors. Mrs. Revson disdained prêt-à-porter and attended our shows at the hôtel semiannually to replenish her wardrobe.

The Portuguese socialite São Schlumberger, an heiress and art patron who resided in a Parisian hôtel particulier, was also present, flaunting dangling emeralds the size of my fist and scarlet lipstick, at odds with our too-tight ivory satin sleeveless gown as she elbowed her way to the front of the buffet queue. Yves detested her, assigning her fittings in the studio to me, though he couldn't evade her demand that he, and he alone, adjust the seams of her purchases.

And the Baroness de Rothschild, her blond hair lacquered

in waves from her face to enhance her magnificent opal-and-diamond necklace, complemented by a flowing sea-green crepe de chine gown with an extravagant bow at the neck and flared sleeves, couture from our so-called Scandal collection. With effortless poise and a welcoming smile on her neutral-colored lips, she sailed through the crowd, greeting everyone by name, the privileged strata parting before her passage like a bejeweled sea.

Though I craned on tiptoes to survey the chattering assembly with champagne in hand and oysters on porcelain plates, Yves was nowhere to be seen. Pierre, however, was here, in an azure velvet tuxedo, his bristling hair tarnished silver at his temples, conversing and sharing cigars with the baron and other men of distinction.

He hadn't attended the dress rehearsal or bothered to seek me out to ask my opinion of it. I couldn't fault him. Had I been given the choice I'd have skipped it, too. Upon my return to the palace, I'd discovered matters had careened from unwieldy to excruciating, the French rehearsal culminating in the abrupt extinguishing of the lights at its conclusion, with Halston bellowing at the indifferent stagehands, who departed. They left the American contingent to stumble through their delayed rehearsal in the dark.

Halston wasn't displaying any ire now. Smoking a cigarette in his black turtleneck and white mink coat, a fringed Hermès scarf looped over his shoulders, he sallied about with his perfect-toothed charm as if he owned the place, received by those who did with polite solicitude and offers of introduction. He zeroed in on the wealthy ladies gathered about Givenchy and de la Renta, his intrusion greatly abetted by Minnelli on his arm. She sported a white Halston pantsuit open to her navel and a megawatt smile.

Yves had apparently absented himself. He'd sent me an envelope that I had no idea what to do with. With the envelope in one hand and balancing my plate of canapés and a cigarette, I found a vacant spot to sit and nibble on the food, when Pat found me.

She looked warmer, the van der Kemp apartments not subject to the glacial restrictions imposed on the rest of the palace. Wearing jeans and a flannel shirt, scrubbed of cosmetics, she stood out like a lioness among peacocks.

A mink coat was draped on her shoulders, however, its pockets bulging. At my raised eyebrow, she chortled. "The fur's from one of the girls. They were too exhausted and depressed to put on another show tonight. They're also starving, so"—she patted the pockets—"canapés for all, courtesy of the baroness."

I choked on my laughter. "I heard they turned the lights off."

"Motherfuckers." She popped a spinach quiche from my plate into her mouth. "They left us there like Helen Keller, groping for the stage. You should have heard him yelling. He's definitely suing."

"I bet." I eyed Halston, oozing compliments to Madame Schlumberger as she wolfed her food. "He should. The entire thing is appalling."

"Isn't that the truth? Rich white people. Drop any of them on a subway to Harlem and see how long they last." Her eyes turned soft. "But, oh my god, Josephine Baker came backstage to talk to us. She was amazing. None of it matters after that. They can kiss our ass. We spoke to Josephine Baker. A bunch of black girls from America met the queen of Paris."

A pang went through me. "Yves isn't here yet, but he'd be shouting right alongside Halston."

"He would, wouldn't he? He's not like them. I'd walk for him again in a New York minute. I loved doing his show."

"He loved having you and Donna in his show," I said.

"But the rich white people didn't." She flipped her hand. "Like I said, they can kiss our ass. Gotta go, Loulou. The girls are waiting back at the hotel. See you tomorrow night. Bring party favors. We're going to need it."

She strode away, looking very much, I thought, like a queen herself.

Then, out of the corner of my eye, I spotted someone I never expected to see.

He circulated with an ice bucket of Dom Pérignon, refilling crystal flutes, a white cloth over his shirtsleeve to dab up spills; his trim figure in the uniform black pants, cummerbund, and bow tie of the catering staff; and his tawny hair slicked back on his skull in his matinee-idol incarnation.

I couldn't believe it. I had to force myself to stop from staring, loitering at the buffet tables to pile pasta salad onto my plate that I had no intention of eating while maintaining covert watch on him. He was ignored by the attendees as they extended their glasses for more bubbly, and he moved on. Not even Pierre took a second look.

By the time he reached me, the envelope in my couture pocket was burning a hole.

J for Jacques.

"Would mademoiselle care for more champagne?"

"What—" I took a breath. "*What* are you doing here?"

"Serving champagne." He gave me an innocent smile that had nothing innocent about it.

"Champagne. Really. Did Karl put you up to this?"

Now the smile was entirely his, racy and capricious. "Karl wasn't invited. No prêt-à-porter allowed at le grand divertissement à Versailles. Or none from France. But he'll be very curious, if I decide to tell him."

Yves had done it. Gala tickets were by invitation only and had sold out within days, at four hundred francs a pop. Clara had expressed outrage at the number of desperate callers ringing her office phone off the hook—lesser-known clients and even Rive Gauche customers—trying to finagle a ticket on the house. Karl could afford the entry fee but hadn't received an invitation. Even if he had, I was certain the pointed contempt for his line of work would have caused him to sniff and organize his own fashion bacchanal.

Yet here was Jacques, a waiter serving champagne at the pre-gala reception.

I had to know why.

"Is he coming?" I asked in a low voice, letting him top off my glass.

"He's hoping to later," he replied with unmistakable innuendo.

Gulping my champagne, I removed the envelope—"I think this must be for you"—and I slid it between his fingers. He pocketed it as if it were a tip. I hissed, "Are you going to the show tomorrow night?"

Jacques couldn't evade detection at the gala if he had a ticket. He wasn't anyone of note in the baroness's privileged circle, and someone, likely her, would remark on it.

"Me?" Laughter husked his voice. "Absolutely not. We thought it would be fun, to get me a job with the caterer and spy on the guests. To laugh about it afterward. It was his idea." He leaned toward me, whispering, "Yves loves his little games. À bientôt, ma chère."

Gliding into the crowd, he reverted into another shadow, hired to ensure the guests were unobtrusively attended.

Yves loves his little games.

A card with a secret key. What was Yves up to?

14

Yves showed up the following day in the late afternoon, in oversized sunglasses, a bulky black wool sweater, and jeans, his hair unkempt but his jaw recently shaved, a cigarette hanging from his lip. He carried a garment bag over his shoulder.

His arrival brought with it visible relief. By now, none of us was sure whether he'd make an appearance or ignore the event. I'd even started to doubt it, knowing how he deemed it an absurdity, and Pierre had advised him to wash his hands of it.

With a quick, approving check of the models and their outfits, he said to me, "The drag queens will get dressed backstage for our segment, but be ready. They're on their way with Zizi now, with suitcases of makeup, after eating everything in Paris. I wonder if they'll even fit into the costumes."

As Anne-Marie immediately set herself to preparing the red velvet 1920s coatdresses with feathered collars and cuffs he'd designed, I said, low in his ear, "You missed the parade of ball gowns and jewels last night. It was the Sun King's mistresses of the court, resurrected."

"I didn't miss it." He gave me a catty smile. "I heard Madame Schlumberger pushed people out of the way to get to the buffet table. Millions of francs in Modigliani and Monet, and she behaves like a famine victim. Thank you for being so discreet."

"He was pouring champagne for them," I said, unable to stanch my giggle, and thinking the mysterious key must have been for a hotel room for them. "Right there, in front of everyone. No one noticed him."

"He has a talent for being someone else, doesn't he?" Yves inspected the female impersonators' costumes as Anne-Marie hung them a rack. "Let's steam out the feathers a bit. They look like chickens about to be cooked. The drag queens might eat them, too."

I burst out laughing. We were due backstage at the theater in less than two hours, the gala scheduled to begin at nine o'clock, though given the exalted guest list, leeway was suggested for late arrivals.

"I'll need to change into my tuxedo after our segment." Yves indicated his garment bag. Anne-Marie promptly unzipped the bag to steam the pleats of his trousers. "Such an overpriced fuss over an old, run-down château."

"Well, it is the royal one. Halston's been on the warpath," I added, as we wheeled the racks into the pandemonium back-stage, where the militant precision, already frayed by the chaos of dress rehearsal, had disintegrated, assistants jostling for room amid sets and half-naked models. "He thinks it's all been designed for his personal humiliation."

The Americans had staked out a corner. Pat and her fellow models took turns on a lone stool with compact mirrors to do their makeup. One of them held a flashlight so they could see as they rummaged in plastic travel cosmetic bags.

Yves paused, regarding them. "I hope Halston and the rest of them put us to shame."

While Anne-Marie directed our models to the bulb-lit, mirrored makeup table set up for the French contingent, I said, "Go sit with Pierre. I can take care of this. We rehearsed the segment yester-day, or we tried to. Might as well enjoy the show."

"Yes, might as well." He took his tuxedo and kissed my cheek. "See you afterward. Let them eat cake."

The show started an hour and a half late, with the arrival of Princess Grace in a white Dior sheath, crimson Madame Grès cape, and a ruby-and-diamond tiara, followed by the recently widowed, emaciated Wallis Simpson, Duchess of Windsor, in blue crepe and sapphires. Mink coats, lynx wraps, and fox-fur-tailed cloaks flecked with the first dusting of winter snow were deposited in luxurious heaps at the coat check, footmen in powdered wigs and livery and gendarmes with sabers saluting the unhurried procession of the regal, titled, and very rich entering the Théâtre Gabriel. The sole official photographer snapped flashbulbed pictures of their persons.

When I peeked out from backstage as the lights dimmed, the glittering jewels atop coiffures and about throats and wrists captured the chandeliers' fading glow. The theater was full, every seat taken.

The orchestra struck up the delicate, violin-laced overture of Prokofiev's *Cinderella*. The curtains swept aside for the fantasy forest and immense cardboard-and-tinsel pumpkin on wires of Dior's presentation, overwhelming Marc Bohan's severe black and beige clothing for the house.

I busied myself instilling a semblance of order and employing plenty of tissues dipped in cold cream to dab the overdone lipstick on the raucous female impersonators, who squeezed into our costumes, cracking bawdy quips about flashing the Princess of Monaco as they adjusted their tucked genitalia under thick, nude-colored pantyhose.

Cardin's rocket-ship set landed in a disconcerting blast of sound effects on the stage. Models in thigh-skimming dresses and black tights, accompanied by men in sleeveless jersey suits overlaid by black vinyl jockstraps and equipped with spacesuit headpieces, marched about to an eerie, discordant symphonic accompaniment.

The ensuing polite applause was what I might have heard at a sedate salon presentation where the ladies were hungry for lunch, and not particularly moved to purchase.

Emanuel Ungaro's Wild West–themed segment opened with actress Jane Birkin, braless, flinging her arms in a skintight white T-shirt and micro-miniskirt with chisel-jawed movie star Louis Jourdan, sporting furred animal ears that defied identification as to the creature he was supposed to emulate. A bass player sawed out a harmonica rendition as the models moved like sleepwalkers in cashmere-and-mink ensembles.

We were next.

Zizi Jeanmaire barreled out singing "Just a Gigolo," with the female impersonators gallivanting against the painted backdrop of the replicated 1920s limousine. Our models, in violet and green bell-sleeved chiffon gowns, draped in feather-trimmed cloaks—unearthed from our sample closet from past collections—attempted to pose and pivot as the impersonators hoisted Zizi in their arms while she belted out her song.

"Mon Dieu," murmured Anne-Marie at my side.

Mon Dieu was right. Having not attended the dress rehearsal, the impersonators were improvising bawdy entertainment, and Zizi, determined to prove her mettle to the international audience and not be overshadowed by a youthful American rival with an Oscar, milked it for every last drop.

There was laughter, though I wasn't sure if it was with or at the jarring juxtaposition of our couture-draped glacial models and the waggling female impersonators.

I slumped in relief as the segment concluded. Zizi took an excess of bows, and the impersonators tromped backstage with their mascara melting from the spotlights.

Givenchy's floral basket, his name emblazoned in petalled paillettes, and his invited celebrity, the actress Capucine, floating among his mannequins in carnation-pink chiffon, took to the stage for the French designers' finale.

Hastening with Anne-Marie to clear the area, I caught Pat's eye. She wore a soft-angled, lettuce-hemmed dress in blocks of color, reminiscent of the coat I'd admired—an iridescent summer leaf, crumpled on her slim body. She winked at me. I held up a circled forefinger and thumb for a good luck charm, and she tapped her nose to pantomime coke sniffing, making me chuckle.

Nureyev was leaping and awing the audience in his fitted silver-tissue doublet, his white-hosed thighs rippling in the pas de deux of *Sleeping Beauty*, as I reached my assigned seat next to Yves and Pierre. I'd heard the temperamental dancer had kicked up a storm that necessitated replacing his female partner at the last minute, but the fragile ballerina held her own.

"A catastrophe," Yves whispered in delight to me. Pierre had gone stone-faced as the fourteen Crazy Horse dancers pranced onstage in furs by the French designers. Gyrating around red-ribboned stripper poles, the dancers teasingly discarded the furs to reveal garters and stockings, spangled pasties, and G-strings.

In her cocoa-tinted, glitter-embroidered catsuit and plumed headdress, trailing a white fur like an afterthought, Josephine Baker then emerged to deliver her throaty "Mon pays et Paris."

The audience cheered her. Released for a brief intermission after two stultifying hours, everyone escaped their velvet loge seats for spirits and champagne in the antechambers.

Pierre gave me a sidelong look. "What a mess. No cohesion, every house throwing their paint at the wall. So much for the best France has to offer."

Yves tugged me out into the hallway to smoke a cigarette with him. "I had to bite the inside of my mouth to stop from laughing," he said, his blue eyes sparkling in teary amusement behind his glasses. "Those drag queens—they stormed onto the stage like circus elephants. And Zizi, shrieking under her top hat. If Dietrich had been here to see it, she'd be mortified."

I began to laugh helplessly. "It was impossible to stop them. I think one broke wind and split his back seam."

"Farting in front of the baroness, Princess Grace, and the Nazi duchess." Yves leaned against me in hilarity, gripping my arm. "Halston can stop worrying. They'd have to show tennis rackets to outdo our embarrassment."

"Where were you?" I said, wiping at my tears of laughter.

He abruptly went somber, wetting his fingertip to wipe mascara from under my eyes. "You know where I was. I gave you the key."

"Yes, but . . ." I hushed my voice as attendees moved past us to return to the theater, nodding at Yves, who straightened his spine and smiled in his charmingly remote way. "You might have given me some instructions with it. What if I hadn't seen him?"

A furtive smile lurked at the corners of his lips. "He knew to look for you."

"Oh. I hope you had fun, while I ate canapés and watched Madame Schlumberger gorge on free oysters."

"I didn't want to leave the bed with him," he said. "Now, let's get back and witness how the Americans make us eat cake."

By now I was exhausted, wishing I could get into a bed and not get out of it for a week, but the moment the lights dimmed and the spotlights hit the minimalist backdrop of the Eiffel Tower, the energy in the theater electrified.

Liza dashed out with a closed umbrella, wearing wide-legged taupe trousers and a camel-colored turtleneck by Halston, the same red sweater I'd seen on her the day before looped on her shoulders, and a fedora hat tipped to one side. A knuckle-indented silver cuff on her wrist and the silver clasps on her wide, low-slung belt caught the light as she feigned awe at the sight of the tower, whirled about, and crooned in her potent alto: "What a lovely night. I'm feeling so fresh and alive . . ."

To her vivacious rendition of "Bonjour, Paris!" the American models cantered behind her like tourists, in varying shades of beige sportswear, pointing at the tower, chattering to each other, pretending to snap pictures with invisible cameras in their hands.

Upswept collared peacoats and sleek trench coats paired with knife-pleated skirts, shirtwaist dresses, cable-knit sweaters slouched over loose-fitted trousers; and all of them in hats, either edged to the side like Liza's or cloche-snug over their ears.

Yves slipped his hand into mine and squeezed it.

Before Liza even hit her last powerful note, her hands jazz-splayed on her umbrella, the audience was applauding and cheering.

Pierre grunted.

Anne Klein's segment was an African safari of cap-sleeved leotards, funneled turbans, and black shirts over abstract animal-print skirts, the orchestra silent as a percussive prerecorded medley that we would have danced to at le Sept had the models kicking up their legs with an exuberance that evoked the memory of Pat and Donna in our salon.

Then Stephen Burrows's designs appeared to Al Green's "Love and Happiness." The funk beat of the music enlivened the models as they filed out in bold colors of matte jersey, a rainbow explosion of body-hugging gowns with haltered tops and plunging neck-lines. Sensuous and swirling, the ragged hems were like foam about their long legs, trains of oceanic fabric drifting in their wake.

Pat whirled out, a dervish with her arms hovering, her gown fanning about her, right to the edge of the stage, where she went still for a beat, arched her neck, cocked her hip, and fixed her huge mascara-lined amber eyes upon the stunned audience.

The other models paused as statues in frozen animation, then surged forward to surround her, snapping their hands and flinging New York street attitude.

Glancing at Yves, I saw a tear slip down his cheek.

The audience roared, throwing their pale blue event programs with gilded calligraphic lettering into the air.

Bill Blass's *Great Gatsby*–inspired tailored wool jackets and slim beaded skirts had the models vamping to the piano at a café, lifting cigarettes to pouty lips, and eyeing broad-brimmed hatted muscular men in wide-shouldered three-piece suits and soft, deconstructed cashmere coats.

By the time Halston arrived with his flowing jewel-toned eveningwear, the verdict was evident. The dramatic thunder of Visconti's score for *The Damned* shifted the spotlight to strike each model in turn, catching her in a defiant or provocative gesture: A transparent sequined sheath clinging to Marisa Berenson, my former roommate's sister, now a world-famous cover model and costar of Minnelli's in *Cabaret*. A sleeveless gown baring another model's entire back to the cleft of her buttocks. A cocoon of satin frothing past a model's ankle-strapped shoes to flood the floor. A lime-green drench of sequins cutting to the navel, exposing the supple curvature of breast.

Halston's muse and jewelry designer, Elsa Peretti, her cigarette poised in a thin lacquered holder, flipped her cuffed wrist like a spurned countess, her bony shape dripping ash chiffon and smoke.

The lights went out. We sat breathless.

Barry White's "Love's Theme" soared, and Oscar de la Renta's segment manifested in a black model, sharp as a knife in verdant gossamer, unraveling a carnation-pink scarf from her long palm with a magician's enigmatic flair. The models danced out to the hip-clenching rhythm in secretive rose chiffon. A lilac scarf unfurled next, and the rest of the models appeared in sunset mauve. Weaving her arms above her in the smoke-filmed spotlight, the black model-magician summoned the girls to graceful gliding, a mesmerizing swimming, the gowns stark and unadorned, like wings on swans.

Liza returned in a bugle-beaded Halston cocktail dress, cut asymmetrically in front to show off her toned legs. She sang "Cabaret," followed by a song with the lyrics "Au revoir, Paris," with the models in black eveningwear by each designer joining her onstage.

When the curtains swooped down, the entire theater was on its feet, stomping and applauding, banging their hands on the gilded loge railings and yelling *Bravo!* in unabashed approval.

Rising with them, his hand still clutching mine, Yves shouted his joy.

"They did it." He turned to me. "They *did* it! They took the cake."

Pierre rumbled, "We'll have to take a slice from their cake. They made us look like outdated seamstresses." He swerved around to watch the audience scrambling to get backstage before the après-show midnight buffet. "And swooping like vultures to place their orders, too."

Yves whispered to me, "Jacques would have loved to see this. He would have wept."

I hugged him. "I did."

"So did I. We must congratulate them."

PAT WHOOPED AND plowed into my embrace. "I don't even need those party favors tonight. Oh my god, we *creamed* the stage with them!"

"Oh, you did more than that," I said, watching as Yves sidled past São Schlumberger, the socialite placing orders on the spot from the American designers.

Halston arched a brow and lit a cigarette, Liza beaming at his side, as he caught sight of Yves, who avoided him to approach a slightly built man standing apart, in ivory trousers with a billiard-ball print, a striped shirt, and an incongruous sailor's cap, round-lensed glasses on his cherubic face.

"That's him," Pat said, her voice choking. "That's Stephen, my brother."

I saw Yves lean toward him, murmuring, then the moment was broken by the arrival of Josephine Baker in one of Yves's see-through black gowns, plastered with strategically placed feathers that left little to the imagination. The American models swarmed her.

"Go," I urged Pat. "The queen is here to congratulate you."

She kissed my cheek. "I adore you, Loulou. Remember, any time. In a New York minute."

"I'll remember. And so will Yves."

Yves now hugged Halston and kissed Liza's hand. She threw her arms about him.

When he returned to me, he was wiping away tears. We proceeded toward the Hall of Mirrors and the King's Apartments, where the après-show buffet was scheduled.

"What did you say to him?" I asked.

He assumed his diffident public persona. "I told him he made beautiful clothes."

"I bet Halston loved that. He's been waiting all his life to hear it from you."

"I didn't say it to Halston." Yves smiled. "Halston already knows he makes beautiful clothes. If he knew it any better, he'd be insufferable. I told Stephen Burrows, the designer Marie-Hélène claims she never heard of."

"He must have loved it even more," I said quietly.

"He deserves it the most. He's an artist." Yves lifted his chin. "Now we'll eat humble pie instead of cake and pretend nothing happened." He gave me a penetrating look. "But we're making changes, Loulou. I've had enough of l'ancien régime."

I discerned his note of resolve and wondered if it meant more than just his approach to fashion.

PART III

THE DEVIL

1973–1977

A devil with Garbo's face . . . He was the opposite of me. He was also impossible and despicable. He was perfect.
—KARL LAGERFELD

15

For the holidays, I flew to New York to visit my mother. Her husband, John, was gravely ill, in and out of the hospital. My brother phoned from London on Christmas Eve, promising to delay his wedding until John was better, though we all knew that he wouldn't ever improve.

I didn't know why I kept expecting Mama to fall apart. It wasn't in her character, but as I watched her accompany John to the hospital for a battery of ongoing tests, and her returns while he stayed overnight, I could see her stoicism taking its toll.

Mixing her favorite martini, I handed her the glass, sat her down on the sofa, and, at her bewildered look, said, "I'm here. You can scream if you want. Throw that glass against the wall. I won't tell a soul."

"Why would I ever do that?" she asked.

"To grieve, Mama. You love him. He's very ill. He's—"

"Don't say it." She gulped her drink. "If you do, I'll never speak to you again."

"Mama—"

"Don't. I can't bear it. Go do something. I don't want you thinking about it or waiting for me to burst into sobs like an operatic heroine. When the time comes, I'll grieve—and not a minute before."

"I could ring Fernando. He's here in New York. Are you sure you want me to?"

"Oh, dear God. Yes. Go see him. If he's that boyfriend who

left you when you started working with Yves, tell him how well you're doing and break his heart instead."

I smiled. "He didn't break my heart. He's gay, remember?"

She finished her drink. "I'm taking a hot bath and going to bed. Call him and stop fussing over me. Honestly, *where* do you get it from? I never fussed over you once in your entire life."

"Maybe we all need a little fussing over, now and then."

"Not me. I detest it. Now, mix me another martini, darling. I'll drink it in my bath. What I need is to get good and drunk. Call the gay not-boyfriend."

I phoned Fernando, who was still designing for Revillon and working on his ready-to-wear line, seeking elusive investors. I modeled the samples he'd had made up, walking the floor in his pied-à-terre, and then we had dinner together at Max's Kansas City, laughing and falling into our usual familiarity as he teased me about Ricardo and my flight to the desert in Marrakesh.

"You must have been hard up," he said. "The man is a complete bore."

"He has a vigorous hard-on," I retorted. "I wasn't fucking him for conversation."

After an astonished second, he lifted his wineglass. "Touché. You must tell me all about it. Vigorous hard-ons are lacking in my life, to my regret."

We collapsed into hysterics.

JOHN WAS RELEASED back into my mother's care by the time I returned to Paris shortly after New Year's 1974.

After months of tireless search, Pierre had finally located a new hôtel particulier for the house: a corner town house on avenue Marceau, with rounded stone edges and white-shuttered windows, built during Napoleon III's reign and lording over the heart of the couture world between the sixth and eighteenth arrondissements—a very expensive, exclusive locale. Pierre hired the decorator who'd redesigned the interior of Christian Dior's fashion house to refurbish the hôtel to its Second Empire splendor.

The reception area was by the ground-floor entrance, beside a grand staircase; the receptionists were ordered to spray Rive Gauche perfume daily into the air. An expansive grand salon for presentations and private showings sat right of the staircase, done in mirrored walls, pale green moiré carpeting, and ruby-red brocade chairs and couches. Plenty of marble, white wainscoting, and workrooms upstairs.

Pierre's new office and our studio were on the second floor, Clara's office ensconced between us. The other two floors contained the ateliers.

Moving from Hôtel Forain proved an epic undertaking. Professional movers were employed for the furnishings, but the couture collections in our closets had to be hand-wrapped in protective tissue and transported separately, overseen by Anne-Marie and the atelier premieres.

As for Yves's studio, he wouldn't entrust his personal belongings to anyone but me, so I packed his lucky framed ten-of-clubs playing card, artbooks, and sketches; Moujik and Hazel's toys and baskets, and his other knickknacks. Not surprisingly to me, he vanished in the weeks it took to move locations, heartbroken at leaving the building where he'd launched his independent career under Pierre's guidance.

I set up my work area in our new studio and then his office, meticulously re-creating the ambience of our old hôtel for him. After two days of not seeing him, though we had our pending prêt-à-porter line to finish, which I'd been put in charge of, I went to Pierre's office to inquire about him.

As I paused in the office doorway, Pierre making a minute

adjustment to the Bernard Buffet painting of Yves hanging on the wall, I heard Hazel yap and Moujik growl from under the desk, which was how the bulldog greeted everyone save for Yves and Pierre, regardless of how long he'd known them. Pierre never kept the dogs with him at work; Moujik and Hazel were Yves's beloved companions, always in the studio with us.

"Excuse me," I said, when Pierre turned to hush Moujik. "Do you have a moment?"

"No." He grimaced. "I have work coming out of my ears. What is it?"

"I called rue de Babylone, but Yves isn't answering. Is he coming in today?"

"How would I know? Call his penthouse on avenue de Breteuil." Pierre didn't glance at me, riffling papers and calling out, "Clara, have those financial reports from the Syndicale arrived yet?"

"Not yet," she said through the ajar door to her press office. "I'll chase them down today."

"Chase them down is right," he muttered. "I'm president of the Syndicale, and it's another mess to sort out. They kept records like their rules: haphazard and archaic."

"Yves has a penthouse?" I asked. Avenue de Breteuil wasn't far from their home, a short walk down boulevard des Invalides.

"He didn't tell you?" Pierre snorted. "He probably forgot. He's in a state."

I tried to not react. "Why?"

"Why else? After Versailles, he claimed he couldn't work at the Hôtel Forain anymore because of all the pending disruption with the move. He has his studio on rue de Babylone—he's taken over the entire upper floor of our duplex and relegated me to the lower one with all my books. Plus the dogs. All of a sudden, he has no time to walk them, and can't find peace and quiet anywhere." Pierre clucked his tongue at the unseen pets ensconced under his desk. "Since the studio here wasn't ready, he rented a one-bedroom for himself on Breteuil. Anne-Marie's been sending updates to him there."

A pang went through me. He hadn't told me. "I don't have the number."

"Here." He scribbled on a pad and ripped out the page, handing it to me. "Though knowing him, he hasn't had a phone installed. He can't find a telephone book, let alone manage to get one connected. His penthouse is on the seventh floor. He's probably holed up in there, brooding. He dislikes cats, but he's just like one: he hates change."

"It's a big change," I said, keeping my surprise in check. "This new hôtel is beautiful, but—"

Pierre made an impatient gesture. "I could have found us a château, and he'd still be in a state. You'd think I was moving us to Bretagne, the way he carries on about leaving Forain. We were stepping on each other's toes there. We can't grow our business out the window because he's sentimental about the location. Clients can find us more easily here. Dior is nearby; so are the rest of them. I can keep my eye on everyone. As the president of the Syndicale, it's incumbent on me to do so."

"Thanks." I retreated to the studio.

Dialing the number, I received a buzzing sound. Either the phone was still disconnected or he'd taken it off the hook. It would be like him, especially if he was, as Pierre said, brooding; but I had an uneasy feeling that propelled me to pull on my coat and hail a taxi to avenue de Breteuil.

THE DAY WAS crisp, winter lingering in the air. The building's creaking elevator rose at a snail's pace, modernized, but barely.

Once on the seventh floor, I faced a closed door. I suddenly felt like an intruder.

I knocked on the door after looking around for a buzzer and it swung open, unlocked.

I stepped into a minimalist bachelor's apartment with garret windows. The walls were freshly painted in lime, accented in white, and the living room furnished with a low glass-topped table, a curved white sofa on stubby metallic feet, and a lone piece of art: Warhol's blue-and-green-washed quartet portrait of Yves, pensive without his glasses. A departure from his and Pierre's lush, antique-cluttered style.

A vase of his favorite Casablanca lilies sat on the table, alongside a tin ashtray like those found on every outdoor café table, a carton of Lucky Strikes, and a crushed bag of marijuana. Traces of rose-tinted powder smeared the table's glass, a razor blade discarded by them. The telephone was tumbled on the cream shag carpet, its receiver off the cradle. A sketch pad had been tossed aside, colored pencils scattered by it.

The apartment was still, too silent. It abruptly struck me: the absence of Hazel scampering about, always clingy with Yves, and Moujik's growl. In all the time I'd known him, Yves never left his dogs behind, except to go out at night and on the now infrequent trips abroad. He'd even started flying the dogs with him to Marrakesh, devoted to them, not wishing to leave them in anyone else's care.

Yet he'd left them with Pierre.

My heart started to pound as I dipped my fingertip in the traces on the table and tasted it. Cocaine. High quality.

In the galley kitchen, dirty glasses and two empty bottles of wine were overturned in the sink behind me. The bedroom door off the living room was ajar.

As I moved to the door, my breath lodged in my throat.

"Yves?" I nudged the door open, the scene hitting me with stomach-churning impact.

The bed's black Egyptian cotton sheets dragged to the floor, colorful mirror-speckled and tasseled pillows from Marrakesh pummeled in disarray. The bedside lampshade had been knocked askew; cigarette butts overflowed in the ashtray. Clothing was strewn across the carpeted floor: his white jeans, a tangled shirt, a pair of stub-toed leather boots, and crumpled leather chaps. The pungent smell of stale smoke smothered the air, the drawn drapes at the window emitting dim illumination from the building's interior light well.

"Yves!" My voice cracked.

A muffled groan from the closet yanked me to it. Pulling open the accordion doors, he spilled out, naked, his wrists bound by a tie, a scarf gagging his mouth.

"Yves, oh my god." Dropping to my knees, I pulled off the binding, tore the scarf out. He had a mottled bruise on his shoulder, his body limp. I shook him, hearing him gasp for air as if he were choking.

"I'm calling an ambulance." I started to rise to my feet when he croaked, "No."

"No?" I looked down at him as he eased up painfully to prop himself against the bed, drawing his knees to his chin in sudden awareness of his nudity.

I averted my eyes from his penis, clasped by a studded leather cock ring.

"Just . . . give me a moment," he said.

"Yves, you need medical attention—"

"No. Please, Loulou. No doctors. I—I just passed out."

"*Just* passed out?" I heard a shrill lift my voice.

"Can you fetch me my robe? This is embarrassing."

I searched the closet, the wood rack containing articles of his clothing, folded sweaters on a shelf. "Where is it?"

"In the bathroom," he said, "on the hook behind the door."

Fetching it, I turned my back as he stood—too thin, his ribs incised under his colorless skin, as if he wasn't eating and getting enough sunlight—and draped himself in the robe, my breath hitching as I heard him unsnap the cock ring.

"Can I get you anything?" I asked hoarsely.

"Coffee, please. There's an espresso pot in the kitchen cabinet and a bag of ground beans in the freezer. I'll just be a moment."

As he stepped into the refurbished lime-tiled bathroom, I went to make the coffee, moving jerkily, noticing absently that he had few plates and cups, only two spoons and forks, and almost nothing in the fridge, as if the apartment was a temporary way-stop.

The espresso pot was percolating on the stove when he entered the living room, his glasses retrieved from the bathroom, the front of his hair damp from water splashed hastily over his face.

"Take a shower if you want," I said, forcing out a smile. "I can go to the corner patisserie for croissants. You should eat something."

"Coffee first. I—I think I owe you an explanation."

"It's none of my business—" The pot began whistling. Turning off the burner, I poured two cups.

He sat on the sofa, lighting a cigarette as I set his cup before him and perched beside him. Fumbling in my pocket, I pulled out my pack of Gauloises, and he clicked his butane lighter for me. "You won't tell anyone?" he said, after a long moment.

"No." I gulped my coffee, scalding my mouth.

"It was a game." His voice was very quiet.

"A game . . ."

"Yes. I like to play it sometimes." He lifted his cup, blew on it to cool the coffee, as he did when we absconded from the studio for a gossip break at a café down the street. "We went to a club last night, and I was excited. I asked him to play it with me."

"Jacques? Jacques did this to you?"

"He didn't *do* it to me. I asked him to."

I drew on my cigarette, the smoke acrid in my throat.

"We don't do it often. I passed out in the closet. I panicked."

"Of course you panicked." Despite my effort to control it, my voice rose again. "You were tied up and gagged."

"He was coming back. He—something must have delayed him." Yves stubbed out his half-smoked cigarette in the mash of butts in the tin ashtray and lit another.

"He *left* you inside the closet?"

"It's part of our game. No, Loulou . . ." His hand reached out to detain my lunge from the sofa. "You don't understand. He wouldn't have left me if I hadn't told him to."

"Why?" I whispered.

He averted his eyes. "I like it sometimes. To be . . . controlled. Dominated."

I inched back onto the sofa. "You didn't tell me you rented this penthouse."

A frown knitted his brow. "I left you the key to give to him."

"The key? I thought—I thought it was for a hotel room."

"It was for here."

"He's living with you?"

Yves smiled—a barely there smile that sundered me. "No. He has his apartment on rue du Dragon. I didn't want to go there anymore. Fernando and Clara, they live in the same arrondissement."

"Yves, Clara can't see rue du Dragon from her place. Fernando's apartment is blocks away. He's been in New York for months, working on his collection."

"Yes, it's very silly of me." He paused, smoke drifting from his nostrils. "Jacques's cousin from Bretagne is staying with him. I rented this place so we could have privacy."

You'd think I was moving us to Bretagne, the way he carries on about leaving Forain.

"Oh."

"I needed my own place." He sat upright, tucking the robe about his bare legs. "Pierre is always on the phone in our apartment; it's always ringing, and he's always yelling when he answers it." He grimaced. "He's president of the Syndicale and issues orders like he's planning a war. It was impossible for me to do any work there. I can hear him from upstairs, bellowing, Moujik and Hazel barking. Then he comes charging up the stairs to tell me about it. I don't care about the Syndicale."

"The studio on Marceau is set up now," I said. "I made sure it's like you want it."

"I know." He lowered his gaze. "I was planning to go there this afternoon, but"—a shaky chuckle escaped him—"you caught me in flagrante delicto. I'm so embarrassed."

I set my hand on his. "There's nothing to be embarrassed of. I won't tell anyone, but this—it can't happen again. If I hadn't come looking for you, you'd have been shut in that closet all day."

"No, he was coming back for me. We have dinner plans this evening. He wasn't supposed to leave for very long. He went to fetch his clothes for tonight. As I said, something must have delayed him. Maybe his cousin. He's been staying with him for a week or so now."

It didn't fit the timeline. According to Pierre, Yves had expressed the urgent need for another private space after Versailles, in late November. Yet Yves had given me the key for Jacques to this penthouse during the gala. The excuse that Jacques had a cousin staying with him for a week or so couldn't be the reason to rent it. It was now March; he'd already had the apartment for at least three months.

But the fact that he hadn't wanted me to know about it was enough for me not to question him. "I'll go buy croissants. A baguette and cheese."

"You really don't have to. I'm fine. I can eat something later. I need to visit the new studio. This afternoon, I'll go there, and you can show me around."

He hadn't yet set foot in the new hôtel, so I nodded. "I'm still bringing you food. Yves, you must eat."

Before he could protest again, I went to the door. "It was unlocked when I got here."

"My key's on the kitchen counter. Take it," he said, veiled in smoke as he lit yet another cigarette and drank down his coffee.

"I'll be right back."

On my quickened walk to the corner to purchase the croissants, baguette, and cheese, adding a quarter kilo of ham and stopping at the corner grocery for milk, yogurt, eggs, jam, and sugar, I tried to convince myself it had been a mishap. A sex game gone accidentally awry.

Yves loves his little games.

I had no right to poke my nose into it.

He was in the shower when I returned to the penthouse. Stashing the perishable items in the fridge, I halved a croissant, inserted ham and cheese in it, and set an egg to boil. Cutting the baguette into slices, I slathered jam on them, munching on pieces myself. I hadn't eaten today, either.

Cleaning and organizing the table, I set out his plate, the egg cooled by water from the tap. He emerged from the bedroom in his robe, a towel wrapped about his head. Less pallid now, but an elongated thread under the terry cloth folds.

"Sit and eat everything." I pointed to the sofa.

He smiled softly. "You shouldn't have."

"Someone has to. I'll see you later at the studio. Okay?"

"Yes." He nodded, started peeling the eggshell. "This is very rustic and comforting. Thank you, Loulou."

"Eat everything," I said, as I put his key on the counter and clicked the door shut.

I had no right to poke my nose into it, but as I hailed a taxi on boulevard des Invalides, I heard myself say darkly, "Rue du Dragon."

16

Jacques's apartment building was close to Café de Flore, not far from the celebrated brasserie les Deux Magots. It was one of the peeled-plaster, age-yellowed structures ubiquitous in Paris, untended for decades, with a turn-of-the-century scuffed portal door and winding staircase lit by a single bulb hanging by a wire.

Tugging at my wool-cashmere coat and removing my wool scarf to stuff into my bag, I raked a hand through my disheveled hair. I'd been unpacking odds and ends in the hôtel when I'd left to locate Yves and was in jeans, an ordinary work shirt, and not a scrap of bijou. After winding my way up the dimly lit stairs, I rapped on the door.

Rustling behind it, then the slap of bare feet on old wood flooring, preceded its opening.

"Yes?" A thin man who seemed younger than me peered with reticent dark eyes behind steel-rimmed glasses, his dark hair brushed from his brow in a semblance of Jacques's style, but springing in tufts at the top, the gel hastily applied. He'd tucked a black gauze cloth at the throat of his white shirt with its upright collar, mimicking a cravat. Again, it evoked Jacques, but clumsily, without the innate panache. He wore loose, cuffed black trousers, his feet unshod.

"Is Jacques here?" I asked, a bite in my voice.

"He stepped out to buy cigarettes." The young man kept peering at me, as if he were struggling to put a name to a face that he somehow recognized.

"I'm Loulou de la Falaise. I work for Yves Saint Laurent."

His eyes widened; he'd heard my name, maybe seen my photograph in a daily or a fashion magazine. "Won't you come inside? Jacques should be back in a moment."

"I will, thank you."

The living room was narrow, a window in a wall by a low, lumpy blue sofa overlooking the light well. Backless shelves on the opposite wall contained leaning stacks of books; a portrait studio black-and-white close-up of Jacques in a plastic slip frame as the matinee idol, his slim ringed hand under his chin against a white satin backdrop; and a dying plant in a ceramic pot. The kitchenette through an open doorway was utilitarian, barely able to fit one person.

To me, the apartment gave off an air of barren transience, a place to change clothes, maybe sleep on occasion, before the next adventure.

"Coffee?" The man moved uncertainly into the kitchenette.

"Are you Jacques's cousin?" Yves had mentioned it, and he hadn't introduced himself.

"Not really." His smile was timid. "I'm a friend of his from the university. I'm José. José de Sarasola. I'm also from the Loire-Atlantique." At my evident confusion, he said, "It's a Breton custom to call your friends 'cousin,' though you're not related."

"Oh. Coffee would be lovely." I managed a smile, itching to barrage him with questions and explore the apartment. I could see an open bedroom door down a tight, short hall, a white-tiled, steam-stained bathroom visible at the end.

It wasn't what I expected. For an alleged muse to Karl Lagerfeld, the styliste who surrounded himself in opulence, Jacques lived like an impoverished Saint-Germain student in a moldering walk-up.

"You've known each other since university?" I said, as he

handed me a cup of instant coffee, undissolved dregs floating in the lukewarm water.

"We were raised near each other. My family's château is about ten kilometers from his family's home, la Berrière. We met again at the Université Paris Nanterre, where we were both studying law. He left in his first year to sign up for his military service."

His unfeigned forthrightness once more struck me as incongruous with Jacques's sophistication—and a chance to find out more about Jacques himself.

He says he's from a rich old family, counts or dukes or something. Karl laps it up, but we think it's bullshit.

Corey, Pat, and Donna believed Jacques had lied about his lineage.

"La Berrière is another château?" I sipped the awful coffee.

"A small one, yes. It has vineyards. Jacques comes from a noble family. Older nobility is better, I think. His family's title is from the nineteenth century. He could tell you more. I barely understand it."

So, Jacques hadn't lied.

"How did you meet up here?"

"I came to look for work in a bank. I was staying in my sister's flat." One of his bare feet moved on top of the other as he leaned against the kitchenette doorway. "I ran into Jacques at Café le Flore, and he told me Monsieur Lagerfeld might need a business manager."

"You work for Karl?" I couldn't disguise my surprise.

"No," he said with another nervous smile. "I mean, yes, I think I do. I'm not sure."

I let the silence settle before I said, "Sometimes working with a fashion designer can feel like you're doing something and nothing at the same time."

"I suppose so. I helped Monsieur Lagerfeld with the papers

to buy Château de Penhoët in Grand-Champ. It's in Bretagne. My parents knew a local notary who prepared the title for him. I don't receive a salary. He pays me with clothes. I'm still looking for a job; I was just about to go and apply for one. I'm not really a fashion person."

He pays me with clothes.

Jacques hadn't arrived. I couldn't prolong my stay.

"Thank you for the coffee." I stood, setting the cup on the small table adjacent to the sofa. "It was very nice to meet you, José." I started toward the door.

"I'll tell Jacques you came by," he said.

"Please do."

Going down the winding staircase, I didn't know what to think. A cousin, but not a cousin. Paid with clothes. The apartment Karl rented for Jacques, smaller and more dilapidated than the one where the Americans had stayed. Karl could have offered that one to Jacques when he kicked the Americans out. He hadn't.

He never had lovers. He showed no interest in sex. He likes to possess things, to show them off . . . Karl always gets bored eventually.

Perhaps for Karl it was a relationship of temporary convenience, an ephemeral amusement, until the next novelty happened along.

I was reaching for the building's doorknob when Jacques came in.

His hair was wind-tossed. There was a splash of color in his angular cheeks, his hazel eyes bright and, I thought, a little feverish, as if he'd been racing to get here.

"Loulou." He halted. It was the first time I'd seen him look disconcerted. "I didn't expect . . ." He paused, the haste in his eyes fading. "I did. Yves told me."

"I found him. In the closet."

"I just went to see him. I was delayed unexpectedly. Karl called me. My cousin needed help with his job application—"

"You left him in a closet. With a gag in his mouth." I stared at him.

Jacques drew me into the building foyer. "Come upstairs. Let me explain to you."

"I was just upstairs. I met your 'cousin.'"

"José? He's still here? He'll be late for his appointment at the bank." Jacques smiled, and it, too, was curiously unnerved. "Oh, well. This is awkward."

"To say the least."

"Come upstairs, please. I want to explain."

Reluctantly, I followed him. José had his shoes on and a navy-blue suit jacket, which, with the inept cravat, made him appear mismatched.

"A tie, José." Jacques led him to the bedroom; I didn't stay behind in the living room.

Like the rest of the apartment, the bedroom was sparse: a Japanese-style futon with a faded satin coverlet on a wood platform; a white ceramic Venetian mask with glitter-rimmed eye-holes, painted with a green dragon breathing cartoon fire, on the wall.

In the overstuffed closet, I glimpsed rows of coats, jackets, and trousers, coordinated by color; shelves with camisole vests in neat piles; and hangers of shirts, ties, and silken robes. Shoe racks on the floor, sagging with footwear.

The luxury lacking in the rest of the apartment was in the closet: a trove of fashion.

"This one." Extracting an azure silk tie that went perfectly with José's jacket, Jacques undid the black gauze scarf, buttoned up and straightened the shirt collar, and expertly fastened the tie with a Windsor knot. He brushed his palms over José's jacketed shoulders in fraternal attention. "Banks don't hire boulevard dandies. Now you look the part. Merde."

The wish for good luck in the theater.

José gave his nervous smile and edged past me to leave.

Jacques turned from his closet. "Can I make us some coffee, or would you prefer to go to Café le Flore? It's just down the street."

I didn't want a repeat of the instant coffee but, likewise, didn't wish to air my grievances in a public place. "Here is fine."

"I'll make us espresso." He removed his cropped light green wool Loden coat, styled with black braiding and buttoned leather-piped lapels, like an Austrian hunting jacket, and laid it on the futon. Underneath, he wore a crisp black shirt with blouson sleeves and a detachable wing-tipped collar; his narrow hips and lean legs were encased in brown leather pants with flared bottoms over stub-toed boots.

"José's family is Spanish, but he doesn't know how to use an espresso pot. He ends up overboiling the water and shoots hot coffee all over the kitchen. Did he offer you anything?" he asked, as I trailed after him.

"Nescafé."

He made a wince. "I thought so. He's very polite, but hope-less."

"He says he works for Karl." I lit a cigarette. He motioned, wagging his fingers, so I gave it to him and lit another for myself.

"He travels with us. He needed something to do. Karl's gener-ous." Jacques spooned coffee into the steel filter of the espresso pot—the same kind I'd made coffee in for Yves—and filled the lower part with water before screwing on the lidded spout top and setting it on the tiny stove to boil.

I refrained from commenting that yes, Karl could be generous—with clothes.

"José is helping me with the new château. Karl hired Patrick Hourcade from *Vogue* to search archives for the original docu-mentation on the house and re-create everything as it was; he's in charge of decorating, too, but there's still a lot to do, so I'm taking care of some of it with José." He opened the minuscule fridge, frowned. "I'm a terrible host. I've nothing to offer you. I'm so rarely here these days."

"It's okay. I ate bread with jam at Yves's new place."

He went still for a moment. "About that."

"It's really not my business."

"It is." He lifted somber eyes to me. "You found him in a compromising position. If I were his close friend, I'd be furious."

Moving to the sofa, I sat down. He brought me an ashtray; after the pot started to whistle, he poured the fresh-brewed coffee and served it on a painted wood tray with a bowl of sugar cubes and a pitcher of cream.

He said, "I told you Yves likes his little games."

"You did."

"It's one of them." Tapping his cigarette in the ashtray, he sat cross-legged on the floor opposite me. All of a sudden, he seemed disarmingly young. Still strikingly handsome, but not contrivedly so. His crisp shirt collar gaped at his collarbones; a hint of dark auburn hair peeked from the hollow of his throat. "He wants to be naughty. He likes to be punished by his papa."

The words were unsettling against my newfound impression of him.

"He likes to be tied up and left for hours in a closet?" Skepticism tinged my voice.

"Yes." Jacques met my regard. "He does. He's not such a good boy."

The world thinks they know me. They don't. I'm not such a good boy.

I swallowed my coffee.

"We went to a club last night," Jacques continued. "Not le Sept. Another place that he enjoys. He was aroused by what he saw.

He wanted us to do it with the other men, but I didn't think it was safe for him. It can get rough, and Yves doesn't know his limits."

Thadée had said practically the same thing to me.

"I promised we could do it at his apartment." He paused, inhaling smoke, blowing it in a plume over our heads. "Are you sure you want to hear this?"

I wasn't. "Not if you'd rather not tell me."

"I don't mind. I'm not ashamed of it." He went silent, as if he were collecting the right words. "He's curious. He likes to experiment. I like it, too. I like having sex with him. He can be like Karl; he wants me to dress up and play a part for him, but it's different with him."

"How is it different?"

"He wants only to please me, and have me please him." Another pause. He finished his cigarette. "Would you like a joint or some cocaine?"

"No." I heard a quaver in my reply. "I have to go back to work."

"You never do drugs at work?" he asked matter-of-factly.

"No. Does Karl?"

"Karl never does drugs. He barely drinks wine."

"But Yves does."

"Yes. We do drugs together. He likes that, too. But he can . . ."

"Go overboard," I said quietly.

"He gets excited. The drugs release his inhibitions. Coke and weed help him stop worrying he'll look silly or vulgar. He thinks about that a lot: how he'll appear to others."

"Don't you?"

"Of course. Everyone does." He toyed with his cup, turning it around on the table. "But it incapacitates him. I like to see him happy, not thinking about it. He has a . . . a kind of innocence.

He writes me these beautiful letters, pouring his heart out on paper, drawings of snakes and hearts; he must express how he feels, or it eats him up inside."

The letter in the envelope left at my hotel in Versailles, the card, and the apartment key.

"I tell him it's not shameful to want to see me naked in chaps, to wear a cock ring, and to ask for what he wants," Jacques said. "Do you ask your lovers for what you want?"

"Sometimes." I was finding it very strange to have this conversation with him, but also liberating. Most people never talked candidly about sex.

"Only sometimes?" he asked.

"It depends on the circumstances, the person. I don't tell strangers what I want."

"Some people find it easier to tell strangers. But do you think it's perfectly normal to have fantasies and want to live them out?"

"I do, as long as the fantasies are consensual and don't hurt anyone."

His expression clouded. "I didn't mean to hurt him. It really was supposed to be a game."

"Do you play these kinds of games with Karl?" I felt as if I'd tripped on a razor's edge.

"We play other games. Karl enjoys fantasy, too, but only if he's in control of it. He prefers to hear me talk about it. He doesn't partake in it."

"Karl doesn't want to be locked in a closet," I heard myself say.

He gave a poignant smile. "Karl wants to lock me in a closet and keep me under glass forever, in a state of perpetual youth and inspiration for him. Yves wants me inside the closet, growing old with him."

"But you weren't inside the closet with him."

"No." He met my eyes. "Are you okay?"

I nodded, though the level of intimacy was starting to unsettle me, like I was looking through a peephole into Yves's bedroom.

"Last night, he wanted it rougher. He was turned on by what he'd seen. I played with him, and then he asked me to punish him. Put him in the closet and leave him there, so he could think about what a naughty boy he is."

Abrupt sorrow welled in my chest.

"It's symbolic," said Jacques. "A closet is shame. He does it to himself." A slight tremor marred his voice. "He thinks he deserves punishment. He doesn't. But I can't tell him that. I can't teach him it. I try to show him it's what we all want—to be true to our desires. I give him the pleasure he asks for because he gives it back so freely. But I can't take away the shame of it for him."

My eyes filled with tears. He brought up a fingertip to trace the spill.

"You were scared for him. He told me."

"It did scare me. He'd passed out."

"He loves you so much. He told me you came into his world and changed how he saw it. You brought him color, life. He says you never care about what others think. He calls you his 'gypsy.'"

I swallowed against the choke of tears. "I love him, too. Very much."

"I know." He drew back. "I'm sorry it scared you. We got carried away. I want him to be happy and forget that he'll hurt himself. I went back as soon as I could. You'd been there already. He was showered and dressed, ready to go to the studio. He wants us to have dinner tonight as planned, but if you don't want me to see him anymore, I won't."

Jacques is dangerous. He likes pain and degradation. Protect Yves. Keep him away.

As Corey's warning went through me, I thought he'd been

wrong. What he'd interpreted as danger from Jacques wasn't the threat. The danger lay in Yves, in his hidden pain.

"I can't—" I shored up my voice. "I can't tell you to do that. It's not my decision."

"He'd listen to you." Jacques contemplated me. "He would listen, and probably agree. He was also scared when I went back to him. He knows we went too far. I told him we can't ever do that again, but when I said we should stop seeing each other, he started crying."

"He . . . he thinks he's in love with you."

"I know. He feels so intensely. To be in love is beautiful to him, but it can also be so damaging." He spoke gently, as if Yves were a fragile object in peril of shattering—not so much protective, but cognizant of avoiding a fissure that might enable the breakage. I also noted he didn't verbally reciprocate the emotion.

"You . . . you're not in love with him," I ventured.

He went quiet, reflective. "It's not something I think about like he does. It's too early, maybe, for me to say." He motioned to my cup. "Is it too strong?"

"No, it's fine." I finished the coffee, then he collected the emptied cups and went into the kitchen to wash them.

Shouldering my bag, trying to dispel the heaviness that had come over me, I said, "I should go. He wanted me to show him the new studio. We'll probably work this afternoon. We have a line to finish."

"Yes, okay. Thank you for coming, Loulou. Again, I'm sorry about this."

"Don't be." I paused, as he went motionless at the sink. "He can decide what's best for him. Or you can decide it together."

"Do you want to see where we go?" His voice was low. "I can take you."

"I—I don't think that's necessary." But I heard myself hesitate, and I wasn't sure why: a strange mix of curiosity and perhaps my unacknowledged guilt at my voyeurism, the feeling I'd intruded in a place where I didn't belong—a place Yves had created for himself, a private space he didn't want to share with me, like the penthouse.

"It might help you understand it better. We can have dinner together and then go to the club." He glanced at me over his shoulder. "It's not shameful. It's just sex, Loulou. That's all it is."

"Let me think about it." I couldn't bring myself to accept his offer, even though it seemed sincere, his way of making amends and easing my mind.

He nodded, dried his hands on a kitchen towel, and went past me to his bedroom. I heard a drawer open, and he came back with a card.

"This is my phone number. I'm not here a lot, but there's a machine. You can leave a message. Sometimes José stays here, so if he picks up, tell him you want me to call you. He's trustworthy. His sister's apartment is smaller than this one, if you can believe it, so he sleeps on the sofa, or I let him use my bed if I'm out with Karl or Yves. I don't spend nights with Karl, but I do sometimes with Yves. He likes me to spend the night with him."

"All right. I'll think about it." I put the card in my bag and turned to the door. Then, before I knew what I was about to say, I asked, "Does Pierre know about you?"

"I think he must suspect something by now." Once more, Jacques sounded mindful of a boundary he couldn't cross. "I'm not sure if he knows it's me. Will you tell him?"

I shook my head. "That's also not for me to decide."

He held the door open for me; as I left, he said, "Yves is very lucky to have someone like you looking out for him."

Out on the street, I exhaled a knotted, pent-up breath.

*He feels so intensely. To be in love is beautiful to him, but it can
also be so damaging.*

Upon reaching the hôtel, where Yves hadn't yet arrived, I shut
myself in his studio. Without warning, I started to cry.

Once more, I wasn't certain why, only that I wished I could tell
Yves to not be afraid of how he felt. We were so close, in so many
ways, but this was unknown terrain between us. I didn't want to
humiliate him further by trying to reassure him he shouldn't be
ashamed of his own desires.

Then I wiped my tears, reapplied my mascara and lipstick,
because Yves liked to see me in makeup at the studio, and
called Thadée.

WE MET AT a local bistro in my district. It was quiet, out of the
way. There was no risk of us running into someone we knew or
who might recognize us.

Thadée wore jeans, a creased white shirt, and a caramel-and-
black houndstooth blazer, his thick hair razed by the March wind
prowling through the city. We always seemed to be meeting in
the wind.

Over drinks, onion soup, and veal cutlets, I told him.

He leaned back in his chair. "He was tied up in the closet, and
he wanted it?"

"That's what they both told me. In the same words: a 'game'
Yves likes to 'play.' Only it went too far this time. Jacques explained it."

"Yves didn't say anything else about it?"

"He came to the studio shortly after I called you. He apolo-
gized to everyone on the staff for his absence, thanked them for
being so thorough with the move, and worked until seven p.m.
with me. He was very apologetic with me as well, for not being

there to help set up the studio, but he didn't mention it or explain anything else."

"He also didn't tell you he'd rented that penthouse."

I lit a cigarette and drank down my white wine. I wanted to get drunk. "No."

"He's been hiding it like we thought. Hiding it from everyone, including you."

"Because he's ashamed of it. He's even ashamed of it with Jacques." I gestured to the waiter for another bottle. "I think that's why Jacques isn't—what's the word? Not 'serious,' but—"

"Committed. He's keeping his distance."

"Yes. He knows how Yves feels, but I got the impression it's too intense for him."

"And there's Pierre. The house. The scandal in the press. Jacques has been photographed enough times at Chloé shows and with Karl for them to be linked. People know there's something going on between them."

He poured us more wine as I said, anger crisping my voice, "Karl's not going out of his way to maintain Jacques. You saw his apartment on Saint-Sulpice. He recently bought a château in Grand-Champ that he's restoring. Jacques has his cousin José staying with him, sleeping on the sofa. He lives like a rat compared with Karl."

"Maybe Karl's offered to give him more, and Jacques doesn't want to take it." He ran his finger around the rim of his wineglass. "Maybe he's maintaining a certain distance with Karl, too, waiting to see what's more beneficial to him."

Karl wants to lock me in a closet and keep me under glass forever, in a state of perpetual youth and inspiration for him.

"I didn't hear that in him. It sounded almost as if he's trapped between them."

Thadée considered, sipping his wine. I told myself to slow

down, as I was already on my third glass, but I didn't follow through. I downed it.

"We should take him up on it," he said at length. "Go out with him to dinner and then to that club. Find out exactly where he's been taking Yves."

I laughed uneasily, the wine hitting me in sudden, dizzying force. "It's a place where gay men have sex. I don't think they'll appreciate a woman showing up."

"If Jacques said he could take you, it must be okay. He also said it's a place Yves enjoys, so they've obviously been there more than once or twice."

I had trouble finding a plausible excuse to that.

"Loulou, it's serious. Very serious, as far as Yves is concerned. And Pierre just invested significant capital to move the house to the new hôtel, because the business keeps growing, right?"

"Yes." Now I felt sick. "We have five new boutiques opening this year. Clara mentioned we have over a thousand people on our invitee list; she thinks our new salon will soon be too small, and we should consider renting a hotel ballroom for the couture presentations."

"Meanwhile, Yves is having an affair that Pierre's oblivious to."

"Pierre can't be totally oblivious. Jacques admitted he must suspect something by now, even if not who Yves's lover is. Yves rented another place."

"Pierre justifies the penthouse like he told you: Yves is upset about the move. As for the affair, to Pierre that's all it is. He doesn't want to know more. It's part of their arrangement: they keep to the rules, and no questions." Thadée didn't sound reassured.

"Did Pierre tell you about their arrangement?" I asked, thinking of when Yves had described it to me.

"No. He never talks about it. But we've been friends for years.

Everyone who's close to them knows they both do it. Pierre has flings; I only know because Clara's arranged hotel suites for him. She manages those expenses. So, yes, he probably suspects. He's seen the signs before. Yves isn't good at hiding it. But not who it is. Or how far it's gone. He's waiting for it to end. With Yves, it always does. Except this one might not."

"Do you think we should tell him?" I wasn't sure what I'd do if he said we should.

"I wouldn't," he replied, to my relief. "What are we going to tell him? 'Yves is seeing Lagerfeld's companion or boyfriend or whatever he is, and goes to sex clubs with him, then likes being tied up and locked in a closet'? 'He's thinking of leaving you for a younger man with nothing'? Pierre will laugh in our faces, then threaten Yves with a sanatorium. Only this time, he'll lock him up in one."

I winced. "So, we call Jacques and try to find out more?"

"I think so. But let's give it time, so we don't look desperate or suspicious. Tell him we want to invite him out for dinner. Don't mention the club. We'll see how it goes."

"Okay." We paid the bill and wandered out of the restaurant. The wind wasn't strong, but it carried an icy underbite, a touch of rain that sobered me somewhat.

"I'll walk you home," he said. "My car isn't parked far away."

At my building door, I rummaged for my keys, my hands numb, my head numb. I dropped my bag. As it spilled lipstick and my cigarettes, my wallet and joints and the keys, and Thadée knelt to pick everything up, a strangled moan escaped my lips.

He stood and, without a word, took me in his arms. "It's all right. It's all going to be all right. We'll figure it out. Everything will be okay."

"I found him in a closet . . ." I said brokenly. "He's ashamed. Hiding from me. I don't know what to do for him."

He cupped my chin, raising my face to his. "You can't do anything more than what you're doing. You can't save Yves from himself."

"Why not?" I could hear the scarred pain of my childhood: how I protected my brother as we navigated an upended world where we were no longer wanted.

His smile was gentle, his fingertip brushing my lips. "You can't save anyone, Loulou. You know that. We can only save ourselves, if we're lucky."

I clung to him. "Don't leave."

"Are you sure?" His voice husked. "I don't want to be an act of desperation or regret. I told you I'd wait, for as long as necessary."

"I don't want to wait anymore." Pulling him into the foyer with my bag still in his hand, I seized his face in my hands, kissing him, pressing against him. I wanted to forget everything, to drown myself in him and feel.

Just *feel*.

We stumbled into the elevator to my flat, my bag falling again at our feet, my hands on his chest, his mouth at my neck, a groan escaping him as I went lower, palming his hardness, unzipping his fly to reach into his underpants and grasp him.

He had me up against the elevator wall, his hands on me, slipping my panties to my knees, slipping his finger inside me.

I started to cry out, and the elevator dinged, startling us, making us laugh. The doors slid open, the grate needing to be released; we kicked my bag to my door. He had my keys in his pocket, rooting them out to fit into the lock. He kept kissing me as he did.

We tumbled into my loft. The night poured through the windows, and he shut the door with the back of his heel, scooping me up and carrying me to the bed.

He stood there, his breath shallow, his gray-blue eyes in

shadow, taking in every inch of me. "I want to know what you want."

I writhed out of my clothes, watching him watch me, and moistened myself with my fingers, arching my spine, playing with my breasts.

"Here, I want you here. And here. Everywhere. Inside me."

He fell on me like the rumble of thunder in the distance, my hands pulling away his shirt to reveal his chest dusted in matted hair, his nipples hardening at my touch. With my heels, I inched down his pants, and then he was warm skin, pulsing against me.

You do want someone you think you shouldn't. But you're brave enough to fight it.

His mouth a cauldron, searing mine. His desire for me, his patience, waiting in hope, and my urgency for him, firing my veins. I'd wanted him from the moment I'd first seen him, and had tried to resist it.

I couldn't resist him anymore.

When he eased inside me, gauging me, I lifted my hips to receive him. His eyes were now full of me, my body full of him; and he started to move, building the tide inside me.

I cried out at our climax, grasping him to me, never wanting to let him go.

WE LAY HEAPED on the bed among our crushed clothes, hands entwined, my head on his chest, my fingers raveled in his chest hair.

"What do we do now?"

His chuckle was low in his chest; I felt it under my hand. "I don't know. It came too fast and furious."

I laughed quietly. "Can you stay?"

A moment of hesitation, then his kiss on my forehead. "Yes."

Untangling myself, feeling as if I were adhered to him, I groped at the side of my bed. "My bag."

"I think," he said, "it's still outside the door."

He got up, a lean sliver, his buttocks flexing as he went to retrieve the bag. I drank him in. He was even more beautiful naked, his hair a spiky thicket on his head and his body a ribbed carving.

"You should never wear clothes," I said, fishing in my bag for a joint and my lighter.

"And turn away all the offers of free clothing from every designer wanting to dress me?" He made a mock halting motion with his hand. "What would Paris say?"

"If Paris could see what I do," I said, lighting the joint and passing it to him, "they'd stop designing clothes altogether, knowing it was pointless."

He laughed, toking on the joint. Sitting on the edge of the bed, he caressed my face.

"I can't stay," he said.

My throat thickened. "I know."

"I will. I . . . I need time to do it. We've . . ." He lowered his face. "It's already over between us. Clara knows it, and so do I. But we've been going through the motions. Yves and Pierre. Betty and François. The house. It's all stuck together."

"The scandal in the press," I said softly. "What will they say?"

"I want this." He looked directly into my eyes. "I want to be with you."

"Me, too." I forced out a frail smile. "Who knew? I never thought I'd want it again."

"My irresistible charm and utter lack of means overcame your better judgment." He smiled, kissing me. "We have time. Take all the time you need. You might not want it later. I want you to be sure."

"Yes." I swallowed against the lumping. "We should both be sure."

He dressed. I threw on my blouse and accompanied him to the door. As we kissed again, he said into my lips, "I am sure."

I leaned against the door as he took the stairs down, seeing him in my mind as he pulled up his blazer's collar and hunched his height, hastening to his car.

Rain pebbled my loft rooftop, streaking the mossy skylight.

I said into the silence, "I'm sure, too."

IN THE MORNING, when I woke alone, my sheets didn't smell of him. I lay in bed listening to the dribble in the gutters from the rain that poured all night, and knew it would cause an unbreachable rift. Clara and Thadée had been a couple, for better or worse, since before I'd arrived, woven into the house tapestry.

It's all stuck together.

I didn't have the courage to tear it apart.

17

I worked on our prêt-à-porter line, overseeing the mockups sent from the manufacturers and consulting with Yves on changes deemed necessary before we approved production.

After the presentation, I spent a week at our Rive Gauche boutique on rue de Tournon. The red walls, transparent display counters, cream leather beanbag chairs, dangling rounded-medallion lighting fixtures, and dresses hanging flat, framing the square interior archway, cocooned me in womblike comfort. I helped the sales staff dress the mannequins in the new line behind the white-mum-busheled display windows, rearranged racks and shelving in the store, and had a framed poster of one of Yves's love cards, magnified to blowsy proportions, mounted at the store entrance.

Going home to change, I snorted lines to rev up for the night, then met with Yves, Pierre, and Paloma and her new beau, an angelic-faced, dark-haired Argentinian playwright. We had dinners at la Coupole and went dancing at le Sept. I had luncheons with Betty, who was content with her two daughters and nonchalant as ever.

Since the day in his Breteuil penthouse, Yves hadn't mentioned Jacques again. I didn't ask, nor did I make it a point to follow up on the invitation from Jacques.

I saw Thadée frequently, at dinner parties and art gallery openings, or nights at the theater and the ballet, when Nureyev danced. Always with Clara, who was invariably polite; but her steel-edged reserve was also embedded in her manner.

Thadée and I did not seek out time alone together. We hadn't made a stated decision not to, but it happened anyway. We kissed each other's cheeks hello and goodbye, and avoided the frisson between us. It was almost as if the night in my loft had never occurred, yet we both knew it had—and like our unvoiced decision to keep a certain distance, it could happen again if we gave in to it.

After a month, on a morning when I woke up earlier than usual, scavenging barefoot in a T-shirt in my kitchen, searching my bag for a fresh pack of cigarettes, my fingers grazed the crumpled card wedged at the bottom of my bag, flecked with tobacco bits.

A simple white card with his black block-lettered name and number.

He picked up, groggy for a moment, woken from sleep, before he identified my voice.

"Loulou. I thought I wouldn't hear from you."

"Is it too early?"

"Not at all. I had a late night, but not extravagantly late."

"Yes, well, I'm sorry it's taken me this long," I said. "I've been busy."

"The spring line was beautiful. I saw a lot of you in it."

He didn't attend our shows, or at least I'd never seen him there. It was an unspoken yet inviolate rule that those of us in fashion didn't intrude on another designer's terrain during a show. But I was always backstage; and our guest list had grown so large, it was possible. I imagined him slipping into the presentation as a seating host or an assistant editor representing a publication, much in the way he'd served champagne at Versailles—an anonymous face, blended into the audience, unobtrusive and unnoticed.

"Dinner," I said. "Are you still available?"

"I am."

"We were thinking of la Coupole."

"'We'?" I didn't detect a discernible shift in his voice; he spoke like when he'd asked me if I ever did drugs at work or if I asked lovers for what I wanted.

"A friend of mine, Thadée Klossowski. I thought it might be nice to bring him along. He's also a close friend of Yves's. They've known each other for years."

"I know who he is." I was taken aback. He must have sensed it or heard it in my pause, because he said, "Not personally. His name. His father is Balthus. Everyone knows who he is. I've seen him at le Sept and other places."

Dance with me, Loulou.

His milky linen suit damp with sweat, his lean body a darker silhouette within the fabric; the stringed neon lights limning him, his hips swerving into mine . . .

"Is it okay?" I asked, closing my eyes to shutter the memory.

"I'd be honored." He went quiet for a moment. "But maybe not la Coupole."

"Why not?" I thought of his student apartment, the overflowing closet. Did Karl pay him in clothes, too, and he didn't want to expect us to pick up the dinner check at an expensive restaurant?

"It's too . . ."

"Lavish?" I suggested.

"Yes." He laughed. His light, boyish laugh. "Perfect description. I was thinking closer to here. Les Deux Magots. Then we can take a cab to rue Sainte-Anne. If you still want to go? That's where the club is."

I didn't dissuade him. "Thadée can take us. He has a car."

"Even better. Tomorrow night, at around nine o'clock? I'll make a reservation and meet you at the restaurant."

"Good. See you then."

Hanging up the phone, I sat on my bed. My hands were trembling.

Then I showered and dressed for work.

BY A MUTUAL accord that hadn't been discussed beforehand, when I met Thadée near the restaurant, he was dressed casually, in jeans and the plain white shirt and houndstooth blazer he'd worn before, a creased black scrap of scarf twined about his neck.

I wore a dark red blouse by Yves and a pleated skirt, with a light knee-length black wool coat and my battered Rive Gauche suede boots. It was a balmy evening; as we moved to the brassiere, he said, "We're keeping it low-key tonight."

"He wanted to eat here."

"La Coupole would be too visible. We're far less likely to bump into anyone we know in a tourist-trap brassiere."

"Even if we do, we're just having dinner."

"We are, aren't we?" He stubbed out his cigarette before we entered the restaurant.

Les Deux Magots had a vibrant literary past as a hangout for the publishing world in Saint-Germain-des-Prés, with various distinguished writers making it their haunt over the years. It epitomized the bohemian iconoclasm of the arrondissement, the restaurant's signature green awning marking the corner of the square, with rattan-backed chairs, marble-topped iron tables, and painted, age-tarnished effigies of Chinese scholars in robes perched in niches inside.

And, I thought, as he stood from our reserved table to wave at us, an ideal setting for Jacques's avant-garde style.

He wore his Loden hunter jacket, a green shirt with a white wing-tipped collar, and scratched tobacco-leather pants, along with a peaked green wool military cap angled on his head and a medallion-studded belt at his hips. His knotted black gauze scarf, the one from José that he'd replaced with a tie, hung on the back of his chair.

Introducing himself to Thadée, we ordered a bottle of red wine and a charcuterie and Auvergne cheese board to start. Cigarette smoke and conversation hung thick in the air as we made small talk, easing ourselves into the encounter.

Over our second course of ham croque monsieurs, he asked Thadée about himself, artfully navigating around the thorny subject of his father's insurmountable fame as a painter and pausing at Thadée's admission that he wanted to write a book.

"You're in the place of inspiration, then," declared Jacques. "Imagine Simone de Beauvoir writing *Les mandarins* in that corner, completely unaware she'd win the Prix Goncourt. Or Hemingway after the war, entertaining Marlene Dietrich with his reporting escapades. Or Verlaine"—his voice adopted a sly note—"high on absinthe and battling with his lover, Rimbaud, over indecent poetry."

Thadée smiled. "I'd be put to shame. I'm much too lazy; I write whenever the mood moves me and will never be remembered for it."

"Do you want to be remembered?" Jacques fit a cigarette into his white filter and reclined in his chair. "The weight of one's own repute can be insupportable."

I thought of Yves, his house becoming his prison, chained to the expectations that every collection must exceed the last, always needing to outdo himself.

"But," added Jacques, as if he read my thoughts, "the weight of words on paper is lasting."

"If anyone bothers to read them," said Thadée. "For every Hemingway and Beauvoir, there are a dozen others who die without publishing anything lasting."

"Impermanence can also be a gift. Create nothing lasting. Leave nothing behind. Live for the present. In beauty, until it ends." Jacques exhaled smoke thoughtfully. "In Latin, *cadere* means 'to fall.' It's the root of 'decadent.' Not as we think of the word now, but a beautiful way to fall. A slow fall, willingly. Like fashion. It never lasts, but for the time it's there, the beauty of it is something we'd die for, though we can never hold on to it."

We sat quiet for an extended yet not uncomfortable moment. Thadée said at length, "That might be the most poetic metaphor for fashion I've ever heard."

"I've had a lot of time to think about it. I'm also too lazy to be remembered."

Clearing my throat, I said, "More wine?"

"I don't think so," said Jacques, and Thadée nodded.

We shared the check—Jacques insisted—and moved outside, the streets full of tourists and students. Checking his slim black-banded wristwatch, Jacques said, "It's still too early for the club. Let's walk around, or go to my flat?"

Without agreeing on a destination, we drifted to his apartment, seemingly larger in the muted light of lamps on the floor, the focal lights on the backless bookshelves switched off by him.

He cut lines of coke for us on the table, spooning out the rosy powder from his miniature enamel box. We snorted it, then smoked a joint, listening to a Diana Ross album on the record player, before he said, "Loulou, we should change your outfit."

Stoned and relaxed, I asked, "Is my skirt too enticing for the club?"

He laughed. "Hands will want to go up it." He glanced at Thadée, sprawled on the sofa, his long legs stretched out before him, feet tapping to the music. "Is that okay?"

"It's not my skirt," Thadée said.

I followed Jacques to his bedroom, where he opened his closet and stood, surveying the racks. "This." Taking a white tuxedo shirt from a hanger, he brought it to me. As I started to unbutton my blouse, he turned away.

"I've undressed for fashion shows a hundred times," I said, "with a hundred people running about."

"Right, of course." He laughed again, lower in his chest, and continued moving hangers, searching.

"And now?" I asked.

He turned around. I stood in my black panties and the tuxedo shirt. It had a scooped hem and fit me loosely, but wasn't overlarge, as Jacques was slim, not much taller than me. Its starch-stiffened flat-front apertures were made for studs, without buttons.

"I think you should go like that. With a bowler hat. A Berlin cabaret performer."

"Then I will. Do you have the hat?"

He smiled. "I do. But . . ." He unzipped his fly, tugged, and wriggled out of his leather pants. He wasn't wearing underpants. Below his crumpled shirttail, his pubic bush, darker than his hair, framed his well-shaped, uncircumcised penis.

Tossing the pants at me, he peeled off his shirt and swiveled naked toward the closet, with only his detachable wing-tipped collar about his throat.

A fleur-de-lis was inked on the mid-upper cleft of his small right buttock.

"My friend Philippe tattooed it for me with an injection needle when we were on a ship during our military service," he said, glancing over his shoulder. "Oh, those look wonderful on you."

His leather pants were warm from his skin, slick on my legs to my hips.

Pulling on a white shirt, he left it open to the dust line of hair on his navel and added a pair of tight, well-washed button-up jeans. He came over to me, adjusting the pants. "Hmm . . . The belt."

He picked up his studded belt from the floor and notched it about my waist, tucking the slight excess of leather above the waistband—he was narrow-hipped, like me, but I was thinner—and then, with a pensive finger at his lips that reminded me of Yves outfitting a cabine mannequin, he returned to the closet.

From a jewelry box, he extracted opaline silver studs to insert into the shirt openings, just up to the middle of my rib cage, the shirt gaping at my breasts.

"You're flat-chested," he said. "You can look like a boy."

"I never wear a bra, if I can avoid it."

"A bra can be sexy. But this is sexier: the illusion of it, when it's not there."

Sitting me on the bed, he went to the bathroom. He returned with his hair slicked back and with a jar of green gel, a comb, and a plastic makeup kit under his arm, similar to the travel bags that the American models used at Versailles.

From the bedside table, he flicked a tissue from a box. "Can I?"

"Yes." I sat still as he unclasped my earrings, setting them in my hand, and delicately wiped away my lipstick, using his butane lighter to melt the end of an eyeliner pencil and draw about my eyes, smudging with his fingertips.

He leaned back, considering, then he nodded and combed back my hair, lathering the gel into it to grease it to my skull.

"Voilà," he murmured. "Un beau garçon."

Rising with him to the full-length mirror on the inside of his closet door, I looked at my reflection as he stood behind me, a smile playing across his lips beneath his thin mustache.

"What do you think?" he asked.

"I look like a Helmut Newton photo."

"My favorite photographer. Black and white. Fantasy."

"Erotic," I said.

"That, too. But unobtainable. He photographs only his obsessions, not ours."

He leaned over my shoulder to apply eyeliner to himself. I reached up, taking the pencil from him. "Can I?"

"I would like it," he said.

I turned to him, so close our bodies touched; wetting the burned tip with my tongue, I painted his eyelids, rubbing in the charcoal dust.

He regarded us together in the mirror. "Like twins."

"In decadence."

Jacques brushed my cheek with his lips. "Falling beautifully."

Thadée was smoking another joint as we emerged from the bedroom. He smiled indolently. "The angel and the devil."

Jacques laughed. "I like it, don't you? Good and evil. The eternal battle."

"I do like it," murmured Thadée approvingly. He stood as we retrieved our coats, his six-foot stature looming in the living room.

"Can you drive?" said Jacques, locking the apartment door after we stepped onto the landing. "Or should we take a cab?"

"I think so," said Thadée. "I've driven higher than I am now."

"Take rue de Seine and Quai Voltaire to Pont Royal."

In the car, we smoked more weed. Jacques dabbed coke on the crook of his hand, leaning in from the back seat to lift it to our nostrils.

Rue Sainte-Anne wasn't busy on a weekday, but le Sept had its usual queue of hopefuls lining up, Fabrice ruthlessly dictating his selections.

"Past le Sept," said Jacques. "Find parking, and we'll walk from there."

After circling for over half an hour, Thadée navigated the car into a cramped space, and Jacques led us past bars and local brasseries, into twisting side streets of what remained of the medieval part of the district.

We stopped at a black-painted door, behind which the soaring strings and warbling electric guitar of Love Unlimited Orchestra played.

Jacques looked over his shoulder at us. "Remember, it's just sex. That's all it is."

Inside was a small neon-lit club with Christmas lights strung from the ceiling and a matte-black bar with mirrored bottle shelving. Men danced on the postage-stamp-sized floor, bare-chested, in unbuttoned jeans and boots. Some wore only jockstraps under chaps like those I'd seen on Yves's bedroom floor. Others were in satiny shorts and mesh tanks, like Warhol's stud-groupies.

The music pulsated. The smell of beer and cigarettes, of pungent marijuana and the metal of amyl nitrate, was dense in the smoky air. We'd left our coats in the trunk of the car at Jacques's advice; now I understood why. The heated musk of close-packed bodies wrung perspiration from my pores. Thadée gazed about curiously, his eyes heavy-lidded. Bearded, mustached men at the bar stared back, eyeing him.

A few eyed me, too.

Jacques wove us through the dancing men to the bar, ordering three vodka tonics. The bartender, a hairy-chested man with a potbelly, in a leather vest, greeted Jacques by name as he served us.

"Do you want to dance?" Jacques said in my ear, the music pounding. I glanced at Thadée, who nodded, sipping his vodka.

We jostled in among the men, into the sweating heart of it. I imagined Yves, his glasses misted, his tawny mane soaking, as he leaped with abandon. No one here to ask for his autograph or deliver unsolicited opinions on his latest collection. Just another beautiful man among others, indulging in what Jacques had called the pleasure he felt he must be punished for.

With our drinks in hand, we danced, the rhythm throbbing in our cocaine-seared veins. Men were kissing and feeling each other around us; it was intoxicating to see, so uninhibited in their freedom, without judgment or condemnation.

The music darkened into a street-based rift with a hip-grinding bass that captured and amplified a sensation of mounting sexual joy. I lost myself in it, pressed between Jacques and Thadée, our glasses discarded and our hands on each other's hips in vodka-steeped hedonism.

The tuxedo shirt was plastered wet to my torso, its wilted starched front clinging to my breasts, when Jacques guided us from the floor and toward an open door past the bar, down a steep, narrow staircase glazed in red-bulbed light.

The basement was carved from medieval foundations, a vaulted brick catacomb that might have had its origins as a wine cellar.

Men leaned at the walls, in jockstraps and calf-high boots, fondling themselves. On mattresses on the floor, others bucked into kneeling partners. A trio was engaged in simultaneous oral and anal copulation.

A muscular man in a harness and undone codpiece approached me. I heard Jacques say, "He's here to watch," and the man turned his attention to him. "Not tonight." Jacques coiled his arm about my waist. "I have what I want."

The man said thickly, "Maybe later, then."

Farther back, leather slings were suspended on chains from hooks in the ceiling, swinging and creaking with naked men spread-eagled in them, bound by their wrists, with full masks on their faces—eye slits of anonymity, leather-meshed mouths groaning—as the men standing between their parted legs inserted lubricated black dildos or oiled fists into them. Those watching kissed each other and masturbated.

Now the atmosphere thickened, ladened with the smell of grease and seed. I felt Jacques's arm tighten about me, heard Thadée's breathing shorten behind me.

Jacques turned us around and led us back up the stairs.

Suddenly, I felt faint, stumbling against Thadée. Without a word, Jacques brought us outside, into the night.

"Something beautiful and lasting now," he said, as I gulped in air. "The Eiffel Tower."

THE STRADDLED WROUGHT-IRON spindle pierced the violet sky. On the loam of the Champ de Mars, we lay with our hands behind our heads, gazing up at the city's electric glow refracted by the distant half-moon.

We hadn't spoken since leaving the club.

Thadée said, "A decadent fall."

"It is." Jacques sat up, curling his arms about his knees. "It can be beautiful."

He turned his red-rimmed hazel eyes to us. Despite our consumption, he appeared sober and, to me, imbued with inescapable sadness.

I reached up to touch his face. He kissed my palm. "Now you know."

"He wants to be free," I said. "To be like you."

"Not like me." Jacques's smile was fleeting. "To not be him."

He came to his feet, humming the overture of Verdi's *La traviata*, Yves's most beloved opera. In a low, smoke-husked tenor, he sang softly,

Libiam, amor fra' calici più caldi baci avrà
Tra voi, tra voi, saprò dividere il tempo, mio Giocondo
Tutto è follia, follia nel mondo ciò che non è piacer
Godiam, fugace e rapido è il gaudio dell'amore.

Drink, love among the warmest glasses, we will have kisses
Among you, among you, I will know how
to divide the time, my playful one
Everything is madness, madness in the world that is not pleasure
Let us enjoy the joy of love, fleeting and rapid.

Standing up, Thadée and I embraced him on the loam, swaying to the aria, his voice drifting and fading into an echo in the night.

WE DROVE HIM home. There were no promises to call, no expressions of gratitude or enjoyment found in each other's company.

He exited the car and walked into rue du Dragon.

Thadée drove to my district to drop me off. As I gathered my bag and coat from the back seat of his car, he said, "This is really not safe for Yves."

"Yes." I pulled on the door handle and slid out. "I know."

18

For our fall couture, we presented modifications on Yves's classics: his le Smoking in light wool with white piping. His peacoat and peasant dress. His translucent-sleeved gowns and billowy chiffon blouses, tailored pantsuits and appliquéd coatdresses.

The business was earning millions. Our Rive Gauche prêt-à-porter, the scents and cologne, the menswear—everything was selling out, as were the licensed products. Even the cigarette brand Yves detested so much he'd refused to approve the packaging concept had sold.

Yet a challenge was issued in the new year of 1975 by Revlon's new perfume, Charlie, whose wholesome girl-about-town scent and athletic, fresh-faced international campaign reaped record profits, eclipsing the venerable and, until now, invulnerable Chanel No. 5 as the world's bestselling women's fragrance.

Not to be deterred, Pierre whipped up a counterproposal for a genderless Yves Saint Laurent scent, spurred by information garnered by his associates that Halston had one in the works, backed to the hilt by Norton Simon Inc.

Halston's signature scent, presented in an opaque tear-drop bottle with a lopsided top designed by his muse, Peretti, was an instant success. He achieved his lifelong ambition to overshadow Yves, if only for a season, and threw a celebratory star-studded party in New York in his own honor, where he invited us to kiss the ring while he gloated.

Our spring trip to New York was spun for the press as a publicity visit for Eau Libre, Yves's new fragrance. But with nothing but Yves's fame to promote it, the fragrance sank under the weight of Halston's ferocity and his corporate backers' boundless advertising budget. But we partied at the Factory and various new dance clubs, staying up till dawn with Fernando and Warhol and his nubile superstars. The overwhelming crowd at our boutique terrified Yves, mobbing us on the sidewalk before we could get inside. When a shrieking fan tried to grab a fistful of his hair, Yves put an end to public appearances.

He'd become too famous. Everywhere he turned, strangers were intrusive; no place felt protected to him, except the studio, the homes of his friends, or le Sept and Régine's, where he could socialize, the proprietors ensuring he'd not be disturbed.

I stayed for a week in New York with my mother. John passed away quietly, after a prolonged struggle, his face beatific in its jaundiced emaciation as he breathed his last, Mama silently holding his hand, without tears.

She'd told me when the time came, she would grieve, but I didn't see it. I worried for her, even though I knew she must be mourning him, in her way. Yet the lack of any evidence of it stirred long-buried resentment in me, as we flew to England after John's cremation for my brother's delayed wedding.

It was a simple ceremony, Alexis determined to not make a fuss. I had to return to Paris to start working on the next collection, and I made repeated offers to Mama to come stay with me for a time.

As we were packing our bags in our shared room in the London hotel, she finally snapped, "How many times are you going to ask? Do you think I'll fall apart at the seams without a husband? I was alone for years after I left your father. You have your work, your own life to live. I don't need you to coddle me."

Her retort was so unexpected, and so seemingly indifferent to my concern, I saw her as I had in my childhood: beautiful and savage. Not a mother. A stranger.

"I know how capable you are." I threw my underwear into my bag. "No one knows it better than me."

She paused. "What's that supposed to mean?"

"Nothing." Belatedly, I scooped out my mess of panties to fold them.

"Just say it." Her tone turned stony. "You've wanted to say it to me for years."

Glaring at her, I said through my teeth, "John died. You're acting as if it doesn't matter. Like Alexis and I didn't matter."

With a sigh, she said, "I left because I took a lover. Your father threatened to sue me for adultery. In France, a wife was guilty if the husband accused her, regardless of the circumstances. They would have taken my children away from me."

"They took us anyway. We were sent to foster families. Boarding schools."

"Your father did that. He took his revenge on me through our children. I was denied custody. What was I to do?"

"Care." I flung the word at her. "Care, and fight for us. But you took a lover. A job in Paris. We didn't fit into your new life."

"Well, I got it right in the face, didn't I?" Pacing to the bedroom side table, she took up my cigarettes, lighting one. "I suppose I deserve it."

"Don't turn this on me. I offered to bring you to Paris to stay with me."

"Your poor, bereaved mother. What a tragedy. Maxime de la Falaise: she used to be somebody. We're not sure who, but we've heard her name in passing. Didn't she design a collection?"

I felt sick to my stomach. "You don't want to come to Paris because of *that*?"

"I want John alive." She flicked ash to the floor. "I want to not be his widow. You judge me for being a bad mother—and I was. I am. But I wasn't a bad wife to John. You judged me for that, too. I saw how you and Alexis fled the apartment on Christmas Eve."

I slammed my suitcase shut, though I hadn't folded a shred of underwear. "You were feeling up his photographer lover. Right in front of us."

"And?" She regarded me with near disdain over her cigarette. "Haven't you ever done something just to please someone else? I loved John, and he loved me. He was attracted to men, so I let him know that I didn't mind. That I understood."

Sinking onto the edge of the bed, I said numbly, "Why did you marry him?"

"Why? Oh, darling. Why do we do anything in life?" She moved to sit beside me. "To be loved, Loulou. To love. You do it for Yves. Every day. You give him what he needs. You sacrifice for him."

"It's not the same. I work with him. I'm never going to marry him."

"Given our track record with husbands, thank God. Imagine the chaos."

I had to bite my lip to stanch a burst of sudden, sour laughter. "I don't sacrifice for him, either. I love working with him. It makes me happy."

"And you love making him happy. You don't see it as a sacrifice, like I didn't see it for John. We're more alike than you think." Standing, she crushed out the cigarette in the ashtray. "I appreciate the offer. I may take you up on it later. But right now, I have his estate to settle. His private collections, his beloved photographs of all that awful Victorian ghoulishness of corpses in caskets, on display in parlors. I need to do that first, and learn to be without him."

"I'm sorry." I felt awful for what I'd said. "I didn't mean it."

She gave me a look. "Of course you did. It was about time. But look at how you turned out without me. Now, go to Paris and be happy. One of us has to be."

AT THE AIRPORT the next day, as we separated for our flights, she kissed my cheeks, in a French goodbye. "Tell him you want to design something. You needn't be a martyr to la maison Saint Laurent. You give him inspiration, so he can return the favor. Really, darling. I designed one collection that didn't carry or make my name, but"—she posed as she had at Christmas, one hand on her hip and her head thrown back, eliciting stares from passengers in transit—"I did it. It's *my* collection."

YVES WAS INSPIRED, bringing in armfuls of sketches, enough for several collections. Scattering them on the studio floor, Anne-Marie and I spent hours with him debating the designs, choosing what we thought might work best, and then rampaging for fabrics in our now-extended shelving.

"For this collection," Yves said, "I want you to design the accessories." He smiled at my astonishment, as if he'd overheard my mother at the airport. "I've seen you making them for yourself after hours, like a magpie. The gypsy earrings and bracelets, those odd, chunky necklaces. Will you?"

I hugged him, overwhelmed by his generosity and his uncanny prescience. I'd never aspired to see my name on the label; if I had, I only needed to look to my mother's example, and Yves's. Everything that could go astray or fall by the wayside, the constant pressure, and what Mama deemed sacrifice. Yet the truth was I had become a designer despite it, through my work with him. "How did you know?"

"Know?" His hand pressed at my nape, nesting my head on

his shoulder. "I like your chunky, odd jewelry. You've designed pieces for our lines. Why not our jewelry?"

"I . . ." My voice flooded.

"Was it very terrible?" he murmured.

"She buried him, and then we went to my brother's wedding." I drew back, looking into his intent blue eyes. "She's devastated. She must learn to live without him."

"I can't imagine it. Bring her here. Pierre would love to meet her. So would I. She worked with Elsa Schiaparelli. Pierre wanted us to hire you because of it. Remember?"

"I do. He brought me that newspaper clipping. And I thought he liked my style."

"Your style was why *I* wanted to hire you. Lobster hats aren't my thing."

I smiled. "I'll tell her. She says she might come later."

His fingertips wiped the smudged mascara from tears I'd almost shed. "She's always welcome here. This is your home, too, my Loulou. It's *our* house."

And for the first time since we'd met, I let myself believe it.

ON AUGUST 1, YVES turned thirty-nine. He didn't want a big celebration, just an intimate gathering at rue de Babylone. Instead, over two weeks of planning under Pierre, it ballooned into an all-night bacchanal, as he kept adding names to the guest list that he believed we couldn't ignore, if not for the monetary value to the house, then for their social significance. Caterers were hired, the duplex steam-cleaned to pristine luster. White lilies were dispersed everywhere in crystal vases.

One of the names Pierre included was Lagerfeld. Yves seemed oddly unperturbed by it, having resigned himself to being the center of unwanted attention. To me, it was evidence that whatever Pierre might suspect, he still didn't know about Yves and Jacques.

To complement the decor, I wore a white bugle-beaded dress from our latest collection, with bulky fake-pearl accessories of my own design. Yves chose a severe black velvet suit and white-polka-dotted bow tie. When I arrived early at the duplex, in case extra help was needed, the catering staff was bustling about, setting up cloth-draped tables on the terrace for a buffet.

Yves pulled me aside with a drawn-out sigh. "It's Capote's black-and-white ball. I don't even like half the people Pierre invited. I wanted a dinner party with my friends and a game of charades."

I kissed his cheek. "It's your birthday. We should celebrate it."

"Why?" He made a helpless gesture. "One year older, and every year, less to say."

I knew aging was frightening for him, as it was for most people in fashion, especially those who reached its echelons. Our business revered youth and depended on it. Even if some of our dwindling couture clients neared their dotage by now, creating the illusion of youthful freshness was essential. Our Rive Gauche customers were mostly young women who idolized him. Our menswear clientele likewise was mostly young and gay; the nude photo of Yves for the cologne advertisement had become a treasured pinup in gay bars. Eternal youth was what we sold. The chimera that it could be bought.

"Chanel was still designing well into her sixties," I said.

"And she was wretched." His smile was wan. "Living in the Ritz, barking at the staff, and eating the same dinner of filet mignon and salad every night."

"What would you do, if you stopped designing?" I'd never asked him before; and as silver platters with canapés were set out on the tables and scented candles lit in glass containers, he gazed toward the city skyline as though he also had never reflected on it.

"We could live in an attic room somewhere in the Marais: you, me, and Thadée. Drink red wine, smoke opium, and write bad plays."

That he'd cited Thadée as part of our trio made my breath catch. He shrugged. "It's very silly of me."

"No," I said softly. "It's not silly. It's wonderful."

Guests began to appear, and he straightened his spine. Pierre, stout in his tuxedo, motioned from the living room for Yves to come stand beside him to welcome the arrivals.

Karl came with Jacques, who wore a black suit and shirt sprouting a white splayed collar, an abstract-patterned green-and-pink Chloé silk scarf about his shoulders.

Seeing them together jarred me. I'd conjured an image of them from what Jacques had told me at the birthday party for Karl: of him costumed as Garbo or Valentino—the raw clay for Karl to mold into an ideal. Yet they had a distinct ease of motion about them, a familiarity that, while maybe not that of a couple, still evoked its secret language.

I had to stop myself from staring to catch them in a furtive act, a quick clasp of hands or prolonged look that would confirm Jacques had misled Yves about their physical relationship. But he and Karl greeted Yves and Pierre briefly, and then divided up, each of them moving to opposite corners of the room.

By then, guests spilled out onto the terrace and crowded the living room, the air filled with cigarette smoke and animated conversation.

Jacques was soon charming everyone with his effortless élan and knowledge of obscure historical scandals. Betty, casually chic in one of our black jumpsuits and an emerald silk pajama jacket, chatted with him for an hour. Clara hugged Karl, sat with him on the sofa, and insisted on being regaled with details of his career, which he seemed to downplay, though we all knew he flourished. His perfume for Chloé had taken him on his own publicity tour in New York, with a fawning feature in Warhol's *Interview*, replete with allegedly candid photographs of Karl, Jacques, and José in a limousine, sporting aviator sunglasses and brandishing fistfuls of dollars.

As I observed Jacques milling through the crowd, stopping to express admiration for a watch or earrings on a guest, I also had the sense that something had changed in him.

It was indefinable, almost imperceptible, as he'd never displayed diffidence in public as far as I was aware. Jacques struck me as someone always in his element before admirers. But his sparkle was less overt, as though he no longer felt the need to attract attention. The interest sparked to him instead, drawn to his youth and elegance, his self-assurance.

Yves's eyes stalked Jacques. The studious way they avoided each other, even when corralled together in awkward conversation by an intoxicated third party, told me everything.

They were still seeing each other.

I wasn't certain how to construe it. Faced with the unmistakable fact that Karl and Jacques must share more than either would admit, I suddenly thought that here might be the danger. Yves couldn't expect a commitment; he had to accept that what had gone on between him and Jacques must eventually come to an end.

Betty sidled up to me, a champagne flute in her hand. "I'm drunk, and I haven't finished my second glass. Children, Loulou: don't ever have them. It spoils your life."

I smiled. "You look radiant. It must be doing something for you."

"Don't say that." She shook her blond mane from her shoulders. "Everyone keeps telling me how wonderful I look. It's like they think motherhood is a miracle fountain of youth. They wouldn't be so complimentary if they saw my tits. I need a crane to lift them up, or I'll trip right over them."

We started giggling, and Yves hurried over to us. "What? What's so funny?"

"Betty's tits," I whispered. "She says she's tripping over them."

"*Tripping* over them?" He blinked in confusion.

Betty yanked down the zipper of her jumpsuit. She wore nothing on underneath.

"They look . . ." Yves paused to scrutinize her fuller breasts, concentrating as if he were assessing a modèle. ". . . sublime to me."

Betty cackled. "This, from a man who never sleeps with tits."

"Betty." He leaned toward her, as if in surprise. "I would have slept with yours, if you'd only asked me."

She pinched his cheek. "Le petit prince. You get away with murder with that smile."

He put an arm around each of us. "My beautiful muses. How can I not want to sleep with, and worship, both of you?"

"Bonne anniversaire, petit prince," we chanted in unison, kissing his cheeks.

A camera flashed. Jacques smiled as he lowered it. "So beautiful."

He gave me a wink and drifted back into the crowd.

Yves tensed, excusing himself to talk to Clara and Thadée, murmuring that he hadn't the chance, bombarded by birthday well-wishers and strangers in his home. I saw him edge a path to where Jacques posed by the white bookshelves, interspersed with terra-cotta Grecian urns. Karl's arm snaked about Jacques's waist as Pierre wielded his own camera to snap pictures of them.

"That young man's very attractive, but also very strange," said Betty. "Like he walked out of a Proust novel." She deposited her unfinished flute on a passing waiter's tray. "He behaves as if we still ride in carriages and leave calling cards."

"I think he behaves as Karl wants him to behave," I said cautiously.

"Hmm." She cocked her hip in an unconscious mannequin's jut. "It seems to me that Karl lets him do as he pleases. I don't see a leash on him."

Her remark spiraled inexplicable alarm in me.

"Anyway," she said with a sigh, "I'm falling asleep on my feet. Pathetic. Two in the morning, and less than four years ago, I'd have been flashing my tits on the dance floor at le Sept. Now I just want my bed and my husband."

"Good night." I embraced her. "Don't be a stranger. Come flash your tits at the studio. Yves and I would love to see you there."

"And face the wrath of Anne-Marie for lewd behavior in the sanctum sanctorum? I wear the clothes and don't set foot near the hôtel until the day of the show, remember?" She searched the crowd for François. "I've ended up with no life anyway, but the studio is a no-Betty zone. There he is. He already has our coats."

Sipping my nearly finished and uncounted flute of champagne, I was moving to refill it when Thadée was suddenly beside me.

"Loulou, we can't keep doing this."

Through my suddenly forced smile, I said, "Do what?"

"This." He spoke quietly, firmly. "Whatever it is we're doing."

"You're asking me *now*?" I glanced at him, unable to curb my flare of anger. "At Yves's birthday gathering, in front of everyone?"

"It's a party. We can talk freely here. No one's paying attention to us." He made a move as if to touch my arm, and I recoiled.

"I need to know, Loulou. Now's as good a time as any. I won't keep hoping if there's nothing for me to hope for."

"Then don't hope." My own words blistered my mouth. "It's what we decided."

His face clouded. "Did we decide it? Or are we just too afraid to decide, so we don't?"

I was starting to panic, glancing about us, thinking everyone must be overhearing. Betty and François had been waylaid in their escape by Clara, glazy-eyed with champagne and loquacious in her red polka-dot bow-tie dress from our recent prêt-à-porter. On her it looked like a staid uniform, and she was fixated on them, not us.

"On the terrace," I said. "We can smoke out there and talk about what we're too afraid to decide."

It was the last thing I wanted to do, but other guests were beginning to depart, sifting around Betty and François, who were holding their coats as Clara warbled. Betty rolled her eyes at me over Clara's head; once she managed to extricate herself, Clara would seek out Thadée to leave, as she had at la Mamounia. I had to face him, even if he was right: I had no idea what we'd decided, and I didn't want to admit it. Because once I did, I might have to stop hoping, too.

The buffet tables had been ransacked; the terrace was empty. It wrapped around the upper floor of the duplex; as I staked a spot at the far end, reaching for my cigarettes in my beaded wrist bag that scarcely held the pack, a joint, and my lipstick, I discerned agitated voices, trying to stay muted. They were just around the corner from where I stood, blocked from my view.

"You told me it was over." Yves, his tone fracturing. "I was desperate."

"I told you we needed time apart. You sent me a dozen letters."

Yves and Jacques, arguing.

A tension-laden silence. Then Yves said, "I called you first. No one answered."

"I wasn't home."

"Where were you?" Another silence. Then Yves, in an audibly ragged effort to preserve his dignity: "I can't do this here."

"You don't have to do this at all," said Jacques.

"Jacques, wait. Tomorrow. Please, meet me at the penthouse." Yves's voice quavered; I could hear tears inundating him. "Will you?"

At Thadée's footstep behind me, I gripped his arm in warning. He went still.

"Yves, don't start crying. It's your birthday party."

"Then you'll come see me tomorrow night? Stay with me?"

"I'll come see you, but I can't promise to stay."

Still gripping Thadée, I pulled him into the shadows of the terrace, hastily lighting my cigarette, forcing out a feigned, drunken laugh.

We didn't speak until Jacques walked past us back into the duplex, followed a few minutes later by Yves, his shoulders slouched and his head lowered.

"They stopped seeing each other," I whispered. "Something happened."

"What?" He took my cigarette from me to puff anxiously on it.

"I don't know. I thought everything had calmed down."

"Yves is in love," he said. "It's never calm. Just the calm between storms."

I resisted the metaphor. "He has to know it can't last."

"Does he? Or is he doing what we are: Delaying? Not deciding either way? He hasn't left Pierre yet. Something happened with Jacques, but you're not saying what."

"Yves—" I swallowed. "He almost started crying. He was begging Jacques to go see him at the penthouse. Jacques said they needed time apart, but Yves kept calling and sending him letters."

Thadée handed me the cigarette, smoked nearly to the filter. "That sounds bad."

I abruptly felt as if I were on the edge of the chasm. "It did."

"Jacques wants to end it, and Yves isn't letting him go. He's obsessed with him."

The chasm crumbled under my feet. What Thadée was saying carried a double meaning. He was saying what we couldn't admit about us—what I didn't dare.

"But what can we do?" I managed to utter. "We tried. We can't interfere again."

"We can ask Jacques directly if he's really ending it. Then we'll know for sure, and we can help Yves get through it."

"He's supposed to see Yves tomorrow. It's too late to—" I saw his expression darken, and I found myself saying, "What are you doing the day after?"

"What I do every day. As little as possible."

"We'll call Jacques." I met his stare. "We take him out again, to ask him."

JACQUES AGREED TO meet us at le Sept. This time, we weren't concerned about being seen. He and Karl had attended Yves's birthday party, along with almost everyone who was anyone in Paris, so it no longer mattered if we were recognized in public with Jacques. His presence at the party marked him as someone we could socialize with.

He arrived dressed in black from head to toe. It turned his eyes under his slicked hair golden in the restaurant's faux-gaslit glow. He'd trimmed his mustache to a mere pencil stroke above his lips. His matinee-idol guise, but more refined. Darker.

Ordering food and drinks, we talked about the party: who'd

shown up uninvited and what people had been wearing, with him complimenting me. "I would have thought white would be too bridal on you, but you wear it beautifully."

A compliment? Or a hint at seeing me and Thadée together? I suddenly felt too exposed to him. We'd invited him into our lives; now the three of us had secrets we shared. I'd never said a word to him about Thadée and me, but how could I have thought he wouldn't notice? He'd danced with us that night at the club. He must have sensed it.

I evaded his remark to broach the subject. "I was going out onto the terrace to smoke the other night at the party. I overheard you and Yves."

He nodded. "I heard you laughing. It wasn't your laugh."

"I've never been good at pretense," I said.

"That's one of the things I like most about you. You don't pretend."

Thadée coughed, reached for his cigarettes. Jacques lit for him a new lighter—rose gold, I noticed. It looked expensive, custom-made, not something he could afford. Then I noticed, as he extended the flame to Thadée, that he also wore a matching rose-gold wristwatch, not his black-banded one. I couldn't bring myself to remark on it, though he'd remarked on my attire at Yves's party; it felt superfluous, and we'd invited him here to find out about Yves, not his new accessories.

But it was on the tip of my tongue to ask anyway. Then Jacques lit his own cigarette in its long white filter, yanking me to attention.

"You must be wondering why we were arguing."

"It's not our business," I said, "but yes, we are. Yves sounded very upset."

"He was. He is." Jacques took in smoke. "I ended it. I did it for Yves."

"For him?" said Thadée. "I think that's the last thing he wants."

"He thinks that, too. For now. But it's better for him to hurt now instead of later, when he's decided on something he regrets."

"Is that really what you want?" I discerned subdued pain in his voice and thought of the cramped apartment, the wealth measured only in clothes. A twenty-four-year-old man without means of his own, fifteen years younger than Yves, who, at his age, had already become a fashion prince. Did he think he had nothing to offer?

"It's too obsessive," he said. "He doesn't understand, but it's hurting him. It doesn't make him happy anymore. He's miserable."

Thadée's foot brushed mine under the table, as if to tell me it was over. But I didn't feel relieved. Jacques was hurting, too.

"I went to see him last night," Jacques went on. "He begged me to stay the night with him. I did. In the morning, he promised me again that he'll leave Pierre."

"You don't think he will," said Thadée.

"No, I think he will." He tapped ash into the ashtray, circling his cigarette tip in it, then dropped the cigarette half smoked from the filter and left it to smolder. "I know he will. That's why I ended it, before he does."

He'd confronted the impossibility of the affair, everything that would be torn asunder; the irreversible step over that invisible boundary, where Yves might shatter.

I started to touch his hand on the table. "I'm sorry."

He withdrew his fingers. "You don't need to be. It's better this way."

In the discomfort following his assurance, we ordered coffee, though he didn't drink his, and by now, we were sieving for words. Fabrice never charged me. None of us in Yves's circle ever saw a bill at le Sept, but as I reached in my bag to tip the waiter,

Jacques said, "Let me," and he removed a wallet from his black damask vest.

The restaurant door swung open. All three of us lifted our eyes to it at the same time. The chatter at the nearby tables faltered and fell silent.

Yves staggered in, his hair tangled about his face, his glasses fogged, in stained white jeans and a black cable-knit sweater, which was too hot for August, and had been wrenched out of shape, as if he'd been tugging and yanking at it.

Thadée came to his feet, moving out of the banquette to let me go to him.

Yves thrust out a trembling hand to detain my advance, lurching to the table, where Jacques sat as if frozen in place. I smelled the reek of whiskey wafting from Yves.

"I—I've been looking everywhere for you." Yves slurred his words at Jacques. Clutching his arm, Thadée forcibly lowered him onto the banquette.

Jacques sidled in on his side of the table to allow me to sit.

"I called your apartment." Yves gazed imploringly at Jacques. "No one answered, so I went there."

The waiter came over with a glass of water. "Would monsieur like to see a menu?"

"Just espresso, please," I said. "Very strong."

Yves was blinking through his glasses; Thadée took them from his nose and wiped the condensation off the lenses. Putting them on lopsided, Yves said, his voice cracking, "José told me you came here with Loulou and Thadée."

He glanced at me—a look of such betrayal that it stabbed through me.

"They invited me," said Jacques. "I wanted to say goodbye."

"Goodbye?" Yves's pained echo brought Thadée's hand to his

leg, squeezing it. In vain, Yves tried to quiet the panic rising in his voice. "*Why* are you saying that? Where are you going?"

Jacques said, "Yves, let's not do this again. Not here."

"Then where?" A sob broke in his throat. "Where do you want to do this? I'll go anywhere. Just tell me, please."

Jacques started to shift past me on the banquette.

Yves covered his face with his hands. "Don't go. Why are you leaving me? *Why* are you doing this to me?"

I met Jacques's eyes, biting my lip, trying to stop myself from crying.

Jacques said, "Yves. You know why I'm leaving."

"I don't know," moaned Yves. "I don't understand anything."

"Can't you stay?" I struggled for a smile as Jacques hesitated. My mouth wasn't moving right; it felt inert. "Forget all this for tonight." At his subtle frown, I forced out the smile, straining my lips. "Let's go downstairs and dance. The four of us, as friends."

Yves lifted his pleading, tear-streaked gaze.

"All right," said Jacques quietly. "After Yves drinks his coffee, we'll go dance."

THE FLOOR WAS packed. The throwing aside of the week's cares, of life's cares, to revel in music, in freely circulating drugs, and in the forgetting of others.

Fabrice had reserved a small table for us, consummate and ever discreet.

Watered-down drinks were delivered, also at Fabrice's discretion. Yves gulped his and tore off his misshapen sweater. He wore a white T-shirt underneath, dampened by his frantic race through Paris, molded to his thin form as he stood, swaying, like a toppling pilaster, and careened onto the floor, shoving into the crowd.

He was recognized—he was always recognized here—and they parted as much as they could for him. Hastening to join him, lest he stumbled or fell, I heard Diana Ross come over the speakers, her breathy defiance in "Ain't No Mountain High Enough."

Yves faltered.

It was a song that had been playing the night we danced here, when he first saw Jacques without his shirt, suckling a finger and trailing it across Yves's shoulder . . .

Thadée and Jacques came onto the floor. As they began to dance, Jacques undulated, the lights splashing neon patches on his obscured form. Thadée drew me away, murmuring in my ear, "Let them be together."

Yves flung his arms over his head, moving frenetically. His hair was soon sopping wet, spraying droplets; he sang the lyrics off-key as he keeled into those around him.

Jacques made as if to steady him. Yves angrily shook him away, and then Jacques's arms, draped in the raven wings of his sleeves, enveloped him. Yves crumpled, his head on Jacques's shoulder as Jacques led him off the floor.

Jacques held him slumped about his waist as Yves began to sob uncontrollably.

"I'll take him to his penthouse," he told us.

"I can drive you." Thadée fished in his pocket for his car keys.

"I'll ask Fabrice to call a taxi. I don't feel his keys in his pocket. He didn't drive here, and he probably locked himself out of the apartment. I still have the key."

Thadée looked uncertain.

Jacques said, "I'll stay with him tonight. He's going to be sick later. He did more than drink. Don't worry. Stay here, have fun."

He didn't wait for our reply, guiding Yves up the stairs.

"His sweater." I rushed to retrieve it from the table, but they were already gone, and I didn't want to cause more of a scene by following them out to deliver the sweater.

Crushing it into my bag, I stood, helpless, gazing at the stairs as people pranced down them, drinks in hand, laughing and pouncing onto the dance floor.

The music faded to an indistinct rumble in my ears.

Thadée said, "We need to let it go. Yves needs to let it go. It's over."

Turning to him, I buried my face in his chest.

I didn't think in that moment that I was showing him how I felt by seeking succor in his embrace against the pain of seeing Yves falling apart, but with the tender grasp of his arms about me, strong and protective, he told me that he knew.

He understood that what we'd just witnessed was something we should never bring upon the people we knew, rending and upending their lives.

Or upon ourselves.

19

I didn't hear from or see Yves for over a week. At this time of year, we'd normally be returning from Marrakesh to prepare our fall couture, or he'd be returning from a trip abroad with Pierre. For the past several years, trips with Pierre had become infrequent; Yves preferred the privacy of Dar el-Hanch, where he could create without strangers recognizing and accosting him.

The studio felt poised in suspense, waiting for his footstep to cross the threshold, the clicking of his dogs' nails, Moujik's ill-tempered growl. Then there would be his gentle inquiry as to how the women's weekends had been, his pause to ask Anne-Marie about her husband and children, and his donning of his white smock, his little sigh as he lifted his chin and started the day's work.

Today it felt as it always did when he wasn't there, except now there was a palpable tension to it, the familiar tapestry on its loom losing a vital thread, the weft unraveling.

When he appeared in the afternoon without advance notice, his eyes hidden behind his sunglasses, not saying a word as he traversed the workroom to his studio, Anne-Marie motioned at the women.

"I want to see those hands busy. Monsieur is here. We have modèles to finish."

Slipping from my stool at my worktable by the window, I motioned at Anne-Marie to have coffee brought and went into

Yves's studio. He sat on his chair behind his desk, a cigarette smoldering between his nicotine-stained fingers.

"The modèles are almost ready—"

"Something's wrong." Ash scattered onto his sketch pad on the desk. "He's not returning my calls again."

Swallowing the lump in my throat, I said, "There's always been something wrong."

He glanced up, sharply, at me. "Why do you say that?"

"Yves, you know how much I care for you . . ."

His posture shrank. The cigarette dropped into the ashtray; he lit another with quivering hands.

"You can't ask him for what he doesn't have to give." I moved toward him. At his flinch, I pulled up the padded stool where I always sat and chattered to him for hours while he sketched. "What's wrong isn't him or you. It's both of you, together."

"Because of what?" His voice was leaden. He knew.

"It's not meant to be. He's twenty-four. He hasn't done anything with his life—"

"You were the same age when I met you, and hadn't done anything with yours."

I let his retort bite into me. "It isn't just that. He's not in the same place as you."

"And?" His eyes lifted, hard and cold, but the pain lurked behind them, bottomless. "I can give him everything he needs. Anything he wants."

"At what cost?" I asked.

"Whatever it costs."

I folded my hands in my lap. The silence grew rigid between us. It was as if our friendship, the honesty that had always existed between us, had been bricked into a wall he'd erected, behind which he could hide, refusing what he understood to be true.

I finally said, "Maybe he doesn't want it, no matter what it costs."

His chin trembled. "Jacques is young. He doesn't know what he wants."

"That's my point. He doesn't know. You do. Something has always been wrong."

He drew on his cigarette, coughed. "You've been seeing him."

"Twice. The night you saw us at le Sept and once before that." I didn't want to tell him about the first time; then I realized he might already know, because Jacques had told him that I'd gone to his apartment on rue du Dragon to question him.

He answered me as if he did. "He likes you. Respects you."

"I like him, too. But that doesn't stop it from being wrong for both of you."

He smudged the ash into his sketch pad, the same act of erasure he'd done when Pierre insisted on us attending Karl's birthday party. "You could talk to him."

"Yves, I—"

"Not to convince him." His eyes teared up, the pain now surfacing, carving hollows. "So he can explain it to me. We—all we do is argue now. I don't hear him. I don't think he hears me. I . . . I get drunk, and then it's terrible for me."

"I think it's terrible for him, too. He doesn't want to hurt you."

"I know he doesn't, but he does." Yves kept pressing his fingers into the ash. "I just want to understand it. Hear him explain it to me. I won't beg him anymore. I need to talk to him without getting angry. To . . . to say goodbye."

I whispered, "What do you want me to do?"

His inhale shuddered through him. "Ask him to come to my penthouse for dinner. Nothing fancy. Rustic, comforting." His fragile smile ached my heart. "Bring Thadée. He wanted to say goodbye to both of you the other night, and I wouldn't let him."

"We don't need to say—" I cut myself short. "I can try. He might not want to."

"No, he might not." He bowed his head.

"I'll try." I stood, leaning toward him and kissing his head. "I'll try."

THADÉE MET ME at the corner of les Invalides. He had brought two bottles of red wine. I carried a sack with baguettes, cheese, and pâté, strawberries and bananas and a jar of honey to make a simple fruit salad, which he took from me and shouldered.

"Did Jacques confirm?" he asked, as I pressed the call button for the elevator.

"I left him a message." I checked my lipstick in my compact mirror. I'd put some on and painted my nails red. I wore my Rive Gauche boots and the iridescent ocher-and-russet cotton peasant dress with the pale saffron swirls and high, ruffled neckline. "He didn't call me back."

He made a troubled sound. "Loulou, this might not be—"

"Yves asked it of me. What could I say? 'No'? 'I won't try'?"

He nodded, and we stepped into the elevator. "I don't like seeing him like this."

"Neither do I."

The elevator opened, and more than its door opened in me. Thadée and I had been assiduous in avoiding any discussion about us; he'd broached it at the birthday party, and we'd gone out to the terrace to talk about what we'd supposedly not decided, and then we hadn't. Neither of us had brought it up again.

It was another wall, one we'd built deliberately, and I didn't know how to break through it. After the night at le Sept and my moment of weakness, I'd also retreated behind it, to hide my longing for what could never be.

"We'll have dinner with him," I said at the door. "Spend time with him. He's lonely and lost. He needs his friends. Then, when Jacques doesn't show up, we'll pick up the pieces until he agrees to go back to rue de Babylone."

"To Pierre, who's too busy being president of the Syndicale to notice Yves is desperate." Thadée returned my gaze. "It's never been that way, either. Pierre has always noticed when Yves goes too far."

"Maybe Pierre knows he can't do anything but let it burn itself out."

Yves answered the door, barefoot, in his laundered white jeans and a tobacco-colored paisley shirt open at his neck. His hair was brushed in soft waves. He'd visited his hairstylist, had his hair cut shorter. I smelled a faint trace of his men's cologne on him as he kissed my cheeks and then Thadée's.

His eyes passed over me, a little smile lifting his mouth. "You finally wore the dress I made for you. It's so lovely on you."

"I thought it was time to wear it." I touched his cheek. "You know me well enough to dress me by now."

He'd set out plates and wineglasses on the living room table, a fresh bunch of his favorite white lilies in the clear crystal vase. White taper candles lit in silver holders. The apartment spotless from a recent cleaning service, and the windows ajar, the tidal static of traffic on les Invalides dampened by the apartment's cul-de-sac location.

A record played low on the stereo, which I hadn't seen during my visits here, but must be tucked inside the white living room cabinetry: Roberta Flack. The speakers had been wired and placed on either side of the sofa.

As her hoarse lament floated through the penthouse, I unpacked the food and started cutting up the fruit in a bowl. He'd bought new dishes, the kitchen cabinet stocked with them. Extra cutlery in the drawers, as if he were setting up a permanent home.

A pang constricted me. I immediately suppressed it.

Thadée sat with him on the sofa, sharing a joint and conversing. I heard Yves chuckle. "No, no. I didn't design that dress. She keeps telling everyone I did, but anyone who knows my work can see it isn't mine. It looks as if it had fallen off a balcony on her by accident, like an overturned flowerpot."

Thadée laughed. I thought Yves sounded more like himself, his wicked asides on fashion faux pas.

"Shall we eat?" I asked, and there was a difficult hush before Yves assented.

"Yes. It's getting late."

We didn't hear the elevator. Thadée and I had taken off our shoes; I'd stuffed my headscarf in my bag and sat cross-legged on the carpet, drinking wine, laughing, telling Thadée, "Jane Birkin was leaping around, showing her thong to the audience, and Jourdan had these bizarre furry ears on. No one knew what they were."

"Cat ears," said Yves. "Or donkey ears. Ungaro makes such exquisite clothes, his tailoring's almost as fine as Balenciaga's, and they stage his segment like *Cat Ballou*. If he'd invited Jane Fonda, she might have saved it."

"Jane Fonda as Barbarella couldn't have saved Cardin," I said, and Yves burst out laughing. "That rocket ship landing shook the entire theater. It was like an atomic bomb. And the dismal music, those vinyl suits: everything in black on the stage, with no lighting to see the clothes. A science fiction funeral."

"But," said Yves, holding his stomach to keep from falling

over in hilarious collapse, "we stole the show. Drag queens in red velvet like circus elephants, stomping around and farting, while Zizi screamed 'Just a Gigolo' as if her life depended on it."

Thadée roared his belly laugh, tears streaming down his face. "I should have been there. I love elephants."

"Who'd eaten everything not nailed down in Paris—" Yves abruptly stopped.

From the door, which we'd left unlocked, Jacques said, "I'm sorry I'm late."

I swerved my head to him. He stood with a bottle of wine in his hand, in a crisp white shirt under a cropped, unstructured black linen jacket and wide-belted button-up jeans, crimped about lace-up walking boots. His hair had been smoothed across his brow. "I'm sorry," he said again, an uncomfortable almost-smile on his lips.

"No, no." Yves started to rise. I came to my feet first, taking the bottle from him.

"Thank you," he murmured, "for inviting me."

"Yves invited you," I said quickly, and then, louder, "We were just telling Thadée about Versailles. Sit. There's still plenty of food."

Uncorking the wine in the kitchen, I watched him remove his jacket and drape it over the back of a chair, then sit on the carpet.

"Jacques served champagne at the pre-gala reception," Yves told Thadée, nervousness seeping in his voice, but not, I sensed, in prelude to a confrontation. He was trying his utmost to instill casual camaraderie that included Jacques. "He saw São Schlumberger wrapping shrimp and oysters in a napkin to stash in her purse."

"She's so *cheap*." Thadée rolled his eyes.

"Millions in artwork." Yves reclined against the sofa, as if to maintain his distance from Jacques—again not aggressively, but to avoid weighting the mood. "And she gobbles up free food whenever she can."

"She also hates us." I returned with the wine to pour Jacques a glass.

"No," said Thadée, incredulous. "Clara says she runs up thousands in couture every season."

"Because the baroness does," pealed Yves and I at the same time.

Yves added primly, "She spies for Givenchy, though she says God forbid anyone should say she doesn't wear me. She'd steal all my dresses for him, if she could."

"She also asks me every time for a discount." I pursed my lips in Madame Schlumberger's garish pout, mimicking her accent. "'Loulou, meu chuchu. Is it possible to reduce the price? The hem is uneven, and the waistline is too tight.'" I scoffed. "She thinks calling me 'her pumpkin' in Portuguese will make me ignore that the waistline is too tight because she gains weight between fittings, and the hem is uneven because she insists on wearing one shoe to check the length in the mirror."

"I never allow her a discount." Yves drank his wine. "I always do for my private clients, but she can sell one of her Matisses. I don't need her money, and I know she rushes to Givenchy to show him my dresses, so he can rip them apart and study them."

Jacques smiled.

"She's not Audrey Hepburn," Yves went on. "She thinks Givenchy is going to dress her in pink-red velvet and shoot her cover for *Vogue* in the Louvre."

"Like you dressed your elephants," Thadée chimed in with a grin.

Yves let out a giggle. "She'd be a perfect elephant, like the ones in tutus in *Fantasia*."

As our laughter faded, the silence intruded.

Thadée checked his wristwatch. "Well."

"No, please." Jacques looked at him and then at me. "Don't go."

The echo of Yves's broken imploration to him in le Sept shivered through me.

"Yes," said Yves quietly. "Please stay. It's all right."

The sizzle of a dying candle guttered the light, etching shadows across his face.

"I brought something special for our gathering." Jacques retrieved his jacket, taking out a gold-latticed porcelain box. "Sèvres. It once belonged to Marie Antoinette."

"Really?" Thadée arched a brow. "Did you serve champagne and loot the palace?"

"It's a gift." Jacques opened the lid, edging his plate aside to spoon out a little pyramid of his rose cocaine. "I would have looted the palace."

"So would Halston," I said, noticing he wasn't wearing his rose-gold wristwatch, while he sliced the powder with a razor blade from the box. Thadée caught my eye; I understood what he was trying to convey: we shouldn't encourage anything, but Yves had leaned forward on the sofa, and the longing in his eyes as he looked at Jacques . . .

I couldn't refuse him this final time.

Jacques produced a thin gold-plated straw, handing it to me. "Ladies first."

I inhaled. It was silky smooth, without a sting or acrid burn. Within seconds, it was spinning in my veins, enhanced by the wine, and softening the room.

Thadée did a line, then Yves, followed by Jacques. From an ivory-inlaid wood African coffer on the table, Yves removed a bag of marijuana mixed with hashish and a sheaf of rice papers, and gave them to Thadée, who started to roll joints.

Lighting a cigarette in the meantime, I poured us the rest of the wine.

Yves lit a cigarette, too, wreathing himself in smoke and drinking, as Jacques spliced more lines on the glass table.

The record on the stereo crackled, the needle snagged in the groove of the last song. Yves rose to open the cabinetry and search a leaning stack of albums. Part of his extensive record collection in rue de Babylone, brought here. He chose one.

Classical music. Sonatas by Mozart.

"So beautiful." Jacques closed his eyes, listing slightly to the violins.

Lacing the joint with a sprinkle of cocaine, Thadée lit it and passed it to me.

The room was suffused in melting candlelight, in the winds over water of the sonata, the smoke of our breaths, and the narcotic surge accelerating our blood.

As we finished inhaling the lines, Jacques dipped his fingertip into the pile, rubbed some on his gums, and inclined to me. "It's cut with a little heroin. Delicious. Try it."

I parted my lips; the powder numbed yet also tingled. In turn, he moved to Thadée and then to Yves. They held each other's eyes for a moment, before Jacques rubbed the rose powder on Yves's lips and said tenderly, "I took Loulou and Thadée to our club."

For a second that became endless, I couldn't find my breath.

Thadée abruptly stood. "I'm sorry, but I have to go. I just remembered something."

I started, looking up at him in bewilderment. Yves had gone immobile, Jacques leaning over him, his finger poised at Yves's mouth.

Taking up his jacket, Thadée smiled at Yves, said, "Good night, mon ami," and went to the door, almost briskly, causing me to stumble to my feet and follow him.

"What is it? What's wrong?"

He shrugged on his jacket in the hallway outside. "They want to be alone, I think. Or Yves does. I don't want to stay."

"Yves asked you to stay." Something in his eyes, a shadowing. "Why are you leaving?"

"I have things to do. Clara. I just can't, Loulou." He started down the stairs, ignoring the interminably slow elevator. "I'll call you later," he said, disappearing.

I remained on the landing, confused, trying to understand. He'd left so unexpectedly, the moment Jacques mentioned the club. Was he uncomfortable with Yves knowing? Embarrassed or ashamed that we'd been out with Jacques, to a place he'd frequented with Yves, because we'd gone without Yves and then kept it a secret?

I couldn't tell. My head was swimming. Without warning, anger surged in me.

Clara. He had something he had to do with her. It was my fault; I'd avoided his request to sort things out between us, too reluctant to breach the wall we'd built. Now I'd unwittingly pushed him to a decision, when there had never been a choice to start.

He and Clara, woven into the weft of the house, like Yves and Pierre.

Reeling back into the penthouse with a brittle smile, I said, hearing my false nonchalance, "Clara. Of course."

"The ball and chain." Jacques's smile scarcely shifted his lips.

"When?" Yves's eyes locked on me, and he spoke as if from very far away. "When did you and Thadée go to that club?"

"It—it was only one time. I don't remember exactly when. Months ago," I said, my voice catching.

Yves shifted his gaze to Jacques. "How . . . ?"

"I dressed her as a boy." Jacques glanced at me. "They liked her. They liked Thadée, too. Didn't they, Loulou?"

"Yes," I said, my voice a thread.

"My Loulou, dressed as a boy . . ." Yves lifted a hand to his throat. "I want to see."

Jacques smiled. "If she wants to show you." He extended his hand to me, a drawing room courtesy. "Do you?"

I looked uncertainly to Yves.

"Show me, Loulou," he whispered. "Let me see it."

Turning to Jacques, I felt his hand enclose mine.

"We'll be a little while." Lifting his jacket from the carpet with his other hand, he guided me into the bedroom, closing the door.

The fresh white sheets on the bed were unfurled. Incense burned the scent of Marrakesh in a painted carved-wood sliver, and the colors of the desert simmered in the bed's throw pillows. A candle on the bedside table had nearly extinguished.

He switched on the light in the bathroom, casting electric glow into part of the room. "You don't have to do this."

His eyes were veiled, but had sadness in them, too. The melancholy I'd glimpsed on the Champ de Mars, the pain of impermanence that he called decadence.

He wants to be free. To be like you.

Not like me. To not be him.

"I want to do it," I said. "For him."

Opening the closet, he withdrew the chaps, the black leather boots, the cock ring—items he handled with intimate familiarity. "It won't be the same."

"It never is." I hoisted my dress over my head in a cloud, stepped out from under it as the fabric floated down to pool at my feet.

He said, "We'll leave your lipstick on."

In my ivory lace panties, my skin expanded at his touch as

he fastened the chaps around my waist, using his belt to fasten them, and laced the crisscrossed sides up my thighs. "We need a robe."

Returning to the closet, he selected a white silk kimono of Yves's. Helping me slide my arms into it, he fastened the tie loosely, as he had his tuxedo shirt on me at his apartment, to partially reveal the curves of my breasts.

"Your hair. He doesn't use gel."

In the bathroom, he wet my hair with a towel, combing it back from my face. Took the eyeliner pencil from his jeans pocket and licked it, painting my eyes.

"Now me."

He shed his ankle boots, jeans, and shirt. Black bikini underwear, low on his hips; darker hair feathered between his flat pectorals, trailing to his abdomen, thickening at the waistband. His sun-bronzed skin softly muscled, firm with youth, but not ridged by exertion: the body of a casual swimmer or aesthete.

Pulling on the calf-high leather boots and cropped linen jacket, a severe demarcation at his waist like night's hem, he half turned, snapping the ring around himself and adjusting the bulge at his crotch. He sat on the bed as I dampened and combed back his hair, then dusked his eyes.

We faced each other. He said gently, "To say goodbye."

THE CANDLES IN the living room flickered as the bedroom door opened; a flame went out. Darkness inked the corners of the room.

When had someone closed the windows and drawn the drapes?

Yves sat exactly where we'd left him, the stub of a joint pinched between his fingers, the spicy smoke floating, haloed, above his head. He was sniffing, wiping a finger under his nose to clean it of residue.

Another set of lines was cut on the table.

Jacques said, "Voilà. Un beau garçon."

A foreshortened exhale issued from Yves. As Jacques circled me, his jacket drifted about his lean waist, his legs taut in the boots, his black underwear sifted lower from the prominence of the cock ring. I kept my gaze on Yves's entranced face.

"Yes." Yves sounded like a child with an unexpected gift. "Loulou, show me."

My hands drifted to the robe, unfastening it, letting it part to hang from my shoulders. With a lowering of my eyelids, I bent one leg in the chaps onto my tiptoes, resting a red-nailed hand on my hip, like his favorite cabine model, Delphine.

"She's beautiful, isn't she?" Jacques trailed his fingers across the backs of my shoulders. Taking his stance behind me, so close I felt the hardening inside his underwear at my buttocks, he posed my other arm up and over to encircle his neck. His thigh brushed against mine as he splayed his booted leg, veining his calf. His hand came under my chin to nudge my upraised head to his chest, his mouth at my throat.

"What do you see?" he asked Yves. His slim-fingered hands spread over my chest, splaying down to my stomach, stopping above the lace rim of my panties.

A moan escaped me.

"Beauty." Yves's eyes filled with wonderous fulfillment, the look he had when a cabine model walked into the studio wearing his design and everything fit, everything was perfect on her, nothing to adjust, no changes were possible: his impossible vision, made into reality. "I see so much beauty."

The scene suspended, Jacques and I inanimate in our eroticized sculpture.

"The angel and the devil," he said to Yves, and Yves stood, his eyelids heavy.

He took a step toward us. Jacques reached out to tug him by his belt. He was taller, seeming to tower over us; he looked so deeply into my eyes that, for a moment, it was just him and me, alone in the room, and I saw his acquiescence.

Then he pulled away, lowering his head so that his hair fell like a curtain. He retreated to the sofa.

Jacques lowered his head to mine, his mouth wet fire.

Slipping like dark water around me, shucking his jacket and coiling his arms about my waist, he stood at my back, my breath quickening, shallowing, as he explored my body from behind, teasing with his fingers, slipping between my buttocks to fondle me.

"Come to us, Yves," he said, and we turned together to Yves.

He'd dropped motionless onto the sofa. I couldn't see his eyes behind the disheveled drape of his hair and his glasses, the guttering candles sheening the lenses.

Jacques shrugged off his boots, moving barefoot, bare-chested, stealthily to where Yves sat; when I saw Yves recoil, shrinking into himself, Jacques motioned to me.

"Show him there is no shame in it."

I went to him. Jacques cupped and tilted Yves's chin. He murmured, "Let yourself go," and kissed him, raveling his fingers in Yves's thicket of hair. Yves clung to him with his arms as, together, we lifted him to his feet, and Jacques slowly undressed him, the shirt floating in a sail from his pallid torso, the white jeans crumpling like melted snow to his ankles.

"You have such a beautiful body," Jacques said, "such a beautiful heart."

Yves was trembling: a famished lion, its cage unlocked.

His skin rippled at our touch and our lips as we took him into the bedroom.

20

A thudding headache stirred me to consciousness.

Floundering from rumpled sheets, I groped for the white silk kimono on the floor and stumbled into the bathroom, sitting on the bidet.

I was aching, sore.

Then it returned to me, in distorted flashes. From the toilet, I saw the discarded chaps, the half-open bedroom door, and a glimpse of the sofa, Yves's jeans and shirt folded on it. Wiping myself and splashing water on my face, I avoided my reflection in the mirror as I opened the cabinet, located a bottle of aspirin, and swallowed three.

I padded past the bed. Yves was asleep, an arm flung across his torso, his profile sketched on the pillow, and his hair fanned in disarray.

In the living room, morning sunlight blinded me. I had to pause while my vision adjusted. My stomach growled at the smell of percolating coffee. The glass table had been wiped clean, the empty wine bottles, plates, and detritus picked up.

Someone was in the kitchen. "Jacques?"

I froze.

Thadée turned to me, in the same jeans and shirt he'd been wearing last night, smoking a cigarette and sipping coffee by the kitchen's ajar window. At my stance, he gave a tight smile and poured from the espresso pot into a mug. The coffee was still hot.

"Here. You look like you need it." He handed the mug to me.

"I needed it, too. What did he put in that stuff? I felt like a bus ran over me."

"Heroin." My voice was a thread, the coffee hitting my stomach in an acidic jolt. I took one of his cigarettes from the pack on the counter, then set it aside. I was too queasy to smoke, and horrified to see him.

"He used more than a little." Thadée turned back to the window. "I've snorted coke with heroin before. One line lasts me the entire night. I never felt like this after."

"We did more than a line." I eased onto the taboret at the counter. "You left." I didn't mean for it to sound accusatory, but it did.

"I told you I had things to do. Things to say."

Taking refuge in my mug, I didn't ask. "Yves is out."

"He needs to sleep." He paused. "You haven't asked about Jacques. Aren't you curious about where he is?"

I went still. "Where is he?"

Thadée drew on his cigarette. "He left. Very early, before dawn. I happened to run into him as I was coming up the stairs. He had his boots in his hands and a bunch of clothes under his arms."

"Clothes . . . ?" Nausea soured my stomach.

He gave me a dry look. "I suppose whatever he'd kept here."

"Oh." I winced inwardly.

"He was wearing what he wore last night." Thadée's voice flattened. "He took every piece of clothing that belonged to him. And his little box of poison, of course."

I couldn't speak. Everything faded into the sudden hammering at my ribs.

"I confronted him, asked him to his face why he told Yves about us going to the club, why he was leaving with all his clothes."

"What—what did he say?" I wrenched out my voice.

Thadée knew what we had done. He'd come back early, caught

Jacques sneaking out. I was here, in the kimono. Yves was asleep in the bed. He *knew,* and he wasn't saying anything.

He turned on the tap to extinguish his cigarette, tossed the butt in the trash under the sink, and lit the one I'd taken from his pack. When he put it to my mouth, I inhaled. The nicotine swam in my head.

"He told me what he'd told us at le Sept," Thadée said. "It's over. He ended it."

To say goodbye.

He met my eyes.

"We—" My hand slipped on the coffee mug, rattling it. "We—we were high." It sounded pathetic to my own ears, a futile excuse. "We got in over our heads."

Thadée's smile was mirthless. "I gathered as much. I shouldn't have left. He put too much heroin in the coke. On purpose. He knew what he was doing."

"It wasn't like that." I could barely maintain his regard. I wanted to shout. Yell that he'd left and gone to Clara, but it wasn't my right. I shouldn't care. I'd pushed him away. Only he might have stayed, shown me that he cared enough to stay. "He didn't force us."

"Maybe not. But he's dangerous. We didn't see it, because we didn't want to believe it. We started out thinking the worst of him, and he made us trust him."

You have such a beautiful body, such a beautiful heart.

Dislodging the knot from my breastbone, I said, "You can hate me. Don't hate Yves. He loves you so much. None of it was done on purpose. It just happened."

His voice softened. "I could never hate you. Is that what you think, that I'm jealous?"

"Are you?" I whispered.

"Not of him. Not of Yves." He put his hand over mine on the

counter; I almost flinched. "This sort of thing doesn't just happen. He took advantage of the situation, of our trust in him and worry for Yves. He deceived all of us. I didn't need to be in the room to know it. Loulou, look at me. I don't hate you. I hate him."

I found myself resisting it, because it would be easier, even simpler, if he blamed me. I could deal with that; he'd pursued me when he shouldn't have, because he was in a relationship with another woman, but in a way, I had pursued and rejected him. I hadn't ever said I wanted more from him. I kept delaying, avoiding it, until this happened.

Maybe if he'd stayed with us last night, if I'd made an effort to tell him I wanted him to stay, it wouldn't have.

The thought that it had been a sordid ploy by Jacques was unbearable to me. My mind was also hazy from the drugs, but I recalled the yearning in Yves. How natural, even innocent, it had felt to give him pleasure. To feel him and Jacques, without any barriers between us. The kinship between them, different from mine with Yves. Muses, and the man who loved us, who needed us to create, to personify his longings. I wanted to think that all Jacques had done on purpose was provide us with a final gift: a moment of release, freed from our constraints.

"It won't ever happen again," I said. "It was a mistake."

He stepped to the counter; his muted eyes focused on me. "I'm not talking about the sex. You don't need to regret it. I'm talking about him. His lies and deceit. He's a sadist. He has an evil twist in him. I only regret I didn't stop him before now."

"You think he's evil? Why?"

"He crept out this morning like a thief. He was very surprised to see me on the stairs. He didn't expect it. I told him Yves would be desperate if he left like that, and all he said was that he had ended it. Nothing else. He ended it."

"He—he didn't know what to say," I quavered. "He also knows we made a mistake."

"Loulou." His eyes were gentle, his voice hitching. "It's not a mistake to him. It's not the same for him. To him, it's a game. That's why I hate him. I love Yves. I—I'm in love with you."

When I didn't speak, he drank his coffee, went about rinsing the pot to make another. "You don't have to say it back. I told you I'd wait, but I couldn't. Not anymore."

My heart capsized in my chest.

"I told Clara last night that I'm leaving her." He turned on the stove burner under the pot. "We've been over for years. I won't live a life lying to myself, existing in a delusion. I've seen what delusion can do, what it's doing to Yves."

"You—you didn't have to—"

His swift turn to the counter silenced me, his hand again on mine. "I do. I'm thirty-one years old. I'm not going to spend the rest of my life pretending to love someone I don't. It's paralyzing me." He didn't remove his hand as he said, "Do you love me?"

I threaded my reply. "I . . . I think so." I couldn't say that I did. It terrified me, the very consequences of it. The tearing asunder in the house, with Clara, and with Pierre.

"Then we'll figure it out as we go. We don't have to rush into anything. You have enough to contend with. Yves is going to be a wreck, and—"

The wail from the bedroom cut him off. We hastened to the door, pulling it open all the way. Yves was naked on his hands and knees, upending the closet, excavating his sweaters from the shelves, his socks and underwear from the drawers, flinging them across the floor; grappling at hangers and tearing them down in a cascade of clothes.

"No. *No.*"

Thadée grasped him in his arms. Yves flailed, shrieking. "*NOOO!*"

"The shower," Thadée barked at me. "Turn it on. Cold."

He hauled Yves, kicking and wailing, into the tub. The cold water drenched him, and he began to gag. I clambered into the tub with him, the shower striking me with icy needles as I held back his hair. He threw up into the drain, chunks of food and rose-tinted bile.

As I held him shivering against me, Thadée yanked at the valve, turning on the hot-water spout in the tub to rinse away the vomit. The old building boiler took time to heat up. My feet were freezing by the time tepid water started to fill the tub, and I slid down with Yves into it, his legs too long, dangling over the tub rim.

He'd gone limp in my arms.

Thadée helped me sidle out from underneath him, removing my sopped robe. "Bathe him. He needs to sober up. He's still high. I'll get your clothes and a robe for him."

Squeezing liquid soap from the dispenser, I lathered his hair, sponged him clean. Every rib showed under the thin envelope of his skin. He was wasting away.

Thadée waited with two towels, wrapping him in one and rubbing him dry, putting on his white terry cloth robe, while I dried myself and scrambled into my panties, peasant dress, and suede boots, raking a hand through my damp mess of curls as we assisted him to the bed.

"Coffee," said Thadée. "Plenty of it. Cheese or pâté, on whatever's left of the bread."

Sitting beside Yves, I held his hand as Thadée went into the kitchen.

He stared unseeing at our clasped fingers. "He's gone. He left me."

"Yves." I fought back my anguish. "Yves, please. We're here. We'll never leave you."

"He's gone . . ." Tears crested down his face. "I want to die."

Thadée came to the doorway. "He needs to move. Let's bring him to the sofa."

I retrieved his glasses from the bedside table, Thadée hoisting him upright, keeping an arm around his waist as Yves treaded as if over broken glass into the living room.

The bread and coffee mug were on the table. Thadée sat him on the sofa, wrapped his hands around the mug, urging him to drink.

I hovered, my gaze locked on Yves.

"You must try, Yves," said Thadée. "You can't let this destroy you."

Yves took a listless sip from the mug.

"That's right. Easy. Everything is going to be all right." He set his hand on Yves's leg. "Eat something, and calm down. We'll figure it out."

The phone rang. The discordant, abrupt chime flared Yves's eyes.

"It's him." His voice shredded in agitation. "It's him. He's sorry. He's coming back—"

He started to rise; Thadée's hand tightened, keeping him place. "Answer it, Loulou."

Though he didn't look at me as he spoke, I knew what he was telling me to do.

I picked up the receiver, trying to find my voice, and Pierre's growl came over the line: "Is he there?"

"Yes, we—" I shot a terrified glance at Thadée, mouthing, *Pierre.*

His expression went grim. He nodded. Yves was breathing fast through his mouth.

"Loulou?" Pierre's impatience scorched me over the wire.

"Yes, he's here." My feigned bright tone was too brittle in my ears. "He just stepped into the shower. We were up late last night, working on ideas for a new collection."

I glanced once more at Thadée; he nodded again. Yves lowered his face in despair into Thadée's shoulder.

Pierre grunted. "I need to see both of you at the hôtel. Now."

"Now? It's Saturday. We—we were going to have lunch later, and then—"

"Now. I came in to finish some business. Something's happened."

I didn't answer him.

"Are you listening to me, Loulou?"

"Yes." I couldn't stop the catch in my voice. "I'll be there as soon as possible."

Pierre snorted. "Is he too hung over from drinking himself into a stupor? Never mind. Of course he is. He needs to hear it, too. I'll tell him later, when he can comprehend it."

He hung up. Thadée looked at me.

"Pierre says something's happened. He wants us at the hôtel."

Yves moaned.

"You go," said Thadée. "I'll see him home. He can't stay here by himself."

He followed me to the elevator, keeping the front door open.

Yves huddled on the sofa.

"They have their butler and staff at rue de Babylone," said Thadée in a hushed voice. "They must have helped him bring some of his things here. He'll have people around him to watch him, so he doesn't do anything crazy."

I punched the call button, the elevator lodged on a floor below. "He says he wants to die."

"He won't. Loulou"—he touched my arm—"it's going to be

very bad for a time, but he has the house. His collections. Pierre and Betty. You and me. We won't let him die."

I shuddered as he drew me into his arms.

"Just listen to whatever Pierre has to say and go home. Get some rest. It's probably Syndicale shit—you know how he is. His emergency is the only one that matters." He kissed my forehead. "I'll call you later. I promise."

As the elevator arrived and I stepped onto it, he remained standing there.

"I love you," he said, the door closing on his face.

TAKING A TAXI to the hôtel, I fumbled in my bag for my compact, applying lipstick, mascara. My face in the foundation-smeared mirror was haggard, my eyes bruised.

Twining the wrinkled Rive Gauche scarf about my head, I entered the hôtel, the receptionist desk empty, and took the stairs to the second floor. In the workroom, the dressmaker dummies were swathed in pieces of our upcoming collection, fabric unrolled on the tables, patterns pinned to the cloth—preparing for the king to return, to conjure the extraordinary.

We are their muses. The raw clay they mold into their ideals.

Pierre was typing, banging at the keys with two fingers, a cigar in the ashtray.

I cleared my throat in the doorway.

"That was fast," he said. "No traffic on a Saturday?"

"I took a cab from les Invalides."

It sounded banal. A meaningless pleasantry. We'd never developed a friendship as I had with Yves—deliberately, I knew, on Pierre's part. I was designated as Yves's friend, his confidante. His muse, though I'd never liked the term. It implied passivity on my part, and I'd worked for almost four years without missing a day.

"Sit." He puffed on the cigar, clouding the air. Grimacing, he stubbed it out. "This is going to be unpleasant." As I sat on the chair before his desk, where his long-suffering secretary took dictation and Clara endured his tirades, he said bluntly, "Lagerfeld's little friend is dead."

My lungs drained of air. I went breathless with panic. Jacques was dead. *How?* We'd just seen him. It wasn't possible. It couldn't be.

"Apparently"—Pierre's mouth twisted—"it was a suicide. Clara heard it first. His body, or whatever was left of it, was found on the train tracks on Tuesday, not far from Vannes station. He lay in a freezer in the morgue till Wednesday night because no one knew who he was. A taxi driver who read in the local paper that the gendarmerie was requesting help to identify the body came forth. He'd taken fares from them, driven them from the train station on several trips to Penhoët."

"Penhoët . . ." My mind reeled. Dead since Tuesday. Relief swamped me. Not Jacques. Someone else.

"In Grand-Champ." Pierre's brusque tone startled me. "Lagerfeld's overpriced seigneurial château. By his own admission, Karl spent the weekend at the château with them. He and his hooligan came back to Paris on Tuesday morning, hours before the body was found. His chauffeur confirmed it."

I'm sorry I'm late.

It slowly, horribly, dawned on me. Timid eyes peering from behind steel-rimmed glasses.

I'm not really a fashion person.

"Loulou, are you hearing any of this? I hope you're not also doing drugs with him. I have enough with his drinking, without you also turning into my problem."

"Yes, I'm—" My stomach cramped, like I was about to throw up. "I'm listening."

"They drove back to the city without this boy. They didn't go looking for him when he went missing. Karl claims to know nothing about it. The news is spreading like a contagion; everyone is horrified. Marie-Hélène called me. She's beside herself."

"Why?" I blurted out. "Did she know him?"

He glared. "Why would she? The Baroness de Rothschild doesn't buy clothes off the rack. He was a nobody who supposedly worked for Karl. But she knows of him. Karl and his nobodies were photographed for Warhol's rag, sitting on piles of dollars in a limousine like gangsters. The boy was completely out of his depth, like that American you and Clara rescued out of the gutter. If the boy killed himself, then Karl led him to it." Pierre slammed his fist on the desk. "That's it. There will be no more associating with Lagerfeld or any of his appalling friends. Am I understood?"

I couldn't speak. I could barely move.

"You don't have anything to say?" His eyes narrowed to slits. "You don't need to. I know already. Yves, losing his mind over Jacques de Bascher." He spat out the name. "He must think I'm an imbecile. His love nest five steps from our home, that gigolo coming and going at all hours. The entire arrondissement knows. Everyone in Paris *knows*."

My mouth parched. I stared at him, immobile.

"I don't care who he fucks." Pierre raked his hand through his thinning, silvering hair, bristling it. "But he's made a fool of himself—and a fool of me. That scene at le Sept, drunk and sobbing. Fabrice called me. Paloma called me. Everyone called me." His voice razored. "Except you."

In the awful silence that ensued, he added, "I told you if you wanted to stay, you work for us. For *our* house."

My expression hardened; I felt it. I heard it in my voice. "I do."

"Do you? Because it doesn't look like it from where I'm sitting."

I kept quiet, smothering the urge to retort that if he still doubted me, I would leave. But I couldn't leave Yves, even if my fury at the accusation nearly overwhelmed me.

"I want every letter Yves wrote to him," said Pierre. "Every note. Every card. Don't say there aren't any, because I know Yves. It's Casablanca lilies by the dozens and 'forever after' until he's bored of it. He did it with me; and he's done it with every lover since. Karl can't be trusted, much less his gigolo. They'll give the letters to the press, to put us on the front page and wipe themselves off it. Get it all back."

I stood on legs that I didn't feel. As I turned to the door, he plunged his next words like a knife into my back. "I'm assuming you don't need his address. You didn't have the phone number for their love nest, but you know exactly where to find him."

Without looking back at him or saying a word, I left the hôtel.

BY THE TIME I reached my loft, I couldn't stop trembling and sank to the floor. The unvented cry in me taloned my belly, clawing up my throat.

José, trampled on train tracks. Almost two days unidentified in the morgue. A taxi driver coming forth to identify his remains.

I'm sorry I'm late.

My phone was ringing.

I overturned my bag, seeing Yves hurling his belongings from his closet in agony, and I smoked a cigarette to the filter, crouched on my threshold like a wounded animal.

The phone stopped ringing. Plunging into the bathroom, the ruffled collar of the peasant dress strangling me, I yanked off my boots and then the dress, dropping them onto the floor.

The phone started ringing again.

I turned on the shower as hot as I could, scalding myself in the downpour.

Rubbing steam from the mirror, I forced myself to meet my reflection.

I want every letter Yves wrote to him. Every note. Every card.

Like a somnambulant, I applied mascara, eyeshadow, rouge to hide my pallor. Lipstick. From my closet, I unearthed a black knife-pleated skirt and silk shirt. Black tights and ankle boots. All black, which I rarely wore, but was now required of me.

The phone rang, insistent, resounding in my near-empty space. Never enough time to properly decorate, except for whatever happened to catch my fancy at a flea market during an idle day off. My bed, a table, two hard-backed chairs. Never here enough to care.

"Yes?" my voice rasped.

"Loulou, are you okay? I've been calling you for over an hour. I took Yves to rue de Babylone. He didn't fight it, but it took some time for him to sober up."

I crumpled where I stood. "José killed himself."

"José?" echoed Thadée in confusion. Then he said, "Jacques's cousin?"

"Yes." I told him what Pierre had flung at me.

"Christ. Have you tried to call Jacques?"

It hadn't even occurred to me. "No."

"Stay there. I'm coming over."

HE ARRIVED WITHIN the hour. The late-August sun gilded Paris in evening descent, but in my loft, night had already fallen.

Thadée took one look at me and said, "The corner bistro."

"I'm not hungry." I sat on a hard-backed chair, my ashtray littered with butts.

"You can't be like Yves. It won't help anything. You need to eat."

We went to the bistro, Thadée ordering whatever was on the

menu à prix fixe. Sipping limonade, the waiter's offer of wine declined, he said, "Did you call him?"

"Multiple times." I reached in my bag for my cigarettes; the pack was empty. He lit one of his Gitanes for me. "He didn't answer. His machine didn't pick up."

"Are you going to try to see him in person?"

"What choice do I have? Pierre wants Yves's letters. Notes. Any cards. I have to see him." I tried to make it sound like an errand, not a humiliation. I had to look Jacques in the face after sleeping with him and Yves, after he left us without a word, and request something private from him, demanded by the man who paid my salary.

"I'm going with you." Thadée paused as the waiter served us plates of roast poulet with pommes frites, tomato slices in olive oil. "I've taken a hotel room nearby. You're not going to him without me. How can Pierre make you do this?"

"He's enraged. I'll get the letters back. And that's all." I made myself start to eat. "Why did you take a hotel room? You can stay with me."

"I think we should wait for that, until matters settle down." At my wary glance, he said, "Not because I don't want to. I do. More than anything. But moving in together with the situation as it is will feed the fire. Pierre thinks you hid the affair from him."

"I did hide it from him." Only now, as I admitted it, did I realize I also hated myself for it. "We shouldn't have kept it from him. He found out anyway. He could have put a stop to it before now."

"We did what we thought was best for Yves." Thadée paused, sopping a chunk of bread in the oil on the tomatoes, biting into it. "Pierre told you Clara called him to tell him about José? That she heard it first?"

"Yes, but from whom?" I skewered a piece of chicken on my fork and couldn't lift it to my mouth.

"I've no idea. But she obviously had an ear to the ground about Karl and Jacques. She did know more than she let on, as you thought she did when Corey left."

"She—she didn't say anything to you about it?"

He gave a terse smile. "I found out when I called you. Eat, Loulou. Please."

"Nothing at all?" The food before me—which, as he'd said, I needed—turned my stomach. I had to force myself to eat.

"She told me last night to pack my things, if that's how I felt. I'll arrange later to collect my father's paintings from the apartment. It was civilized. She was expecting it. But she told Pierre about José, so she must have told him you'd asked her about Jacques when you came to see Corey. Probably the very next day, before we'd even gone to Karl's birthday party."

"All this time . . ." I dropped my fork onto my plate, nauseated. "You think Pierre knew it was Jacques all this time?"

"Given how he's behaving, he knew more than he let on. Like her." Thadée's voice edged in anger.

"God. I can't imagine going to work. I can't look her in the eye."

"She won't say a word to you. The house is sacrosanct. You work on the couture collections with Yves, manage the lines for Rive Gauche. Design accessories. You're indispensable, so she'll keep her feelings to herself."

I wasn't so sure of it, recalling her invitation to lunch and her upbraiding of me shortly after I was hired, but I let it go. "And Pierre?" I asked. "He's furious at me. I might lose my job over it."

"He's more furious at himself. He blames everyone right now. He'll get over it. You won't lose your job. Yves won't allow it. Whatever Yves wants, Pierre gives him."

Again, I wasn't so sure.

"I'll stay with you tonight," said Thadée. "Tomorrow, we go to rue du Dragon. I want to look *him* in the eye."

HE WASN'T AT home. Thadée buzzed repeatedly at the portal, shouting his name. Upstairs neighbors threatened to call the police, so we went to Café le Flore, to calm down.

"He knows," said Thadée.

"He must. He and José were friends."

"No, he knows we're looking for him." The muscle in Thadée's jawline clenched under his skin. "He knows we've figured it out."

I froze in my seat at our outdoor table. "He had an affair with Yves. He left. His friend killed himself. There's nothing to figure out."

"Loulou." He regarded me steadily. "I understand you liked him. I did, too. And I understand how Yves still feels about him. But he was hours late for our dinner, and it wasn't to make an entrance. You know it as much as I do."

To say goodbye.

"José's body was in the morgue for nearly two days before that taxi driver came forth," Thadée added. "The driver took fares from them; he drove them from the train station several times to Karl's château. Isn't that what Pierre told you?"

I nodded, abruptly voiceless.

"The driver recognized the body. He wouldn't have known a name. The gendarmerie didn't have any next of kin to notify. Just a boy, seen in a taxi with Lagerfeld, who owns the château. They called Karl before anyone else."

My expression must have betrayed my incredulity, for he reached across the table to grip my hand. "Clara found out once the news started to spread, which apparently was yesterday. Maybe Karl was the one who told her, to make himself look better, because it was going to get out anyway, no matter what. The gendarmerie must have called him sometime on Thursday; José's family would have been notified immediately after. Jacques already knew it when he went to see us on Friday night. He knew when he—" His voice hardened. "His friend was dead, and everything that happened . . . he did it anyway. Like no one had died near that château."

Despite the humid heat of the day, a chill frosted me.

"He . . ." I searched for a reason. "He might not have been able to say anything. José's next of kin, his family—they wouldn't want him to tell it. He was in shock."

"Shock." He released my hand. "Did he seem like he was in shock to you?"

My gaze darted to his building, its front door visible from the café. "He has to come back. He lives there."

"And I'm going to wait until he does." Thadée flicked his lighter on and off, the flame flashing and dying in his hand. "I don't have anything else to do. I also know where Karl lives."

"We can't—" I took in his resolved expression. "We can't sit here for however long it takes." My lungs felt short of air, the square wavering in the heat. "I have to go to work tomorrow. We've a collection to finish. Yves—he won't be coming in."

"There's a phone booth over there." He pointed at it. "As soon as I see him, I'll call you, at the hôtel or your loft. He'll show up. When he does, he's not leaving again until we get Yves's letters from him."

21

The following days in the studio were so heavy with tension, I imagined being able to take a pair of scissors and slice through it.

Yves was sequestered in rue de Babylone, not taking calls, barricaded by Pierre as word of José's suicide spread and became a lurid drama—an innocent from the provinces, lured into glamorous peril, scaling to precarious heights and plunging to his death.

Dismay and horror were avidly bandied about, but Karl was still seen dining about town, and there were more important issues for front pages: The ongoing oil crisis. An attempted assassination of U.S. president Gerald Ford. Other world-shaking events.

The death of a young man whom no one outside fashion circles had even heard of scarcely warranted a footnote.

I worked long hours at the hôtel, avoiding le Sept and every other place where fashion people congregated. I'd completed most of my accessory designs, and the couture sketches were approved; Yves had designed the collection weeks before. Anne-Marie and the atelier premieres had chosen the dresses and outfits to make and were working on them. The splicing of delicate fabric, the threading of needles, and the susurration of embroidery were a humming hive. The king's absence was felt everywhere, but everyone employed at the house knew their responsibilities. By now, we could put together a collection without him, even if doing so was inconceivable.

I consulted with the upstairs ateliers on producing my accessories. Independent artisans often requested appointments with us to show their samples, hoping to catch our eye. Yves was always gracious and welcoming; we'd often taken the appointments together, also hoping for something to catch our eye. I had a Rolodex filled with people to call on, eager to be associated with the House of Yves Saint Laurent.

I would not fail Yves.

THADÉE CHECKED IN to have dinner with me. He'd had no sighting of Jacques. He was on the hunt, staking out both rue du Dragon and Karl's apartment on Place Saint-Sulpice. Disturbingly to both of us, he'd seen movers entering Karl's building, evidence that Lagerfeld might be preparing to vacate his apartment.

Then Thadée called to say Jacques had returned to rue du Dragon.

I DIDN'T HAVE time to change out of my work clothes: baggy jeans, a beige blouse I'd been wearing for days on end. Yves wasn't present to gently chide me that he liked to see me with lipstick, coiffured, and in heels.

Grabbing my bag, I took a taxi to Saint-Germain.

Thadée met me at the front door of the building, his eyes pocketed in shadows; he was visibly drained, running on nervous energy. A week tracking Jacques, while contending with his separation from Clara, had exhausted him. As had contemplating a future that neither of us felt we could discuss until we finished what we'd started.

"Ring his apartment," he said. "He's here. I saw him go in. He hasn't left."

Tugging at my peacoat, a chill roving the evening air, or maybe just a chill in me, I pushed the buzzer.

It took him several minutes to respond. "Yes? Who is it?"

"Loulou," I said.

A long pause, then the buzzer opened the door. Thadée entered the foyer with me. He fished in his pocket. Alarmed, I grasped his arm.

He smiled. "My cigarettes. Did you think I brought a gun to shoot him?"

"It crossed my mind for a second," I admitted.

"It's crossed my mind, too." He flicked his lighter to his cigarette.

"I'm going to do this alone," I said. "You're too angry at him. Wait here."

He nodded. "I will. Tell him I'm right here."

Climbing the winding staircase, I pushed aside my sentimentality, my hope that it had all been a terrible misunderstanding. A moment when we were caught up in each other, in the longing of it; our awareness it was to be our last time together.

Not a ploy. Not a game.

His door was ajar. I nudged it open and paused, the apartment dismal as daylight from the interior well diminished. Jacques said from the bedroom, "I'm in here."

I halted in the living room. "Let's talk out here."

He came out barefoot, his black shirt untucked over his jeans. I saw at once the change in him: his face thinner, his mustache untrimmed, and his hair unkempt. His fastidious attention to his image, his alluring projection of it, had always been such an integral part of him that, for a moment, he looked like someone else.

A stranger, whom I might not have noticed, had he passed me on the street.

"I'm happy to see you,'" he said. "Let me make you some espresso."

"It's not necessary."

Though I tried to contain it, my voice was schooled. Aloof.

He nodded, sat on the lumpy blue sofa where José had some-times spent the night. "Are you angry with me?"

"I'm sorry about José." I perched on the sofa's edge, refusing to admit, now that I was seeing him, that I wasn't angry. I'd just take the letters and leave. I didn't want to hear any explanations. They wouldn't change anything.

He swallowed; I saw the subtle movement in his throat. "He left me a note."

My breath stalled.

"He . . ." Jacques folded his hands—now veined from exertion, I thought, with an onyx gold ring on his pinkie. "We left him at the château because he wanted to stay. He was helping me with the decor. Karl offered us the gatekeeper's lodge by the gardens to decorate on our own. José wanted it to be eighteenth century. I—"

I found myself wanting to comfort him.

"I wanted something different. José and I argued about it, nothing exaggerated. He said he'd take the train later. Karl had his friend Anna Piaggi visiting." His eyes lowered to his hands. "He'd been sketching her in the gardens, wearing things we'd found in the attic. Old, moth-eaten cloaks, torn-up dresses. She looked so beautiful in them." His smile was evanescent. "Karl wanted us to leave that day, so we did."

I knew I shouldn't ask; it would unlock something I should never want to know. "What did José's note say?"

"That he was in love with me. I showed it to Karl before we left. He got impatient, said José was becoming a nuisance. He wanted him gone, like Corey."

I went utterly still. Corey. He'd also fallen in with Karl's clique. He'd been ejected from it, precipitating his downward spiral.

"What do you mean, 'like Corey'? Was Karl sleeping with him?"

"No." He gave me a flat look. "Karl doesn't sleep with anyone. Corey must have met someone else. I don't know who. We never saw him again."

"But he was with Karl and you. In your group."

"For a while. Karl got impatient with him, too. Corey wanted to model for him."

"And only you model for him." My fingers on my bag flexed. "You shouldn't have left José alone at the château. He wrote you a note saying he was in love with you."

"I didn't think he'd kill himself over it. He never even told me he liked men. I don't understand it." Jacques paused. "But you're not here because of him, are you?"

"I met him once. I'm here for Yves."

He stiffened. "I told him it was over."

"You came back. You were there, with us, that night."

"I came back to say goodbye." He met my eyes. His gaze was different now, and I couldn't interpret it. "You told me Yves could decide or we could decide it together. You didn't say I could decide by myself. I did."

My fingers coiled into my hand. "I need his letters."

"Why?"

"Don't ask me that. I need you to give them to me."

He remained quiet for a long moment. "I don't have them."

"You must. I know he sent you at least one, with a card and the key to his penthouse. I gave it to you in Versailles."

A shadow crossed his face. "Did Pierre send you to me?"

I thought of lying to him. "Yes."

"Pierre has the letters," he said, "and the key."

My vision wavered, the room dissolving around me.

"You didn't know." He twirled the pinkie ring with his thumb.

"Pierre followed me here that day, after I left the penthouse. He told me if I didn't give him the letters, he'd see me run out of Paris and tell everyone Karl and I killed José. So, I gave them to him."

. Pierre had laid a trap for me. He already had the letters in his possession when he'd called avenue de Breteuil from the hôtel. A test of my loyalty—to him. He wanted to see how far I was willing to go, as only someone who knew Jacques and about the affair from the start would dare ask for the letters' return.

The light in the window darkened. Everything blackened around me.

"If you want something to get back at him," I heard Jacques say, as if from across an abyss, "he also fucked me that day."

My eyes locked on him. "What?"

"He wanted to. He said he wanted to know what was driving Yves mad. After we did, he said he'd had better." He shrugged. "I have, too."

My entire person recoiled. "How—why would he do that? Did he force you?"

I needed to believe it, to cast Pierre as the aggressor, until Jacques gave me a strange smile, as though he wished he could let me believe it.

"I told you why. He wanted to know. I could have refused him. I wasn't raped, if that's what you're thinking."

Without knowing how I managed it, I pitched to my feet. "You—you did it because he wanted to *know*? A man who despises you, after you broke up with Yves?"

"It was just sex, Loulou. The same thing Yves was doing with me."

"How *could* you? You were with us the night before. Yves— he loves you."

He gazed up at me. "Yves doesn't love me." His voice was

inflectionless, not cold. Like his eyes. That was what I couldn't interpret; he was removed from any detectable emotion. "He loves the fantasy of who he wants me to be. It was never about me. It was always about him. What he needed from me."

I backed away from him, toward the door.

"They wanted me to play the parts they assigned: Yves needed a lover to make his fantasies come true. Pierre made me into a devil who destroyed their relationship and took advantage of Yves. Do you remember what we talked about at Karl's party?"

"No." I was diminishing into a yawning pit in my stomach.

"The creation of our imagined selves. Who we yearn to be, and how we live to fulfill it." He watched me pause, caught in a storm I couldn't escape. His voice softened, almost soothing. "You really don't remember? You said fashion is how we reflect who we want to be. But it's more than that. We hide our weaknesses behind it; we hide what we secretly desire and fear. We objectify ourselves, and others with it. It's a weapon."

My voice unraveled. I was up against the door, cornered by his words. "We—we trusted you. You lied to us."

"I never lied to you. That night was a fantasy for Yves, what he couldn't ask for himself. You knew it before it happened. I told you I'd ended the affair. It was our gift, to him."

Our gift. What I'd desperately longed for it to be, but never like this. Never a complicit act of destructive delusion that devastated Yves.

When he stood, my hand was gripping the doorknob. "Did you ever care for him?" I whispered. "Was any of it real?"

Jacques tilted his head, as if my question were unexpected. "What do you think?"

It's not the same for him. To him, it's a game.

I turned blindly, yanking the door open.

"An illusion, Loulou. That's all I was to them. Only Karl sees me for who I am. He accepts me, without expectations or re-proaches."

As I stumbled onto the landing, he said again from behind me, "I never lied to you."

THADÉE SAW IT on my face. He was on the stairs before I'd reached the bottom step, his arms about me, taking me outside, embracing me as my tears finally broke free and I wept against him, my sobs racking me until I had nothing left to shed.

And then, in the wake of my torrent, as Thadée gazed furiously at the building, I finally said, in a broken voice, "I do love you. So much. I'm so afraid of it."

He kept holding me close. "You don't need to be afraid." He brushed my wet cheeks with his fingertips. "We'll be okay, I promise you. We'll get through this. Together."

Nodding, drawing back from him to collect myself, I said, "He doesn't have the letters. Pierre does. He had them before he called the penthouse."

His expression turned hard. "We're going to rue de Babylone."

WE ARRIVED AS night dressed the city, the glimmer of light scattering sequins across the velvet skirts of the Seine.

Yves's butler answered the door, about to send us away before he saw who were.

Silently, he took our coats and brought us upstairs, into the living room with its gilt-framed, spotlighted paintings by Gauguin, Renoir, and Cézanne; a black-and-white lithograph and abstract sculpture by Paloma's father; the Mondrian color blocks that inspired Yves's seminal dress in 1965; archaeological artifacts, African masks, ivory tusks, and ebony caskets; shelves of first-edition books; and glass cases of rare manuscripts—the eclectic, exquisite accumulation of a seventeen-year symbiosis.

Pierre turned from the bar, a tumbler of cognac in his hand. Yves sat on the crimson silk brocade couch with its bamboo-leaf embroidery, his black knee-length linen tunic and loose drawstring pants—comfort clothes from Marrakesh—floating on his frame.

"Well?" Pierre asked. "Did you get them?"

I returned his unblinking stare. "No."

He snorted, and Thadée said, "Pierre, stop it. You know—"

"Don't." Pierre kept his voice level. "Don't interfere, Thadée. We have years of friendship. I don't want it to end in this sordidness. It isn't your concern."

"It is my concern," replied Thadée. "Leave it be. It's done. Finished."

"Is it?" said Pierre, as I moved to Yves. He didn't react to my fingers on his hand.

Turning to the bar, Pierre poured two more cognacs, handing them to Thadée, who brought mine to me, while Pierre staked his distance, keeping a long, narrow sandalwood table with a small alabaster bust of a Roman emperor between us and him.

"I trust this is over, then. I don't want to hear their names again in this house or at the hôtel. As far as I'm concerned, they're as dead as that boy they killed."

Yves lifted his eyes. "Not to me."

"No?" Pierre's smile knifed his mouth. "You're going to continue to make a cuckold of me and throw yourself at a nobody who doesn't want you?"

Yves's hand spasmed, withdrawing from mine. "He loves me."

"God." Pierre gave a brusque laugh. "You truly are insane. You sent him letters—love letters—spilling your guts to him, saying you'll die without him. You think he cared about you? He and Karl read your letters aloud to each other, on the way to their château."

"No," cried Yves. "He would never show anyone my letters!"

"Ask Loulou. She went to try to get them back from him."

Yves gave me a desperate look, his face ashen.

"He didn't give them to her," said Pierre. "Do you know why? Because I took them from him first. He was very willing to give them to me; he didn't try to keep them."

My hand closed on Yves's fingers as Pierre downed his cognac, glancing in warning at Thadée, who looked as if he might strike him, and then directed himself again at Yves.

"Look at yourself. A drunk. A drug addict. About to become a laughingstock. The great Yves Saint Laurent, in love with a whore paid for by Lagerfeld. While they plan their next party, their next dead boy."

Yves half rose from the sofa. "You're jealous," he hissed. "You despise him because he's everything you're not. Because he's young and beautiful. Because he's *mine*. You can't stand it, because you think you own me."

"I do own you." Pierre's reply was lethal in its precision. "Everything you are is because of me. The house. The villa in Marrakesh. Every piece of art in this apartment. Every design you show in the salon. Your very genius is mine, because without me, you'd be in a lunatic asylum, making paper dolls. Or dead in a sewer from all your vices."

"Pierre." Thadée started toward him, enraged. "That's enough."

Pierre held up a hand. "I told you not to interfere. He will hear it. I've worked my fingers to the bone for him." Stepping to the sandalwood table, his eyes like rusted shards, Pierre stared at Yves. "He never gave a shit about you. And I know it because I fucked him. In his apartment. He was also very willing to do it. He came in my hand. He liked it."

The sudden silence roared in my ears.

With a howl, Yves lunged to his feet, seizing the marble bust from the table. Thadée rushed at him as he flung the bust at Pierre. His aim was unfocused, the bust veering to strike the wall, denting the red-painted plaster. I reeled up and back, gasping, as Pierre stood perfectly still, the bust rolling, chipped, behind him.

When he eventually spoke, it was with terrible finality. "You want him so much? You can have him. Choke on his lies, his malice. I'm done with it, done with you. But before I go, I'm telling him to his face so he understands that unlike you, I'm nobody's fool."

"You're the one who's nothing without me," shrieked Yves. "*Leave us alone!*"

"I will." Pierre's voice was icy, a tone I'd never heard from him before.

Thadée grasped Yves by the waist to hold him back, his cries dissolving into wails as Pierre barked at the blanch-faced butler, who'd appeared at the sound of the commotion, "Have my car brought around."

Yves screamed. He struggled against Thadée's grip, collapsing to his knees as Thadée engulfed him and pulled him close.

"Yves—" I heard Thadée's voice break. "Please, no more. You have to let it go."

I couldn't move a muscle. I couldn't draw in any air. I was suffocating.

Thadée lifted his gaze to me. "Go to Pierre. I'll stay here with him."

"Don't leave me, Loulou," pleaded Yves. "Please, don't leave me."

I reeled away, down the staircase and through the black-and-white-checkered entry, into the blast of sundered night.

Pierre waited by the curb in his hat and coat. He raised stony eyes to me. "You knew about it from the start. You let it go on until this had to happen. You *knew*."

My heart caved into my ribs. I'd never paused to consider the pain it would inflict on him. Thadée and I had debated its discovery by him, but not his suffering over the loss of Yves, whom he loved and still loved, and was fighting for even now, in his rage.

"It must have been amusing for you," he said, "to steal Thadée from behind Clara's back, while that hooligan fucked Yves behind mine."

"No. Pierre, we never meant to—"

"To deceive me?" He chuckled in arid contempt. "You cozied up to Karl's tramp to be close to Thadée and cover up for Yves. What did Yves promise you, eh? My office? My job? You and he, running the house, after I slinked off with my tail between my legs?"

I took a wary step toward him. "Please, believe me. It was never like that. Thadée and I were trying to protect Yves. He said he was in love. He—"

"He thought he could elope with Prince Charming. How does it feel, to know Prince Charming and his king drove away from the castle, leaving a dead boy on the train tracks? Does that seem like happily ever after to you?"

"No," I whispered.

"But the boy's still dead. Yves is raving mad. I will see them pay for it."

The Rolls-Royce pulled up with its chauffeur. Pierre gestured to the back door. "You want to protect Yves? Get in. Show it—to me."

I slid into the upholstered leather back seat; my hands knotted in my lap as we drove in complete silence to Place Saint-Sulpice.

Pierre emerged from the car and strode to the entry, punching the bell. I stood shivering beside him without my coat. My blouse sleeves brushed like sharp insect wings against my arms, wrapped about my midriff.

The buzzer sounded, admitting us. Taking to the marble

stairs in militant resolve, once he reached the double doors to the drawing room, Pierre shot a glare at me. "We do this my way."

He shoved the doors open. The room within, with its high windows overlooking the church, where we'd celebrated Karl's birthday, where we'd danced and gotten high and danced, was a ghost, the few remaining furnishings draped in sheets. Wood crates stamped with an auction house insignia were piled by the marble-fronted fireplace.

A clack of heels preceded Karl. "This is a surprise." A hint of teeth glittered within his spade-shaped black beard. "To what do I owe the unexpected visit?"

"Where is he?" Pierre met Karl's impassive stare. "Where's your whore?"

"Oh my. Are we truly at that stage? He's not here. Feel free to see for yourself." Karl stepped aside in a rustle of black leather. "Only me, locking up our den of inequity."

Pierre scoured the room behind Karl with a savage sweep of his eyes. "You think you can hide him?" he sneered. "Or is the coward too afraid to stand up for himself?"

"He has no reason to 'stand up for himself.' This isn't a duel in a saloon." Karl glanced coldly at me. "Jacques isn't here. You have my word."

"Your *word*?" Pierre burst out laughing—like a claw scraping stone. "When has your word ever mattered? You brought that devil into our lives."

Karl lifted his chin. "I believe Yves is responsible for bringing the devil into your lives. But let's not argue, shall we? It's beneath us. You can accept my word or not. In that respect, yes, I'm afraid it doesn't matter. I will honor it, regardless."

"*Where* is he?" Pierre snarled.

"That also doesn't matter. Not to you. Jacques is no longer your concern."

Pierre bunched his fists at his sides. "If I ever see him near us again, if one word of any of this leaks to the press, I'll tell everyone what he did. And how you let him do it."

"No." Karl's reply was composed. "You will not. Neither will I. We will behave like gentlemen. You see to your business, and I'll see to mine."

"You think you're a gentleman? A copycat for hire, who designs for houses that aren't yours? You imitate and steal. You're an imposter. A parvenu. The son of a German industrialist. Your father was a fucking Nazi."

Karl's expression didn't shift. "How petty of you. Not every German was a Nazi, though you're obviously incapable of distinguishing the difference."

"What do you know about me? You can keep pretending you do, but I know you for what you are—a liar. He comes within my sight, and I'll see you both dragged through the mud. I run the Syndicale. By the time I'm done, you'll be a pariah. Chloé will fire you. No one wants a murderer with a cokehead gigolo on their payroll."

Pierre spun away, tromping down the stairs. In a haze of disbelief, I started to follow him when Karl said, "Loulou."

I froze on the landing.

"Jacques will miss you. He's very fond of you and Thadée. Under other circumstances, who knows? We might have all been good friends."

"He misled us." I ripped my words out. "He never cared. He's incapable of it."

"Ah, but that's part of his charm, isn't it? How well he plays the part." His voice warmed, but his eyes were like Jacques's— detached. Indifferent.

"You deserve each other." I was trembling in anger. "He chose you because of it."

"He didn't choose me. He chose himself. He chose not to be someone's toy." Karl's tone turned crisp. "And as far as that boy everyone seems to think we led into perdition—Jacques has his faults, I'll admit, but José killed himself. An unfortunate risk of aspiring to more than what we're meant to be. We never know how far we may fall. You aspired, too: to be someone with Yves. Unlike José, you knew how to survive. I wish you and Thadée the best." His smile creased his lips, like a cracking of granite. "And Yves, of course. I've never wanted anything else for him."

"Keep him away from us," I said. "Away from Yves."

"You also have my word." With an incline of his head, Karl closed the doors.

I clamped down on my rage, moving to where Pierre waited by the car.

We never know how far we may fall.

22

1977

Swans glided on the Seine, their white feathers like obscure mirrors, capturing the colored reflections of the red-lit lanterns on the gardenia-garlanded skiffs, transporting our guests to the bucolic isle in the Bois de Boulogne.

Their laughter echoed in the July twilight; little shrieks as someone's hem slipped over a skiff side to trail in the water. Willows wept into the ground. The restaurant of Chalet des Îsles rang with the chimes of champagne flutes and porcelain plates overflowing with buffet canapés for the wedding ball festivities.

Thadée and I waited on the terrace to welcome our guests, canopied by the trees, and with a marquee backdrop of white hydrangeas twined with green-and-white ribbons, designed by Yves. My new husband wore white, also designed by Yves—a double-breasted suit and a satin tie, with a pink rosebud plucked by Yves and inserted into the buttonhole of his wide satin lapel. His thicket of hair had been tamed for the occasion, but sprung up in the humidity; he held my hand as if it were his anchor.

I'd changed from my Marrakesh-inspired wedding outfit, designed by me and Yves: white jacket and harem pants, sashed in red silk; a high-collared lace blouse with ropes of fake pearls; and a bejeweled turban, sporting red-white feathers. For the reception, I kept on my silver shoes and donned another Eastern-themed whimsy.

Paloma disembarked with her Argentinian beau, her hourglass figure regal in one of our black velvet couture gowns with wired-gauze cap sleeves, a choker dangling amber at her throat, and her expressive dark eyes enhanced by her flamenco bun of slicked dark hair.

"Congratulations, Loulou." She kissed my cheeks. "The ceremony was beautiful."

Betty arrived with François, in a shoulder-strapped emerald silk top and slinky bell-bottomed trousers, with a gold leather hip belt and no other accessories, which were superfluous on her statuesque person.

"Well." She planted a hand at her hip, rail-thin as ever, her skin milky in the dying light and her silver-blond mane loose. "You did it again. They say the second time is the charm." She pinched Thadée's cheek. "Be a good husband to her. She divorced one already, and he had a castle." Thadée laughed, and Betty leaned to me to whisper, "No children. It spoils your life."

Fernando, trim in a tuxedo with a black bow tie, and breathless: "It's infernally hot. Black tie, when we should all be in Speedos, throwing ourselves into the river."

"The night is still young. You might meet a boyfriend," Thadée said with a grin.

"I need to meet one. Desperately." Fernando ran a hand over his cropped curls, graying at the temples. "Not that I will here."

"You never know." I kissed him.

He made a scoffing sound. "I've met everyone here more times than I care to count, and I don't want to see any of them in a Speedo. Except you," he said with a wink at Thadée. "Save me a dance, Loulou."

Marie-Hélène and Baron Guy de Rothschild, her arm looped in his. She wore pleated-sleeved midnight-azure chiffon Saint

Laurent couture, sapphires in her immaculate honey-blond hair and at her wrists. A moment of surprised pause.

"I'm wearing the bride's color. It's unforgivable. No one told me."

"I changed after the ceremony," I said, smiling.

"Is it a sari? Such a wonderful color for you: blue as midnight. All those stunning gold bangles on your arms, like snakes. The crescent moon in your hair and star in your ear. You're a Hindu goddess."

"I made the moon myself." Thadée nudged me mischievously as I added, "With cardboard, glue, and diamanté in the studio," lest she might think, in the dusk, that I wore actual jewels.

"How enchanting." She pecked my cheek. "Such style and heritage," and she drifted with her baron into the lantern-lit chalet.

"Oh, no," Thadée muttered under his breath, as São Schlumberger clambered from a skiff in her white satin couture, ostrich plumes in her hair, and her hand flashing an enormous diamond ring as she harangued the skiff driver:

"I almost fell overboard. Very clumsy of you. This dress costs more than you'll make in a lifetime."

"She wore the dress that costs more than he makes in a lifetime at Versailles," I said, watching her yank at the moistened hem. "It's a repeat performance."

"So cheap." Thadée rolled his eyes.

"Loulou, meu chuchu." A hasty air-kiss, her overpainted eyes keen on the baroness, eclipsing her own entrance into the chalet.

"How many more?" Thadée's other hand riffled in his pocket. "I want to get high."

"We invited three hundred," I reminded him.

"Two years for us to decide to get married, and they wouldn't let us do it quietly." He chuckled. "Six hundred turn up at the party. We'll be here all night, stung by mosquitoes."

"My feet won't withstand it." I cast a rueful glance down at my silver high heels.

More guests congratulating us. Thadée finally succumbed and lit his joint.

Mick Jagger clapped Thadée on the shoulder, his whippet figure in scarlet velvet, his tuxedo shirt unbuttoned over his bony chest, dripping with necklaces.

"I brought you this, mate." He thrust a bag of cocaine at my husband, who pocketed it. "No smack in it. Hate the stuff."

Bianca gave him an exasperated look.

"Your dress is gorgeous," I told her. It was: a confection of pink tulle that on a different woman would have been garish, but Bianca could wear anything.

She made a naughty moue. "Oops. It's by Bohan at Dior."

"Yves will be beside himself." I laughed.

"No." She eyed me knowingly. "He'll do something to alter it."

He would.

A skiff landed among the others; a solitary, square-shouldered figure stepped from it.

My hand tensed in Thadée's as he walked toward us, a peculiar mince in his gait. His muscular build was encased by an ivory smoking jacket, his thick neck in a high-collared shirt with a bow-tied black cravat, and his athletic torso fitted into a pale bloodred damask waistcoat with gold buttons and edged in gilded braid. His jet-black hair had grown longer and been swept from his brow, grasped in a ponytail also tied with a bow. His clean-shaven complexion was dusted with talc, like a matte mask.

He didn't remove his tinted sunglasses when he said. "The very best to both of you."

"Thank you, Karl," replied Thadée tightly. "We're glad you could make it."

"I wouldn't have missed it." Through the sunglasses, I felt his gaze fix on me.

"How is he?" I asked. It seemed like the only thing to say to him.

"Oh, very well. He's enjoying the flat on Saint-Sulpice enormously. You know Jacques; he adores entertaining, and there's plenty of room for it."

"Yes," I said. "I do know how he loves to entertain."

Karl nodded and moved toward the chalet.

"The balls on him," muttered Thadée, as soon as he was out of earshot.

"Pierre insisted he had to be invited." I squeezed his hand. "He's head styliste at Chloé. He has his ongoing contract with Fendi. According to Pierre—"

"Thirty-eight licensing deals." Thadée put the joint to my mouth so I could take a toke. "Pierre never tires of reminding everyone of how lucrative Karl's business is, and how much he hates him, but he invites him anyway."

"Pierre probably hoped he wouldn't show up. We can't ostracize him; everyone in fashion knows Karl. Besides, Pierre paid for our reception tonight. You know it's his way of apologizing to us. He can't say it, but he also insisted on it."

"I wish he hadn't," Thadée grumbled. "I told Yves we didn't need a party."

"They wanted to give it to us." I rose on my tiptoes to kiss him. "It's our wedding night. Let's go dance."

IN THE LATE evening, the five hundred guests—a hundred fewer than Thadée surmised, but with stray wanderers among them, including a trio of green-mohawked punks in tartan and piercings, whom everyone thought were very chic—had satiated themselves on buffet and Bollinger champagne. The baroness and Madame Schlumberger were holding court on the terrace, while others sneaked off into the bushes to satiate more fleshly needs.

Yves touched Thadée's shoulder on the dance floor. "May I?"

Thadée laughed, stepping aside. "You're the host. Of course you may."

Yves slipped his arm about my waist. "Dreams" by Fleetwood Mac was playing, and in the heartbeat of the night, he lifted his hand to my cheek and asked gently, "Are you happy, my Loulou?"

"Yes." I kissed his fingers. "Thank you for all of this."

He was better now, healthier. He'd put on weight and wasn't drinking; his ongoing stays for depression at the American Hospital in Neuilly, ordained by Pierre, had helped ease his anxiety and feelings of futility, as well as the public rumors of a fatal illness, incurable addiction, and suicide attempts. He could live in rue de Babylone with the staff or spend time in his villa in Morocco without us worrying he might do harm to himself. He could lose himself in his work with me in the studio again.

"Pierre and I wanted you and Thadée to have a night to remember."

"It is. We'll always remember it." I leaned into him. "How is it with Pierre?"

"Strange. He keeps his suite at the Athénée, but it's as if we're still living together." I heard a wistful note in his voice. "He comes to have dinner with me every night, after we've seen each other all day at the hôtel. He tells me about new licensing contracts for the house and the tedium of the Syndicale. Sometimes he forces me to go with him and Clara to the opera or ballet. You know how he is. He won't take no for an answer."

"He loves you," I said. "He always has."

"Yes." He gazed into my eyes with the shy tenderness I'd glimpsed in him on the first day we met. "You still love me, too, don't you?"

"Always." I embraced him as we swayed on the floor. "Forever, my petit prince."

"And I love you, my gypsy." His arms tightened around me.

Epilogue

1978

The audience awaits in the immense ballroom of le Grand Hôtel, waving their programs as improvised fans. A heat wave in Paris chars the sky to a burned shield, wilting the chestnuts and evaporating fountains in the Tuileries. Even at midmorning, the show scheduled to evade the exhausted somnolence of afternoon, the city simmers.

Anticipation builds like a lover undressing. Whispers volley as eyes lock on to the archway of white lilies, with its red spotlighted backdrop where his spiked initials are entwined. The raised catwalk screened in ruched moiré is a sumptuous novelty that makes them wonder at the spectacle to ensue. Photographers are stationed around the catwalk, armed with long-focus lenses behind cordoned barriers.

The rumor is that nearly a million francs have been lavished on the presentation, the most expensive in couture history. As anxiety in the audience thickens the air, a hunger to see for themselves if the clothes deserve the expenditure, the overture of La traviata begins.

The ballroom chandeliers dim.

Violins soar as, one by one, the models sweep out, flowing in saffron satin coats with majestic ballooned sleeves and fringed shawls woven on peasant looms. Cinched, wasp-waisted black velvet bodices girdled by crushed-rose-petal sashes, dangling braided tassels over capacious gold lamé, jade, or emerald petticoats, bright as summers in Marrakesh and deep as Parisian nights of betrayal. Lynx-trimmed metallic boots and lush sable hats; headdresses veiled in coins and turbans coiled like dragons. Sweeping cloaks forged of tawny autumn sunsets and icy winter evenings. Diaphanous blouses that cling to skin like icons, and cropped silk jackets embroidered in scarlet wounds—a voluptuous intoxication, a decadent beauty, enraptured by insatiable longing.

The aria of the courtesan who defies doom's approach lifts high in the stunned whisper of weeping mousseline and envious taffeta.

Everything is madness, madness in the world that is not pleasure
Let us enjoy the joy of love, fleeting and rapid.

In the shadows, the king watches, his muse at his side.

Afterword

Loulou de la Falaise worked with Yves Saint Laurent until his retirement in 2002—a devoted colleague and friend whose flights of fantasy and imitable sense of drama were instrumental in many of his iconic looks, which continue to be reinterpreted by fashion to this day. In response to her appellation as his muse, she said, "For me, a muse is someone who looks glamorous but is quite passive, whereas I was very hard-working . . . I certainly wasn't passive." Years later, she reassessed, saying she liked being called "the muse" because she understood she was integral to, and part of, Saint Laurent history.

Loulou was fifty-five years old when Yves retired and closed his couture house. She opened her own house, featuring her designs and jewelry, with two boutiques in Paris. But the fashion world had undergone monumental changes, and she couldn't replicate her successful collaboration with Yves. She remained a fashion muse, her eclectic whimsy a fount of inspiration for others. Loulou and Thadée had a daughter, Anna. Loulou died in 2011 from lung cancer, at the age of sixty-four.

Thadée Klossowski de Rola published his memoirs, *Vie rêvée*, in 2013. He lives in Paris.

Maxime de la Falaise's cookbook, *Seven Centuries of English Cooking: A Collection of Recipes*, was published in 1973. She never remarried after John McKendry's death, but she did go to Paris and did some designing for Yves, after she reputedly complained that his collections were looking "too Madame." She acquired a home in Provence, where she died in 2009, at the age of eighty-six.

Yves Saint Laurent became the first living fashion designer honored with a solo exhibition at the Metropolitan Museum of Art. He was awarded both the ranks of commandeur and grand officier de la Légion d'Honneur, and in 2002, he and Pierre founded their Fondation Pierre Bergé–Yves Saint Laurent to preserve their house's legacy. Yves spoke openly of his struggle with addiction and depression. Coupled with age, he became reclusive, though close lifelong friends, such as Loulou and Betty, remained constant. Yves died in 2008 of brain cancer, at the age of seventy-one.

Pierre Bergé dominated French fashion, arts, and philanthropy. His romantic relationship with Yves ended in great part because of the events fictionalized in this novel, and he never lived again in their shared home. Years later, he engaged in a feud of words with Karl Lagerfeld, accusing him of dispatching Jacques to seduce and destabilize Yves. In turn, Karl—unintimidated by Pierre's power in the industry—fired back that Pierre had also fallen in love with Jacques. Pierre vehemently denied it, citing that while Yves most certainly had, he did not have "bad taste." Nevertheless, nothing severed his bond with Yves, forged in the fire of their youth into a lifelong reliance on each other. Pierre remained stalwart at Yves's side and at the house they created, as partner, confidant, and ally. He upheld their legacy until his own passing. His philanthropic contributions included financial support against AIDS, architectural and artistic renovations in Paris, as well as contributions to UNESCO. Pierre died in 2017, at the age of eighty-six.

Karl Lagerfeld reigned as a survivor of the titans of fashion. His accomplishments and foibles are too numerous to cite here, but as Yves's star waned, his rose. In 1983, he was hired as the artistic director for Chanel, a then moribund brand, which he resurrected in a series of spectacular, seemingly never-ending collections. He became legendary, as much for his rigid work ethic and voluminous output as for his personal eccentricity and, at times, tone-deaf insensitivity. Karl died in 2019, at the age of eighty-five.

Jacques de Bascher has become synonymous with depravity, dancing as fast as he could toward his own demise; in a shallow way, it might be deemed an accurate representation, if a condemnatory one, that fails to take his youth and the era into account. Like so many young people then and now, Jacques was hedonistic, living for the moment. To his friends, he was charming, generous, and loyal; it's almost impossible in hindsight to unravel him from the tangled web of his affair with Yves, whose subsequent suffering eclipsed the complex neuroses of their liaison.

Jacques's sexually licentious, drug-heaped parties culminated in the infamous Moratoire Noire, held in Karl's honor on the night of a Chloé show. Four thousand of the fashion elite gathered in a warehouse, where gay S&M acts enacted on a motorcycle-decorated stage foresaw the fetish for butch leather that would enthrall fashion in the early '80s. Organized by Jacques and financed by Karl, the latter refuted any knowledge of the goings-on, even as he no doubt delighted in the controversy.

In 1984, Jacques tested positive for HIV. At the time, the diagnosis was almost always a death sentence, with agonizing physical deterioration. Jacques endeavored to keep his status a secret, and Karl provided the best medical care available in the hope of saving him. Toward the end, Karl slept on a cot in the hospital room where Jacques died in his arms of AIDS-related complications in 1989, at the age of thirty-eight.

Karl bought a house near Hamburg that he named Villa Jako

and, in 1998, launched a fragrance called Jako, in Jacques's memory. Decades after Jacques's passing, Karl broke his silence on their relationship. While he refuted a sexual component to it, Jacques was indeed the love of his life. Despite their nineteen-year age difference and antithetical personalities, Karl's magnanimity of heart with Jacques is unquestionable. Karl Lagerfeld never had another acknowledged life partner.

Betty Catroux lives in Paris and continues to be a fashion icon. Her husband, François, died in 2020.

Fernando Sánchez found success in the 1980s with his lingerie-style ready-to-wear dresses, worn by Tina Turner, Cher, and Elizabeth Taylor, among other celebrities. A fixture on the New York social scene, he maintained his friendship with Yves and Loulou throughout his life. Fernando died in 2006, at the age of seventy, from a cardiac arrest due to complications of leishmaniasis, a sand flea–borne illness.

Clara Saint worked for the House of Yves Saint Laurent until her retirement.

Pat Cleveland and Donna Jordan continued to model; by the early 1980s, Pat had become known as one of the first "supermodels." Corey Tippin became a photo stylist.

In 1998, the prêt-à-porter Rive Gauche line and its licenses were sold to a conglomerate in a multimillion deal for Yves and Pierre. The first artistic director for the YSL clothing label, Tom Ford, paid homage to Yves in his sexy, 1970s-steeped collections. Ford left YSL in 2004 to be a film director. The Saint Laurent style is still revered, his silhouettes reappearing in collections by Marc Jacobs and Ralph Lauren, as well as other designers. The namesake brand still exists.

MY INTEREST IN Yves Saint Laurent started in my adolescence, when I dreamed of working in fashion—a career I pursued in the mid-1980s, until the impact of AIDS on my community propelled me to join the fight against it. I spent the next twelve years of my professional life in the HIV-related public health arena. Therefore, the opportunity to write this novel was one I embraced, as it contains elements from my past in fashion that I treasure.

As it turned out, of all my novels, this book proved the most ambitious. I found myself confronted by a story I passionately wanted to tell at this time in my life, yet discovered I lacked some of the time-honored tools I've come to rely on. It's ironic, given that I've delved into more distant centuries where extant historical records are also confounding, that I was stymied in my resolve to unearth every detail for a novel set in the twentieth century.

Documentation about Yves Saint Laurent's work abounds. Surprisingly, there are significant silences and tenuous contradictions in his personal record, while Loulou de la Falaise hasn't been the subject of a full-length biography. The ephemeral nature of fashion—its compulsion for constant reinvention, discarding or transmuting the past—results in a cornucopia of imprecise recollections and cocktail chatter of diverging opinions. The ultimate allure of fashion is impermanence, a celebration of beautiful superficiality. Those who dwell within it adopt its ever-changing hues to craft their own mythologies.

I didn't set out to write a biographical novel of Loulou, but rather to capture an incandescent moment that will never come again, when the excesses of an era collided with its innocence. Loulou de la Falaise entered this moment at the age of twenty-four, damaged by childhood, with aristocratic lineage and bohemian flair, ascending to its heights. In bearing witness to Yves Saint Laurent's genius and torment, she became his muse in far more than inspiration. Loulou personified the rebellious daring, perilous ambiguity, and evanescent indulgence of the era—and together with Yves, their work transcended it.

To depict a time before our current-day awareness of the addictive nature of substance use, mental health issues, and the ravages of HIV presented unique challenges and joys for me. I knew this time briefly in my own youth, and how intoxicating and dangerous it could be.

No one in these pages was a devil or an angel. They were human beings, fallible and driven by emotions that we all share, however we choose to manifest them. My insight into the characters is my fictionalized interpretation, not intended to portray a biographical standard. I've distilled their essence into a dramatized account without claiming unimpeachable veracity. Any errors I've made are inadvertent, if inevitable. My goal was to depict how it may have been, as we can never know how it was unless we lived it. Even then, we filter it through our individual perspective. To live in any given moment is also impermanence.

While I endeavored to adhere to facts and documented personalities, besides those already mentioned I admit to liberties, such as shifts in time or place, to facilitate the narrative, as well as the omission of people and events to maintain cohesive pacing. I hope I've done this story justice. For me, writing this novel was a personal labor of love.

I RELIED ON a variety of sources for my research. While not intended as a full bibliography, the following list includes the works I consulted most often:

Benaïm, Laurence. *Yves Saint Laurent: A Biography*. New York: Rizzoli Ex Libris, 2019.

Drake, Alicia. *The Beautiful Fall: Lagerfeld, Saint Laurent, and Glorious Excess in 1970s Paris*. New York: Little, Brown and Co., 2006.

Givhan, Robin. *The Battle of Versailles: The Night American Fashion Stumbled into the Spotlight and Made History.* New York: Flatiron Books, 2015.

Massey, Sarah, ed. *Yves Saint Laurent: The Scandal Collection, 1971.* New York: Abrams, 2017.

Menkes, Suzy. Introduction to *Yves Saint Laurent: The Complete Haute Couture Collections, 1962–2002.* New Haven, CT: Yale University Press, 2019.

Petkanas, Christopher. *Loulou and Yves: The Untold Story of Loulou de la Falaise and the House of Saint Laurent.* New York: St. Martin's Press, 2018.

Rawsthorn, Alice. *Yves Saint Laurent: A Biography.* New York: Nan A. Talese, 1996.

Acknowledgments

It's often said there are no coincidences in life. I've always resisted the adage, as it implies a lack of control over our choices. But this novel was written after a period of personal tumult that reflected the subject I explored, so perhaps it isn't a coincidence.

My beloved cat Boy passed away as I drafted the initial chapters. He was there at the beginning and in spirit to the end. Our other cats, Maus and B.K., remind me that nothing in life is more important than naps, good food, and love. My agent, Jennifer Weltz, has steered me through crises as an agent and a friend, and she encouraged me to persist through the shoals of this work.

Rachel Kahan has taken me under her wing in times when my professional future seemed bleakest; she offered guidance on my proposals, then stepped aside in trust that I would deliver. As with my previous novels *Mademoiselle Chanel, Marlene,* and *The American Adventuress,* I'm privileged to have her as my editor. I owe special thanks to Nancy Tan.

Publishing and bookselling confront similar challenges to those that haute couture faced in the early 1970s, as ready-to-wear took hold. Curated exclusivity has lost its luster before widespread availability; those who continue to work in the book business do so with passion for the written word. Democracy in publishing isn't a setback. Progress is part of change, and I hope publishing in all its iterations can thrive in our social-media-addicted, here-today-gone-tomorrow, soundbite world.

Most of all, I thank my readers. Your enthusiasm inspires me to continue this unpredictable career. I hope to entertain you for many years to come.

I remain an advocate for sexual and gender equality in its infinite forms and committed to ending the suffering caused by intolerance, hatred, and discrimination. Our planet is under siege, and we're driving it. We must learn to live in harmony with one another if we wish to survive. We must never forget that we are one people, with one home, and to love unconditionally is our only means to transcend the brief stay of life.

Each of us must make a difference.

Thank you!

Discover more from C. W. Gortner and William Morrow

"No one writes bright, bold, bad, and beautiful women of history like C. W. Gortner, and he outdoes himself with his latest heroine: Jennie Jerome, American heiress, royal mistress, and mother of Winston Churchill. *The American Adventuress* shines on every page with Jennie's irrepressible thirst for adventure, love, and everything else life has to offer!"

—Kate Quinn,
New York Times bestselling author of *The Rose Code*

A lush, dramatic biographical novel of one of the most glamorous and alluring legends of Hollywood's golden age, Marlene Dietrich—from the gender-bending cabarets of Weimar Berlin to the lush film studios of Hollywood, a sweeping story of passion, glamour, ambition, art, and war.

"Deliciously satisfying. . . . Gortner tells the epic, rags-to-riches story of how this brilliant, mercurial, self-created woman became a legend."

—Christina Baker Kline,
New York Times bestselling author of *Orphan Train*